W9-AQB-988

GUARDED HEART

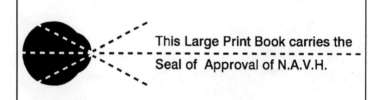

This Large Print Book carries the
Seal of Approval of N.A.V.H.

GUARDED HEART

JENNIFER BLAKE

THORNDIKE PRESS
A part of Gale, Cengage Learning

GALE
CENGAGE Learning·

Detroit • New York • San Francisco • New Haven, Conn • Waterville, Maine • London

GALE
CENGAGE Learning

Copyright © 2008 by Patricia Maxwell.
Master at Arms Series.
Thorndike Press, a part of Gale, Cengage Learning.

Thorndike Press® Large Print Romance.
The text of this Large Print edition is unabridged.
Other aspects of the book may vary from the original edition.
Set in 16 pt. Plantin.
Printed on permanent paper.

LIBRARY OF CONGRESS CATALOGING-IN-PUBLICATION DATA

Blake, Jennifer, 1942–
   Guarded heart / by Jennifer Blake.
      p. cm. — (Master at arms series) (Thorndike Press large
  print romance)
    ISBN-13: 978-1-4104-0639-2 (alk. paper)
    ISBN-10: 1-4104-0639-3 (alk. paper)
    1. Widows — Fiction. 2. Swordsmen — Fiction. 3. Large type
  books. I. Title.
  PS3563.A923G83 2008
  813'.54—dc22   2008009044

Published in 2008 by arrangement with Harlequin Books S.A.

Printed in the United States of America
1 2 3 4 5 6 7 12 11 10 09 08

For LaDell,
sister-in-law, friend and driver par
excellence,
with thanks for enduring with me the
mildewed
charm and authenticity
of an ancient Vieux Carré town house,
and for always being there.

ONE

New Orleans, Louisiana
January 1844
"I require your expertise in order to kill a man."

Gavin Blackford paused in the act of taking a glass of Madeira from a tray on the side table. Such a clear yet low-voiced request was unexpected during a courtesy call for *Réveillon,* the celebration of New Year's Day. It was particularly surprising from a lady.

A multitude of boisterous conversations went on without pause beyond their isolated corner, token of the conviviality of this occasion where men were required to go from house to house among the ladies of their acquaintance, accepting a drink at each stop to toast the New Year. This was his tenth visit of the afternoon, his tenth glass of wine or rum punch while slogging here and there through the pouring rain that fell beyond the French doors of the elegantly appointed

7

salon. Gavin was not at all certain that his pleasantly bemused senses had not somehow garbled the words just spoken to him.

"I beg your pardon?"

"You heard, I believe."

Replacing with care the glass he had meant to offer to Madame Ariadne Faucher, Gavin turned, surveying her in the flickering gaslight above them. She was tall for a female, of upright carriage and an elegant form costumed in rose silk with deep flounces draped in black lace which whispered of the latest mode from Paris. Her gaze was steady, holding a shadow of consciousness but no real sign of discomposure. The rich brown irises of her eyes appeared almost black by grace of large pupils and a deep gray outer ring. Her hair of shimmering ebony was caught up in a simple chignon set off by a spray of rosebuds and softened by errant wisps that curled at her temples in the evening dampness. The skin of her face and shoulders was fine-grained and pale, with an incandescent quality that made it appear as if dipped in pearl nacre. Though it would be bad form to lower his gaze to the milk-white curves revealed by her décolletage, the acute edges of Gavin's vision told him these lovely curves had the same soft gleam. This gave rise inescapably to the question of whether the remainder of her body carried a similar pearl-like sheen.

He had thought Madame Faucher agreeably sophisticated, a little too strong-featured for the current ideal of wan and delicate beauty, but intriguing. That was as his hostess, Maurelle Herriot, had introduced them before moving off to see to her other guests. How was he to guess she harbored a deadly turn of mind?

"Forgive me, madame," he said with a brief inclination of his head. "Though I confess to a certain pleasure in the more honorable forms of mayhem, my habits don't run to murder."

"Debatable, I would say, in view of your reputation on the dueling field."

It was not a reminder he appreciated. "Nonetheless, my sword is not for hire."

"I was led to believe you are a *maître d'armes*," she said with a frown between her winged brows.

"A respectable and quite legal occupation, if somewhat déclassé."

Her lips thinned a trifle before she answered, a shame given their rose-red shade and their luxuriant curves. "My purpose is not outside the law. I require lessons in the use of a sword."

"You require lessons." The words were

blank as he readjusted his thinking.

"Is that so difficult to accept?"

"You will admit that, like a kitten warding off a bulldog with a kitchen knife, it is not the usual practice."

"But not impossible."

Gavin was assailed, abruptly, by the image of the lady before him stripped for fencing in the manner of his male clients, wearing only a simple bodice open at the neck and a pair of pantaloons to allow free movement. Her cleavage would expose delights never seen in the bachelor haunt of his atelier, and any vigorous lunge would display every inch of what he suspected were delectably long legs.

His mouth went dry, while a stirring in his groin warned of the need to keep his thoughts on a more-elevated plane. Annoyance brushed him. He usually had better control of such responses.

"Not impossible in theory," he allowed after a moment. "I know of one or two ladies who spar with a father or brother from time to time."

"Hardly what I require."

"Still, if your husband should care to come to me, he might see to your instruction."

"I am a widow. My father and my brother

10

are dead as well. If they were not, I should have no need to embark on this matter myself."

Her voice, cool and even, did not match the dark pain that welled into her eyes, the warm color that bloomed across her cheekbones or the pulse that throbbed in the soft hollow of her throat. She was, he thought, less sanguine and perhaps younger than his first estimation, somewhere between twenty and twenty-five. For an instant, he was beset by the need to offer comfort. That was as unacceptable as her request, since she was obviously of the *haut ton,* the upper echelons of the narrow French Creole society on whose outskirts he moved. She would undoubtedly be scandalized at any hint of it.

What was it Maurelle had said as she presented her? He had not been attending with any closeness, being too taken up by the remarkable nature of it. Women of Madame Faucher's position did not consort with sword masters as a rule, so were seldom formally introduced. He thought there had been some mention of her recent arrival from Paris but could not be sure.

Rallying his thoughts, he said, "My condolences, madame. Am I to understand you are alone in the world?"

"In a manner of speaking."

She glanced toward a mustachioed gentleman of bear-like form, the silver-white hair of the prematurely gray and a supercilious expression who stood in a group not far away. Gavin noted the gentleman's stare in their direction with a swordsman's honed instinct for possible trouble. "There is no one, no one at all, to exact satisfaction for any insult you may have suffered?"

"Just so."

"The problem of taking up the matter yourself, you realize, is that no gentleman worthy of the name will accept the challenge of a lady."

"I did not say he was a gentleman."

"All the more reason for rethinking this bloodthirsty ambition," Gavin said with a frown.

"You can call it that when you have killed on the field of honor?"

The point seemed of importance to her since it was the second time she had mentioned it. "As a last resort only, or by accident. A mere show of blood usually suffices in matters of honor."

"That is also a possibility in my case."

He was not sure he believed her assertion given the grimness of her expression. Several reasons came to mind for the lady's craving

12

for satisfaction: a past injury to her dead husband or a slur on his memory, being cheated by a mountebank, the rejection or betrayal of a lover or the mistreatment of a physical nature by him. Regardless, women did not usually pick up a sword for reprisal.

Before he could speak, she went on with a flash of contempt in her eyes. "Can it be you hesitate from the belief that only males should seek redress for their injuries?"

"I fear it's the way of the world." He lifted a shoulder. "There can be no honor in vanquishing a foe who may not be one's equal in weight or reach of the sword arm. Yes, and who may be as tender as a young lamb when spitted, so the mind recoils from the thrust. Besides, feminine reprisal is usually more subtle."

"But not as satisfactory."

"On the contrary," he answered in quiet certainty, "it can be, often is, far more devastating."

She ignored that while searching his face with narrow-eyed intensity. "Then you refuse my request?"

Gavin inclined his head in assent, even as he caught the movement of the gentleman of imperious manner and silver hair as he detached himself from his acquaintances and started in their direction. "It pains me to be disobliging to a lady . . ." he began.

"But naturally, he refuses," the newcomer interrupted in assured tones. "How should it be otherwise? Did I not tell you, *ma chère?*"

The man's words, for all that they were directed at Madame Faucher, were meant for him, Gavin thought. Though spoken in excellent French, they had the harsh accents of Russia allied to a definite note of command. He felt his hackles rise. He did not take orders well, even from those with the right to give them.

Ariadne Faucher swung to face the Russian with annoyance in her fine, dark eyes. "This does not concern you, Sasha. Have the goodness not to interfere."

The man drew himself up as if on parade, an impression reinforced by his cutaway tailcoat of white worsted ornamented with bars of gold braid in the military manner, the unfashionably close crop of his hair that glinted in the gaslight, his luxuriant mustache and the scar of a saber cut that slashed his left cheek. "Anything which touches you concerns me, *ma chère madame*," he declared in fervent tones. "This obsession with swordplay goes beyond what is reasonable. You may be injured, and a scar to so lovely a face or form would be tragic."

14

"I should like to think I am not so clumsy," Gavin murmured, though he could not but agree with the sentiment.

"Now it is you who interferes, monsieur," the other man said with barely a glance in his direction. "Do not, I advise you."

"The conversation, poor thing though it may have been, was between the lady and myself. It is you who are unwanted, *mon vieux.*"

The look Madame Faucher sent him was startled, as if she might be unused to anyone lending her support and was marginally grateful for the effort. That struck Gavin as a thing to be encouraged, though he was aware in some dim recess of his mind of the absurdity of it.

"It would be best if she did not speak to one such as you on any subject," the Russian said through his teeth. "You may leave us."

"Sasha!"

"Now that," Gavin said, "I cannot."

"I beg you won't," Madame Faucher said quickly. "At least, not until we have come to an agreement."

The Russian clenched his fists at his sides, speaking with hauteur that hinted at noble bloodlines. "There will be no agreement."

It was quite the wrong attitude to take

with the lady; Gavin could have told the overbearing oaf as much on the strength of five minutes' acquaintance. Ariadne Faucher did not strike him as one used to obedience any more than he was himself. Magnificent in her anger, she stood straight and proud in her silk and lace with color staining her cheekbones and resentment in the black depths of her eyes. Abruptly, something hot, acquisitive and quite unexpected lodged in Gavin's chest, closing off his breath.

"You are not my keeper, Alexander Novgorodcev," she said with precision. "I order my life now, I and no other. If you wish to continue being numbered among my friends, you will allow me to know my own mind."

The message could not have been more clear; the Russian must accept her ultimatum or forfeit her friendship. The struggle it took for him to accede to her will was plain on his broad, rather cruel face and in the angry purple of the scar across his cheek. He summoned a stiff smile. "It shall be as you wish, *ma chère madame,* as always. I will leave you to your arrangements."

It was as well done as could be expected under the circumstances, Gavin acknowledged as he watched the pompous gentleman execute a heel-clicking obeisance and walk away. That it also removed the hovering prospect of a duel between the two of them was gratifying since he had no wish to disturb Maurelle's New Year's reception with a challenge. Nevertheless, he was left with the thorny problem of how to tell the willful lady in front of him that he still couldn't oblige her.

Yet why could he not? A female client might be unconventional, but that need not be a consideration for him if it didn't trouble Madame Faucher. She certainly couldn't come to him in the Passage de la Bourse, that pedestrian byway given over to lawyers, barrooms and fencing salons; venturing there was not done, at least by ladies of good repute. Regardless, some accommodation might be found.

"Well, monsieur?"

He must indeed have had too much to drink on this first day of the year since the idea of a female client was beginning to seem not at all unreasonable. The race of the blood in his veins because of it was even more intoxicating. Long months had passed since anything had stirred his interest in quite this way. Nonetheless, something in the lady's manner and honed instinct for danger made him wary of committing himself.

"Like the bashful choirboy with an angel's voice, I may appreciate my own skill but thought it known only to heaven otherwise," he said in quiet irony. "With more than fifty sword masters in New Orleans from which to make your choice, why come to me?"

"You were highly recommended." Ariadne Faucher glanced down at the black lace fan which dangled from one gloved wrist, flipped it open and waved it back and forth to cool her face.

"By whom, if I may ask?"

"Our mutual friend, Madame Herriot, if you must know. She might have suggested one or two others of her acquaintance, so she said, but they no longer keep their fencing salons and their wives might object to the late hours."

Gavin thought she avoided his gaze as she turned her appraisal from her fan to the charming salon around them with its ombre-striped wallpaper, Louis Quinze furnishings upholstered in cream brocade, and its marble fireplace, and the chattering guests, ladies occupying the settees with their delicately colored skirts spread like flower petals around them and their male partners in convivial groups behind them. It could mean she was being less than truthful, but might also indicate she was not as

18

oblivious to the unsuitable nature of her aim as she pretended. It was an instant before he could drag his attention from his own assessment of the lady and the shadows made by the silken fringe of her lashes in order to grasp what she had said. "Late hours?"

"You would have to come to me, of course, and calling too often during the day would not do."

"Indeed," he said in dry agreement, "though dropping in at midnight must be no less scandalous."

"You would not be visiting me, of course, but Maurelle. She says such visits would be unexceptional, particularly if your friends are added to the company from time to time."

"In other words, she has offered her house as a place of assignation."

If he had thought to test her composure with that hint of the clandestine, he must have been disappointed. Closing her fan, she met his gaze without flinching. "As you say."

What did it matter to him how it was arranged? She had every right to protect her good name, and he was quite aware that he was not socially acceptable in his present guise. Regardless, slow anger rose inside him.

He had not always been quite so beyond the pale. As the younger son of a marquis, second in line to the title behind his brother, he had moved among the cream of London society. His birthright had been accepted without question, his company with pleasure. All that prevented him from gaining the more exalted circles around the young queen and her Saxe-Coburg prince had been the double handicaps of a tendency to abandon decorum at odd moments and the whispers about his past. His descent from such a charmed circle had been his own choice, made on the day he left England's green shores, but that did not make the exile less galling.

"Who is this man you hate so much that you would take such risks?" he asked, his voice flat. "How did he wrong you?"

"That is my affair." She lifted her chin with a quick movement that caused the gaslight from the nearby wall sconce to shimmer over her hair, highlight her cheekbones, pool in the delicate hollow of her throat.

"Still, it might be useful to know whether he is some bumbling fool or a swordsman of note. To meet the first might leave you some hope of victory. The other would be suicide."

"My need is to be schooled for the meeting. The outcome need not concern you."

He could think of many things in which he would like to school her during evening lessons held in private, none of which involved a sword. At the same time, he was disturbed by the fervor of the impulse. He was not prone to wayward fantasies. A man who could not control his imagination was a danger to himself on the dueling field.

"You are mistaken," he answered. "I have the reputation of my atelier to consider. And I refuse to be responsible for the death of an innocent."

She opened her lips to answer. Then she closed them again, compressing the soft curves in a tight line. Her hands clenched on her fan, and the tearing sound as its painted silk pulled away from the ebony sticks seemed loud in the quiet. Drawing a deep breath that lifted the gentle curves of her breasts a fraction from their silken prison, she looked down at the damage, then smoothed the tear with a trembling finger. "I see. You will not help me."

"I regret most sincerely . . ." he began.

"Perhaps you can name another who might be suitable."

21

Reluctance gripped Gavin. He could name a dozen others, though only one or two he might trust to impart the skill the lady required without taking advantage. The *maîtres d'armes* of the Passage de la Bourse were honorable in their fashion, but numbered few saints among them.

"On second thought, don't bother," she said, tilting her chin. "Monsieur Novgorodcev will be all too happy to instruct me. I was persuaded you might have a different level of skill, perhaps more finesse compared to what he might have acquired during training at a military academy, but his will have to suffice." Swinging away from him with her heavy gown rustling as it swirled over her petticoats, she began to walk away.

"Wait." The request was dragged from him, graveling his voice with reluctance.

She paused, turned slowly with brows lifted above eyes as black as a winter storm yet burning with life and, perhaps, hope. "Monsieur?"

To agree was madness. He would regret it, without question. What drove him was not entirely his annoyance with the Russian or any doubt of her safety with him or any other sword master. The fact was that he was bored. He required stimulation, new interest, new purpose.

His male friends in the city had settled into marital bliss in the past year or two, and though they invited him to their homes, he was far too aware of being outside their family circles to be comfortable. The Brotherhood, that loose collection of swordsmen organized some four years earlier to offer protection to women and children who received none under the shaky legal system of a city divided into three separate municipalities, had dwindled to a mere shadow of its former self. The past activities of the original trio — Rio, the Conde de Lérida, the Irishman Caid O'Neill and Gavin's half brother Nicholas Pasquale, along with himself — had met with such success that few incidents now required their intervention. It seemed the challenge posed by Madame Faucher might be an outlet for his bottled energy.

Then there was the lingering contempt in the lady's eyes. Vanity was not, he felt sure, his most obvious sin, but he was used to at least a modicum of respect for his deadly skill if not for his breeding. To adjust her opinion seemed a worthy ambition. Above all, however, was his need to know why she was so desperate to be instructed in the art of swordplay, particularly by him.

"I will attend you here tomorrow evening,

madame. If Maurelle, Madame Herriot, can arrange a fencing strip, I will supply the remaining equipment."

Something bright and fiercely triumphant flashed in her eyes before she lowered her lashes to conceal it. "Excellent. I will await you, monsieur."

She turned and moved away with languid grace. Gavin watched her go while the blood sang in his veins. It was not only admiration and anticipation that crowded his chest, however. Layered with them was an inexplicable and icy trickle of dread.

Two

Ariadne put half the room and a large portion of Maurelle's guests between her and the English sword master before she turned her head to look back at him. He had not been at all as she expected. His manner was polished, and his person as well, creating an image of aesthetic refinement at odds with her view of his chosen profession. The fit of his blue frock coat and gray pantaloons was impeccable and his waistcoat of embroidered silk was notable without being ostentatious. His hair had the sheen of old gold coins. His brows, a shade or two darker than his hair, were thick without being heavy and his face was neatly shaven in its entirety, minus the whiskers or bits of side hair affected by most gentlemen these days. His boots had a glassy sheen, his buttons and fobs were plain yet well-polished. In short, he was burnished to such a gloss that it seemed a deliberate attempt to deflect

25

unwanted attention or else a facade behind which he might hide his true nature.

Then there were his eyes, as blue as the seas of the Indies, vivid with intelligence and an intimation of mockery for everything and everyone around him, yet shadowed as if by hidden shoals. He had seen too much of what she thought and felt, she feared, though how that could be she could not imagine. An instant later, his face had turned impassive, closed to human emotion while remaining as compelling to look at as that of some powerful angel sent from heaven by God's displeasure. The memory of how he scrutinized her, as if able to plumb her every secret, chilled her so a shiver ran down her spine with a prickling of goose bumps, making her knees feel almost unhinged beneath her gown.

She had approached Gavin Blackford and emerged from the encounter with his promise for what she required. The die was cast.

"So, *ma chère,* the English sword master agreed?"

The question came in Maurelle's rather sultry voice as she rustled to a halt beside Ariadne. In an evening ensemble of pale gold taffeta with cream lace and a parure of citrines and diamonds, she wore her hair in braids placed to emphasize the prominent cheekbones that prevented her face from being entirely rounded. A full-blown camellia in style, like those of creamy white she wore in her hair, she was comfortable in her curvaceous embonpoint, and majestic with it. The lady was a widow and, as with Ariadne, comfortable with that circumstance as well.

Ariadne gave her a wan smile. "With some persuasion."

"Amazing. I would have wagered anything you cared to name on his refusal."

"I thought the same for a few moments."

"What convinced him?"

Ariadne looked at her fan, folding it to conceal the damage she had inflicted. "I wish I knew."

It was as well she had watched him from a distance to take his measure before asking that Maurelle present him, she was sure. Because of it, she had let him know more of her purpose than she had intended, perhaps more than was wise. Maurelle, and even Sasha, thought her whim was to play at fencing. Only she and Gavin Blackford knew her final purpose. And he did not know the whole of it.

"I should warn you, he will call tomorrow evening," Ariadne continued after a moment.

"To begin, you mean? So soon? *Parbleu,* what an impression you must have made!"

"Meaning?"

"Not only is he most selective in his clients, but the waiting list is long for those eager to face him on the fencing strip."

Ariadne allowed herself a cynical smile. "Perhaps it's the novelty."

"Or he could anticipate a novel reward," Maurelle said with an amused curl of her full lips.

"He will be disappointed."

"Oh, I don't know. You are a widow and he is made to a marvel, yes? The hours these swordsmen spend on fencing strips make them sublime of form, with wide shoulders and firm thighs far beyond those of other gentlemen. And I'm sure he's the soul of discretion."

"I . . . have no time for games of that nature." Ariadne ignored as best she could the small, hot thrill that rippled through her at the thought of Gavin Blackford's expectations, the jangling of her nerve endings like a careless hand sweeping across harp strings. "Besides, it's you everyone will be talking about if it becomes known that he visits with any frequency."

Maurelle tilted her head as the amusement faded from her eyes. "At first, possibly. But then a more likely explanation may occur to the gossips." She paused. "Are you quite sure you know what you're doing, *chère?* It's one thing to take up a Bohemian attitude, but quite another to forfeit your good name for a caprice."

The warning was gentle yet serious. Maurelle should understand the problem as well as anyone, Ariadne knew, since she had performed the difficult balancing act of living freely for years while maintaining her good repute. Married at a young age to a man much her senior, she had embraced her eventual widowhood with gratitude and a vow to cling to it. Though careful never to transgress upon the conventions too far, she entertained a wide circle of friends, many of whom, like the *maîtres d'armes,* were forbidden entrance to the more conventional households of aristocratic New Orleans. Some whispered that she had at least once taken a sword master as her lover, but the arrangement had apparently not been allowed to disrupt her peace or her life.

It was in Paris that Ariadne and Maurelle had met three years before. Maurelle had been in the city on her yearly pilgrimage to visit relatives and replenish her armoire, while Ariadne had just begun to go about in society at the insistence of Jean Marc, her

29

husband of only a year who had been ill even then with the consumption which killed him. Their paths had crossed at some soiree, and Maurelle had asked permission to call upon her.

During that afternoon visit, she had received from Maurelle the story of the house party at Maison Blanche, her country plantation where Ariadne's foster brother, Francis Dorelle, had been killed in a duel. It had been a tearful occasion, but the beginning of their companionship. That she and Maurelle were both from Louisiana, both of independent natures and both victims, in a sense, of arranged marriages to older men, made common ground between them. They had become fast friends, often providing necessary chaperonage for each other.

Even after Jean Marc died and Ariadne had retired from society in the manner required by her two years of mourning, Maurelle had visited with her in Paris, keeping her current with all the tittle-tattle of New Orleans — which lady had given birth to a child that looked nothing like her husband, which was known to be traveling in Europe at her husband's command, what gentleman was keeping the latest ballerina from the Theatre d'Orleans. They decided that, when the time was right — when Jean Marc's estate was settled and the mourning period over — Ariadne would come to Maurelle for a new beginning.

That prospect had kept Ariadne sane during her time in black bombazine. Paris had seemed dull and gray and her husband's family much the same, when they were not exuding disapproval. They were incensed that she had inherited the fortune Jean Marc had accumulated as primary stockholder in an international banking concern. She had influenced him unduly, they said, causing him to leave it away from his brothers and sisters, nieces and nephews who had more right to it. She was much too young and inexperienced to have sole management of such wealth. She should remain in Paris where she might benefit from the wise council of Jean Marc's brother, now head of the family, and, not incidentally, where they might make certain any future alliance she contemplated met with familial approval. What purpose could she have in going elsewhere? Her family in Louisiana, her parents and her brother, were no longer alive, *n'est pas?* She could have no call whatever to return to such a pestilential and uncivilized place.

They had been wrong on almost every count.

Now she said, with a wry smile, "My good name? Who is there to care? Well, other than you, my very dear Maurelle."

"You, *chère,* as you will discover if it should be lost to you."

It was good of Maurelle to be so concerned. Worry and guilt that she might be dragging her friend into something she would not like clouded Ariadne's mind. Maurelle had not wanted to present her to Gavin Blackford, knowing as she did that it had been his sword which had killed her foster brother. She had agreed only because she harbored some small hope that familiarity might lead to understanding.

"Shall I find another place for these lessons?" Ariadne asked. "I can always remove to a hotel or other lodging if it will make you more comfortable."

"Don't be an imbecile." Maurelle caught her close in a jasmine-scented hug. "The very idea, as if I'm not dying to see how you progress with Monsieur Blackford. Indeed, this promises to be the most exciting *saison de visites* in years."

Ariadne returned her friend's embrace with gratitude, though she was not entirely satisfied. Indeed, she hoped the affair would not become more exciting than either of them could bear.

THREE

Ariadne was consumed with impatience as she waited for the sword master to arrive on the following evening. She had envisioned this moment for such a long time. That it was almost upon her seemed not quite real.

Everything was in readiness in this bedchamber of the Herriot town house's *garçonnière* wing. Whoever had planned the room must have had a large family of boys for it was long and narrow, on the order of a dormitory, with white plastered walls above a wainscoting of durable cypress wood. Its six single beds had been removed and several candelabra on floor stands brought in to line the walls between the windows; though the main reception rooms boasted gaslight, Maurelle was too frugal a housewife to extend it throughout the town house. The tall window sashes were wide open and the shutters thrown back for air, in spite of the winter coolness and incessant rain which fell into the courtyard on one side and the street on the other. Wine and water sat ready in case of need. A strip of canvas perhaps five-feet wide and fifteen paces long, and marked at the middle and on each end, had been laid down the center. This was the fencing strip, the piste upon which the lessons would take place.

Ariadne could think of nothing more that might be required. Now she paced, the skirt of her old gray walking costume swishing around her feet and her hands squeezed together in front of her until they were numb, as if the tightness of her grip could hold her being together.

Maurelle's other guests were in place; she could hear the distant sound of their voices and laughter and the slap of cards. Why had the *maître d'armes* not yet arrived? What was keeping him? Had he decided he could not be bothered to instruct her after all?

"Monsieur Blackford, madame."

She whirled to see Solon, Maurelle's tall and dignified majordomo of many years. With the grace of an aristocrat he dipped his graying head before stepping aside to allow the Englishman to enter. The manservant carried a sword case under his arm which he had apparently taken from Blackford along with his hat, cane and rain-damp cloak. These items he placed on a table, then bowed again, his angular features rigidly correct, as he offered refreshment. When it was declined, he presented the compliments of his mistress and asked that they ring if anything more was required. Then he departed.

Ariadne, left alone with the sword master, stared at him for a suspended instant. He was dressed for the evening in a double-breasted coat and trousers of dark blue worsted, a waistcoat with a subtle cream plaid and white silk cravat. His sartorial choice was doubtless suitable for the gathering of Maurelle's friends that he was supposedly attending but seemed to indicate little chance for more. It could mean that he did not intend anything serious in the way of a fencing demonstration.

Her movements stiff, she came forward, finally, to offer her hand in its short glove. "It's gratifying to see you at last, monsieur. I had begun to think you would not put in an appearance."

"I did give you my word, Madame Faucher." He inclined his blond head over her fingertips but did not release them. Straightening, he shifted his hold to clasp her hand as he might on greeting a man. "Tighten your grip," he said, "as much as you are able."

"Monsieur?" The warmth and intimacy of his firm grasp sent a tremor along her arm while it seemed she could feel the steel-hard ridges of his swordsman's calluses through the layers of their leather gloves. Vexation stirred inside her. Touching this man in anything more than the most civil of greetings had not been a part of her plan.

"You cannot hurt me," he said, his smile whimsical. "Or if you do, I'll make certain you never know it."

His eyes were so very blue seen at this close range. Quiet humor shifted in their depths like rays of sunlight striking through clear seas, giving him an unexpected attraction. The mingled scents of starched linen, spiced shaving soap and clean male skin drifted toward her like a subtle invasion, so she had an almost irresistible urge to jerk away from him. That she did not had less to do with self-control than it did with the knowledge that it might prove impossible. She had no wish to appear ineffectual, now or ever.

"Nor," he added in quiet assurance, "will I harm you."

He thought she was afraid of him, or at least wary of his intentions. That she could not allow.

"No," she said with a quick lift of her chin. "I'm sure you will not." She grasped his hand then, clamping down with all her strength. He maintained his hold but did not return the pressure. If he felt anything at all of the compression she exerted, he gave no sign, just as he had promised.

She was not quite so sanguine. The heat of his warm, hard palm nestled so close against the sensitive surface of hers was distressingly intimate in spite of their coverings. She could sense the surging power, rigidly contained, inside him. He was too close as well; it was all she could do to remain where she stood instead of stepping away a safe distance.

"Excellent," he said after an instant of assessment. "You should have no trouble keeping a grip on your weapon."

She gave a short nod and relaxed her grasp. He released her at once, which was something of a surprise since she had half expected him to prolong the moment, possibly even make some flirtatious remark. Most gentlemen of her acquaintance would have done so as a matter of form, because they thought it expected if for no other reason. She was glad he recognized that she had no interest in such meaningless flirtation.

"Have you any experience at all on the fencing strip?" He spoke over his shoulder as he moved to where Solon had placed the sword case.

"None whatever."

"Yet you have chosen a sword as the method of your retaliation. Why, if I may ask? A taste for sharp objects, or is it the pretty silver chasing that sometimes appears on the blade?"

Annoyance for his condescension gave a bite to her voice as she answered. "Neither. It seems suitable as it's the gentleman's chosen weapon."

"Which presupposes some skill on his part." He unfastened the catch of the rose-wood case and laid back the lid. Taking a long and slender foil from it, he held it up, sighting down its length as if checking for straightness. "And you are still certain this is what you want?"

"Quite positive."

Abruptly, he turned and sent the foil spinning in her direction. Horror took Ariadne's breath as she saw it arching toward her, twirling — an elongated top surrounded by yellow-orange candlelight, making a swirling nimbus. To fling up her arm was purest instinct. The foil's hilt struck her gloved wrist a numbing blow. The glittering blade rolled down her skirts, clattering to the floor where it spun in a half circle before coming to a stop. She stood rigid, staring at it.

"The idea," Gavin Blackford said in soft reproof, "was for you to catch it."

She shuddered, pushed away the blackness that hovered at the edges of her mind. She had never handled a sword, never thought to do so until a few short months ago. For an instant, she was torn with doubt. How was she to go through with this? It seemed impossible. Yes, but how could she not when her soul's peace depended upon it?

Reaching for anger as both goad and shield, she said, "You might have warned me of your intention, monsieur. I'm not here to play games."

"Nor am I," he answered, his voice hard. "Fencing is a craft requiring strong nerves and instant responses as well as strength and skill. If you are going to scream and cower away from any weapon that comes toward you, then we may as well abandon the exercise now. It will save valuable time for us both."

What right had he to test her? She was paying him to impart his skill, not to judge her fitness. Yet he had a point, even if she didn't care for it.

Stooping with careful fortitude, controlling the tremor in her fingers, she reached to pick up the foil then rose again to her full height. "Thank you for the object lesson," she said, her voice taut and her gaze on the blade she held. "I shall not display such weakness again."

He did not reply for long moments. It seemed she could feel the heat of his regard as he searched her half-averted face. She was far too aware of its intensity and the intelligence which drove it. For a single instant, she felt a thrill of fear that he might penetrate her defenses, discover everything there was to know about her. Angry panic rose into her throat, threatening to choke her.

"If you can manage that," he said finally, his voice laced with grave amusement, "then you will do better than most."

Her relief was so great that she almost sagged with it. She was also annoyed with herself. He was surely not so perceptive as all that, could not be given his history. If he had been, she would not be here. "Then you may depend upon it."

His brief nod indicated his satisfaction before he went on. "I should tell you, perhaps, that you have certain advantages on the fencing strip because you are a woman."

"You surprise me."

"Permit me to enumerate," he continued with the lift of a dark gold brow, perhaps for her ironic tone. "Because your lower limbs are in more equal proportion to your torso, compared to men with their longer legs, you will be more stable as you move up and down the strip, less likely to stumble or be forced backward against your will. Women are neater in their movements, generally speaking, also not given to wasting effort with showy moves that have no purpose. Some masters feel that women are better able to divide their attention during contests, to concentrate on what their opponent is doing while planning their next attack."

If he was aware of the sacrilege in speaking to her of lower limbs, he seemed not to recognize it. That fact allowed her to ignore the heat in her own face. "And the disadvantages, since I'm sure you mean to point those out to me?"

"A shorter reach in the lunge for most females, merely because their arms are not as long in proportion to their bodies. Added to that is an ingrained reluctance to attack when the opportunity presents itself or to take advantage of an opponent's weakness."

His smile twisted. "The last two are traits to be encouraged in future wives and mothers, of course. You will have to overcome whatever lessons you may have learned in that direction."

"I'll endeavor to do so. Is there more?"

He tipped his head in assent as he turned to lift the other foil from its case. "Look at your weapon, if you please."

"Yes?" She held it in imitation of the way he handled his, with her right hand grasping the handle and the tip balanced on the fingers of her left.

"This is a foil, the practice weapon of fencing, lighter than an épée, more limber by far than a sword. It will become an extension of your arm, another finger on your hand."

What followed then was careful instruction in the various parts of the fencing foil — handle and pommel, guard, crossbar, blade and blunted end — plus its care and cleaning. He then fitted the one she held to her hand, adding padding so the handle would not be too large, and showing her exactly how to hold it. She was introduced to the idea of the canvas chest padding which protected vital organs and the screen mask which prevented facial injury — these last by description only since they were not on hand this evening. When that was done, he directed her attention to the canvas fencing strip where he pointed out the exacting etiquette which applied there at all times, including the salute to an opponent and other aspects of sporting conduct.

Ariadne listened to every word as if her life depended on it, which it might. As he spoke, her gaze rested on the face of the sword master. It was plain that he took special pleasure in the details of the profession he had embraced. His thoroughness also hinted at why he was a master of it. She could respect that, if nothing else.

She had no wish to respect him, nor did she care to stand listening to the rhythm of his deeply mellow English voice which gave his French such a musical lilt. He was much too personable, too utterly sure of himself and his skill. The set of his shoulders and tilt of his golden head, the superb athletic control with which he moved, his manner of dress and the excellent fit of his clothing — everything about him set her teeth on edge. She could feel the magnetism of his masculine presence aligned to an effortless charisma which seemed to draw her to him. The way the light in the long room fell across his face — gilding it, picking out hollows, angles and shadows — was far too intriguing. The caverns of darkness beyond the candle's glow and the clattering rain outside the windows closed them in together in a most disturbing manner. If they did not soon get down to the business at hand, she would scream.

"Monsieur Blackford," she said at last. "I have no desire or plan to set myself up as a female teacher of fencing. The intricacies of the art, while no doubt fascinating to its devotees such as yourself, are of little use to me. All I require is the ability to face a man with sword in hand."

"Also to live to tell about it later, or so I assume. Or do you intend merely to sell your soul at a dear price?"

"Whatever my purpose may be, lectures on the manners and graces of the dueling field seem unlikely to advance it."

"The way a man dies, or lives as the case may be, is surely as important as the fact of it."

She frowned at him even as the quiet intensity of his voice played havoc with her nerves, making her feel a little breathless while tightening the tips of her breasts. She had not expected such an idealistic attitude from him. "No doubt that's so," she said in tart rebuttal, "or it should be, in a bout between equals over a point of honor. The meeting I envision is quite otherwise."

"A mere chastisement — swift, vicious and, if need be, underhanded."

"I didn't say that."

"As with a downdraft of carrion crows falling on dead meat, some things naturally follow."

"Monsieur!" She could hardly believe that he had just compared her to a vulture. He had, hadn't he?

He went on without pause or change of expression. "But don't think I delay for the sake of your sweet smiles. These preliminaries, tedious as they may be, are quite normal. It was only after a long month of such dull lessons and other exercises that I was first allowed to take sword in hand."

He had received no smiles from her, sweet or not, which meant he was baiting her. That he dared did nothing to soothe her irritation. "What you may have suffered is of no concern to me since I have only one meeting for which to prepare instead of a lifetime of such things," she said as she whipped the air before him with a singing hiss of her blade. "Could we please get to the true use of these foils?"

He moved so swiftly it was a mere blur in the candlelight. One moment he stood at ease three paces away, the next she was lodged against his hard length, pressed to him from breast to knees with her wrist in his grasp and her foil held well away from their bodies. The breath left her lungs for a stunned instant. Then she inhaled sharply, jerking against his hold.

"Never take a swipe at a man with sword in hand unless you mean it," he said with biting precision as he glared down at her. "A swordsman's instinct is for instant, unthinking defense. His very life depends on it. If he holds a sword of his own, the attacker could be spitted before he sees whether it's friend or foe, man or woman. He might, no doubt *would,* cry out to heaven at the pity of piercing so soft a breast as yours, but you would be no less dead."

She could feel the thud of his heart, the hard muscles of his arm as they pressed into her through the stays at the back of her bodice, the firm columns of his legs where he had waded into her skirts. His body heat seemed to seep into her pores, routing a chill she had not known she felt. A shiver caught her unaware, and she struggled briefly against his hold. It was stronger than any she had ever known, far more inescapable than any her husband had ever employed. It seemed to sap her will, so it was all she could do to remain stiff and unyielding in his grasp instead of leaning into its steel-like support.

"Release me," she said between her teeth.

"On the instant, if you will tell me you take my meaning."

"I may have been careless, but I'm not stupid. I understand perfectly."

A short, silent laugh shook him; she felt it. "Valiant and vinegary. It must suffice. Because it does, I will speed the lessons to reach a match with foils as soon as possible. First, however, there are a few more details you should know."

As abruptly as he had caught her to him, he let her go. She swayed a little, seeking her balance. He put out a quick hand in aid but she only glanced at it, uncomprehending.

Being held in his arms should have been loathsome and her release a joy. That neither was true stunned her into immobility. She had been surprised by his swiftness, angered by his daring, stirred by the heated hardness of his body but not, unaccountably, repulsed. To be set away from him gave her a hollow feeling in her stomach, as if she had been rejected. It was disconcerting in the extreme and, yes, even a little frightening. What manner of woman was she that she could be affected in this way?

She had planned so carefully. She had known Gavin Blackford was attractive to women. Why had she not taken that detail into consideration?

The truth was, she had thought herself immune. Because she had known no man in a physical sense except her elderly husband who roused mere compassion, had met none in the salons of Paris who caused her heart to beat faster, she had discounted the possibility of a physical response. That had been an error, one to be avoided from this point onward. She truly did learn from her mistakes.

"Madame?"

She lifted her lashes to search his face for triumph, amusement, some sign that he recognized her dilemma. The blue depths of his eyes were clear, his firm mouth with its sensual curves and tucked corners unsmiling; a quirked brow expressed nothing more than polite inquiry.

He had taken her foil as he stepped away, firmly removing it from her possession and placing it on the side table. It was just as well. She had greater need of a living teacher than a dead one.

"You spoke of other details," she said, her voice strained.

He was still for a long moment before he

gave a short nod. "So I did. Let us talk of stamina and breathing, the placement of feet, chalk lines and, above all, control."

"Control." She had taken a deep, reviving breath while he spoke and was glad to discover that her voice was now reasonably well-modulated.

"Of both our weapons and ourselves," he answered, going on without pause, "Come, take your place here on the piste."

He didn't touch her, but only indicated with a smooth gesture of one hand where he wanted her to stand. Lips compressed, she moved to where he directed, turned to face him. It seemed, with his talk of control, that he might have noticed her confusion after all. That would not do. The last thing she wanted was for him to think there was anything personal in her approach to him. Pride would not permit the use of feminine wiles as a trap. Neither could she see any satisfaction in it.

"Now," he said, his features serious as he joined her on the stretch of canvas, "hold out your arms in this manner."

She did as he illustrated, spreading her arms away from her body and as straight as the tightly fitted sleeve of her walking costume would allow. He shifted until their fingertips overlapped a few inches. Then, as she watched, he turned three-quarters toward her and dropped into a crouch with knees spread, right arm still extended and left bent at the elbow with his hand held at the level of his head.

"Face me and take this position with your right arm extended."

She followed the directive, though she could feel a flush burn its way from her neck to her hairline. All her life long she had been told that a lady never sat or stood with her knees apart. To deliberately spread them, and in front of this Englishman, was like abandoning all modesty. It felt suggestive, even erotic, though she recognized the stance as the typical swordsman's crouch often seen in the mock swordplay of opera and theater.

"Lower," he said. "Bend your knees more. Lift your arms higher."

Her skirts puddled on the floor around her as she complied with the first command, but her tight sleeves prevented elevation of her arms much above the level of her waist. She snatched at the cloth constricting her shoulders, attempting to drag it higher.

He shook his head. "Let that go for the moment, though you will need to wear something with more ease as we progress. Now. Raise your heels until you are on your toes. Lower again. Raise and lower. Again, and yet again. Excellent. This is the movement you will do a hundred times each morning, and again each evening, in order to strengthen the leg muscles. You see?"

"I see." What she saw was the flexing of the long muscles in his legs and the faint impression of manly parts at his crotch. That was before she dragged her gaze upward to where amusement glimmered in his eyes. He apparently understood her discomfiture but thought it misplaced, or else that she had brought it upon herself so had no right to protest. Nor would she, though she clenched her teeth until the muscles of her jaws ached.

"*Bien.* Now lunge toward me — like so."

He launched himself, hand closed as if he grasped a foil. The movement was well-oiled, from thousands upon thousands of repetitions, as natural to him as breathing. It was swift, silent and so powerful that his fist came within inches of her chest. His features were set and his eyes suddenly opaque, as if he had closed off all feeling, retreating inside himself to a place where none could reach. If there had been a sword in his hand, she knew without question that she would be dead.

She had not flinched or moved. It was

some consolation.

Sudden anger boiled up inside her as he retreated to his former stance. She surged in his wake with her own imaginary sword gripped tight. Her aim was low, held by her sleeve and so angled downward. When she stopped, her tight fist grazed his groin.

They stood in frozen tableau. An instant later, his lips twitched and bright hilarity leaped into his eyes. With a crack of laughter, he reeled away, his upper body racked by chuckles that had a rusty sound.

Mortification held Ariadne immobile for long seconds. She spun then, clapping her hands to her fiery cheeks as she put her back to him.

She knew, oh, she *did* know, what lay behind the smooth front of his pantaloons where her knuckles had grazed him, knew the meaning of the steel-like firmness she had touched. That she'd had the temerity, or the bad luck, to land just there was one thing, but that he could laugh at her for it was quite another. She saw nothing remotely funny about it.

That something in the lesson thus far had aroused him left her aghast as well. Men were indiscriminate in their passions, or so she gathered from her sojourn in Parisian society, but this was most unsuitable. How was she to continue if she had to worry that he might press unwelcome attentions upon her?

Even so, she was aware of the slow, hot shift of some half-realized feeling inside her. Part of it was gratification that a man of such dangerous reputation could see her as desirable. For the rest, she preferred not to look too closely.

Passions of the fevered, desperate kind portrayed between doomed lovers in her favorite operas were foreign to Ariadne. She had been fond of her husband in a mild fashion, had honored him for his kindness and attention to her comfort. Allowing him to make love to her had been a duty, one never too onerous or particularly unsettling. Afterward, he had always been so grateful, so very loving that it was nearly enough. Yet sometimes when he had fallen into snoring sleep, she had lain staring into the dark while her body jerked with nerves and unsettled yearning and tears tracked slowly into her hair. And she had wondered then, as she did now, if it might not have been different with another man.

But not this one. No, never, ever this one.

FOUR

Her face, her face . . .

Gavin choked, trying to control the unholy amusement that shook him. His glacially superior pupil could not have looked more appalled if she had discovered he had a jungle snake in his pantaloons. He was sure she would have preferred it.

Regardless, her lunge had been well-executed. She had taken him by surprise as no one had in many a long day, not since he first stepped onto a fencing strip. Her form had been excellent, particularly given the handicap of petticoats, corseting and the ridiculously close-fitting sleeves which rendered a woman helpless in the current fragile and wan style. It was possible she might turn out to be a credit to her *maître.*

Not that the possibility was an object with him. His purpose from the moment he entered the *garçonnière* had been to discourage her ambition to become a swordswoman. On second thought now, he was inclined to go forward with these visits. He could not remember when he had been so entertained. And if the truth be told, he wondered what it would take to bring the lady to touch him with willingness, perhaps even pleasure.

No small amount of that inclination was brought on by the flash of awareness he had caught once again in her eyes, some flicker of hot emotion that roused his curiosity. He had the distinct impression that she would not have cared if she had emasculated him. It was a novel idea, given her remote attitude, one he was inclined to put to the test if the situation arose.

Schooling his features to suitable gravity, he turned back toward his pupil. "Forgive me, Madame Faucher. My sense of the ridiculous sometimes runs away with me."

"You are saying that I . . ."

"No, no, you mistake me," he assured her. "Ferocity in the attack is a fine thing, but requires a weapon to complete it. Perhaps we should take up the foils for this session after all."

"You mean it?"

"I do," he answered, and stepped to where the foils lay on the table with candlelight glimmering along their blades. Choosing one at random, he presented it formally, with a bow and the hilt across his wrist.

The lady met his eyes for a long moment, her own darkly pensive, as if she wondered at his purpose. He could hardly blame her since he was not sure himself. Testing her further might be no more than an excuse to prolong the lesson. No matter; he would do it still. Like the war it resembled, a bout with crossed blades brought out the true natures of those engaged in it. There was little he would not know about the young widow Faucher when they were done.

She lifted her chin as if accepting the challenge she saw in his eyes. Then she took the foil from him and stepped back with the quickness of distrust. He could not but approve. She had more reason than she knew.

Instead of picking up his own foil, Gavin reached for the buttons of his double-breasted frock coat and slipped them from their holes before shrugging off the close-fitting garment and tossing it aside. Removing his watch and chain from his waistcoat pockets, he let them slide from his hand onto the table. He could have stopped there with perfect comfort, but it did not suit him. She was watching, he knew, for he could see her set and pale features from the corner of his eyes. With leisurely movements then, he freed his swirled-glass waistcoat buttons from their holes and stripped away that layer. It was a solecism for a gentleman to appear in his shirt sleeves in front of a lady, of course, and he half expected her to turn her back, make some protest, even leave him. She did none of those things, but stood waiting with a suspended look on her face.

His impulse, to see if he could shake her nerve, was undoubtedly base, but he would not be deflected from it by her valiance. With a rueful smile curving his lips, he reached for his cream silk cravat, pulling it loose and discarding it, then removed, in fine deliberation, the two top studs of his shirt.

"Unconventional, I will agree," he said in answer to the curl of her lower lip as he began to fold back the cuffs of his sleeves, "but I do not, as a rule, fence in full evening dress."

"Only when honor demands it, I do understand. You must not regard my presence."

"Oh, I don't since this is hardly a social occasion."

"Precisely."

It was a reminder, if he needed one, that there was no basis for the two of them to meet socially. None was required. Folding back the other cuff, he took his foil in a hard grip and stepped back onto the strip.

"This," he said, tapping the canvas under their feet with the blunted tip of his blade, "is our world for the moment. If either of us steps off it, the bout is ended and the one who transgressed is the loser. If you want to concede at any time, you have only to say a single word: stop. If I touch you with my foil, you must acknowledge the hit by the classic signal of calling out touché. I will naturally do the same. We begin with a salute, after which we assume the guard position you have been shown. When I give the order, we will raise our weapons and cross them at the tips. I will then provide the signal to begin. Your object during this first lesson will be to touch me, no more than that. All targets are to be above the waist." He paused then ended in soft promise, "And my purpose, of course, will be to touch you. But . . . only above the waist."

Her eyes blazed at him, hot as the fires of hell as she absorbed the innuendo, and rich color bloomed across her cheekbones. He was satisfied. Annoyance with him would perhaps compensate for whatever self-consciousness she might feel due to lack of skill and, just possibly, remove any curb she might be inclined to put on her natural instincts.

He had not brought the usual chest padding and masks since he had expected to have no use for them this evening. It occurred to him as he stood there that without them this initial bout, or *phrase d'armes,* had the feel of a duel. It made no difference. He had no intention of harming a hair on the lady's head. That she could touch him was so unlikely that he hardly considered it at all.

"Ready?" he asked with the lift of a brow.

Her nod was positive, the grip she took on her foil like a stranglehold.

"Good." His foil whistled as he swept it up before his face, then out in a wide arc as he made her an ironic bow. *"Salute!"*

Eyes narrowed, she copied his action. He thought her lips trembled a little at the corners, but she compressed them and stood waiting.

"En garde."

He raised his blade, holding it steady. She lifted her arm, but could not quite meet his steel for the restriction of her sleeve. Obligingly, he lowered his foil tip a fraction as a concession to her problem.

Frustration crossed her features and she reached with her free hand to pull at the tight gray sleeve. The result was plainly inadequate and she scowled as she tried two of three times to stretch higher from the shoulder.

The current fashion seemed likely to defeat her. Gavin stepped back out of the engaged position.

"Wait. Please," she said without quite looking at him. Curling her fingers like claws, she dug them into the cloth of her sleeve and gave a hard wrench. A dull rip sounded, and the stitches holding it at the shoulder seam gave a fraction. She pulled again to break those remaining, then peeled the tight tube of fabric down her arm and tossed it behind her. A cool smile tipped her mouth and she turned to face him again.

Gavin stood in his tracks, his gaze on the bare skin of her arm where it emerged from the ragged armhole. He had wondered if the rest of her had the same warm-pearl bloom as her neck and bosom. Now he knew. Oh, it did indeed. And the nonchalant way she had exposed her arm to his gaze, as if it mattered not at all that he saw, stirred his blood to a slow boil. What would it be like to stand and watch while she ripped away layer after layer of clothing, emerging in naked, incandescent splendor? Would she dare him to touch her or beckon him near?

"En garde?"

She was waiting for the rise of his sword arm. If he was lucky, she would not notice that condition had already been achieved by another portion of his anatomy. Removing the concealment of his coat had been a monumental error, a bit of provocation she had trumped without trying. He would do well to remember it next time he sought to disturb her composure.

With a short nod, he lifted his foil, crossing the lady's at the tip. Her blade felt steady, as if she might have gained confidence from the small respite. That was just as well for her sake, he thought with conscious benevolence.

"Begin," he said with an encouraging nod.

She struck straight for his heart. Lips tight, teeth clenched, she came at him with every ounce of her strength and murder in her eyes. No tentative beating of blades or delicate forays, no exploration of his competence or the force of his objectives, just a lunging attack at his vitals that came close, too close, to succeeding.

His guard came up before his brain kicked into motion. Slapping her point aside, he parried, defending with a scrape of blades that rained orange sparks onto the floor. There was only one thing to be done after that, and he did it with ruthless competence.

Swirling his wrist in hard riposte, he caught her steel, bending, binding, lifting as he stepped into her guard.

She cried out. The foil flew from her hand, describing a shining arch before it struck the floor with a hollow thud and went spinning away across the room.

"God's teeth, woman, what do you think you're doing?" He slung his own blade onto the table with a hard clatter before turning back to face her.

She was holding her wrist, rubbing it, her face pale, almost bloodless. "Fencing," she answered tightly.

"Committing bloody murder is more like it."

"Isn't that the point?" The words had a strained sound.

"This isn't a duel and I'm not your enemy. You're here to learn to defend yourself. Slashing and stabbing in a wild rage won't do it." He paused, nodded toward her wrist. "Did I hurt you?"

"It's only numb." She shook her hand then let her arms fall to her side as she raised her eyes to his. "Perhaps it will be best if we stop here."

She was furious that he had disarmed her. He had expected no less. Still he had not thought she would give up so easily. "As you wish," he said, and began to fold down his cuffs. "Consider this evening's lesson an experiment, one without charge."

"And tomorrow evening?"

His fingers stilled. "You expect to continue?"

"Of a certainty. You said I was to say stop to end our passage at arms, not to end the lessons."

She despised him and seemed to scorn his methods. She was not, insofar as he could see, here with him this evening because she hoped for a passionate affair, nor had she a titillated inclination to make love to a man with blood on his hands as did some women he had known. He had done what he might to discourage her ambition, and thought she disliked it intensely. Yet she suggested another assignation.

What did she want of him? That there was something, he knew very well; he could feel it with every instinct he possessed. Whatever her game, he should refuse to play.

Oh, yes, he should refuse, but where was the pleasure in that? As alive and intrigued as he felt at this moment, it just might be that whatever she wanted from him, she could have with his blessing.

"It is best to rest a day between lessons until the muscles become accustomed to the exercise. I will be here the day after tomorrow then, madame. And you? Will you come to me all armored with woe and anger — oh, and something less in the way of petticoats?"

"Wait," she said without a smile. "Wait, and you shall see."

Gavin inclined his head. It was puerile, stupid and entirely selfish under the circumstances, perhaps, but he intended to do that very thing.

Nothing whatever could prevent him.

FIVE

"*Mon cher!* How early you are out and about. Have you eaten? Do you care for coffee? Solon, another cup for Monsieur Blackford."

Gavin surveyed Maurelle with a satirical smile since it was midday. He was fully able to appreciate the rakish picture she made, however, dressed *en déshabille* with one of the soft Oriental turbans so fashionable this season covering her hair and an exotic *blouse volante,* or Mother Hubbard, flowing in copious amounts of russet and gold silk around her lush form. "I trust I am not disturbing you, *chère madame,*" he said at his most ingratiating. "Time is a slippery beast — I thought it later as I've seen half a dozen clients already this morning."

"Such energy and stamina, particularly on a gray morning that is perfect for lying abed." She shuddered while watching her butler place a cup for him and pour twin streams of hot coffee and hot milk into it. "And after a late evening, too. So heathen of you, *cher*. Have a roll to sustain you while you tell me why I am being honored with this visit."

Gavin waved away the roll, but took the café au lait and sipped from it before making an indirect reply. "Madame Faucher lingers among the sheets still?"

"That one? No, no, she is nearly as mad for morning light and rain as you. I am told she and my maid Adele are out making a round of the shops. Her own maid remained in Paris, you realize, being positive she would be menaced by wild savages should she venture across the water. I believe dear Ariadne mentioned something about an ensemble appropriate for fencing lessons, but I was half asleep at the time. You wished to see her?"

"But yes, and at any time," he answered in the prescribed formula, "though it suits me to speak with you alone. Have you any idea why she wants to carve the guts from some poor devil and serve him up with an apple in his mouth?"

Maurelle, apparently startled in the middle of a smiling approval of his pale yellow cravat held by a turquoise pin, lifted her eyes to meet his quizzical gaze. "What makes you think she might?"

"Being attacked in the gentleman's stead. I don't regard sundry sword cuts in the midst of fevered play, but would prefer they be expected."

"She didn't!"

"No, though she tried. Perhaps you can tell me whether aiding her is a matter of mercy or folly."

"She cannot have thought she could best you."

"If she did, she does so no longer." He paused a moment, frowning at his inability to say with any exactness what Ariadne Faucher did or did not think. She should not have remained such a mystery after their short bout. It was annoying that he had not been able to tell what drove her or the lengths she was capable of going to achieve her aim. Sheer surprise at her ferocity had wiped all else from his mind during those few seconds of play. That riled him even more. "So, should I wear my padding back-to-fore?"

Maurelle touched a languid hand to her temple. "Please, *cher,* do not be obscure so early in the morning for I'm not up to it. If you mean to ask is she mad enough to stab anyone in the back, the answer is no. No indeed. She's quite sane."

68

"Only enraged past all bearing. Why?"

"I'm sure I don't know. She presented this fencing arrangement to me as a whim or perhaps a small attempt at setting a fashion."

He leaned back in his chair, his gaze watchful as he toyed with his cup. Maurelle was avoiding his gaze now, and he would swear she had grown pale about the mouth. "If you suspected more, you would not tell me?"

"Now, *mon cher.*"

"Would you?"

She put a hand to her turban, pushing it into a more becoming drape before reaching for a roll. "Certainly not without permission. I do try to be loyal to my friends."

So she did, he conceded as he appraised her through his lashes. Maurelle loved gossip as she loved life, but had her own personal code in such matters, one as stringent as that governing the conduct of sword masters. "You must have known the lady for some time for her to be so near and dear."

"A number of years, yes. We met in Paris during one of my sojourns there."

"Her accent is not Parisian."

"Her family is from Louisiana, somewhere upriver, I believe. She had just been married to the head of a banking family of some renown in France when we became acquainted. Her parents had returned here, leaving her behind, and she was lonely since she knew no one in the city, scarcely knew her husband."

"An arranged marriage, then."

"And an excellent alliance, though he was ill with consumption. Jean Marc Faucher was a distant relation of her father's, a kind and gentle man of great intelligence and understanding. He thought perhaps to sire a child to live after him, though it was not to be."

"He hardly sounds the kind to give his wife a distaste for men."

"Certainly not."

"What of her father? Did he force her to accept the match?"

Maurelle's smile had a wry edge. "What a romantic you are, *cher.* But I must tell you that Ariadne revered her father. It was ever an object with her to please him, and she made no objection whatever to the marriage. In all truth, she was . . ."

"What?" he asked as she trailed off, a conscious expression flitting across her face before she hid it in her coffee cup.

"She had no other attachment and was just as happy to be in France."

"Leaving scandal behind, or did she drag it, whining, at her heels?"

"Nothing of the sort! She had been living quietly in the country."

"A difficult thing to imagine," he said, recalling the soignée lady he had met on that first evening.

"I assure you it's true. If you must know, she was taken abroad because her parents thought her too subdued."

"All pale and forlorn, possibly pining after a lost love?" He tipped his head, waiting to see if Maurelle would respond to that assessment.

"After her brother, rather, with whom she was quite close. He had come to town for a little polish, leaving her behind at home."

"Here to the Vieux Carré, you mean."

She gave a brief nod. "So, there you have her history, *mon ami,* dull as it may be. All I can say is you must have given her the wrong idea concerning the use of the foils, or else so incensed her with your obstinate manner that her feelings overcame her."

"Perhaps," he allowed in pensive tones.

Maurelle raised expressive brows. "What did you do?"

"Nothing that I recall, which means I may have to repeat what passed between us in order to discover it."

71

"Monsieur Blackford!"

"Oh, never fret, *chère madame.* She will be safe, if not particularly subdued, in my hands."

She watched him while an odd expression, half gratified, half disapproving and wholly captivated, appeared in her fine eyes. When she spoke, her voice held tones as ripe and mellow as a winter pear. "You are *épris.* Who would have thought it? All the ladies who have paraded themselves before you, and what piques your interest? One who cares only for swordplay — which is her appeal no doubt, other than that she has no use for you beyond your expertise. If you had but known, you might have made a fortune as a tutor of female clients."

"Or not," he said, his voice dry. "One seems more than enough."

"You don't deny being smitten?"

"Of course I deny it, *mon amour,* for what good it may do me. Curiosity was ever my downfall, and now that I have awakened from my ennui, I discover you on my trail. I must surrender at once and take what comes to me."

"Especially if it may be the lady, I do see," she replied with a moue of irritation for his blithe manner. "No, I won't help you there. Ariadne has had enough to overset her without adding a daring English devil to the list."

"Other than the passing of her husband you mean?"

Maurelle tipped her head in assent. "Her parents are no longer alive, nor her brother."

"Oh, yes, so she told me. An epidemic of misfortune, it seems." He went on with barely a pause. "So now she is alone."

"In a manner of speaking."

His hostess hesitated, but shrugged whatever she might have added away as if too unimportant to mention. Gavin let it go as well. Rising to his feet, he moved to the side table where Solon had left his hat and cane. "But she has you, madame. And I shall do my poor best to see that she is not injured by whatever misbegotten specimen of manhood has earned her dislike. That will, you perceive, be my sole contribution to making her visit useful and long, a thrill everlasting."

"Will it?" Madame Maurelle Herriot murmured, tapping her teeth with a fingernail and staring after him when he had bowed over her hand and taken himself from the breakfast room out onto the gallery overlooking the courtyard where rain still pattered down. "Will it indeed?"

Gavin heard the quiet comment but did

not bother to look back, much less answer
it.

Six

On her return to the town house, Ariadne sent the maid Adele, young, spritely and charming in her white, kerchief-like tignon and gold earrings, to the kitchen where she might dry her skirts before the fire. Pausing on the gallery outside the salon, she removed her bonnet and gave her rain cloak into Solon's keeping so it would not drip on the carpets. She smoothed her hair and shook out the skirts of her walking costume of forest green broadcloth, then moved to join her hostess whom she had caught sight of through the French doors.

Maurelle looked up from the letter she was penning at her *secrétaire* to give Ariadne a quick smile. "There you are at last. I expected you back an hour ago, *chère*. Are you quite drowned?"

"Very near it," she answered on a low laugh. "I'd almost forgotten how it rains here, great plopping drops so different from the civilized sprinklings of Paris."

"Pour a cup of chocolate to warm yourself. Solon brought it just this moment so it's quite hot."

"So he told me," Ariadne stepped to the tray where a chocolate pot painted with a spray of carnations was set out with matching cups and a crystal cake stand piled with meringues. Filling her cup, she strolled with it to the fire that burned in the coal grate beneath the mantel of white marble, holding a hand out to the flames. "He takes good care of you, your Solon."

"I hardly know what I would do without him." Maurelle sanded her letter then folded it. "You had a successful expedition?"

"Most successful."

"You found a fencing costume then?"

"Commissioned one, rather." Her smile was roguish. "I can hardly wait to see your face when you behold it. I don't know who was more shocked at my request, Adele or Madame Pluche."

Maurelle gave her a resigned look. "What have you done now?"

"I shan't tell you for fear you'll insist I cancel the order. You'll have to see for yourself."

"*Mon Dieu.* As if fencing lessons and midnight meetings with dangerous swordsmen weren't enough. Keep this pace, and even your besotted Russian may desert you."

"If only he would. How do you discourage a man who believes himself indispensable to your existence?"

"With ease, if you are certain it's what you want. I have been meaning to ask what passes between you, *chère*. I knew this Sasha, as you call him in the Russian way of pet names, danced attendance upon you in Paris while I was there, but had not realized matters were serious between you."

"Nor are they except in his mind." Ariadne sighed.

"Why not, pray? Rumor in Paris was that he is a cousin to the czar, in spite of having a French mother."

"So he is, though he left St. Petersburg under a cloud. I don't know the details, but it seems to have been too close an association with those involved in a failed coup or some such thing. His exile is a great grief to him, especially being parted from his family. As for our first meeting, he appointed himself my *cavaliere servante.* This was while Jean Marc was ill, you know, and quite had my husband's approval since he was unable to take me about and preferred I have some protection. Sasha has never stepped over the line and always executed the duties of his role most faithfully."

"Which is why you hesitate to wound him, I suppose." Maurelle's wise gaze reflected her understanding of the usefulness to a married lady of such an admirer. Quite accepted in European capitals, so-called servant cavaliers put in an appearance on visiting days, acted as escort on shopping excursions or outings to the theater or a soiree when the husband was indisposed or disinclined, made themselves the bearers of their lady's cloak, gloves or fan, and regularly presented such trifles as books, flowers and bonbons. Though the pose was one of selfless devotion, not unlike that of the knights of the ancient Court of Love, the gentleman's attachment was only half serious in most cases, serving as a convenient shield against the wiles of nubile females and their matchmaking *mamans.* While a love affair sometimes developed, dread of *la scandale* was usually enough to assure a mere platonic attachment.

"He was there when I needed a friend," Ariadne answered in wry agreement.

"I do see the difficulty. But you may have one even more pressing now."

"Meaning?" Her attention was caught by the unaccustomed seriousness of Maurelle's voice. Motherly concern was not usually her friend's style.

"Monsieur Blackford did me the honor of calling this morning."

Ariadne felt as if someone had yanked her corset's strings so it squeezed her chest. "And?"

"You seem to have aroused his interest, something not easily done. Are you sure you know what you are about?"

"He was asking questions?"

"Quite pointed ones," Maurelle agreed, and went on to give examples. "I accused him of being infatuated but he avoided an answer."

"So I should hope!"

Even as she spoke, Ariadne recalled with searing vividness the few minutes when the Englishman had removed his coat and waistcoat in front of her while a smile hovered at one corner of his beautifully molded mouth. His dexterous fingers had slipped the studs from his shirt, leaving the strong column of his neck exposed at the front, along with the barest hint of dark gold chest hair. He had known she watched and minded not at all, as if he thought her a woman of experience who might be entertained.

It made her temper rise merely to think of

it. How dare he assume such a thing? And the way he had disarmed her, with a mere flick of his wrist? Infuriating.

Nonetheless, she had been transfixed for a long moment, stunned into immobility by the perfection of line and form and intimation of raw power to be found in a man's body. Her husband had never undressed in front of her but always came to her bedchamber in darkness. Whether it was to save her blushes or because he knew his illness was wasting his muscles and virility she had no idea. The result was a great deal less experience with such scenes than Monsieur Blackford might suppose.

She was not the kind of woman to be influenced by flagrant masculinity, however. She preferred men with tender and gentle manners who appreciated music and poetry and the more graceful aspects of life. Sweaty power and the ability to kill did not make her heart beat faster. No, not at all.

"Giving Sasha his *congé* could be premature," she said after a moment.

"You feel your Russian may be some protection against Monsieur Blackford's interest? As much as I dislike causing you worry, I assure you Sasha will be of little use should the Englishman decide to pursue you. He holds few things sacred, recognizes fewer barriers to his desires or even his caprices. On the other hand, I cannot imagine him making a fool of himself over a woman who holds him in disregard. He has too much pride for it."

"Or too much arrogance?"

"Oh, I'll grant that he holds himself as high as any swordsman in the city, but he allows little to touch him personally."

Ariadne gave her a direct look. "You seem to know him well."

"He has been in and out of this town house along with the other sword masters and their wives I've spoken of so often, Nicholas Pasquale and his Juliette, Caid O'Neill and his wife Lisette, the Conde de Lérida and his *condessa*, Celina. Yes, and the American, Kerr Wallace, as well — it was Monsieur Blackford who introduced him to me and they are often together as neither has a household beyond the rooms above their ateliers." Maurelle lifted a plump shoulder. "Still, he is a most private man. I'd not presume to say I know him."

"By his choice, I'd imagine."

Her friend's expression turned pensive and she set down her chocolate cup before turning back to Ariadne. "About these lessons between you, there is something I must know. Can you really have said you intend

81

to use any skill you gain for revenge? If I'd thought for an instant you had any such idea, I would never have presented Monsieur Blackford. Tell me, I beg, that he misunderstood what you said to him."

To lie went against the grain, yet it was impossible to admit Maurelle into her confidence. She of all people would understand at once who the target must be and would surely move to stop her. Ariadne tried to look mystified. "He must have, mustn't he?"

Maurelle gave her a long look, but was prevented from further questions by a commotion on the gallery outside the salon door. An instant later, Solon bowed a lady into the room.

"Madame Savoie," he announced.

The new arrival was a monumental female made more so by the generous width and carpet-brushing length of her lavender velvet cloak. A large hat of purple felt with an upturned brim and a lavender-dyed feather swirling around the crown topped her head, and her hair beneath the confection was drawn back in a severe style like a helmet of polished copper. Clinging to her shoulder was a green-and-yellow parrot that leaned forward, bobbing up and down and whistling with piercing effect. As she cast her outerwear into Solon's waiting arms, she was seen to be clad in purple satin with a laced, Elizabethan bodice that barely confined her magnificent bosom. Drawing attention to it was a necklace of amethysts and diamonds of a size that should have cried paste but looked amazingly real. Her nose was commanding, the cast of her chin and cheekbones from a heroic mold, and her voice as she spoke had such resonance that it rattled the china ornaments on the marble fireplace mantel and roused echoes in the salon's high, plastered ceiling.

"Chocolate, *chère* Maurelle, for the love of God," she pleaded. "I smell chocolate and must have it this instant. My landlady is a paragon among women but has only coffee and I am like to die of craving the sweet elixir of life, that nectar of the goddess. Oh, please, let me have chocolate!"

"At once," Maurelle said, rising and embracing the vision, then turning to pour from the chocolate service. "Ariadne, permit me to present a diva of talent *extraordinaire* who will be singing at the Theatre d'Orleans. Zoe, here is another of my dear friends, Ariadne Faucher. Sit, sit, both of you, drink your chocolate and let us be comfortable together."

Maurelle moved to the settee beside

83

Ariadne, giving Madame Savoie the fauteuil she had been using so they made a circle around the low table where the chocolate tray sat. Madame Zoe began at once to demolish the pile of meringues on their stand while she and Maurelle caught up on the latest scandals and quarrels in the theater, the bankruptcies and gaming losses among its backers and the problems with upcoming productions. The opera star was witty, outrageous and often ribald, but not snide or spiteful in her opinions. Ariadne liked her at once.

"You must come to see me in my benefit performance next week, Ariadne. Maurelle has a box and will bring you. Yes, Maurelle? There, all is arranged. And you will both invite as many handsome men as you may find, if you please. I do adore looking at them when I sing of desperate passion — one must have inspiration, you know. Some of these sword masters of yours will do nicely, Maurelle, married or unmarried makes no difference since I mean to look instead of seduce, more's the pity. Of course, I might make an exception for the Englishman, Blackford."

"Le diable!" the parrot chortled, presumably to himself. At the same time, he lifted a foot and scratched vigorously at his ear, as

if clearing his hearing.

"What a charming companion!" Ariadne said, certain the bird's comment had been accidental even if describing Blackford as a devil did seem particularly appropriate. "Have you had him long?"

"Oh, forever, fifteen years at the very least. Napoleon was given to me by an admirer in Havana. Unfortunately, his vocabulary had already been corrupted when he came to me. Pay no attention to him." The parrot, perhaps hearing some inflection which allowed him to know he was the subject of conversation, stretched his neck to preen the feather on his mistress's hat. "Stop that, you fiend, or I'll put you in the pot like a chicken," she scolded with affection in her voice. To further dissuade him, she handed him a piece of meringue which he took in one claw and immediately began to crumble upon her shoulder.

Eying the bird's beak that seemed as tough as a horse's hoof but with a much sharper edge, Ariadne asked, "Does he never hurt you?"

"Not I," the diva said with a deep laugh. "He thinks I'm his inamorata or else his mother, which one I've never been precisely sure. He is most caressing, I promise you. He never soils me — not that you asked, but so many do. Most other people he views as prey and pinches with his beak. The exception is Monsieur Blackford whom he tolerates, barely, for the sake of the pecans he brings him."

"He visits you, the Englishman?"

"In my dressing room, yes. He comes to see me every season I am here, regardless of the production. Not that he sheds tears like the beautiful swordsman Rosière, but I shiver, positively shiver, to hear his shouts of 'Brava, Brava!' in his so English voice. It's lovely to be appreciated, do you not agree? Naturally, I send to invite him backstage, and we have an occasional dinner."

"Naturally," Maurelle murmured.

"You begrudge me?" the singer inquired with the lift of a brow. "You want him all for yourself? But *chère,* he is so fascinating with the quickness of his mind that advances, parries and ripostes like the flashing of his sword. I listen with my mouth catching flies. And the subtlety of his insults, like the cut that only begins to bleed long after it is made. So droll he is, too, at times, yet he has such pain inside him."

Ariadne looked up, her expression openly skeptical, or so she feared. "Pain?"

"He has not had an easy time of it, but

then who among us has? We all have a cry-ing child trapped inside us, one we must feed chocolate to stop its tears." She held out her cup for a refill, her green gaze wry even as she lifted a shoulder. "Or give the poor dear something even more delicious as she grows up, like love."

"Oh, love." Maurelle was politely amused.

"But yes," the diva answered, her eyes sparkling. "We are none of us *jeunes filles* here, lacking the experience to understand that physical love can soothe more than a mere itch."

Maurelle chuckled. Ariadne mustered a smile but could not see that the sally re-quired comment. "It appears you are in the gentleman's confidence."

"A little, perhaps," the diva allowed. "People talk to me, you see. I don't know why it is, but there you are."

"Merde," the parrot muttered with his eyes on his meringue.

It was probably the lady's abundant inter-est and tolerance, Ariadne thought while watching the bird's antics, and perhaps her profession that was not known for its re-spectability. She might receive adulation, be feted for her achievements, but, rather like the sword masters, would never be accepted into the rigid ranks of aristocratic French

Creole society. The prohibition might make her willing to overlook things that would shock those within the select and protected circle. Ariadne felt herself drawn to the diva, though what she really wanted of her was some indication of weakness in the gentleman they discussed, something that might be forged into a weapon.

"Handsome, healthy, of good family in England," she said with a twist of her lips, "what could possibly plague Monsieur Blackford?"

The diva gave her a clear look. "As with so many others, his family connections rob him of peace. A mother whom he seldom saw as a child, a statesman father who was almost never in England, a grandfather who reared him but despised his preference for books and the sword instead of hunting and guns. Then there was his older brother, the heir apparent, intent on stepping into their grandfather's shoes and titles, after their father, so he aped the old gentleman in all things. They fought, of course, as brothers do, but particularly when one is intent on making the other feel inferior. As the heir was seven years older, it was an uneven contest, with the younger of the two getting the worst of it. Except when it was a war of words. It was in these, I'm sure, that he learned the uses of biting wit allied to circumlocution."

Ariadne could easily imagine it, the two boys facing off against each other, the smaller one tearing the character of the older to shreds with lilting phrases, the older frowning, bull-like in his lack of understanding, unable to answer the high-flown invective except with his fists. Afterward, the younger boy lying bruised and bloodied, but grimly satisfied that the last word had been his.

Abruptly, she shook her head. She didn't want to think of it, didn't want to envision Gavin Blackford's sorrows and defeats or to be forced to feel sympathy because of them. What had happened to him as a child had nothing to do with his conduct as a man. At some point every person had to discard the past and all the grim things that had happened, to pick up the threads of their lives and weave them into a different pattern, one nearer the ideal they carried in their mind. Events of long ago could not be used as an excuse for whatever occurred, all the things people allowed because they could not, or would not, summon the will to make it otherwise.

For a stark instant, she was reminded of the grief she had known and how it haunted her still. But she was doing something to put it from her, was she not? She had left Paris, the comfort of her husband's home and the supervision of his relatives, to come here. She was attempting to make what had taken place more bearable. She wasn't wallowing in her misfortune or lying supine with a cloth soaked in cologne on her forehead while others dealt with the details of living. No, not even if her husband's family would have preferred it.

Jean Marc's brother had offered his hand in marriage. She was still astounded by that bit of hypocrisy since she well knew the purpose was to keep the fortune she had inherited in the family. His sisters had pleaded with her to accept the proposal, had wept and sworn they could not bear to be parted with her. Perhaps she had grown hard and cynical, but she could not think there was a word of truth in anything they said.

Remaining with them would have meant lingering in a past made dreary by grief and remembrance. She had to move forward, to break free so she could live again.

"Chère?"

It was Maurelle who spoke, putting out a hand to gain her attention by touching her arm. Ariadne gave her a wan smile. "A thousand pardons, my thoughts were else-where. You were saying?"

"Zoe asked if you wished to attend a soi-rée tomorrow evening, and offered tickets to her benefit later in the week."

The diva gave a decided nod that was echoed by the parrot. "The manager sponsors this soirée, you perceive, to introduce the opera company here as the season comes into its own. The food and wine will be excellent and the company the best." She kissed her fingertips in an extravagant gesture. "Her benefit is, well, beneficial to my purse."

"The last sounds lovely but I must miss the party. I have another engagement."

"Do you? And what might it be?" Zoe gave her a droll smile. "Perhaps I may prefer to do something other than smile and smile and be obliged to sing before the night is done."

"Nothing of great interest." The fewer who knew of her appointments with a fencing master, Ariadne thought, the better it would be.

"You may as well tell her, *chère*."

"Indeed?"

"Being in and out of the house so often she is sure to stumble onto the truth."

"Mais jamais!" the parrot screamed.

It was again astonishingly apropos, almost as if the parrot understood the conversation, though it might also be on account of his having eaten the last of his meringue. With a small shrug, she said, "I am to have another fencing lesson. Maurelle has been kind enough to allow the use of a room for the exercise."

"But how brave of you!"

"Not at all. More patience than courage was required at our last lesson." She drank the last of her cooling chocolate, trying to appear blasé.

"Our lesson?" Zoe watched her, her eyes bright and a little too knowing for comfort. "You have a fencing master for instruction then. Which, if I may ask?"

"Monsieur Blackford. You see the reason for my interest in his past."

"Oh, *ma chère,* I could almost envy you. These bouts are private, yes? To be closeted with the Englishman, to face him as he is stripped for action — *là,* my heart runs away with me to think of it." The diva put a hand to her ample chest, her eyes bright with exaggerated humor.

"It is nothing so very exciting." Ariadne was conscious of the warmth in her face even as she made the protest.

"Don't tell me it is all mere thrust and

parry! I shall not believe it, don't want to believe it. No, no, it is all of the most romantic, I'm sure. I shall do myself the honor of attending on Maurelle the morning after, just to see how you progress."

"Vache!" the parrot said.

Ariadne, politely smiling, could only agree. Holy cow, indeed. The last thing she had intended was to draw more attention to her meetings with Monsieur Blackford. At the rate things were going, she might as well nail announcements to the lampposts and charge admission.

She must learn what she needed to know, then end this affair. The sooner, the better.

SEVEN

"Practical, most practical," Gavin said as he turned with the lazy lift of a brow to observe the ensemble Ariadne had chosen to wear for their second fencing session. "Also provocative. Is it meant to show your dedication or as a distraction?"

"The idea was simply to be able to move with more ease. And you did suggest fewer petticoats."

She closed the door of the long *garçon-nière* chamber and came forward, much more aware than she wanted to be of the plain muslin *canezou* blouse she wore this evening which pulled over the head through an opening that plunged deep unless the overlapping ends at its front were securely fastened beneath the belt at her waistline. She had rolled the shirred sleeves to her elbows to free her gloved hands, in imitation of the *maître d'armes,* then used the pull cords running through the skirts of *tan d'or* twill — ordinarily used to lift the hem of the walking costume to avoid mud puddles — to raise it above her ankles in their soft leather half-boots. She had left off her heaviest petticoat with its stiffening of woven horsehair, or *crin,* retaining only a single underskirt for modesty. If Monsieur Blackford thought the resulting display of wrist and ankle provocative, she could hardly wait to see his reaction to the ensemble she had ordered yesterday morning.

Not that it mattered what he thought, of course. It was only that how he saw her, what he thought of her, might be useful.

Nevertheless, the heat she noted in the dark blue depths of his eyes made her so self-conscious it was difficult to move with any kind of grace. She was too closely reminded that no corset confined her waist and only the clever seaming in her camisole supported her breasts so they moved as she walked forward, brushing against the fabric with a tingling sensation in their sensitive peaks. That she and the sword master were alone once more, isolated by any number of rooms from Maurelle and her guests for the evening, was not lost on her either.

She should have insisted that the maid, Adele, attend them. The idea had crossed her mind only to be dismissed. It was pride that made her reluctant to have anyone as witness, at least in part. She was a novice at this sport, after all, and must naturally be somewhat inept. Then she was not some young girl requiring constant supervision, and it seemed best not to set a precedent. The time might come when she would prefer to have no witnesses.

"Thoughtful, possibly, but not simple," he said as he watched her approach. "Still, if you don't mind the draft, I don't mind the view."

Her lips tightened. Let him look, for what good it might do him. She would even return the favor so he might see her lack of concern. He had made his preparations again in the manner she had copied, and stood now in his shirt sleeves with the candlelight gleaming in the dark gold waves of his hair and creating leaping flames in his eyes. The only change was that he wore trousers this evening instead of pantaloons, with straps that fastened under boots of supple leather that had thin soles which would doubtless slip more easily over the fencing strip.

"Shall we begin?" she asked, then cleared her throat of its unaccountable huskiness. "I'm sure you will be glad to have done with this task so you may enjoy the rest of your evening."

"Now there you are wrong. This evening is my *raison d'être* and only solace. Prolonging it is my object. Do you doubt it?"

"Frankly, yes," she said. "Or will you leave me armed for more than an instant?"

"You are still annoyed over that, like the brick-mason's helper reprimanded for sloth who had only two naps all day, each four hours in duration. Passion without politesse does not a fencer make. You must control your emotions, madame, or they will defeat you."

A hard knot formed in her chest as she absorbed his meaning. Was there another message in the words? It seemed possible; he was not a stupid man. Oh, but surely not. He could know nothing of her real purpose.

"I shall endeavor to remember," she said finally.

"Cry peace and hosanna but no quarter, and let us arm ourselves."

He turned to where chest pads and masks lay ready next to the case of foils on the long side table. Handing the smaller of the two pads to her, one shorter at the lower front than his own, he showed her how to manipulate the buckles, also how to pull the wire-grid mask on over her face. Then he stepped back, leaving her to it while he donned his own protection.

The concealment made him seem a different man, she thought, watching covertly even as she struggled with the metal fastenings of the chest pad. It removed personality and identity, concealed the changes of expression that might indicate imminent attack or vulnerability, exultation or pain. His eyes were only a blue glimmer, a bright hint of mockery that might have been for her but could also be for the arrangement, or even for himself.

He was as much aware of her as she was of him, for he swept off his mask and strode back to her, removing his gloves and tucking them under one arm. "Allow me," he said, and reached to brush her hands aside, fastening the buckle that had stymied her with quick, competent movements.

"Thank you." The words were uneven. He was so close, much too close. His scent of starched linen, night freshness and warm maleness enveloped her.

"Reluctant gratitude," he said mildly, "is often worse than none. Breathe."

It was a frowning instant before she realized he wanted to check the fit of her padding. It was, she saw as she lowered her gaze, down-filled and white, no doubt the better to show blood if sliced by an accidental blow. She filled her lungs with air to show that she could, in fact, breathe without unusual effort.

The movement lifted the padded vest. He reached to catch the front edges, tugging them into place. His gloved knuckles grazed her abdomen in shockingly intimate contact. She inhaled more deeply, a soft sound in the quiet, while something warm and tenuous swirled inside her before settling heavily in her lower belly.

He met her eyes, the dark sapphire depths of his own rich with contemplation and something more that hovered, tightly restrained, behind it. The moment stretched, marked only by the flutter of a candle flame and the distant clip-clop of passing carriage horses in the street beyond the windows. She was almost painfully aware of his virility and inherent power. She wanted to step away but could not move, could find nothing to say even in protest.

His gaze flickered downward, lingered. Following it, she saw that his adjustment of the padding had pulled the opening of her *canezou* blouse lower, exposing the upper curves of her breasts. Something she saw in his face caused the heat in her midsection to leap higher, flushing her throat, scalding her face. Yet she would not acknowledge it, would not call attention to her exposure by attempting to cover herself.

He released her abruptly and turned away, ducking his head as he pulled on his mask again. Reaching for his gloves, he drew them firmly into place then picked up his foil from the nearby table as he stepped to the strip.

She followed more slowly while pressing the leather of her own gloves tighter between her spread fingers. She had thought they would protect her from any chance contact, but she had been in error. The question that occupied her mind was just how intentional the sword master's aid just now had been, how unavoidable. She had the distinct impression that he did nothing without a reason. What possible purpose could he have for touching her except, possibly, to unsettle her?

The leather-wrapped hilt of the foil and its metal guard felt cold as she took it up, and the blunted blade was weightier than she recalled. However, she would not show it, but moved to her place on the piste with as much impassivity as the man who joined her there. Even as she stepped on the canvas strip, a troublesome doubt unfurled inside her. Was it possible she had miscalculated?

Ariadne turned to face the sword master. He swept up his blade in salute and down again, his eyes a watchful flicker behind his mask. She followed suit, then waited with her foil tip resting on the strip for what might come next.

"We will begin," he said, "with a series of taps at the tips of our two blades, taps as soft as a lover's sigh, as tentative as a first kiss. It will be a gentle exploration of intentions and desires, no kind of assault. You understand?"

"I believe so."

"Good," he replied, his voice like warm honey; then he continued without change, *En garde.*"

She reached out to cross his foil tip with hers. Scarcely had they touched when he gave the office to begin. They exchanged the beats he had described for several seconds, their blades chiming together in measured rhythm as polite and steady as a metronome. Abruptly, he launched into an advance that pushed her blade aside, sliding past it to immediately touch her chest padding. It was a careful nudge, one that barely curved his blade, but she did not make the mistake of believing it was not rigorously planned.

"Touché," she said, her gaze level.

"Excellent," he said with a nod. "To acknowledge a touch is always a matter of honor. A fencer should never call out his own claim to a touch made upon his opponent for that's vainglory. Nor should he inquire about one that has not been acknowledged. If you should happen to concede a touch I don't believe is valid, I will decline credit for it by saying *pas de touché,* not a touch."

"I understand."

"We begin again. This time, *you* will advance."

She did as he directed, but her small foray was instantly flicked aside so she defended once more. Again and yet again they went through the movements while their blades chimed and clanked until, abruptly, he swirled into a riposte and she felt the thud of his buttoned point against her padding again.

"Touché." She had to unclench her teeth to make the acknowledgement.

"Just so. Again." He waited only until she had raised her foil before he continued. "Fencing, you should realize, can be like a silent conversation, one in which you come to know your opponent. You sense the strength of his wrist, the power of his will, the extent of his training, his physical condition, whether he views himself as invincible or merely competent. These things can all affect the end of a *phrase d'armes.*"

"Yes, I see." Insofar as she could tell his strength was unyielding and his physical condition superb if the disturbingly well-oiled flexing of the muscles in his shoulders and thighs was any indication. She was no judge of his training but thought he most certainly had no doubt of his invincibility. The almost negligent ease with which he controlled the passage between them was beyond annoying, well beyond.

"Or consider it in the light of a flirtation," he went on, his voice lilting above the measured tap and clack of the blades. "Just as you would not reveal your every feeling to a suitor, it's bad strategy to permit that advantage to an opponent. Hold something of yourself in reserve so he is left guessing. Allow him to wonder, to doubt, to feel that he has no chance."

The image he conjured up was disturbing, while some tender current within the deep timbre of his voice sent a shiver along her arm. It seemed best to put an end to that. "And if he becomes importunate?"

He gave a short laugh. "Then you are allowed a slap to remind him of his place."

"This is the method you use to teach

young men to defend themselves?"

"By no means. Instruction is much more direct in their case."

"Why make an exception for me?"

"You suspect condescension? Or is it the comparison to flirtation that offends?"

She would give much to see his face. It was frustrating to be unable to guess whether he was flirting in all truth or merely goading her. "Neither," she answered. "I only seek the true value of the lesson."

"Done," he said, his voice even. An instant later, he touched her again, a gentle probe of his sword point that landed squarely on her padded nipple. He stepped back, surveyed her for a long moment, gave a nod.

They began again.

Now his comments were an unending dissertation on the advance, the parry, the riposte. He called corrections for her form and how she moved, and as regularly as a ticking clock, he invaded her defenses for a light, expert touch.

It was maddening.

Her right arm felt on fire. Her lungs worked like a bellows and the fog of her breath slicked the inside of her mask. She wanted to cry quits but stubborn pride would not allow it. And she hated the man who faced her with a fierce heat that was the only thing that allowed her to lift her foil again and again.

"So you would be a Boadicea with your enemy lying dead at your feet," he said after a small interval of silent combat. "What has this man done to make you long to shed his blood?"

"That is no concern of yours." It was all she could do to rap out the words as her heartbeat thundered in her ears and she struggled to draw enough air into her lungs.

"Even if I forge the weapon of his doom?"

"You do the same . . . for men every day. What is . . . one more?"

"An excellent question, one I would debate at length another time. My more pressing concern is that this enemy of yours may leave you lifeless on the ground or lay open face or breast. Where then is the glory of justice? Or my absolution?"

"I should hope . . . absolution is not required." Fury that he gave no sign of strain, much less laboring, made a red haze at the edge of her vision.

"Oh, a consummation to be wished, but is there basis for it?"

His words were followed, inevitably, by another touch. This one was directly upon where her heart shuddered in her chest.

Her anger boiled suddenly into rage, even

as she stepped back for the usual pause in their play. "You must see to it," she said in biting tones.

"Preparation without guidance is folly. It could be beneficial to know what drives you."

"Nothing you would understand."

"Make the attempt. I may surprise you."

The words were whimsical, but his stance was not. He faced her with challenge in every line of his body, every hard muscle of his form, even the way he held his foil and the tilt of his head. He stood waiting for her to speak, so armored in his strength, so certain that nothing she could say or do would affect him that she wanted to annihilate him. She also wanted, quite suddenly, for him to know the answer to his question.

"He killed my brother."

"Killed?"

"Cut him down in a duel so unequal as to be legal murder."

He stood perfectly still. His gaze seemed to pierce the grid of her mask. In the quiet could be heard the splattering of renewed rain as it fell from the eaves of the house into the courtyard. Finally, he stirred. "*Unequal.* That suggests superior skill on the part of the murderer, and yet you expect to succeed where your brother failed."

"I do."

"Then gird your loins, my warrior queen, and sharpen your blade, for you will need everything I can teach you. That is, if he meets you."

He thought she would be defeated. The need to prove him wrong drove her forward the instant he gave the signal. And he engaged her, meeting her advance with effortless grace and concentration, the point of his foil a glittering blur as he executed parry and riposte with narrow-eyed vigilance but made no attempt to pierce her guard.

He could have. He could and she knew it, which was more infuriating than his constant touches had been. Her anger burned higher even as her strength flagged, draining away so her lunges became mistimed, almost clumsy. Still he would not end it but let her flail and hack at him while her breath rasped in her throat and rage turned her vision as red as blood.

Just as she began a last desperate advance, one of the cords holding her skirt above her ankles slipped its knot. Her hem dropped of its own weight. The toe of her half-boot caught in the fabric and she plunged forward. Steel flashed before her eyes, whispering past her, caressing her arm as she fell. She dropped her foil with a low cry as she reached out to catch herself.

Strong hands broke her fall, cradled her in a firm hold as she settled to the canvas strip. For a stunned instant, she allowed it and was even grateful. Then she struggled to her knees, trying to pull from the grasp of Gavin Blackford as he rested on one knee before her.

"Be still," he said in hard command. "Let me see where I cut you."

It was only then that she realized he held her arm in a tight grip just above her glove cuff while jewel-like drops of blood squeezed between his fingers. She froze in place, staring at him as she faced him there on her knees, caught by his rigid pose and something in his voice that grated like footsteps on broken glass.

He reached up and dragged off his face mask as if it were in his way. Dropping it, he turned his attention to her glove. Loosening the fingers one by one, he slipped the soft leather from her hand. Slowly, then, without quite releasing his clasp, he uncurled his hard grasp from her wrist until he could survey the damage.

Ariadne looked not at her arm, but at the man who held it. His face was drained of color, leaving the bone structure in stark relief while the sockets of his eyes seemed suddenly deeper, half-concealing the glittering blue of his eyes. His hair was flat where the band of his face mask had compressed it, and hung in gold, perspiration-damp spikes against his nape. He seemed hardly to breathe, yet his fingers where he held her were rock-steady.

An imprecation, whispered and scurrilously inventive, feathered the air between them. Closing his fingers again, he leaned away from her to snag his coat from the nearby table with his free hand. He took a folded handkerchief from an inside pocket and shook it out. Draping it over his thigh, he folded it with a few precise moves of one hand then pressed it quickly to her injury. Laying her wrist across his bent knee, he released his grasp while he wrapped the handkerchief around the cut and tied the ends in a neat, flat knot.

"The slice isn't deep and it damaged no artery, I think," he said, his lashes shielding his gaze as he tucked the knotted ends under a fold, "but it may be painful."

"It doesn't matter."

"It does to me. Cow-handed and imprecise I may be on occasion, but I don't usually maim my clients."

"The fault isn't yours," she said, driven by fairness and some peculiar inner disturbance brought on by the self-flagellation in his voice.

"No?" The look he gave her was bleak. "My tongue can be, often is, my undoing. I thought to demonstrate the necessity of holding anger in check. Instead, I am shown my fallibility. Again."

"You could not know I would trip."

"I should have foreseen the possibility. At least you will now understand why this exercise is unsuitable for a female. Scars do not become the softer sex."

"I will heal," she said evenly.

"Oh, yes, and a sleeve may hide the result *parfaitement,* but what will cover my soul's wound, or heal it?"

The mask obstructing her view was suddenly intolerable. She wanted, needed, to see what caused the anguish she heard beneath the low murmur of his voice. More than that, the wire screen seemed to be interfering with her breathing. That had to be the cause of the lightheadedness that gripped her, the weak sensation that made her arm that still lay upon his knee tremble against him.

With her free hand, she reached up to wrench it off. Her hair, loosened from its pins by her exertions, caught in the band. The long swath of it tumbled free, raining pins into her lap as it unfurled down her chest padding.

It was then that the door from the gallery swung open and a man stepped into the room. He stopped as if he had run upon a sword point.

"A fencing lesson, is it?" Sasha asked, his voice corrosive with suspicion. "I don't remember my own instruction being so tender."

EIGHT

It only needed this, Gavin thought with profane resignation. It wasn't enough that he had goaded and driven the lady into a misstep which drew blood, but he would now be required to explain it to the stiff-rumped Cossack who had designated himself her protector. That should be an interesting exercise since he hardly knew himself how it had come about.

There had been a sickening moment when he had been much too vividly reminded of the dawn meeting four years ago when his opponent, a young poet of overweening pride and minimal skill with a sword, had tried a clumsy attack that broke his sword so he plunged forward, slipping in the rain-wet grass of the dueling field. In a sequence that played in memory as horrendously slow, he had flailed, falling, impaling himself on Gavin's rapier before it could be disengaged.

The object had been to teach the young fool patience and consideration, not to take his life. It was a senseless death. His own jagged wound from the broken sword had long healed before he could put it behind him.

He had thought he was over it except for an occasional nightmare revisited in the dead of night. To discover it was untrue was sobering.

No doubt it was the association of accident and inexperience that had affected him so badly just now, that and the natural disinclination to harm any member of the gentle sex. Ariadne Faucher gave little indication of the tender sensibilities that description brought to mind. Still she was valiant, proud and most definitely female, and did not deserve to have her blood drawn for no cause.

If the mention of her brother's death in a duel had any bearing, Gavin could not see it. So far as he knew, the young poet of his meeting, Francis Dorelle, had been the only child of parents who were nearly middle-aged when he was born. He had heard them described in that manner, seen them from a distance at Maurelle's Maison Blanche plantation when they came for the body of their son.

"What are you doing here?"

It was the lady who made that demand of the interloper. Snatching her wrist from Gavin's knee, she bundled the darkly shimmering mass of her hair into a knot and secured it, then began to climb to her feet.

Rising with less encumbrance, Gavin put a hand under her elbow until she could disentangle her feet from her skirt hem and stand beside him. He released her then, stepping away a pace to allow room for retrieving and wielding his blade should it become necessary.

"I become curious about your progress while calling upon our hostess," the Russian answered, his eyes narrow under lowered brows. "What have I interrupted, if I may ask?"

"You may not ask," she answered, her gaze on her glove she donned once more, "particularly in that tone. I will tell you, however, that you came upon us after a small mishap."

"To you?" His gaze rested on the few drops of blood that spotted her skirt. "I must see the damage."

Gavin resented the look of condemnation flung in his direction, also the Russian's assumption of proprietary interest and the way he took hold of Ariadne's hand and

114

brushed her sleeve higher. He had no right to resent anything, though that knowledge did nothing to lessen the instinctive response. It was some consolation to see the lady snatch her arm away again since it suggested she was no more pleased by the Russian's touch than she had been by her instructor's.

Her spirited answer to the gentleman's accusations was also unexpected. Gavin was not accustomed to anyone stepping between him and the prospect of unpleasantness. The novelty held him bemused.

"It's the merest nothing," she said, unfolding her sleeves and fastening them into place over her bandage.

"It's a sacrilege. You must cease these sessions at once."

"We have had this conversation before. I will not go into it again."

Novgorodcev turned to Gavin, his gaze imperious above his bristling white mustache. "Continuing after this incident is clearly impossible. If you are any variety of sword master, any man at all, you will excuse yourself from the lessons at once."

"Nonsense," the lady objected.

A moment before, Gavin might have agreed with the Russian. It was the perversity of human nature that it now loomed as impossible. He examined his fingertips, brushing his thumb over a small smear of the lady's blood, rubbing it into his skin as if it were a precious unguent. "I am at the command of Madame Faucher since I owe her due recompense for injury. If she requires my services in any manner whatsoever, how am I to refuse?"

"Why, you English popinjay," the Russian began as he started toward him.

Ariadne Faucher stepped between them. "Don't be an imbecile, Sasha. You can hardly expect Monsieur Blackford to accept your interference without retaliation. He means nothing personal by it."

The other man seemed unconvinced, but allowed himself to be turned away with a hand on his arm while the lady continued in more soothing tones, suggesting he returned to his claret and cakes in company with Maurelle and her other guests until she had improved her appearance enough to join them.

Gavin, left standing on the fencing strip as they moved from the room, picked up his foil, stared at it an instant, then swept it up to his face and down again in a fast and derisive salute.

The lady was mistaken about his intentions. They were personal indeed, though, with luck, she might never discover it.

She had also aroused his curiosity past bearing. That was, quite possibly, her greatest error.

NINE

Madame Zoe Savoie's benefit performance promised to be a triumph. Carriages lined the street before the Theatre d'Orleans to disgorge passengers. The rain had abated for the evening, so those who lived within walking distance crowded the banquettes. She would be pleased, Gavin knew, not only because of the addition to her purse — the point of the affair after all — but also for the indication of her enduring popularity in the city.

She had chosen Davis's theater, known to all as simply the opera house, in part for its location in the heart of the Vieux Carré, but also from friendship. Her association with the émigré from Saint Domingue who had built the edifice was a long and profitable one to hear her tell it; certainly, she had spent many winter seasons filling the space with her magnificent voice. The St. Charles Theater uptown in the American sector might be newer and more impressive, but Zoe did not forget her friends. Neither did the aristocratic French Creoles of the Quarter who were intensely loyal to the old theater, once the grandest in the country. Davis, wily entrepreneur that he was, catered to their needs for all he was worth; next to the theater was a hotel, a restaurant and a gaming house built for just that purpose. It was said he could lodge you, feed you, amuse you and fleece you all in one city block, though Zoe insisted that he used the profits from gaming to subsidize his beloved opera house, including the importation of Europe's finest singers and musicians to perform there. Naturally, she counted herself among the luminaries.

Gavin thought he might dine at Davis's restaurant after the performance, it being handy and supposing he might run across Kerr Wallace or another of his friends to join him. In the meantime, he had staked out a corner of the lobby as his own while watching the flow of arriving music lovers — the ladies in their silks and satins and velvets and the gentlemen in formal tailcoats, all of them chattering and laughing with animated gestures and anticipation of the evening's entertainment. Most were in family groups, fathers and mothers with their stair-step array of offspring in tow and often a marriageable daughter tricked out in virginal white with camellias or a white aigrette in her hair. No few were young married couples, easily identified by the dutiful husbands carrying cushions and fans and extra wraps. The voices rose above the sound of the orchestra tuning up inside, echoing against the high, coffered ceiling. Gaslight from flickering sconces along the walls played over them, glittering in faceted jewels, shining on high-piled curls, catching the sheen of excitement in women's eyes. The faintly sour smell of the coal gas drifted in the air with the fragrances of perfume and the floral offerings carried by the ladies. Dampness from the river and the rain-wet streets outside swirled with the cool wind through the open doors.

Gavin was not often made aware of how solitary he had become; it was his natural state and seldom questioned. The sense of isolation that crept in upon him now was an unwelcome reminder of things he would as soon forget, chiefly the days of his boyhood in his grandfather's household.

He had never been certain how that arrangement came about, whether by the old man's decree or because his parents, satisfied with having assured the family line by producing offspring, had placed them with him before going their separate ways. He and his two brothers had been too far apart in age to be companions, with some six years between the elder and himself, and nearly a dozen separating him from the younger. Their grandfather had disdained Gavin's bookish habits and lack of enthusiasm for hunting. An Irish nanny, Maggie, had provided sympathy and a soft bosom during his younger years but when he was six she had been replaced by a tutor with a taste for the cane. That he had cried for Maggie in the night for long months afterward was a secret he had confided to no one.

Sometimes, sitting with his legs dangling from the carved pew of the parish church that was decorated with the names of his ancestors, he'd watched the families, mothers and fathers who smiled and touched their children, straightened their clothes and ruffled their hair, and wondered why no one cared about him.

Strange how some things never changed, he thought now with conscious irony. It was a relief when he spotted Caid O'Neill wending his way toward him against the flow of human traffic.

They dispensed with the subject of the

unending rain which had turned the area beyond the principal paved streets of the Vieux Carré and uptown into a muddy and malodorous quagmire, also the chance of flooding if it did not stop soon. Gavin asked after the health of the children fast filling his friend's nursery, a son, Sean Patrick, and the little daughter with whom Lisette had been confined a short time before, Celeste Amalie.

Caid was regaling him with a comical story about Sean Patrick's interest in the baby's nursing habits when a shift in the crowd gave Gavin a glimpse of Ariadne Faucher. Gliding toward him on the arm of her Russian admirer, she was vividly alive in burgundy velvet that was caught up in swags at the hem to show an underskirt of pink silk edged in gilt lace and complemented by a parure of garnets set in gold. She spoke over her shoulder to Maurelle who followed closely behind her, features animated in anticipation of pleasure, instead of drawn with the strain that appeared during their lessons.

Tightness invaded his chest. He was here tonight at the command of Madame Zoe. That Ariadne might appear was a possibility he had also taken into account. Would she acknowledge him in this public arena or pretend she didn't see him, had no acquaintance with a notorious swordsman from the Passage de la Bourse? He wasn't at all sure he wanted to find out.

The rich color of her gown was reflected on her skin in much the way a string of pearls mirrored the color in their surroundings. It gave the soft cleft between her breasts such an appearance of passion's flush that his mouth tingled with the need to taste it. To counter that impulse, he lowered his gaze to the pair of wide bracelets of garnets and gold that encircled her wrists in the current mode. Did the one on her right cover a healing scar or a festering injury? There was no way to tell. The combination of lust and pain that assaulted him was so strong it was all he could do to make the proper admiring replies to the new father beside him.

"How goes it with the lovely widow?" Caid asked in an abrupt change of subject as he followed the direction of Gavin's gaze.

"Excellently well, when she isn't trying to cut my throat and I'm not opening her veins. Which is to say," he went on before Caid could speak, turning to him as Ariadne moved out of sight, "that it doesn't go at all. I haven't seen her these past three days while she recovered from my last ham-fisted swipe."

"You cut her?"

"A clumsy error though superficial in its results, always supposing it heals without complication."

"Clumsy is one thing you are not. There must be more to the story."

"For which faith your name and progeny shall be blessed. In truth, the lady is a puzzle."

"And brilliant with it, if gaining your attention was her object. Is it?"

"Doubtful," Gavin said in dry amusement. "To all appearances, she despises me."

"The devil you say. She's one of those, is she?"

"Oh, I don't believe she holds herself on too high a form. It's more personal than that."

Caid scowled. "Personal?"

"Some damned sod gave her a grudge against men for whom a sword is the weapon of choice and now she holds us all in contempt. That I bled her like a surgeon is unlikely to improve her opinion."

"You need not continue with her as your client."

"How can I bear to desist? And don't, please, accuse me of too fevered attraction.

I've had that from Maurelle already."

Caid gave him a considering look. "The situation seems likely to land you in trouble before it's done. If there is no reward, why take the risk?"

"I never said it was without reward."

"You'll forgive me, but —"

"But you fear for the lady and her reputation? Both are safe enough with me."

"You mistake me. I was thinking of you and yours. Are they safe with her?"

"That is the question," Gavin allowed, his gaze pensive. "When I discover the answer, I'll let you know."

The performance began in good time, the gaslights lowering in dramatic style, the audience rustling into quiet attention, the curtains moving with well-oiled precision on their pulleys, folding back upon themselves to frame a garden scene. The footlights glowed as they were turned higher, revealing the diva in all her magnificence. From a pose of contemplation with her back to the audience, she turned with perfect dramatic timing. Her voice poured over the assemblage like molten honey laced with the finest of Napoleon brandies.

Madame Savoie proved in fine form as the evening advanced. Moving gracefully about the stage, her height and size beautifully proportioned in the removed and foreshortened view across the footlights, she held the audience in thrall. Favorite arias were met with applause as their familiar melodies soared forth, the less well-known with a quiet that was even more telling. Still, cries of "Brava! Brava!" rang out again and again, echoing around the great crystal-and-bronze chandelier overhead and stirring the smoke from the footlights.

Gavin strolled with Caid from one vantage point to another, with the prowling male contingent that waited, as usual, for the intermission when it would be acceptable to visit the boxes of ladies not of their own family. He had no object in view other than dropping in at Maurelle's box to make his bow and discover the state of his client's injury. He didn't care to call attention to his interest, however, so intended to mask his approach by visiting first at the box of the Conde and Condessa de Lérida.

He allowed Caid to go ahead of him through the rear curtains when the time came, standing back while the Irishman approached the Condessa who had been Celina Vallier. He glanced past where his friend was saluting the lady's hand, his eyes narrowing on the box on the opposite side of the theater. Madame Faucher sat there

126

next to Maurelle, half-turned in her chair as she spoke to the three or four gentlemen who were crowding into the box, laughing up at Novgorodcev where he stood behind her chair. The muscles in Gavin's jaw clenched as he absorbed the easy manner of that hefty, white-haired gentleman, as if the place he occupied was his by right. Also the casual way he placed his gloved fingertips on the lady's bare shoulder near her nape.

Celina addressed a question to him, something about Napoleon, Madame Zoe's notoriously unfriendly parrot. It was all he could do to concentrate enough to answer her. When he was free to return his attention to Maurelle's box again, he saw with disturbing gratification that Ariadne had shifted in her chair enough to dislodge the Russian's hand. She faced forward with her opera glasses to her eyes as she scanned orchestra seats, inspected the tiers of boxes.

Light flashed on her glasses as she directed them toward the box where he stood. She paused in her inspection. Was the movement too elaborate? Did she know he was there? Or was it mere curiosity about Spanish nobility in the guise of Rio and Celina that had arrested her attention? Gavin had no idea, but the prickling at the back of his neck let him know he was under scrutiny at the moment. Gazing into the lenses, he inclined his body in a bow.

The opera glasses almost fell away from her eyes. As the lady turned with jerky movements to speak to Maurelle, he permitted himself a hard smile. She did not intend to recognize him. He had expected nothing else, yet was aware of blighting disappointment.

But she was turning again, her chin tilted at the brave angle so vividly remembered from their last meeting. The movement stiff, measured, almost defiant, she bent her head in his direction. She did not smile, but it was definitely an acknowledgement. The constriction in his chest dissolved so abruptly that he made a short sound between a laugh and a grunt.

"You said something?" Caid asked, glancing over his shoulder.

"Not a thing," he answered without removing his gaze from the other box. "Nothing at all."

It was then he saw a lady of perhaps fifty in an evening gown of rather countrified frumpishness enter the Herriot box. She jarred to a halt, searched the faces of its occupants. Her gaze centered on Ariadne and she put a hand to her breast before gliding forward. Her lips moved and something about her expression and the way she clasped her hands in front of her, gave the unheard greeting Gavin witnessed the look of supplication.

Madame Faucher stared at the newcomer for an aeon, or so it seemed, before rising slowly to her feet. Her face drained of color and Gavin thought she swayed where she stood. The Russian reached out as if to take her arm but she shook him off.

"Condessa," Gavin said, breaking in on the conversation of the lady and his friend Caid without compunction, "are you by chance acquainted with the woman to whom Madame Faucher is speaking?"

Celina turned to stare across the way an instant. "She has been pointed out as the wife of a planter from upriver, though I can't quite recall the name. I believe she has a daughter she is presenting this season."

"Madame Arpegé," Caid supplied after a cursory glance. "Her husband and I are acquainted. She and Monsieur Arpegé have a houseful of daughters if the truth be known. Lisette holds the lady up to me regularly as an example of fecundity she has no intention of duplicating."

Even as they spoke, the woman could be seen turning away from Ariadne. She had not, apparently, been offered a chair or encouraged to linger. "What connection has she to Madame Faucher?"

"Who can say? From her appearance, she might easily be a cousin of some degree."

It was true enough, Gavin thought; there did seem to be some resemblance. Nothing was more likely. Creole families were large and their branches torturously intertwined due to frequent marriages between cousins during the long years when the city was an isolated colonial outpost. As he watched, however, the intruder put a hand to her mouth, then turned and departed with drooping shoulders.

"Not a close connection apparently," he commented.

"So it would seem." The agreement came from Caid.

"More might be brought to light with the exercise of guile."

"Or you could abandon it and just ask Maurelle," his friend answered, his voice dry.

"The trouble with that suggestion is that she seems equally at a loss." It was possible only Ariadne could satisfy his curiosity. And the chance of that happening was about as likely as having her respond to his more carnal inclinations.

"Madame Zoe might have some idea," the Irishman said after a moment. "She's met practically everyone during one winter season or another."

"So she has." Gavin was thoughtful. The idea had one merit not present in the direct approach. Contrary to his client in the opposite box, asking the diva was not likely to result in an attack with a sharp weapon.

It might be just as well if he didn't approach the lady this evening after all. He could see she suffered few ill effects, if any, from her wound. Inspecting it could wait for a less fraught, and considerably less public, occasion.

Accordingly, he and Caid gave up their places to other gentlemen waiting to pay their respects, withdrawing with Rio and also Denys Vallier, Celina's brother, to the corridor outside the box. They stood in a male huddle where they talked of the latest news dispatched to reach the city, particularly those that dealt with the war drums that rumbled along the Mexican border.

"You heard, I suppose," Caid said, "that Santa Ana was so irritated by the last message sent him from President Tyler, he issued a decree expelling all United States citizens from California and New Mexico?"

"Also that old General Waddy Thompson,

our American minister, threatened to demand his passport and quit Mexico if it was enforced," Rio said with a nod. "The decree is said to have been revoked within twenty-four hours, but that may be wishful thinking."

Caid tucked a thumb into his waistcoat pocket as he shook his head. "We can only hope Thompson doesn't actually resign. The Mexican fleet has apparently set out for Vera Cruz for refitting in the midst of this little contretemps. It would be nice if we had somebody there to say whether it's in preparation for war. Yes, and to prod Sam Houston into reporting the latest border activity to Washington in hope Congress will get off its collective asses."

"A dangerous tactic if they decide to let him fight his own battles instead."

"Tyler is disinclined to allow too great a British influence in Texas, I think — which may happen if London decides to come to Houston's aid." Gavin felt sure it was in the minds of his friends but would not be aired to avoid offending his English sensibilities.

"Is that likely since Texas refuses to abandon slavery?"

"I suspect the answer depends on governmental self-interest rather than moral verities," Gavin answered. Slavery had been abolished in Britain and its territories some ten years back, with more than a million pounds paid out in compensation to owners. It was his considered opinion that the abolitionists who shouted so loudly for the same in this country would make more progress if they loosened their stranglehold on the national purse strings as well. To expect people with their life savings and the promise of wealth and ease for their children to give up their human chattel as a mere moral gesture seemed ingenuous, if not downright simpleminded. Still, he was a foreigner with little right to comment.

"In the meantime, the Louisiana Legion is losing members as time drags by with no fight and no solution either." This came from Denys Vallier.

"Some are quitting, but quite a few have jumped over to the new Washington Battalion of the Americans."

"I saw in *L'Abeille* that it's the Grenadiers and the Grays that are transferring," Gavin observed. "Not that it seems to matter. Being mostly from the Second Municipality, they didn't understand commands in French anyway."

"Too true." Caid chuckled. "Since they left, the main question seems to be which uniform will be commissioned in case of war, the one with the most shine to attract enemy fire or the one with the wildest color to hide bloody wounds. Heaven forbid the legion should be mistaken as part of any mere Federal army."

Caid could talk because he, Rio, and Nicholas were no longer associated with the Legion, Gavin knew. The obligations of their growing families, abandonment of their *salle d'armes* in the Passage due to these increased responsibilities and natural waning of their taste for armed combat accounted for it. Gavin had never joined, being too solitary in his habits and inclinations, but he thought Celina's brother, Denys Vallier, still marched on the parade ground with his friends.

"Please, *mon ami*," Denys said now with mock offense. "The uniforms proposed most recently are of the noblest tradition, one borrowed from a perfectly acceptable army."

"Which would be?" Rio's dark gaze rested on his brother-in-law with some skepticism.

"Why, the exalted Janissaries of the Great Sultan of Turkey!"

Caid groaned. "We might have known."

Denys gave him a grin and a bow. "You may be sure I am doing my best to encourage a more sedate example."

They spoke of other things, including the shake-up in the British parliament during the autumn that brought Sir Robert Peel to power, and the current engagement of British troops in India against an enormous force of Sikhs led by Lal Singh. Gavin tried to explain what was happening with his home country, but was just as happy when Rio turned to something closer to the Vieux Carré.

"I saw the Russian friend of Madame Faucher in the Passage yesterday. He was asking for you."

Gavin met his friend's gaze for an instant. The warning he saw there sent wariness prickling along his nerve endings. "Was he indeed?"

"It not being your day for receiving clients, he made do with a bout at Rosière's salon. His strength was formidable."

"And his technique?"

"Adequate. It might be more threatening if he depended less on power and rote moves, or so it seemed from my observation. Facing him could be different."

Gavin had a healthy respect for Rio's opinions. He had been one of the great masters of the Passage and was still a swordsman around whom others tread lightly. He filed the information away for the future.

To face the Russian, sword in hand, was not an object with him. Still the life of a sword master was uncertain at best and could slide quickly into dangerous waters. It was as well to be prepared.

TEN

Ariadne sat rigid in her chair. She hardly knew where to look, could think of nothing to say. That Maurelle continued her languidly flirtatious banter with the gentlemen standing here and there in their box was something for which she was grateful since it allowed her a few minutes to collect herself.

Her mother.

The woman who had approached her just now was her mother. Not her foster mother whom she had learned to think of in that light, now dead these three years and more, but rather the woman who had given birth to her.

Who could have guessed she would appear after all this time?

Ariadne drew a deep breath and let it out in a slow and silent attempt at composure. She had not been particularly polite, she feared. It was the shock of it. And the risk.

The Englishman in the box across the way had missed nothing of the meeting, she knew. What if he learned its import? It would be only a small step from there to her true identity. Then to her purpose.

Her mother.

The woman had given her away as a child of two, tearing her screaming from her neck and thrusting her into the arms of Josephine and Etienne Dorelle who had adopted her. Ariadne had looked into the woman's face just now and felt grief and rage allied to a longing so strong that she still shook with it.

She had not known she could care, or at least care so much. How had it come about when she had adored her foster parents and been content with them, wanted only to please them?

Oh, she knew the tale. Nothing of it had been kept from her, nor was it particularly uncommon. Her mother had married out of convent school and become a dutiful wife, presenting her husband with eleven children in fifteen years, all daughters. Josephine Dorelle, a cousin once-removed and dear friend from childhood of her mother had been barren still in spite of marrying in the same year. For a woman so blessed with children to give one to a woman bereft of that boon was seen as a generous impulse of the heart. The gratitude of Ariadne's new parents had known no bounds. That it took the form of a sum of money which tided Ariadne's parents over a bad sugarcane season was incidental.

But as often happens with adoptions, the woman whose womb had been so empty miraculously conceived, a fine son was born in due time and named Francis. Ariadne had been enthralled with the baby, treating him as her personal plaything and dearly beloved younger brother. They could not have been more inseparable if they had shared the same blood. In fact, they had never been apart until Francis decided he must seek the literary circles of New Orleans.

Well before that, the closeness between the two mothers had soured. The sugar plantation of Ariadne's birth parents failed, in spite of the loan, and they moved up-river. Ariadne's father had died and her mother remarried. In the midst of her new life with her second husband, a Monsieur Arpegé, surrounded by her other daughters, including two from the second marriage, it seemed she no longer thought of the one she had given away. Years passed. The marriage to Jean Marc was arranged. Francis was killed in his duel. Ariadne had not seen her mother in such a long time she had almost forgotten her face.

Why had her mother approached her now, without warning and in such public view? she wondered in silent anguish. Had she thought she might otherwise be rejected out of hand? Yes, and why did the Englishman have to be a spectator at the meeting? It had been the one thing that made a rebuff inevitable.

What did the lady want of her? Did she expect to take up where she had left off all those years ago as if nothing had happened? Or had she heard, perchance, that her daughter was now alone in the world and a wealthy woman?

Ariadne pressed her lips together with a small shake of her head. She didn't like thinking such things, wasn't really that hard and cynical. Yet few people acted without first consulting self-interest.

Her mother would call at the Herriot town house; Ariadne had collected herself enough to suggest that much. They would speak in private in two days time, since her mother would be busy tomorrow with the arrival from upriver of her husband and yet another daughter. What would happen then was more than she could say. So much depended on the golden-haired man who watched her so closely.

A shiver ran over her, one so strong it took her breath. She drew her cashmere evening shawl more tightly around herself, huddling into it.

"Are you well, *chère?* You aren't catching *la grippe?*"

Ariadne, warmed by the concern in Maurelle's fine brown eyes, summoned a smile. "No, no. It was nothing, merely a goose walking over my grave."

The brush of cloth against cloth sounded behind her as the gentlemen leaning over Maurelle's chair changed positions. A moment later, she felt a touch on her shoulder and Sasha leaned over her. "I venture to say this goose is your sword master," he said, his voice a low growl near her ear. "Am I wrong?"

She turned a little in her chair. "I don't know what you mean."

"Pretend innocence with your provincial friends if you must, but we are from a wider world, you and I. This affair with the Englishman does not progress well. He grows too bold, openly saluting you across the theater. He is dangerous, not only to your lovely skin but to your reputation. You would have been much wiser to apply to me."

"To be added to your conquests? I think not."

"I would make an exception in your case. It may be time I thought of marriage."

Bestowing a wan smile upon him, she asked, "And if I have no wish to become a wife?"

"A cherished mistress then. I can give you jewels, carriages, a castle — anything you desire."

"Suppose I desire nothing?"

He smiled, his ego untouched. "How tantalizing you are, *chère,* but I am not fooled. You are a woman of deep passions. The trouble is only that you have yet to decide what you desire."

"If you think so then you know me not at all."

He caressed her shoulder while his large, mobile mouth lifted in a superior smile. "Or it could be you do not know yourself."

Before she could shift away from his touch or form an answer to his incredible presumption, he straightened and turned away. No doubt he expected her to stare after him, impressed by his knowledge of women and their emotions. She spared him hardly a glance. Her gaze, instead, turned toward the opposite box where Gavin Blackford was leaving, strolling out with his friends. Clouding her mind was the recollection of the moment she had discovered him there. The gaslight had flickered over his hair with golden gleams, caught the high molding of his cheekbones and given a blazing white radiance to his linen. It had illuminated the grace of his bearing and the refined strength of his shoulders and hands. And it gleamed for a bright blue instant in his eyes as he turned to meet her gaze before inclining his head in a discreet bow.

Oh, yes, he was bold.

She should have ignored him, pretended she didn't see him, did not know who and what he was or his exact place in the circle within which they moved. It was impossible. Against her will, against her best intentions and better judgment, she felt her lips curve into a cool smile as she tipped her head in return. And all the while, her heart had jarred against her corset stays with such force that the edging of gold lace on her velvet bodice trembled with it.

It beat that way still.

ELEVEN

The rain continued to hold off the following morning, though it seemed the respite might be short-lived. Gray, scudding clouds littered the sky and a cool wind blew from Lake Pontchartrain, bringing with it the smell of brine. Ariadne was determined to take advantage of the break to stretch her legs. Persuading her hostess to join her was not easy given Maurelle's natural indolence, but they finally set out.

She and her hostess were not the only ones attempting to escape the indoor stuffiness. The banquettes were crowded with men intent on business concerns, servants on errands for their masters, and ladies with baskets on their arms and veils of common green *barèges* over their faces to protect them from chance sun rays. Vendors plied their wares on every corner so the air was alive with the cries of the knife grinder and rag man, and offers for shelled nuts and green vegetables, pralines and yams. Moving more than a few paces at a time seemed impossible as it was constantly necessary to stop and pass the time with one acquaintance or another of Maurelle's. Even when they were able to make progress, they must still exchange bows with passing gentlemen, smile and nod at the priests and nuns they met, wave to older ladies enjoying the air on their balconies and sidestep the children playing around doorsteps. At Maurelle's suggestion, they turned in the direction of the river and the levee promenade that was usually less crowded.

The promise did not hold true since half the town seemed to have hit upon the same solution. More than that, the masters of the sailing vessels and steamboats tied up at the docks along the river were using the break in the weather to load and unload cargo. Ariadne persevered in spite of the hubbub around the loading sheds of wagons and drays, rumbling barrels and shouting stevedores. She would not be denied her walk nor a look at the river, swollen by rain and awash with debris brought down by the storms, that hurled itself toward the gulf on their water side.

"Look, *chère*," Maurelle cried after some few minutes. "Your sword master and his friends. What felicity."

"Hardly *my* sword master," she murmured, leaning close.

"You know what I mean. They intend to stop, I believe, so do cease scowling and be pleasant or they will think you hold yourself above them."

"They can't be that sensitive, surely."

"You have no idea." The words were spoken quickly and under her breath as Maurelle moved forward with both hands held out. "Monsieur Gavin, the handsome brother Nicholas and charming Juliette, my friends, well met! Ah, and you have young Monsieur Squirrel with you as well. *Bonjour, mon petit.* Is this crush not amazing? I was reluctant to set out when Ariadne mentioned it, but wouldn't have missed it for worlds."

Ariadne smiled valiantly as she was presented to the couple she had not yet met. She had heard much from Maurelle about this handsome Italian and his wife who had been a nun, or very near it, before their marriage, so felt she knew them well. The boy she addressed was actually called Nathaniel, rather than the old *petit nom* of Squirrel. A young man of some seventeen or eighteen years, it transpired that he was serving an apprenticeship of sorts at Gavin Blackford's atelier.

Even as she sorted out the newcomers, she was aware of the close scrutiny of the Englishman. So distracted was she by it that it was an instant before what Maurelle had said penetrated her consciousness. "Pardon? What was that? Monsieur Blackford's brother?"

"Just so, and his sister-in-law, our own Juliette, née Armant." Maurelle smiled upon the couple as if nothing could be more commonplace than an Italian and an Englishman being related.

"I didn't realize you had family here," Ariadne said, surprised into speaking directly to Blackford.

"We are half brothers to be exact," Nicholas Pasquale answered in his stead, giving her a smile of exceeding charm. "Our father was widely traveled, you see. Not that it matters a particle — blood alone is not the thing that makes a brother."

He was a fantastically attractive man, the Italian, in a tender yet masculine fashion. For an instant, Ariadne could see no resemblance between him and Gavin Blackford, one being so dark and the other of lighter coloring. On second glance, she could see the similarity, not only in their height and the width of their shoulders above narrow waists and flanks but, most of all, in the deep set of their eyes behind barricades of thick lashes.

She suspected a story behind the co-incidence of their joint residence in the city. Before she could inquire into it, a hail came from behind them.

The arrivals turned out to be more of the swordsmen and their wives, this time the two couples Maurelle had pointed out to her at the opera the evening before, the O'Neills and the Conde and Condessa de Lérida, along with the mulatto sword master, Bastile Croquère, and another Italian, Gilbert Rosière. The two groups merged without noticeable effort. No constraint seemed to trouble any of them and certainly no formality, Ariadne thought, as they exchanged greetings and quips, queries and friendly insults. Among these swordsmen and their wives, and even Maurelle, was such easy friendship and complete trust that nothing said one-to-the-other was meant in anything except the most pleasant conviviality. They chattered and laughed and touched each other with casual gestures and warmth in their faces while the wind whipped the skirts and bonnet strings of the ladies and the gentlemen held on to their hats. Now and then a strong gust made it necessary for a man to give his wife a protective arm. This was done instantly, with the briefest of conspiratorial smiles that whispered of quiet and passionate intimacy.

Only Ariadne was left out of the charmed circle. It was oddly disquieting to find it so. Somehow, she had never been quite among the chosen, never secure in her place there. Yet she had longed to be, longed for the comfort of such unquestioned acceptance.

A species of angry despair shifted inside her, settling around her heart. It wasn't that she had any desire to join the select circle of the *maîtres d'armes* and their women. Oh, not at all. No matter how inviting it might appear, or how comforting, she knew it was built on the unhappiness and grief of others. It must be that way. Still, the sense of isolation remained.

"Dazzling, daunting and with blooms in your cheeks — you can't, I think, be expiring of blood poisoning."

The comment came from Gavin Blackford as he moved to her side, speaking beneath the continuing discussion around them. She tipped her head to see his face from under her bonnet rim. "Did you think I might be?"

"Not after last evening. May I?"

Without waiting for permission, he took her hand and, shielding his purpose with his broad back, peeled down the cuff of her glove. Ariadne jerked against his hold; he was too close, his grasp too disturbing. She was far more aware of the masculine force of him than she wished to be. He did not release her, but whispered an imprecation as he saw the angry red slash across the top of her wrist.

"It heals," she said, her voice tight. "I removed the bandage just last night."

"And used garnets in gold as a substitute. At least the stones are said to promote healing. Or is that amethyst? I can never recall. I would have presented myself at Maurelle's door to inquire after the injury, except it seemed best not to call attention to it."

"For the sake of your reputation." She would not allow herself to think about how closely he must have watched her across the theater that he had noticed her bracelets. Nor would she consider the conundrum that flashed through her mind — a swordsman so disturbed by a cut to his opponent that he called it a soul wound but who killed without compunction on the field of honor. What if he was equally as penitent . . . No, no, such reflections had no bearing.

"Yours, rather. How can you think otherwise?"

"Oh, yes, you keep your fencing salon as a whim rather than necessity."

"Is that what Maurelle told you? It's true only in part, though I am no less serious in the pursuit of true expertise. And you?"

"The same," she said shortly as she realized he was questioning her dedication to gaining skill with a sword. "I am ready to resume lessons when your schedule permits."

"My whole design in speaking to you — to make our plans. Need I say that my time is wholly yours?"

What he was saying was that flirtation had not been his aim. She might have been more annoyed except for the bright amusement that lurked in the blue depths of his eyes, as if he dared her to doubt him or to comment on the hidden messages beneath their polite discourse.

How very odd that moment seemed, with the yellow-brown river lapping against the levee mere feet from where they stood, the gray winter light in the sky and the wind brushing her skirts against his polished boots. Her bonnet brim bent in the gale and his eyes were narrowed to mere slits while his cravat slapped across his lapel, torn loose from its tucked place and anchored only by its sapphire pin. A tenuous connection greater than her hand in his seemed to tether them to the spot. Ariadne could not look away from his steady gaze as the laughter faded from his eyes, could think of nothing to say to break it. For this moment, there were only the two of them in the windy world and nothing but rare concord between them.

Abruptly, she drew a deep breath. This would not do.

"Excellent, then," she said in brisk tones while tugging against his hold once more. "We will continue tomorrow evening."

"*À votre service, madame,* as always." His eyelids came down, closing off his expression. He released her as he bowed his head. When he straightened, his features were somber again.

Just moments later they heard the strident scream of a steam whistle. It was no ordinary blast, but continued in long bursts, as if the captain hung on the chain that operated it. They swung around to see a steamboat with funnels streaming black smoke making toward the levee at full speed. It was the Natchez packet, the *Mary Jane,* not due on her regular run until much later in the afternoon. Something had caused her to race downriver ahead of schedule.

"The captain wants the way cleared for a fast berth," Caid O'Neill said with a considering frown.

"A problem on board," Gavin answered while running his gaze over the passengers who crowded the steamer's rails and the crewmen who stood ready to run out the gangplank the instant the boat landed.

"Shall we?" The Conde gathered the others with a quick glance and tilt of his head toward the spot where the craft must land. "Ladies?"

The last was an indication that the women were expected to join them rather than remain behind unattended. Ariadne was just as pleased since she had no intention of hanging back.

By the time they reached the spot where the oncoming steamboat approached the levee, drays were being hitched up and hastily moved and barrels rolled out of the way. Men crowded close, reaching out toward the gangplank, ready to fasten it to the dock stanchions the instant it was run out. On board, the captain, white-faced, his hair blowing in the wind, called out to the shouting, rumbling crowd, gesticulating behind them toward the town.

"What's he saying?" Maurelle asked,

frowning as she lifted a hand to her ear.

"A doctor," Ariadne answered above the waterfall rush of the boat's paddle wheel, the continuing blast of the steam whistle and the rumble of the growing crowd. "He wants a doctor sent for at once."

"It's cholera, I suppose. Or yellow fever. Perhaps we should back away a bit."

"I don't believe that's the problem," Caid O'Neill said, his voice grim.

Ariadne could only agree. They could see more now as the boat eased closer to the dock and was made fast. Behind the captain, where the passengers shifted out of the way, could be seen rows of people lying on makeshift pallets — shapeless bundles of humanity with skin exposed, raw and hideously eroded, as if boiled from the bone. The odor of cooked flesh drifted, swirling on the wind. Cries of pain could be heard as the boat bumped the levee.

"Mon Dieu," the Condessa de Lérida whispered, raising a hand to her mouth. "It must be . . ."

Her husband completed the thought for her. "A steamboat has exploded and these are the survivors. The *Mary Jane* must have picked them up on her downriver run."

Not only the survivors. Beyond those who still lived was a long row of covered forms that were apparently rescued bodies of those killed in the accident.

The occurrence was not that unusual. Contracts to transport goods and passengers were awarded to the steamboats with the best speed records between ports of call. Personal competition between boat captains was high as well, with frequent races between rival boats. Corners were sometimes cut to gain speed, including tying down safety values to increase the pressure in the boilers and adding lard, bacon and other combustibles to their furnaces for increased heat. Sometimes the risks paid off. Sometimes they ended in tragedy.

The sword masters needed no explanation and waited for none. Moving as one, they took charge. One pair of them commandeered carriages and wagons and directed them into a line, ready to take the injured, while another pair began to gather grass sacks, canvas, sails, poles and planking from the dockside to construct makeshift litters. Gavin and Nicholas jumped to the Natchez steamer's gangplank before it was fully seated, moving among the rows of hurt and maimed. As one doctor arrived, and then another, the *maîtres d'armes* called out, indicating the moaning figures with the most pressing need of medical attention.

Within minutes, or so it seemed, the chaos settled into an orderly removal of those who still lived, as well as the shaken passengers and crew. Finally, as the doctors and all who could be saved were hurried away toward the newly refurbished Maison de Santé on Canal Street, the Charity Hospital and private hospitals, the dead were brought ashore.

One of those brought off first was a young woman, to judge from the dark hair that spilled in waving tresses over the edge of the litter borne by two stevedores. As they turned toward a waiting wagon, the wind whipped away the sheet that covered her. She was young indeed, hardly more than thirteen or fourteen. One side of her body appeared undamaged, but the other was waxen in its steamed destruction, and her twisted features spoke of agonized last moments.

Ariadne turned sharply away while sick pity rose inside her. She had seen death before, had been at her husband's side as his difficult breathing stopped; it wasn't that she was shocked. Still, it had not been like this, a painful wrenching from life, dreams, promise and all that was bright and good in being alive. It had not seemed so very final or so tragic.

"Come, permit me to escort you to the town house," Gavin said, his voice low as he appeared at her side, taking her hand and tucking it in the crook of his elbow. "You should not be here."

He was the last person she wished to see her in her weakness, so of course it was he who noticed. "Yes, certainly," she answered, her voice husky as she gathered the tatters of her composure around her. "If Maurelle is ready."

"She will go ahead with Caid and Lisette. The others are naturally seeing to their wives. You are, perforce, left with me."

"I . . . must thank you then." What else was there to say?

He bent his considering gaze upon her. "It's not to be wondered at that you are upset."

"I'm not upset."

"No, certainly not. Why should you be, after all? Death for a stranger is less than nothing. It touches no part of the heart or mind, rouses no contemplation of chance events or future loss. One life, more or less, is only a droplet spilled from the bucket brimming with souls, endlessly replenished from the well of life and loving."

"Do be quiet," she said, her voice thick in her tight throat. She would not look at him for fear he could see the tears that crowded the corners of her eyes.

"I am silent," he said, "but not, praise all the gods, as the tomb."

He was being deliberately irritating to distract her, she realized after a glance at his set face — a startling insight under the circumstances. Yet to presume to know how she felt was a great impertinence. Ariadne turned to blast him for it.

It was then she saw the middle-aged woman running toward the levee. Her eyes were wild, her mouth opened in a silent cry, and tears streamed down the lines of her face. Her bonnet slid back from her head, held only by its strings as it flopped against her back. She lifted her skirts high as she ran, unmindful of the exposure of petticoats and ankles. Reaching the young girl, she fell to her knees with a moan while grabbing at the arms of the litter bearers, forcing them to lower their burden to the ground. She searched over the girl's body with wide tear-filled eyes, touched a trembling hand to her waxen cheek, then fell across the stretcher with a great rasping sob.

Ariadne stood perfectly still. The woman was the same one who had come to Maurelle's theater box, the woman who called herself her mother. She had said — What had she said? Something about her husband and her daughter arriving in town this evening, she was almost sure. The girl on the litter — might be, must be, her half sister.

"You really are ill. Shall I find a hackney?"

Gavin Blackford took her hand from his arm, holding it while he put a strong arm at her back. She could feel the warmth of him seeping into her chill skin, was grateful in that instant for his support. "No," she answered in shuddering distress. "Just . . . just take me away. Take me away now."

He made no answer, asked no questions, but steered her in the opposite direction from the scene of grief and horror. For these things, too, she was grateful.

The remainder of the day passed for Ariadne as in a dream. The sword master did not stay on reaching the town house, but gave her into the care of Maurelle and politely took his leave. Her hostess, on learning what she had seen, was all concern, insisting that she lie down while she made a tisane of soothing herbs for her with her own hands. Later in the afternoon, Maurelle sent a servant to learn how Ariadne's mother fared and discovered that her stepfather, Monsieur Arpegé, had perished along with her youngest sister. Her mother and the daughter whom she had brought for her debut were in deepest seclusion, receiving no visitors. According to the hotel servants, they were in disarray, too lost in grief as yet to know whether they would have the double interment in the city or transport the bodies back upriver for burial in their home cemetery.

Ariadne was no more decided concerning her own conduct. There would be no call upon her by her mother. She had dreaded that interview, so should be relieved she need not face it. It was odd to recognize that she was not. Something inside her regretted the lost opportunity to learn more of the woman who had given her birth. Something within longed to know why she had been handed over to someone else like the unwanted kitten in a litter.

Should she pay a condolence call now, leaving her card if not admitted, or just let it go? The blood relationship was undoubtedly there and some things were a matter of common decency. Regardless, she had never met her stepfather or any of his daughters by her mother, did not know them at all. Her mother might have sought contact before, but would she wish it in her sorrow? What possible use could she be to her blood relations at this time? What comfort could she offer? It seemed purest hypocrisy to visit now when she had been so very determined to avoid them. Yes, and did she really wish to become enmeshed in their lives when she had other concerns, other aims of her own?

What did the social conventions require of her in this peculiar situation? Did filial duty enter into it at all?

Going back and forth in her mind with the choice was driving her mad. She could not think what she wanted to do, much less what was required of her. Still, it seemed she should do something.

She could not get the scene she had witnessed out of her mind. Her mother's grief remained with her, weighed on her. Her obvious love for the girl who had died, her horror-stricken despair over the manner of it, had been so very piteous. Ariadne could not help wondering if she had felt even a portion of that desolation over her own removal to the Dorelle household. She had not died, it was true, but she had been just as lost to her mother. Somehow, she had never considered how the woman who gave birth to her might have felt about giving her away. She had always assumed she had been glad to be free of the burden.

That need not be true. She might have grieved.

Had she misjudged her mother all these years?

What else might she have misjudged?

Ariadne's head ached with the confusion inside her. She wasn't sure she was capable of leaving the town house for fear of being sick. She hovered constantly on the verge of tears when she had thought never to cry again after weeping so much for Francis and then Jean Marc.

Rising from her bed, she went to the armoire. She pushed aside her gowns to expose a long case that lay at the back. Lifting it from its hiding place, she carried it to the bed. It was of highly polished ebony wood inlaid with silver, a sword case of fine craftsmanship. She unfastened the catch, opened the lid and laid it back onto the mattress.

Nestled in the case, in a bed of black crushed velvet, was a pair of matched rapiers, traditional dueling swords, with their black leather sheaths beside them. Beautifully made, they had leather-wrapped handles and swept-back hilts of ornately wrought metal plated with silver and black enamel. The maker's mark, a fleur de lis, was stamped into the upper blade which was also chased for a few inches with a design of leaves and vines. She had purchased the set in Paris after walking past the window of a weapons store where they had been displayed. They appealed to her on a visceral level she could not have explained if her life depended on it. Owning them had given solid form to her vague idea of retribution for Francis's death.

She touched the chasing on one blade, thinking of Gavin's disparaging suggestion that she was attracted to fencing for the sake of such beautiful metalwork. He might be more correct than he knew, though the deadly power of the sword also satisfied something inside her. Unladylike as it might be to dwell on such things, owning the means to protect herself, as well as exact recompense for injury, made her feel stronger inside.

Could she really use one of the blades? The anger that had driven her seemed to burn less bright. Everything was more complicated than it had appeared from a continent away. The depression of spirit occasioned by the tragedy she had witnessed that morning made it all seem too great an effort.

This uncertainty would pass, she was almost certain of it. The question was how she might feel when it was done. Closing the sword case lid again, she put it back in the armoire.

Gray skies gathered, lowering, becoming steadily darker as the day advanced. Candles and lamps had to be set alight by mid-afternoon. Ariadne, in the attempt to break free of the impasse that gripped her, dressed and took her needlework, a petit-point fire screen, into the salon.

Maurelle was not there. She had grown sleepy after a strenuous morning followed by a dreary afternoon, or so Adele said when Ariadne discovered the maid loitering on the gallery. She was resting in bed.

Ariadne set a few stitches in her canvas while sitting before the salon fireplace, but could find no real interest in the pattern. When the rain began to fall, she laid her handiwork to one side and went to the window where she stood leaning on the frame, watching the wind-whipped sheets of water that blew down the street and the silver streams that poured from the eaves onto the balcony outside.

She was still there when a visitor was announced. At the sound of a masculine tread, she turned quickly, her eyes wide.

It was only Sasha. He shook the raindrops from his hat and thrust it under his arm with his cane as he came forward. Unlike the sword masters who were more familiar in Maurelle's house, he kept to the European visiting style which limited calls to a scant fifteen minutes. In token of this short stay, a gentleman did not give up his belongings but kept them in his grasp.

It was bizarre to be disappointed that the caller was not Gavin Blackford. She was surely not in such an odd humor that the prospect of sparring with the Englishman could be preferable to her own company or that of any other. Was she?

"How kind of you to call when it is so wet out. I had not thought to see anyone for what is left of the day." Ariadne's greeting as she gave him her hand was, perhaps a shade warmer than it might have been to make up for her lack of real welcome.

"Should I stay away when you require a friend, *ma chère?* I came the moment I heard how overset you were after witnessing this morning's sad events."

"You heard? How was that?"

The tops of his ears turned red as he waved a careless hand. "These things are bruited about, you know. The important thing is that I am here."

"As I said, it was good of you to trouble."

"What disturbs you must rouse the same emotions in my breast, fair one. Tell me what you require for solace and I will bring

165

it to you. Only command me, for I am at your service."

À votre service.

The English sword master had said the same not so long ago. The words Sasha had spoken seemed but an echo of another voice, another promise.

"I hardly know which way to turn," she said with a small shake of her head. "In truth, I'm almost persuaded there is nothing to be done."

"You know best, but I fear you are more disturbed than you will admit. Why else would you allow the escort of Blackford on the street, or suffer that he should touch you in so public a manner?"

She moved away from him, returning to the settee before the fire, staring at the coal lumps like small glowing pillows behind the ornate grate. "Is that what this is really about? That I was seen with the *maître d'armes?*"

"You must admit it was indiscreet," he said, standing at rigid attention.

"I will do nothing of the sort. How dare you suggest —" She stopped, took a calming breath. "Please sit down, Sasha. We must talk."

"I am not sure I care for the sound of that." His gaze was wary as he lowered himself to the fauteuil that sat at a right angle to the settee.

"Possibly not, but it must be done. We have known each other for a number of years, have shared good times and bad. I am grateful for your constancy and the way you stood by me while Jean Marc was ill. I care for you . . ."

"And I adore you, *mon ange.*"

"Allow me to finish, if you please." She waited until he subsided. "As I was about to say, I care for you as a friend, which makes this difficult for me. It is immensely flattering that you followed me here from Paris. I am fully aware of the honor you have paid me. It may be that I even encouraged you in some fashion, though unwittingly, I swear. I have told you time and again that I have no interest in being married again, also no inclination to indulge in . . . in an affair."

"But why, adored one?" He moved with a flexing of heavy muscles to join her on the settee, sweeping aside the needlework she had left there and dropping his hat and cane on top of it. Picking up her hand that lay in her lap, he cradled it in his own. "What have I done to offend you?"

"Nothing, you've done nothing," she declared while resisting the urge to remove her cool fingers from his damp and too warm grasp. "The fault is in me. My nature is not . . . not passionate." The memory of her enthrallment at being snatched against the Englishman's hard body intruded, but she pushed it from her thoughts.

"I could undertake to convince you otherwise if you will only give me leave."

"Unlikely, I assure you. More than that, I'm certain my attraction for you is simply that I am not disposed to fall into your arms as do other females."

"You wound me, madame. I am not so shallow."

"I don't say it's the challenge to your manhood alone. The novelty intrigues, perhaps."

"I love you, this I swear." He carried her hand to his lips, his pale blue gaze intense above it.

Ariadne took a breath and let it out again as she thought how much easier it would be if she could accept his devotion. She could not. She was not even sure if he believed in it himself or if the pretense was only a habit. "You think so because you have had no chance to grow bored with my close company. It will pass."

"Never."

His mustache tickled her palm before he flicked it with his warm tongue. It was all she could do not to jerk away and wipe her skin dry. "Sasha, please."

"I cannot live without you. Your skin is so pale and fine, the curve of your elbow so delicious." He kissed his way from her wrist to the turn of her arm. "I am enraptured by the grace of your neck, so like a dancer's or, better, a proud swan."

She drew back, placing her free hand on his chest to hold him off as he tried to draw her close enough to nuzzle the skin at the turn of her neck. "Swans are dangerous birds, you know. They attack when capture is attempted."

"Attack?"

"I assure you. A slap, so I am told, is permissible under such circumstances."

He frowned while the scar on his cheek darkened. "Who said this?"

"The *maître d'armes,* if you must know."

Abruptly, he released her. "Is that why you prefer the swordsman, because he teaches you these defenses?"

"I prefer him, as you would have it, because he doesn't make them necessary. He would never attempt to instruct me in anything other than the use of a sword."

"Then he cannot be much of a man."

"If this is how you view my misjudgment in seeing you alone, as an opportunity to prove your masculinity, then I must ask you to leave," she said, rising to her feet so he was forced to stand. It was not so much that she thought he might seek to overpower her, but rather that she was reluctant to prolong what had become a disturbing interview.

"You will regret this, Ariadne. So will your paramour."

She stepped away from him. "Threats and insults, Sasha? They are unbecoming after all this time. And if you would speak ill of Monsieur Blackford, you might remember his sword is always close at hand."

"I could cut that yellow-haired popinjay in half with a single blow."

"So you might, if you could touch him."

The instant the words left her mouth, she regretted them. It might sound as if she dared him, and she did not mean it that way. It was only that she had seen Monsieur Blackford's skill first hand and could not allow it to be disparaged. She was also fond of Sasha, or had been, and did not like to think of him facing off against the sword master.

The Russian drew himself up to his full height. "I may be no maître, but I am not without skill."

"I am aware, and did not mean to suggest otherwise." She clasped her hands tightly at her waist, torn between the need to soothe his bruised ego and her longing to speed his leaving. "There is simply no need to go to such lengths. Nothing in my association with Monsieur Blackford requires it."

"Nor will you allow me the right to resent it if it should, in spite of what has been between us."

"The only thing between us was friendship which conveys no rights."

"We shall see, my Ariadne. We shall see." Snatching up his hat and cane, he stalked from the room.

Ariadne stared after him with a frown between her brows. She had thought only to make her position clear. Instead, she seemed to have made the situation worse.

Should she send to warn the sword master? How vain it would sound, that Sasha was so jealous of her company that he might issue a challenge over losing any portion of it. Added to that, it was not certain he would actually seek a meeting. What would be the pretext, after all? His temper would likely cool in the winter rain and that would be the end of it.

She hovered, staring at nothing, while her heart thudded against her ribs with slow, sickening beats. She felt both cold and hot at the same time, and it was difficult to breathe. Of what was she afraid? That the sword master would be hurt when she had longed for months for nothing so much as that he should know pain? Or only that Sasha might steal the revenge she plotted?

It was ridiculous to be so affected. She would make no move to intervene then.

But what if she was wrong?

What if she was wrong?

TWELVE

Gavin stared at himself in the mirror attached to the wall above his washstand with something less than his usual detachment. He had cut himself shaving, something so rare as to be unheard of. It wasn't that his hand was unsteady, he knew, but rather that he had been trying to scrape his beard too close.

"I coulda done better."

That pithy observation came from Nathaniel, his young apprentice who stood holding Gavin's redingote of gray merino with silver buttons and black velvet collar. It was a new acquisition. That he had chosen this evening for its inaugural wearing was part and parcel with the blood congealing on his chin. He really should have more sense. Madame Faucher was unlikely to see him in the new coat for more than the few seconds it would take him to strip to his shirt sleeves.

173

"I don't doubt your prowess with a blade," he answered while dabbing at the blood with a length of damp toweling, "but you are not my valet, *mon vieux,* nor are you likely to be."

"I do for you. We agreed."

"You keep the salon clean, make the morning coffee and run the errands that annoy me, such as summoning the washer-woman." Gavin gave the gangling sandy-haired young man, once a street boy called Squirrel, a severe glance in the mirror. "You do not act as my personal servant since I am no babe needing its chin wiped or bottom washed. In return, I have undertaken to teach you the finer points of swordsman-ship and, not incidentally, French and English. That," he finished with emphasis, "was our agreement."

"You had somebody to do for you back in England."

The boy, always touchy, had turned obsti-nate of late. He was growing up, must be — what? Around seventeen now, though he looked older. Life on the street was not kind to beasts or children, Gavin thought. Na-thaniel had filled out considerably in the year or more spent in his employ but could still use a few pounds.

He looked back at him in the mirror. "I

had a gentleman's gentleman in England, true, a man well-trained for the job. But I am not, you will note, in England."

Alarm crossed Nathaniel's expressive face. "You ain't about to go home!"

"Aren't," he corrected. "Banish the thought. The dubious pleasure of cleaning the cuspidors and ridding the salon floors of tobacco juice shall be yours for longer than you'll want it."

"That's all right, then, though I'd like it better if you had fewer Americans as clients."

"Agreed. A great reason to love the French in this fair city, that they scorn chewing tobacco as a heathen habit."

Nathaniel grunted, his idea of adequate conversation among gentlemen. As Gavin reached for the redingote, Nathaniel held it up for him. "You going to teach the Widow Faucher again?"

"To brave the harridan, rather, and see how much can be accomplished without a bloodletting."

"Yours or hers?"

"Brat," Gavin castigated without heat while sliding into the long, full-skirted coat and fastening the double-breasted front. It had been a mistake to confide in the boy, he suspected. He had made a habit of it in

175

the last few months since it was not unlike talking to himself.

It was Nicholas who had asked as a personal favor that he take Nathaniel in and instruct him. It was not something he could have refused his half brother even if he had wished, which he did not. The lad had native wit, initiative and a prickly sense of honor all his own which made him a pleasure to know. In doing his possible to help him grow into a man of worth instead of a street tramp, Gavin had come to look on him almost as a younger brother. In his more introspective moments, he thought the relationship a deliberate cultivation, to compensate for his past loss.

"Want I should wait up for you?" Nathaniel asked, putting his shoulder against the door frame and crossing his arms over his chest.

"Ready to greet me, all bleary-eyed condemnation, on my return? I think not. Beside, I have no idea how late I shall be."

"You plan more than a lesson then."

"Remove your mind from its former home, guttersnipe. I plan nothing."

"You sure of that?" Nathaniel squinted at him, as unfazed by the insult as he was by the occasional compliment.

Gavin wasn't sure at all, which had formed

another part of his momentary distraction with his ivory-handled razor in hand. He had a matter or two to discuss with Ariadne Faucher this evening, including her interest in the lady whose daughter had been killed, also the identity of the man who had raised her deadly ire. What happened afterward could depend on the answers.

"I go to my fate," he said, reaching for his gloves and sliding them on. "Whatever that may be is in the lady's hands, as it must always be in any meeting between a man and a woman."

"And if it's not?"

"That, stripling, is one reason you learn to wield a sword, to see that a lady always has a choice."

He left the atelier with a jaunty step and twirl of his cane that came, he recognized in wry amusement, from anticipation. Though Ariadne, Madame Faucher, had been upset when last he saw her, there had been no message canceling their lesson this evening, and so he must suppose it would proceed.

It might be better if it did not; this particular client was absorbing far too much of his time. Not that their meetings had been lengthy; rather, they were so often on his mind. The lady, what she wanted of him and what she intended, was fast becoming an obsession.

The way she moved, the turn of her head, the curve of her breast and the faint impression of a nipple under the linen of her shirt flashed across his mind a thousand times a day. He seldom gave an instruction or illustrated a point on the piste without some thought of how he might present the same idea to her. Sleep was only possible if he exhausted himself with teaching bouts, and his dreams were haunted by encounters that woke him with a racing heart and state of arousal so painfully acute it seemed it might become permanent. If he had an ounce of intelligence or self-control, he would sever the association this very evening. Unfortunately, those qualities had deserted him.

The rain had ceased for the time being, but the streets, even those paved with stone, were awash with mud. Further away from the central Vieux Carré, where the paving ended, they were bottomless quagmires. Not for nothing were the city blocks called islets, or little islands, as they were often surrounded by streets of running water. Treading the banquettes of the streets beyond Rue Royale, he took extra care. Made of wood taken from the gunwales of discarded keelboats, the sidewalks were known as dandy traps since the heavy wood lay half afloat in muddy water and an unwary step could force a geyser of it upward to splash pantaloons and polished boots.

Gavin arrived at the Herriot town house unscathed. It was not Solon who opened the door to him, however, but a maidservant he had not seen before. The butler was laid up with a cold in his chest from doing the marketing in the rain, she said, and would the so beautiful monsieur care to step into the salon while she went to fetch her mistress?

This was a change from the discreet entry of his prior visits, but Gavin thought it might serve to bolster the impression that his was merely a social call upon Maurelle. He followed the girl's switching skirts up the stairs and tread lightly into the room she indicated.

His client was not present. Instead, it was Zoe Savoie who occupied the salon in solitary state, with her feet in scarlet leather boots propped on a stool and a chocolate pot at her elbow. "Monsieur Blackford, what a delight," the diva exclaimed as he strolled toward her. "Pray come sit next to me and tell me something scandalous. Maurelle has just now descended to the kitchen to see to our supper so there is no one to prevent you from regaling me with your worst. Or failing that, you may give me your critique of my last performance, though I warn you I pout at anything less than fulsome compliments."

"Pure as the nightingale, soft as the dove and all as required — you were in excellent voice as you very well know," he said, bowing over her hand. "On the subject of bird life, where is Napoleon this evening?"

"At home with his head under his wing. He doesn't care for night air, you know. Was I truly all right? You did not hear the flat note in the second aria?"

"I refuse to believe you could be flat in any respect," he answered at his most droll as his gaze brushed her rounded form.

"Devil." She dimpled at him, not at all insulted. Then she sighed. "I hope you may be right about the note. It's only that I know I cannot go on forever, and I hear faults from dread of failure. Still, I have had a nice long run and should not complain."

Candlelight glanced across her strong face, caught in her fine, clear eyes to illuminate the diffidence inside her. As with most great artists, Gavin knew from some years acquaintance, she had little concept of her enormous gift thus was in need of constant reassurance. "You have no peer, madame," he said. "And have had none these many years except, perhaps, an angel or two singing in excelsior."

She laughed, a gratified sound. "Yes, and I am also madly fond of you, and for good reason, *mon brave.* I would even share my chocolate with you, if you insist, though I prefer to direct you to the wine decanter."

"I would not dream of depriving you." He had embarrassed her, he thought, though she hid it well. Moving to the wine tray on a side table, he kept his gaze on the glass of cut crystal as he filled it with the red-brown sherry. "Where is Maurelle's houseguest this evening?"

"Ariadne? Dressing, or so I believe. Something to do with a special delivery from the fine needle of Madame Pluche. She may not join us. She has had a shock, you know."

"Yes. Regrettable, that she should be at the levee when the Natchez packet came in. But I had not thought it a personal misfortune." He spoke over his shoulder, keeping his tone carefully noncommittal.

"Then you do not know? But I understood you were there."

"I was present when a young girl was brought off the steamer, also when her mother claimed her. That the lady's grief was trying to watch, I can attest, but it should not have been shocking." He paused with the wine decanter still hovering over his glass. "Unless . . ."

"Just so, *mon ami*. Unless the woman and her daughter were known to Ariadne. Which they were, you comprehend."

He had suspected as much. Turning to face the diva with his wine glass steady in his hand and his lashes shielding his eyes, he said, "I meant to ask if they were among your acquaintance, since the elder lady was the same who appeared in Maurelle's box at your benefit."

"I did not see that, being otherwise occupied, though Maurelle told me of it later." Madame's Zoe smile was brief. "The woman is the ambitious mother of several daughters. She has apparently married off a number of them but exhausted the husband possibilities of her home ground upriver so came to the Vieux Carré for fresh hunting. Her husband and youngest daughter were to join her, but now, alas . . ."

"And her name is Madame Arpegé."

"Does it convey nothing to you?" She sipped her chocolate, her eyes brightly watchful above the rim.

"I depend upon you to enlighten me."

"She is Ariadne's mother."

He had half expected something of the

sort as his brain quickly made sense of face shapes, voices' textures and long, loose tresses of familiar shining black. And yet he was puzzled. "I thought her mother and father — all her family, in fact — dead these two years and more."

"That was her foster family."

"Which one acquires, usually, when there is no other. Or am I missing something?"

She told him then, speaking in tones from which all sympathy and meaning were so carefully expunged that they struck his mind like blows. Rosebud-tender Ariadne, given away like an unwanted kitten, spitting and mewling in helpless fear. Petted and cuddled close through tender girlhood, she had then been mated to an old tom for the absolute safety of it — until she became as still and hidden inside herself as a sphinx, a she-lion of the desert which can rend and feel nothing for the victim.

When Madame Zoe's voice stopped, finally, he stared into his glass for inspiration but could find no reason to avoid the pertinent question. "The name of the foster parents?"

"They were her *marraine and parrain,* the godparents chosen for her at birth from among cousins of her mother, thus all in the family so to speak. Monsieur and Madame Dorelle were their names."

"The honored parents of a young man late of this city, one Francis Dorelle." His voice, he hoped, was rigorously even. He had made every effort to keep it that way.

"So I believe. He died . . ." The diva stopped, her face blanching a little while her eyes darkened with sudden comprehension.

"Yes, at my hand. To my infinite regret."

"How very strange," she said, her voice tentative.

"That I should now instruct his foster sister in the use of the sword? The jest of a malignant fate, you think? Or is it merely my folly?"

"I wonder," she said, her expression impenetrable as she brought her chocolate cup to her lips.

Gavin did not wonder at all. The outline of a daunting peril gathered shape in his mind, the contemplation of which brought a silent but virulent curse to his lips.

Madame Zoe glanced at him and her mouth opened. Then she turned away, proving herself a woman of great good sense by remaining decently silent.

Maurelle joined them a few minutes later. Gavin summoned his usual fulsome appreciation and urbanity, at least on the

184

surface. He said nothing of his discovery, in part because he had no idea how much the widow Herriot was in the confidence of Ariadne Faucher, but also because he was not yet certain what he meant to do about it. He was still contemplating the possibilities when a trio of musicians, among them the fabled violinist known as Old Bull, crowded into the salon. While Maurelle discussed with them the program of entertainment for what was apparently to be a musical evening, he made his excuses and escaped to the *garçonnière* wing.

She was waiting, the lovely Madame Faucher. At the opening of the door, she turned toward him in the full blaze of four-dozen candles dancing on their wicks in the draft, capering as well in their reflections in the windows on either side of the long room.

His blood paused in his veins. All coherent thought was wiped from his mind as cleanly as if someone had polished a silver server.

"You are late," she said, her voice far more dulcet than the look in her black, black eyes.

"Detained, rather. Was it for the sake of the spectacle?"

She unfolded her arms from over her chest and pushed away from the table where she leaned, coming toward him with a lithe glide made all too obvious by the form-fitting pantaloons of tan doeskin which encased her lower limbs. Spreading her hands, the better to display the wide corsair's sash of multicolored silk that cinched her slender waist and held fast the lovingly fitted linen of her masculine shirt with its diving décolletage unfettered by cravat or scarf, she asked, "You don't object, I hope?"

"By no means, not being bred from idiot stock." The wonder of it was that he could speak at all, given his view of hips and long, long legs that had heretofore been a petticoat-protected mystery. Had he not pictured her just so at their first meeting? It was as if she had divined and brought to life his most secret fantasy. It was gratifying beyond imagining, but also disconcerting. "Your tailor is to be congratulated, *mon vieux.*"

Her smile turned crooked as she absorbed the masculine form of address, but she did not take him up on it. "My dressmaker, rather. You agree the ensemble should make injury less likely?"

"It should indeed, being singular enough to stop any opponent in his tracks."

"By singular, I take you to mean vulgar."

"Oh, assuredly."

"So you disapprove."

She was almost urging him to say it, or so it seemed to Gavin. Closing the door behind him, he began to unfasten the big silver buttons of his redingote with their bas relief of St. Michael triumphant over the dragon. "I am not just any opponent, so endorse the change wholeheartedly. It will take more than an alteration of dress to stop me. Unless that is a secondary purpose?"

She arched a brow. "I would not think of it."

He hesitated in the act of tossing the outer garment over a chair seat, his attention on some faint shading of provocation in her voice. An hour ago, he might have thought it sensual in nature. Now it fringed the edges of his soul with ice.

Dropping the redingote, he slipped his cuff links from their holes and rolled back his sleeves, then turned to the table where their equipment lay ready. Taking the foils from their resting place, he handed one to his client and then stood testing the other in his hands while his thoughts took a circuitous path to reach a straightforward conclusion. At last, he lifted a hard gaze to her face. "Are you quite certain you wish to continue this game, madame?"

"You mean because of our last meeting and the small hurt you could not help?"

"Because of one that I could, and should," he answered at his most cryptic.

"I don't understand you, monsieur."

Nor did he entirely, but he must at least make the attempt at fairness. "Duels of the kind you intend are not fought by the faint of heart. They are the province of sweaty men with bad stomachs, insufferable pride and the Herculean method of unraveling knots of honor. There is no exaltation in it — no laurels for the victor and precious little real satisfaction on either side. You may feel, like a Spartan harridan with her shield, that a breast is a small price to pay to rid the world of whoever has injured you, but that will be no consolation to a future babe in arms."

Color mounted to her cheekbones, flames of rose-red that spread over her pale skin. "You are suggesting I abandon my vengeance?"

"Or allow me the honor of collecting it for you."

"You . . ." she whispered as her eyes grew black with the expansion of her pupils.

"Appoint me your champion and I will see that your enemy pays whatever recompense will best satisfy you."

A flicker of pain crossed her features. "Even . . . even death in that sweaty contest you just described?"

"If you demand it." Gavin's breathing was light, even, barely moving his chest, as he waited for her answer.

She searched his features with care, meeting his eyes with such steady appraisal that he could see himself in her dark irises as a figure who seemed on fire from the candle's glow behind him. Then her lips opened and a single word emerged like a sigh.

"Impossible."

It was, he was certain, the exact truth as they both now knew it. Impossible, yes, because she was who and what she was. Impossible, because of the past which lay behind them. Impossible, because he could not seek revenge against himself. Impossible, because he, Gavin Blackford, was the man who had killed her foster brother. Impossible, because, despite all his skill and strength and a thousand other advantages bred into the bone, he was still the man she meant to kill.

"En avant, madame," he said with a sweeping gesture toward the fencing strip that ran down the room before them. "Let us have at one another for as long as the lessons last. And while they do, you will be well-advised to guard your person with care."

THIRTEEN

The man facing her this evening was different, Ariadne thought. Watchfulness lay in the sea-dark depths of his eyes, and the corners of his mouth were firmly tucked, almost grim. His movements had lost their casual grace, becoming more purposeful. His stance, when he had moved to the strip to begin their first *phrase,* held a distinct threat, one she responded to on some primal level she had not known she possessed.

Finally, or so it seemed, he had become serious about her training. Heated excitement spread through her, beating up into her brain, flooding the lower part of her body. She tingled with it in an exquisite prickling of goose bumps, more alive than she had ever felt in her life.

He saluted her as she stepped forward to join him, a movement she copied exactly before standing at ease. Then she waited while glorying in the freedom of movement in her masculine-style pantaloons, and also the wafting of the night wind through the open windows as it glided around her hips and thighs. She was dressed as a man but could not remember when she had felt more womanly.

"Anger in a passage at arms being a liability," Gavin said, recalling her attention, "we will attempt to avoid it this evening with an oblique approach and without padding or masks as in our last lesson. I will hold my foil unmoving and you will come to me. Lift your blade, like so."

She complied, stepping lightly toward him and taking the stance she had practiced again and again while alone in her bedchamber. Once in place, she raised a brow in inquiry to make certain she was correctly placed.

He nodded as his gaze moved over her, a thorough appraisal that lingered here and there. The intentness of it created an odd tingling in her breasts and at the apex of her thighs. She narrowed her eyes.

"Now," he went on after a moment. "Using only the end of your blade, you will touch mine. Gently, gently and only at the point."

She complied, though it seemed rather

tame. It was necessary to watch the spot where the two foils came together, to make certain she maintained contact.

"Slide the end of your blade a little so you feel the smoothness of the steel. Notice the temper and hardness of it. You can, if you try, feel my pulse vibrating through the length, almost count my heartbeats."

His voice was hypnotic in its quietness. And he was right, she discovered in some amazement. The power of his hold on the sword in his hand seemed to communicate itself to her, traveling through her fingers and up her arm to lodge in her chest. A quiver, instantly suppressed, shook her wrist and elbow. To cover that small movement, she inched her foil up and down in a delicate, questing caress. His steel was silken, unyielding, poised for instant use yet severely contained, held in abeyance by his stringent will.

Could he feel the thudding of *her* heart? Was he aware of the trembling inside her? Did he realize the peculiar analogy that bloomed, irresistibly, shockingly, in her mind?

"Look at me," he instructed, his voice dropping to a deeper note. "Watch my eyes to judge what I will do next. Allow your blade to move by instinct alone. Don't think, but only respond to that stimulation. Let go of all attempt to control the outcome and permit yourself to be guided by the simple need to survive anything I may do to you."

She attempted to follow that last directive. It wasn't easy while his foil feathered up and down over hers with a musical hum and it seemed that she could feel the heat of him burning against the palm of her hand, even through her glove. Nerves tightened her throat, making it hard to form words, but it seemed imperative she say something to break the odd spell he had cast around them. "This . . . hardly seems like fighting."

"Oh, it isn't. This is its prelude, one not unlike what comes before the physical act between lovers. For the most perfect consummation, it is necessary to first know each other in deepest intimacy — to test will, desire, fortitude and promise to their limits."

He did know; she might have guessed. "As one such overture ends in death and the other in life, the comparison seems less than apt."

"You think so? Yet the apogee of love is called *le petit mort,* the little death. And with the end of life, we are assured, comes the resurrection. No," he commanded as she parted her lips to refute his claim, "you are thinking too much. Come to me now, slowly, one step at a time while keeping our contact unbroken. Come, while I retreat a step. And two. Now I will come to you. Retreat in your turn or maintain the position of your blade, even press against it, as you will. Yes, like that. And again."

Did he understand what he was doing to her? Was there actual carnal intent behind it? She thought so, but could not be sure. The prospect left her breathless, with an aching heaviness in uncomfortable areas as they glided back and forth in incongruous harmony, never losing the touch which connected them. And from the distant salon came the sweet melody of violin, harp and cello in a rapturous sonata that acted as tempo and guide.

"Come closer now as I move into your . . . your area of safety. And away again. Close, yes. And away. Begin to beat your blade against mine, softly, like a heart throb. Yes, like that. Slow. Even. Steady and unceasing while we advance and retreat. Follow my lead. . . ."

Whatever his game, he was not immune to its effect, she thought. His eyes had darkened as the black circles of his pupils expanded. A sheen of perspiration glazed his forehead in the candle's glow and the linen of his shirt caught damply on the taut muscles of his sword arm. Ariadne increased her pace, allowing her blade to cling to his as she made a small lunge with her arm straight while giving him a brilliant smile. "Do I have it, now, *mon maître?*"

"To precision, I believe," he answered even as he swirled into a parry and riposte that captured her weapon in his control, grasping it with the leverage of his own while sliding, grating in a thrust that still did not disengage. She took that powerful response and returned it with such concentrated effort that her breath sobbed in her throat.

And their movements quickened, gaining speed and impetus while their chests heaved with their laboring lungs and their booted feet whispered over the canvas strip, back and forth, back and forth, never losing their tenuous yet frantic contact.

Ariadne's wrist and arm burned and her leg muscles quivered on the edge of cramping. A red haze rose to veil her eyes. The thrum of her blood in her ears was like a drumbeat that drove her, applauded her until she thought he must hear. And she could not look away from Gavin's eyes, so hotly blue, so stark with what seemed an incontrollable need to draw her closer — close enough to touch, to hold, to invade in single-minded possession that she could not, would not allow.

Yet all the time, the end was never in doubt. She was not his match in strength or hardiness, in experience or pounding force. She could not sustain the wild effort, could not prevent the sudden, unwilling capitulation that brought him within her guard, with her sword arm raised above her head and her body, shuddering with every gasping intake of air, pressed against his hard form from breasts to knees.

Their abrupt stillness was like a blow. The candle flames leaped, then burned higher, brighter on their wicks. Outside, the wind died away. The music from the other room had stopped. No sound penetrated from the rest of the town house, as if all within it had fallen silent to listen. The movement of Gavin's firm chest against hers as he breathed nudged Ariadne's tight nipples to aching buds while cradled against the fluttering muscles of her belly was a firmness that was unmistakable. Every inch of her body tingled, yearned, while the faint trembling of anticipation gripped her. Her heart beat with a crazed rhythm and the blood poured through her veins like a river in flood, beat with feathery pulsations in her ears. She inhaled his scent of clean linen, bay-scented shaving soap and over-heated male while her gaze fastened on a small slash mark on his chin from which oozed a ruby-colored droplet of blood.

Sanity and awareness returned in a fiery wave. She closed her eyes in search of excuses or absolution but could find neither. Without looking up, she disengaged with the contraction of overtaxed muscles which threatened, for an appalling instant, to refuse her bidding.

Speaking from a safe distance, she said, "I didn't cut you . . . that is, please tell me it was not my blade that nicked you."

He swung away, putting his back to her. Placing his foil on the table with both hands, he kept his shoulders hunched, his gaze on the long fingers of his hands that held it. "Be at peace. Alarm is not required, contrition not expected." He looked up then, his gaze finding her reflection that stared back at him from one of the dark window glasses that marched down the chamber. "In this *phase* of our meetings, at least, any wound received was self-inflicted."

FOURTEEN

"So. This is where you are hiding."

Accusation layered Sasha's voice as he pushed open the door without ceremony and walked into the long *garçonnière* chamber. Ariadne had caught the sound of his footsteps and thought it might be Gavin returning for some reason. Closer attention told her it was not, even before the Russian appeared; the footsteps were far too heavy.

"Where else, since it's the evening for my lesson?" she answered, turning back to her task of replacing the foils she and her instructor had used earlier in their satin-lined case. Her voice was curt. She wished Sasha at the devil or in some other place equally distant. She was not ready for this kind of confrontation. And if it was disappointment that caused her to be so waspish, she refused to acknowledge it.

"The Englishman failed to appear?"

"What do you think?" She wondered

briefly if Sasha had thought to find him there, if he had intended to discover some pretext for a challenge where there was no audience other than herself. Or, conversely, if he had waited, seen the sword master leave, so knew there was no chance of it.

"I have difficulty believing he could drag himself away while you are dressed — or should I say undressed? — in such a fashion."

She had almost forgotten her male attire in her concentration on other things. Now she glanced down at her pantaloons before giving Sasha a straight look. "I consider the fashion practical. Men appear to find it so."

"They may find it far too alluring on you, though I'm sure your sword master will convince you he thinks it ravishing."

"He has seen the ensemble," she said with a crooked smile. "He pronounced it vulgar."

Sasha looked down his nose. "A man of sense, after all. He has already gone then?"

"He had other matters requiring his attendance."

"I suppose it was better than admitting the need for escape."

She frowned down at the blade she was polishing free of fingerprints with a cloth laid out for that purpose. Was that a faint slurring she heard in Sasha's voice? With his accent, it was difficult to be sure. "From my unladylike display, you mean to say?"

"Rather from temptation." He moved closer, his gaze resting on the deep neckline of her shirt that had fallen open on one side, exposing the white curve of a breast.

It was a possibility she had not considered. Blackford's departure had followed close on the end of their lesson. Could Sasha be correct? She would like to think so, but was not quite so sanguine.

"The gentleman has better control," she said as she reached to close the gap in her shirt. "He would not allow his emotions to run away with him."

"He is a man, isn't he?"

"He is a *maître d'armes* above all, a different thing altogether."

"If I did not know better, *chère,* I would say you admire him."

"It's possible to admire skill and dedication without admiring the man who possesses them." She went on without pause. "You wanted something, that you sought me out here?"

"That is a most leading question. Would you prefer the chivalrous answer, which is that I wanted to see you? Or would the truth serve me better? In view of your mode of dress, I believe I will tell you that what I desire now, and have from our first meeting, is your delectable body that is so frankly displayed."

Anger, mixed with guilt rose inside her, making her feel hot all over. That was added to the flush brought by his too-personal gaze as it moved over her, resting on her lower body where her perspiration-damp pantaloons nestled with particular fidelity. She might have been even more incensed except she was certain now that he was the worse for drink.

Sasha had a considerable capacity for strong liquor courtesy of the revels enjoyed by young men of his class at military academy. There were also times when it caught up with him. She could not help wondering if he had sought courage from a bottle before searching her out.

"My mode of dress," she said evenly, "has no bearing whatever on my character or my likelihood of being flattered by your declaration. You were not meant to see it, nor was it intended for your convenience."

"Only for your swordsman's."

"Rather, for my aid to free movement and safety on the fencing strip."

He gave a weak laugh that wafted alcohol fumes into her face. "You expect me to believe Blackford saw it as nothing more."

"Sasha, for the love of heaven!" She might have been more exasperated except for the mental image of what had taken place earlier in the long chamber.

"Tell me he didn't notice. Tell me he had no reaction, made no advances."

She could not do that, though she had to wonder if she might have imagined the ardor that had run like a molten river beneath his instructions and actions. "He did not touch me other than the usual brief contact of fencing. I resent any implication that it might be otherwise."

"He is a fool or a monk that he missed the opportunity. I am neither."

Sasha took the last long step that would bring him within arm's reach. One massive hand closed on her upper arm and he swung her to face him.

Instantly, Ariadne jerked free of his hold while whirling away, snatching the foil she had been polishing from the table. When she completed her turn, she faced him with the blade in her hand and its tip pointed at the center button of his frock coat.

Surprise at her own action gripped her for half a second. She must have absorbed more of Gavin's instruction than she realized. She had not stopped to think, but only acted. It was an exhilarating thing to recognize, as exhilarating as the knowledge that she was now able to protect herself from unwanted advances.

Nevertheless, she could not help contrasting her reaction to Sasha's encroachment with that of her closeness to Gavin Blackford. Her very bones had seemed to dissolve as she stood pressed against the master swordsman. The core of her body had ached with an emptiness that was beyond anything she had ever imagined. Never had she been so aware of a man or of herself as a woman with needs, desires and the potential for pleasure.

It would not do, must not happen again.

"You forget yourself, Alexander Novgorodcev," she said with the steel of that resolve threading her voice. "I did not give you leave to touch me."

He licked his lips, watching her with intent, pale blue eyes in which lurked chagrin shaded with misery. "My mistake, for which I would ask forgiveness. Though I will point out that your foil is blunted."

"That doesn't prevent it from making a nasty cut."

"Ariadne, *chérie* . . ."

"Don't call me that, if you please. It does nothing to redress your wrong. You may make your apologies in form another time.

For the moment, all I require is your absence."

"You must know I meant no harm. My feelings were simply too strong to . . ."

"They overcame you, added to whatever you have been drinking. This is understood. I bid you good-night."

It might have been what she said and how she said it, the foil in her hand or the recognition of the futility of arguing with an armed woman. It could have been that the bombast he depended on to carry him through most events had deserted him. Whatever the cause, he gave a wavering nod of his head that dipped into a bow, then he turned and walked with careful dignity toward the door.

Ariadne followed him with her gaze, keeping her guard. She was still watching when he turned back.

"Just then, *ma coeur,* you sounded very like the Englishman. You are spending too much time in his company, and so I warn you. I told you before that you would regret it. I tell you so again."

She stood for long moments after the door had closed behind the Russian. He had no power or authority to order her life. There was no one to whom he could appeal who might influence her in any way. His only recourse, then, would be to apply to Gavin Blackford. Threats seemed unlikely to dissuade the sword master since they had not prevented him from taking her on in the first place. That left only one thing, the event she most feared.

Distress rippled over her as the specter of a duel rose in her mind. Why did it have to be this way?

Why was Sasha becoming so difficult? He had never been importunate before. After she was widowed, he had remained in the post of her faithful servitor as a matter of habit, she thought, declaring himself on occasion in heavy-handed flirtation with little expectation that she would return his devotion. She had been surprised when he followed after her to New Orleans, but thought it had more to do with his creditors in Paris than desperate affection for her. She had expected little impediment from him in achieving her design.

That had been naive of her, she realized now. Even so, she could hardly believe this scion of a Russian noble house had serious pretensions to her hand. It appeared that, like a dog with a bone, he had become possessive because a man appeared whom he saw as a rival.

Perhaps she was being too cynical and he

truly was in love with her. She had done nothing to encourage it; she was not so heartless as to raise hopes she had no intention of fulfilling. Their acquaintance had been comfortable to this point, a mere social convention. Such things sometimes ended in affairs, as everyone knew, but she had a purpose which precluded emotional entanglements. That was even if she had desired a closer relationship, which she did not. Nor did remarrying interest her. She might one day consider it for the sake of children but could see no other reason.

No, the change in Sasha had been triggered by her association with the sword master. She had never been indiscreet while married to Jean Marc, never shown any hint of extramarital yearning. Sasha could not understand her interest now, therefore it was suspect. Added to that, he had walked in on her in the fencing costume she had ordered that was something less than demure.

She could not blame him for his suspicion, but did fault him for acting on it. She was no less who she had always been while clad in pantaloons. Until she indicated otherwise, her inclinations were the same as when she wore the concealment of her skirts.

Or was that mere self-deception?

She should have guessed how Sasha would react, should have dealt with him before now, she thought, lifting a hand to rub at her temple where an ache was starting to throb. No matter how she tried to get around it, whatever happened between him and Gavin Blackford would be her fault.

How had everything gone so wrong?

When it seemed clear Sasha had left the house, Ariadne sighed and put away the foil again then closed the lid upon it and its mate. All at once, she was deadly tired. All she wanted to do was sleep, sleep and forget.

She hardly closed her eyes all night. Her thoughts ran in circles as she lay staring into the darkness. What would Sasha do? How would Gavin Blackford meet any threat he mounted? Did the sword master suspect who she was? How long did she have before he discovered it? What would she say if he confronted her? Was it really possible for her to gain the skill to defeat him at his own game, or to gain it in time? And even if she did that, could she strike the fatal blow?

She had been so firm in her purpose while in Paris, so certain that rage and grief would supply the strength to carry through with her plan. That she was beset by doubts now seemed a betrayal of Francis.

Oh, but would he approve of her dangerous quest? Or would he, tender, poetic soul that he had been, deplore it? Would he object to such a tribute and fear for her in its execution? Had she been a little deranged following his death and Jean Marc's lingering demise that she could think it might be otherwise?

It was Maurelle, next morning, who forced her to face the greatest of her fears.

"What have you decided, *chère?* Shall it be the bombazine or no?"

The question jerked Ariadne from her headachy reverie where she and Maurelle sat at the breakfast table with café au lait and buttered brioche in front of them. It was an instant before she could think to what her hostess referred, much less bring her mind to bear on the problem.

"I don't know, I really don't," she said on a sigh as she propped her head on her hand. "Do you think I should really go into black for a stepfather and stepsister I never saw while they were alive and certainly can never claim to have known? I am not unsympathetic, but I foresee only problems." What she could not tell Maurelle, of course, was that she wished particularly to avoid curiosity on the part of the sword master.

Maurelle bent a judicious gaze on the brioche in her hand. "I do understand what you are saying, but that isn't the point. You remember the old saying, *Si un chat mourrait dans la famille, tout le monde portrait de deuil.*"

If a cat should die in the family, everyone would be in mourning. Ariadne's lips curved in a wan smile as she nodded.

"It's a gesture of respect, you understand. No one must be behind hand with such things, it just isn't done. It's also from the knowledge that the next to take the ride behind black horses wearing black plumes might be you. One would not like to make the journey alone."

"I realize, and don't object in principle," Ariadne said seriously. "Oh, but then there is the condolence call and everything else."

"Yes, though I think you can avoid the ordeal of sitting with the remains through the night. That is, unless you prefer it. As for the burial, I am told arrangements are being made to transport the bodies and mourners back upriver to their place in the country."

Ariadne had hoped for that outcome. To hear it confirmed was an enormous relief. As embarrassed as she might be by that obvious self-interest, one question concerning it stood out above the rest.

"You think my mother will return to New

Orleans afterward?"

"No one knows, though I should think it unlikely." Maurelle reached for her coffee cup, cradling it between her hands. "She will hardly rejoin the social round while in mourning, even if she should wish to continue the pursuit of a husband for your sister. The girl herself could attend only the most staid of entertainments, so may as well remain at home."

Had her problem been so easily resolved? Ariadne hardly dared accept it. After a moment, she asked, "What of the condolences?"

"Calling on your mother at once will be best. At least you may choose the time and duration of the visit and will not appear backward in your filial duty. As for whether to join them on their sad homeward journey, you must please yourself."

"Yes, I suppose so," Ariadne said gratefully. Leaving New Orleans was the last thing on her mind.

"You will naturally wear black for the visit. Afterward, I should recommend gray at the very least."

Gray seemed a workable compromise. Being a fashionable color this season, it might easily pass without remark by a certain swordsman, at least for the short time required. "Do you think many know of the connection?" she asked after a moment.

"Perhaps not at present, but this tragedy may resurrect the memories of those who knew of your adoption. It is sure to be grist for the gossip mill in time."

She could only hope that it was later rather than sooner, Ariadne thought as her lips tightened. As for the rest, Maurelle might be a fairly free spirit but no one knew the refinements of the New Orleans social code so well. If she thought a condolence call while in black was necessary, then there was no escaping it.

"You will accompany me for the visit, I hope."

"If you like," her hostess said, though there was a question in her direct gaze.

Ariadne was not sure whether her request was made from a need for support or merely for the sake of company in her misery, but she smiled and thanked her friend, regardless.

They set out during the afternoon, Maurelle in subdued gray with lavender piping and Ariadne in a gown and bonnet rushed from the nimble fingers of Madame Pluche who kept black ensembles on hand for just such emergencies. They walked, since the rain was in abeyance for the time being and it was only a few blocks to the Hotel St. Louis where her mother was in residence. A note had been sent asking if their call was convenient, given that her mother was in seclusion. The reply was brief, but in the affirmative. At least they could expect to be received.

They entered by the side door reserved for ladies without male escorts, nodding to the porter who held it open for them. Another time Ariadne might have been annoyed at the extra steps required to reach it, but in this case she was happy to use the more discreet entrance. It allowed her to avoid the front door which opened on the Passage de la Bourse and a chance sighting from the gentleman who had his atelier there.

The suite they entered was in chaos. Beyond the open doors of the two bed-chambers connected to the sitting room, trunks could be seen with their lids flung open. A pair of maids bustled here and there with clothing over their arms and collections of oddments in their hands from button hooks to sewing boxes. The opulence of the hotel room with its swag-and-fringe-laden draperies, Brussels carpet and brocatelle-covered furnishings, seemed to suggest a change for the better in the circumstances of Ariadne's mother since her remarriage. It was an impression aided by jet jewelry which complemented the deep, lusterless black worn by her and the daughter of marriageable age for whose sake she had been in the city.

One of the maids was sent for a tray of refreshment from the hotel kitchen while the other withdrew, muttering, into one of the bedchambers, shutting the door behind her. Ariadne and Maurelle were left in the sitting room with Ariadne's mother and her half sister.

"It's very good of you to come," Madame Arpegé said with great dignity when the greetings and introductions were out of the way. "I would not have had it be under these circumstances for anything in the world, but —" She stopped, pressing a black-edged handkerchief to her eyes.

"No, nor would I." Ariadne swallowed an unaccountable knot in her own throat before she went on. "My every sympathy is with you, I assure you, though you must realize that I hardly . . ."

"No, no, of course you don't know us, I quite understand that. We have lived apart for so many years, so very many years." Her mother summoned a smile which lifted the lines of her face, making her seem endearingly familiar to Ariadne for an instant, as if she might recall that expression from childhood.

Ariadne's half sister moved closer to where their mother sat on the settee, reached out to take her free hand, holding it between both of hers. This was Sylvanie Renée who had not been born when Ariadne was given for adoption, daughter of the stepfather who had died. She appeared fifteen or sixteen perhaps but mature with it, not at all an unusual age for the marriage market. Though not quite as tall or as thin as Ariadne, she had the same pale skin, and dark eyes and hair, the same steady way of looking at people. Yes, and even the same expression of mistrust.

"Oh, but I expect you are wondering why I tried to contact you at the theater the other night. It was the call of a mother's heart. I didn't mean to intrude but saw you and had to speak to you, to explain. No matter how many children a woman may have, the loss of even one must forever be felt inside. Hardly a day has gone by in all the time since I gave you up that I haven't regretted parting with you, regretted even more the move which took me, took all of us, so far away."

Ariadne leaned forward in her chair. "Why

214

—" She stopped, cleared her throat. "Why did you?"

Madame Arpegé met her eyes, her own drowned in tears. "How to explain when it was so many things, really. I was so tired, you see; that is the first thing. I loved your father desperately and the babies came almost every year, one after the other. You were barely two and I was already increasing again. A hurricane ruined the sugarcane harvest and we could not repay the money we owed against it. Your father gambled away the last of our reserves trying to recoup the loss, then was so distraught I feared . . . feared he might do away with himself. My cousin Josephine, your *marraine,* came to visit and fell in love with you. She begged so to have you, and her husband, your *parrain,* offered . . . offered a loan that seemed our salvation. I thought . . . I thought . . ."

"Please. I understand."

"Do you? I'm not sure I do. I've wondered so many times how I, your mother, could . . ." Her mother made a helpless gesture with her handkerchief. "We lost our home anyway, the next season, you know. By then, Francis was born. I pleaded that you be returned to me but Josephine wouldn't hear of it. You had become hers

215

and you adored baby Francis. He needed a sister, she said, she might never have another child. In the end, we went away."

"I never knew . . . was never told that you asked to have me back." Ariadne could see why it had been kept from her; still she wondered if everything might not have been different if she had known. Hearing it now, she felt the easing of a hard knot of old resentment.

"Josephine was afraid you would hate her, I think, and so . . ." Her mother lifted her shoulder in a fatalistic gesture. "But it must have seemed strange to you, our desertion. I quite realize that now. At the time, it was simply less painful to go away where I need not see your sweet face, would not be reminded. Then your father died, and it was like . . . like a judgment upon us."

"Please, you must not upset yourself further," Ariadne said, her voice not quite even. "It's all in the past now."

"Yes, and then you were sent farther away, to Paris," her mother continued as if she did not hear. "All thought of ever seeing you again was ended, or so I thought. But by chance, the most astonishing chance, I heard you had returned to the city."

"It's fortunate that you were here as well." For a brief moment, Ariadne remembered her suspicion that it was Jean Marc's fortune that had brought her mother to her, and was ashamed.

"As to that, your oldest sister lives here now. You know that you have nine living sisters as well as three stepsisters? Three were lost as children to fever soon after we moved upriver, and then you know of my poor, darling Cecilia and the horror of. . . ."

She trailed off, searched for a dry corner on her handkerchief, used it again. Ariadne looked down at her hands fighting her own tears. It was Maurelle who took up the conversation.

"You say you have a daughter in residence here?"

"But yes, since last year, my Beatrice. It's she who has been helping with invitations for Sylvanie during this season. Her husband is a cotton factor with an office in the Passage de la Bourse."

Ariadne shared a quick glance with Maurelle even as she felt the hair rise on the back of her neck. The Passage was not a long street, being only a pedestrian alleyway leading from the business district of lower Canal Street to the Hotel St. Louis and through its great central rotunda onward to the Cabildo where records were filed and legal business transacted. Any sort of office

217

would be only a step away from the *salon d'assaut* kept by Gavin Blackford.

"How providential for your Sylvanie. I am assuming Beatrice's husband has family connections here?" Maurelle asked with a pleasant smile in the girl's direction.

Madame Arpegé made a distracted sound of agreement before turning back to Ariadne. "What I have told you — it isn't all what I meant to say, *ma chère* . . . You don't mind that I address you so?"

Ariadne shook her head, too anxious over what else her mother might tell her to voice an objection.

"I wanted to see you, most of all, because word came to me that you were alone in the world. No one should be without family, especially when there are those of their blood waiting to take them in their arms. Family is everything, *n'est pas?* Monsieur Arpegé, my dear Theophile, quite agreed. He doesn't . . . didn't . . . care for the city, but felt he should join me here, the better to convince you. Oh, but now . . ."

Ariadne put a hand to her throat where her breathing was suddenly constricted. "You are saying he died because of me?"

"No, no, there is no blame! I didn't mean to . . . it's only . . . oh, please, please don't think so! It's merely the terrible sadness of

218

it. He adored having a family of girls, loved seeing them in their new finery as they tripped down the stairs to show him." She shook her head, mopping tears. "He so looked forward to adding you to their number, one who could speak to him of Paris where he studied as a young man during his grand tour."

"I'm . . . sorry that I shall not have the pleasure of his acquaintance." It was actually true, Ariadne realized as she said it. He sounded like a gentleman it might have been a privilege to know.

Her mother wiped her eyes yet again, keeping them closed for a long instant before she released a sigh. "Yes. Oh, yes. He will be greatly missed by us all. As for our Cecilia . . . but I must not think of that or . . . Our time is short, and I should tell you that you are an aunt, yes, several times over. You were my fourth-before-the-last child, so have older sisters who have been married these several years. The count is six nieces and four nephews to whom you must be introduced."

It was too much, being presented with such a large family after thinking of herself as solitary. Ariadne could not quite take it in or decide how she felt. The close relationship was not something she could claim

while pretending to be without family connections. Gavin Blackford already knew too
much about her; if she turned up with a
long-lost mother, he could well begin to put
together her past.

She rose to her feet with a swiftness which
so startled the maidservant just coming
through the outer door that the china rattled
on the tray she carried. "You go too fast,
Madame Arpegé —"

"Maman, your *maman.*"

"My *maman,* the woman I knew by that
name, passed away almost four years ago. I
must tell you that I have a life of my own
now, one I cannot abandon in an instant
because of an accident of birth."

"Of course, you do. I would not . . ."

"You can't simply take me back and
expect everything to be the same," Ariadne
continued a little desperately. "I must have
a choice this time, since I had none when I
was small."

"Oh, *ma chère.*" Her mother shook her
head in distress while Sylvanie Renée stared
at her in reproach.

"You gave me away as if I was a doll with
no rights or affections. I cried after you, but
still you went away and left me."

Her mother's face crumpled. "You were
so young. I didn't realize, didn't think you

would remember."

"I'm not a child any more. I am a woman in my own right with plans, hopes, needs, things that must be done before I can rest." She went on in near incoherence. "I have much to accomplish before I can even begin to think of what else I may do."

"Yes . . . Yes, I see. You will not be traveling home with us then?"

Ariadne made a helpless gesture. "It's impossible."

"As you say." Her mother seemed to age before her eyes. Tears dripped down her face and she let them, as if she had forgotten the handkerchief she shredded between her fingers. Then she squared her shoulders and rose to face her visitors. "You must do what you will, my Ariadne. You will see that I won't give you up this time; I bore you and will always feel the connection of blood between us. When you are clear in your mind, and if the decision is in our favor, you will be welcome wherever I am and you will be loved as always. And now, I must bid you good afternoon. I have much to do and steamboats and funerals will not wait."

Mere moments later, Ariadne was back out on the banquette with Maurelle walking at her side. Disturbance rang in her mind more loudly than their footsteps. She had said nothing she did not feel, and yet her voice echoed in her own ears as shrill and anguished, like a child protesting unfairness in a world where nothing was fair. If her mother had taken her in her arms . . .

But no, nothing would have been changed, nothing made different. It could not be.

Nothing seemed to be going as it should with her plans. No one was turning out as she expected.

Her mother had been magnificent at the end of the visit; that she freely admitted. Perhaps something of her own determination and clear-speaking had been derived from her. It would have been nice to know what else she might have inherited. Only thinking of it left her in a pall of regret. It also made her afraid in some manner she could not quite grasp.

It brought Gavin Blackford far too vividly to mind.

She had returned in spirit a thousand times during the night before to their *phrase d'armes* in the *garçonnière.* The mere thought of it made her heart beat faster while heat suffused her. Like partners in a dangerous dance, they had moved together with her following his lead. It had seemed right that it should be so at the time, though she wondered now at her acquiescence. It was as if she had been in a thrall; she could think of no other explanation.

He fascinated her, no matter how she might deny it. How powerfully he moved, the muscles of his legs and arms flexing, elongating, gliding to the direction of a superior intellect. His gaze was mesmerizing, so concentrated, as if nothing existed except the moment and their place, with the two of them in it. No movement she made escaped him. That he approved of her form, her style, could not be doubted, since he was quick to point out her errors otherwise. The knowledge was exhilarating, almost intoxicating in its way.

Not that she was under his spell or anywhere near it. She noted his formidable strength and approach to swordplay for the use such knowledge might be to her later. That was all. Most certainly, that was all. If she was sometimes confused, sometimes wondered if she could cling to the vow of revenge made before she left Paris, well, she was female after all and subject to the same mixed feelings as the rest of her sex. Second thoughts in the dark of the night were only natural.

Did he know? Was it possible?

These questions obsessed her. Could Gavin Blackford have learned in some man-

223

ner that he was her enemy, the man she had sworn to kill?

Surely not, for what man, knowing, would or could continue as if nothing had changed? Why would he appear for their lessons while aware he was instructing someone who longed to press a sword's point into his chest?

It had been a mistake to tell him anything of her design in the beginning. And yet, he would never have agreed to take her on as a client if she had not used it to rouse his interest. She would not have had the shadow of a chance to defeat him.

Yes, but what chance had she now?

That doubt whispered at the edges of her mind, wrapping around the warm and beating center of her heart as she walked homeward beside Maurelle. For it, there was only one answer.

The risk must be taken.

FIFTEEN

Gavin awoke to the beat and clang, snick, slide and measured pauses of a bout with épées. The sound blended with a fading dream in which he faced Ariadne again with sword in hand though they were both as naked as the day they were born and his mind sang a paean to breasts as white and pink as a winter sunrise kissing mounds of snow. He groaned and squeezed his eyes shut again.

The noise that woke him came from his salon beneath his third-floor bedchamber. Apparently Nathaniel had found himself a sparring partner. Excellent. Let him wear out some other would-be swordsman while developing his hand and eye. Only why in God's heaven did he have to do it at the crack of dawn?

It was no later than that, judging from the pale and watery light through the window. Certainly it was far too early to be so energetic. The average French Creole gentleman seldom rose before mid-morning due to the late nights of Latin habits; it would be hours before clients began to appear. Gavin rolled over, dragging his pillow over his ears and closing his eyes again.

At once, the image of Ariadne in her outrageous attire rose in his mind. Why it should be that a man's pantaloons and linen shirt should make a woman's form a thousand times more exotically feminine he could not tell; he only knew that it did. The silken folds and damp hollows were so different from the normal anatomy concealed under broadcloth and worsted that the very thought of them scorched his brain.

Acute and heavy discomfort assailed him, and he wrenched over on the cotton-stuffed mattress, flopping onto his back with a sound of disgust. Intemperate passion was not his normal style. Besides, he was supposed to have more control. What had become of it was a mystery, though not more of one than his virulent attraction to Madame Faucher. Who could have guessed that obsession could be aroused in him by a woman who wanted nothing from him except his death?

Well, the lady also meant to learn the exact way to bring that death about from the man most knowledgeable in that regard. Namely him. It was a novel approach to a kill, if nothing else.

God's teeth, but what was he thinking that he was actually attempting to show her? It was madness, beyond logic. She must be a sorceress that she could persuade him to it.

Deadly angel or witch? She was both, and more. Lost child, unawakened widow, terrified lady — he saw all those things in her eyes. He longed so to remedy them that the venture seemed worth any cost.

He did not discount the danger. She was female, tender and sometimes confused, but her purpose burned inside her with perilous brightness. And her cause, he knew to his sorrow, was just.

The tremulous courage of Francis Dorelle as he faced him, sword in hand, on that rain-washed dawn four years ago bloomed in Gavin's memory. With it also came repentance so scorching that it blistered his mind.

Abruptly, he flung back the covers and surged from the bed. Padding on bare feet to the washstand, he poured water from a china pitcher into its matching bowl then, plunging his hands into it, splashed his face again and again.

As he reached for a linen towel, he caught

a glimpse of his face in the mirror. The cut on his chin was marked this morning only by a dried scab. Ariadne had seemed aghast that she might have caused it. That recollection, as he blotted dry the small spot of soreness, was the single glimmer of hope he had that killing him would not be easy for her.

On descending to the salon, Gavin discovered that Denys Vallier, brother of Rio's wife Celina, the Condessa de Lérida, was the man Nathaniel was engaged with on the strip. Both young men were sweating like mules from the exertion; Denys's hair was damp and curling around his hot face and Nathaniel's stood out in wet, sandy tufts. The shirts and pantaloons of both clung with every lunge, and the close room smelled like a cockpit on Saturday night. Gavin walked to the French doors that gave onto the balcony overlooking the Passage and swung both sets open to the morning freshness. Then he turned to watch the two on the strip.

They were well-matched in size, better than he might have expected. Denys, being older by six or seven years, had only an inch or so of reach and a few pounds over the younger boy, advantages Nathaniel made up for by dogged determination. Their extensions were nice, advances clean and with good control of their weapons; their speed was well-calculated, footwork excellent and parries without excess motion. If neither showed any propensity for intricate wrist work, it was explained by the fact that this was a friendly bout and nothing more.

Proof that it was amicable was amply provided by the fact that Denys was holding back. His was the greater skill by a marked degree, since he had studied with his brother-in-law, the great Rio de Silva, before and after Rio became the Conde de Lérida, and was no stranger in the other salons up and down the Passage. Gavin did not make a habit of meeting his friends on the piste, but he had enjoyed a friendly phrase or two with Vallier, so knew his merit.

Nathaniel seemed to believe there was no higher calling than to become a *maître d'armes*. Gavin hadn't the heart to disabuse him of the idea — or else, as he sometimes thought, he needed the boy's high certainty to compensate for his own disillusion. To watch Nathaniel's pleasure in a well-executed touch, to see his confidence improving every day along with his gain in muscular strength, was like seeing himself at the same age: determined, involved, certain that might and right could be the same thing.

The question, as he was well aware, was how long the occupation of sword master would be a viable one. Dueling, with its code that drove men to perfect their swordsmanship, was in decline in the rest of the world. The preference for pistols, and the American view that revenge rather than the preservation of honor was its purpose, had taken the heart out of it. Only here in the Vieux Carré of New Orleans where the code of the gentleman still prevailed was its grip unbroken. Something inside Gavin yearned after this last remnant of bygone chivalry and sought diligently to preserve it.

It was not that he was unaware of its abuses, the hot tempers it fostered, the needless deaths of stiff-rumped idiots too stubborn or too proud to admit a fault, the subtle blackmail made possible by exceptional skill. He had seen all these things at close hand, and participated in some of them. Still, he had grave doubts of what society might be like if there was no recourse for a gentleman who felt he had been wronged, no way for a private individual to prevent men who lacked fundamental respect for their fellow human beings from preying on them.

Abruptly, Denys executed a parry in low

quarte at terrific speed, swirling immediately into a riposte that allowed him to skim forward and press the point of his épée to Nathaniel's chest padding so it bent in a gentle curve. Gavin abandoned philosophy to begin a measured applause.

"Touché," Nathaniel acknowledged in disgust.

Disengaging, stepping out of position, Denys stripped off his face mask and tucked it under his arm with his épée before turning to Gavin with his usual warm grin. "Did we wake you? If so, I tender my apologies. I'm only up myself because Celina's latest brat has the colic. Hardly three months old, the poor mite, and I expect any day to hear that my sister is *enceinte* again, considering the way she and Rio make eyes at each other across the breakfast table. It's enough to put a man off his food."

"Tell Rio," Gavin recommended, his voice dry.

"Thank you, no. I like the arrangement of my face as it is. You wouldn't care to take on the task?"

"Not without full armor and a clanking great herd of pachyderms to drive before me." He went on without pause. "If the reference to breakfast was a hint that you have not had your morning coffee, then consider yourself invited to join us. Nathaniel?"

"Yeah, I know," the boy answered with a roll of his warm brown eyes. "Café au lait, at once. Don't talk about nothing interesting till I get back." Taking the masks and chest pads that he and Denys had removed, he set them back in their proper places then made for the stairs which led to the ground-floor kitchen.

"He improves," Denys said with a nod toward the doorway where Nathaniel had disappeared as they moved to one of several tables which ringed the open room.

"He should, since he's certainly dedicated enough."

"And has an excellent teacher."

"If only he'd pay as much attention to attempts at correcting his language."

Denys's eyes gleamed with amusement in his olive face. "His coffee is nearly as lacking. I daresay we shall be able to read *L'Abeille* through the dregs. Why do you permit it?"

"Because," Gavin answered as he seated himself, "he so enjoys making it. And I prefer it to the mud you call coffee that seems constructed to make a man's bowels shudder. But no matter. Colicky offspring and connubial jealousy aside, what really brings you out so early?"

"Rumors," Denys answered promptly, his features taking on a serious mien. "Did you really parade down the street with your arm around the lovely Widow Faucher?"

"In support only, after she had seen assorted people parboiled like so many succulent shrimp. Is that what the gossips are saying?"

"Not with such graphic detail." Denys winced before he continued. "The consensus seems to be that the lady is ruining herself by keeping company with the fast set Madame Herriot has around her, particularly keeping late-night assignations with a certain gentleman of the sword."

"Nameless, faceless and insubstantial as air?"

"Not so you'd notice, unless ghosts are yellow-haired and whistle their way homeward."

"Bloody hell," Gavin said with feeling.

"I thought you might feel that way, which is why I let it be known that you are a particular friend of Madame Herriot's."

"For which favor, like a hound bringing a partridge to place at his master's feet, you require a pat on the head. Or are you hunting for explanations?"

"Neither are required," Denys answered,

his cheerfulness unimpaired. "I bring the tittle-tattle to you in case there is something you care to do about it. Other than annihilate the messenger, of course."

The different but no less painful possibility that formed on Gavin's tongue remained unspoken as footsteps pounded on the stairs. Slower and firmer than the gallop preferred by Nathaniel, they signaled either the arrival of another guest or an extremely early client.

It was the first, in the person of the large American, Kerr Wallace. With him came the aroma of fresh-baked bread emanating from the pair of baguettes he carried under one arm.

"Breakfast," the tall, russet-brown haired gentleman said by way of greeting as he whipped out one long loaf and brandished it at them like a sword while amusement gleamed in his slate-gray eyes. "Tough as whet-leather and sits in your stomach like a rock, but I've taken a liking to it." His voice turned hopeful. "I don't suppose you have butter?"

"Nathaniel can produce a bowl, no doubt." Gavin, reconciled to playing host, waved toward another seat at the table.

Soon they were all enjoying the simple morning repast, including Nathaniel who was uncharacteristically quiet as he sat with his shoulders straight and face flushed with his pleasure at being one of them. Conversation was brisk but general. They mentioned a mysterious white leather trunk currently being advertised in *L'Abeille* as part of some thief's recovered booty which should be reclaimed by its owner; moved from there to the duel of the concerts being held between the two famous violinists wintering in the city, Old Bull and Vieux Temps, then on to the fate of the hospitalized victims from the explosion of the steamboat which had been identified as the *Bluebell* out of Shreveport on the Red River. Two had died of their terrible injuries, it seemed, but those remaining were expected to recover. Finally, Denys told a tale of an impromptu duel outside a quadroon ball resulting in injuries to both parties that was then followed by a hilarious champagne supper which drowned the differences of the combatants in drink.

Kerr, leaning back in his chair, holding his coffee cup with his fingertips, fixed Gavin with his crooked smile. "Speaking of jumped-up duels, how fares the Brotherhood these days, friend? I've heard precious little of late about that merry band."

Denys answered before he could speak. "That's because there's little to tell, thanks to the depredations of Blackford here. Well, and Croquère. Most gentlemen are on their best behavior for fear of attracting their attention — or else they take good care to keep their worst deeds hidden."

They referred to the informal cadre of sword masters who had banded together a few years back to strike a blow for those left with scant protection by lax policing, primarily women and children. The conditions had been occasioned by the division of the city into three separate municipalities with each having its thin but competing force of gendarmes. Matters had improved somewhat in the past year or two, but were still less than ideal. The Vieux Carré, or Old Square, known to the Americans as the French Quarter, was designated the First Municipality as was right and proper considering it encompassed the original limits of the city laid out by Bienville's engineers. It was here that the sword masters concentrated their efforts since it was where they plied their trade.

"The bogeymen you want are Caid and Rio, with Nicholas Pasquale," Gavin corrected. "They have long since made their mark."

Denys gave him a droll look. "But they are now mired in domestic cares which they have no wish to escape. They seldom leave their houses, much less trouble themselves with the righting of wrongs. No, no, we are all aware who fills the gap."

"I had heard," the Kentuckian drawled, "that you, my lad, might have been sworn into the pack."

"For what good it did me," Denys complained with a sparkling glance from the corners of his eyes at Gavin. "All the best watchwords beginning with a V were taken, I promise. Vigilance was Rio's, Valor was for Caid, Vengeance went to Nicholas and for our friend here, Verity. What was left for me except Virtue?"

"Vex, or maybe Vainglory," Gavin suggested, his voice dry.

"Or Virility? I could have had that, now I think of it," Denys said, as if much struck.

"What of Victory?" Kerr asked.

"Trust a Kaintuck to hit upon that one." Denys tilted his curly head. "It could be yours, of course, if you choose to join us."

"I'll think on it. I've considered setting up as a sword master."

Denys regarded the American with interest in his eyes. "Why not, pray? You've haunted the salons enough, and honed your skill to a nicety."

"Problem is, the lowlife I've been looking

for these two years and more may yet turn up. I've not given up on it, not quite."

Kerr Wallace's quest was well known to them as they had all, at one time or another, helped him chase leads concerning the man who had caused his brother's death in the ill-fated Santa Fe campaign. So far, these had come to nothing. The last anyone had heard, it seemed the man might have traveled overland to Natchitoches near the Louisiana-Texas border, then made his way to the Rio Grande Valley and across the border into Mexico. If the purpose was a business venture, as was said, then it was unlikely to be legitimate. It would also be difficult to trace.

"Ah well," Denys commented with a shrug. "As I was saying, there are precious few daring deeds now left undone."

His tact, in addition to his unfailing good humor, was the reason he liked young Vallier, Gavin thought. "A fallacy, but let it stand. I have discovered in myself a great reluctance to teach manners to the unmannerly, as the Brotherhood has been wont to do, or give further lessons in the art of keeping one's tongue between one's teeth. The result can be entirely too grim, and sometimes irreversible."

"Not a question of nerve, I take it?" Kerr's

gaze was direct and not without concern, robbing the question of anything that could or should be resented.

"Intent, let us say. Given a choice between swatting a fly and shooing it out the door, we usually settle the matter in permanent fashion. But pity the poor fly which lacks direction, principles and choice but dies regardless."

Kerr cocked a leaf-brown eyebrow. "You still don't want its droppings in your plate."

Gavin laughed, even as his attention was caught by the sound of yet another arrival climbing the stairs. He glanced at Nathaniel who flushed and shrugged in token of his having left the street entrance unlocked after admitting Kerr Wallace. It was no great matter given that clients would be arriving in due time. Still, Gavin drank the last of his coffee and rose to face the door.

The caller strode into the salon with the solid tread of cavalry boots, a double-breasted topcoat swinging around his ankles and the light of battle in his pale blue eyes. His cane, of heavy silver and topped by a dog's head, was held like a club in his fist, and his jaw muscles bulged with the clench of his teeth. Ignoring the men assembled, he bore down upon Gavin as if he meant to trample him underfoot.

Gavin stood his ground, allowing Alexander Novgorodcev to come to him down the long room. To anticipate the mission of Ariadne's friend — this gentleman she called Sasha as a *petit nom* indicating a close degree of familiarity — did not seem polite. Besides, he might be wrong.

The Russian stopped, removed his bell-crowned top hat, tucked it under his arm like a helmet and executed a parade bow with a click of his heels. "Blackford. I have a matter I would discuss with you. Let us be private."

Gavin noted the lack of a title of respect. To leave this off among friends was one thing, but among virtual strangers it held implications of a superior addressing an underling. Added to it was the gentleman's failure to acknowledge Gavin's other guests before attempting to dismiss them. Gavin had grown used to the exquisite politeness of the French Creoles, particularly their delicate attention to matters of form and address which made the lack now doubly noticeable. For himself, it mattered little, but he resented it for his friends.

"You will have noticed that I have visitors, monsieur. Permit me to present them to you." He gave their names, including that of Nathaniel who bowed with far more respect than the Russian deserved. Then he went on. "As for being private, we lack that degree of friendship between us and are unlikely to achieve it. You may state your business, or not, as pleases you. Unless you come from Madame Faucher, in which case, I will hear you at once."

"Never would she send me to you," Novgorodcev said with scowling certainty.

"So I would imagine, as she has her full share of mother wit. Still, I can envision no other cause for you to exert yourself by climbing my stairs."

"You are an embarrassment to the lady. She no longer requires your expertise. You will not return to the town house where she is staying so long as she is in residence."

"How obliging of me," Gavin drawled, "particularly when I suspect the lady will be unable to recall giving that command."

"I speak for her."

"And have been reprimanded for it as I remember. Think clearly. Will you risk that again?"

The purple-red of rage spread under the Russian's fair skin. "To be rid of you I would venture it a thousand times."

"Now why? I wonder. I'm no threat to whatever pretensions you may have regarding the lady." The words were soft but carried a warning.

"You flatter yourself by the suggestion," Novgorodcev answered with a twist of the mustache above his full, red lips. "She has better judgment."

"Also fewer requirements, being widowed and thus shy of another entanglement. I do understand. Do you?" At one edge of his vision, Gavin saw Kerr exchange a questioning look with Denys who gave a Gallic shrug. Nathaniel, by contrast, seemed to follow the exchange with ease.

"Better than you, having served her since before her release from marriage."

"But no more than that? Remiss of you or wise of her. I wonder which."

"You are insulting." Ariadne's cavalier breathed hard and fast through his nose, the sound harsh in the tense quiet of the salon.

"Oh, only speculating, unless you care to resent it?" It was clear the Russian had come seeking a meeting. The question was why he had not flung down his card and taken his leave. The suggestion just made was Gavin's oblique attempt to discover the answer.

"Only if you have not been . . . remiss in the course of these lessons."

Gavin held his hands lightly clasped

behind his back, his control complete. "You are asking if she has been wise? My affairs are not a matter for conversation, unlike some. As you are in her good graces, you may guess what has passed between us."

"Such discretion comes a little late, Englishman. Far from protecting her, you have sullied her good name in order to acquire custom for this miserable little fencing salon of yours. It would not surprise me to learn you suggested the man's costume she wore last evening."

"You saw that," Gavin said, all annoyance banished from his voice, or so he thought, though Kerr gave him a look not unlike a ship's gunner told to check a cannon misfire.

"After you had gone. She was still a trifle overheated. What I might have interrupted if I had come sooner is hardly in doubt."

What was without doubt was that the noble Russian wanted, nay required, to receive any challenge that might be given this morning. The reason was not hard to find. As the offended party, he would have the choice of weapons, presumably something that would weigh the scales in his favor. It would be foolish to fall into that trap, and yet caution as a tactic had lost its luster.

"You malign the lady and me with her," Gavin said evenly. "If my three friends here will serve me as seconds, the matter may be settled at a time and place to be agreed upon between them and whoever may act for you."

Nathaniel's eyes widened as he stared at him. "Monsieur Gavin! I never . . . I mean, you don't want me!"

"None so much." Gavin sent the briefest of smiles to his apprentice. He also collected nods of agreement from Kerr and Denys.

"Excellent," the Russian said with satisfaction. "I believe the matter of weapons is left to me. My preference is for sabers on horseback since I was trained for the cavalry. You may pray before or after setting your affairs in order, monsieur. Or both."

It seemed excellent advice, Gavin thought as he watched Novgorodcev turn with a wide swing of his coat hem and tramp from the salon.

The Kentuckian unfolded his long length from his chair and came to join him. Staring after Gavin's opponent, he said, "A rather large fly there, seems to me. About his principles and direction I can't say, but he sure had a choice."

"So he did."

"As did you."

"There you are wrong," Gavin answered, his voice devoid of anything other than the lightest of contention. "For me, there was no choice at all."

Sixteen

The notes from the violin rose toward the high ceiling of Madame Touton's salon, piercingly sweet, haunting in their sadness. The violinist swayed and writhed with his face a mask of what appeared to be pain, as if he dragged the music from the depths of his body. Ariadne was affected by Vieux Temps's performance though she could not help smiling a little at the fervor of it. The romantic anguish of his selection struck a melancholy note inside her, an ache for everything missing from her life, everything always just beyond her reach. The intimation of tears that swelled in her throat wasn't terribly surprising. She had been on the edge of tears a dozen times since the meeting with her mother.

Ariadne had debated for some time over whether to attend this musical. Should she appear in public or should she not, considering her state of quasi-mourning? It was

Maurelle who had finally made up her mind for her. The chance to hear music transcended all else in the city, or so her hostess said; no convention, however sacred, was proof against it. Accordingly, here she was in her demi-mourning of silver-gray satin, perched on a spindly chair in the close room and wishing she was somewhere, anywhere, else.

She unfurled a fan of silver lace, using it to stir the air around her face. Sasha, standing behind her, reached to touch her shoulder, a brief caress of one gloved hand, before resting his fingertips on the back of her chair. She sent him a brief upward glance before looking away again.

His attitude seemed particularly self-satisfied and possessive tonight. Something must be done about it once and for all. He simply had to see reason so her plans could go forward without interference. Apparently, she needed to be more forceful.

Now was not the time. It would be as well to have privacy in case the discussion became too heated.

Vieux Temps's final selection of the evening died away on a note of sublime purity. It was a relief when the muffled applause of gloved hands began. After a moment, his listeners rose with their ovation,

Ariadne among them, and some few moved forward to surround the violinist with their awe and appreciation. The hostess for the occasion spoke in almost tearful gratitude for the lovely music, before she turned away, signaling for her servants to begin offering refreshments. Conversation became general as small groups formed like schools of fish separating and coming together again in the music room of the Spanish-designed mansion.

Ariadne stood talking to Madame Savoie for several moments. Minus her parrot on this musical evening, the diva was still eccentric in a magnificent fashion in an ensemble of brocade in shades of blue-green and a turban centered by an aquamarine the size of a robin's egg. Even as the two of them spoke of this and that, Ariadne was aware of Sasha hovering within hearing distance. His expression was strained beneath its habitual hauteur, and he alternated between rubbing his fingers over his mustache to smooth it, scratching at his wrist under his glove and clasping both hands behind his back. All the while, his brooding gaze remained upon her.

She was thinking of taking leave of her hostess in order to escape the surveillance when Maurelle arrived at her side, laying a hand on her arm. "Come with me a small moment, *chère*. There is someone I want you to meet." She turned her smile upon the diva. "You don't mind, Madame Savoie? It is an object with me to expand the circle of Ariadne's friends so she will not think of leaving us."

"No, no, by all means," the diva said, moving away with a magnanimous wave of a hand heavy with a collection of tinkling bangles. "For Ariadne to be established is most important. Besides, I see a platter of shrimp puffs just arrived from the kitchen and must have a taste before they vanish."

Ariadne turned from watching the majestic departure of the diva to smile at Maurelle. "So where is this personage I am supposed to meet?"

"Forgive me, *chère*. It was a small ruse as I wished to speak to you alone." Maurelle, her gaze on Sasha, drew Ariadne away a short distance then lowered her voice. "I would not upset you for the world, but I have heard there is to be a duel which concerns you."

The gravity in Maurelle's face sent dread skittering down Ariadne's backbone. Lifting a hand to her throat, she asked, "The principals?"

"Your Sasha and Monsieur Blackford."

She felt her heart alter its rhythm, stuttering a little before it began again. It was what she had feared, what she most dreaded. "You mean Sasha challenged the sword master over my lessons?"

"So one might suppose. But no. Apparently it was Monsieur Blackford who issued the challenge."

"It makes no sense. Why would he do such a thing?"

"I've no idea," Maurelle said with a quick shake of her head, "but that's the way it was told to me."

Ariadne flung a quick glance over her shoulder at Sasha. He had not moved, but stood staring in their direction. "By whom? I mean, how came you by the tale?"

"One of the sword master's wives told me. She had it from a street boy, or so I believe."

Ariadne removed her arm from Maurelle's grasp, afraid her friend might feel the fine trembling that ran along her nerves. "I must speak to her immediately. Could you take me to her?"

Maurelle's lips tightened and she shook her head so the candlelight gleamed among her curls, shone over the pearls that beaded the combs which held them. "She knows no more. Besides, she spoke in confidence, because of my friendship with the English-man."

"And would not be pleased to learn you had passed on the information to me." How frustrating it was, all the conventions that enwrapped females. "I wish I could be sure it wasn't some mistake."

"If she had not been certain, she would not have spoken of it." Maurelle's eyes were dark and liquid with concern. "Be easy, *chère*. To disturb yourself is useless. There is nothing to be done."

"Even if a man's death may be on my head? Monsieur Blackford is a sword master. Sasha could be killed."

"As to that, the outcome is far from certain. The weapons are to be sabers and the contest to take place on horseback."

Dread moved over Ariadne in a sick wave. Sabers, the weapons of cavalrymen, were heavier and more lethal than the rapiers used by most duelists. Sasha had been trained in such fighting at his military academy. It had been a saber that slashed his face in one of the drunken meetings so favored by the students of such places, a mark of honor and courage according to his lights. He had served for a time in the horse guards, the elite troops which guarded the czar, so was experienced at fighting from the saddle.

The match favored the Russian to an amazing degree. Had Blackford given away his advantage in the interest of fairness or had the choice been forced upon him?

How very odd that she could even ask herself such a thing when a few short days ago she would have denied that he possessed any such code of honor. Oh, but she had no time for such questions. She must know at once how this meeting had happened.

It was one thing for Gavin Blackford to challenge Sasha for the sake of some arrogant pronouncement or assumption, but something else again if Sasha had forced this duel upon the Englishman with the idea of ending her lessons. He had no cause to take such a mission upon himself, no right to interfere at all. It could not be tolerated, not if she was to succeed in her purpose. Something had to be done.

Clearing her throat of an unaccountable huskiness, she asked, "When did you say this duel will be held?"

"I didn't say," Maurelle answered warily.

"In the morning, I presume?"

"What are you planning, *chère?* You can't interfere, you mustn't."

"No, certainly not," she agreed while

252

wondering frantically who it might be best to confront, Sasha or the sword master.

An instant later, she realized there was really no question. Sasha was here this evening, and it seemed he might have some interest in speaking to her. Before, she could not imagine what ailed him. Now she had a strong idea. And if she suspected the Russian might be more easily swayed than his opponent by her arguments against this duel, that was surely her secret.

To speak to Sasha required nothing more than a smile in his direction accompanied by a beckoning movement of her hand. He came to her side where she had stepped into the relative privacy of a window alcove.

"You require something, madame? Only tell me how I may serve you."

The words were humble enough but his expression did not quite match them. She had noticed that contrast before, though it disturbed her more now.

"A delicate matter has come to my attention," she said as evenly as she was able. "I believe you have an engagement with the Englishmen on the field of honor."

"Now, *mon ange,*" he began with a ponderous frown.

"Is it true?"

"These affairs are not fit subjects for such

fair flowers as yourself."

Anger poured like acid into her veins. "Don't be tiresome, Sasha. I fear you have forced a quarrel on the gentleman from concern for me. Am I wrong?"

"The gentleman, as you style him, has given cause enough for a meeting without touching on your association with him."

"You dislike his manner toward you, is that it? You feel he should be more deferential?" Sasha would, as a matter of course. Most men were his inferiors in his view.

"He is entirely too bold in all things."

"Come, Sasha. Admit that his refusal to bow to your dictates incensed you. You went to him, forced him to challenge you so you might defeat him in a fight where you have the advantage. This business of sabers on horseback is appalling."

"As to that, I am told he is of the landed gentry in his native England so should be able to ride. He holds himself my equal. Let him prove it."

She clenched her fist on her fan. "He has had no military training that I'm aware of. Tell me why you are so determined to be rid of him."

"I have explained . . ."

"Don't take me for a fool, if you please. You are interfering in my life and I will not

254

have it. You must cancel this meeting."

"I am the challenged party, *chère*. It's Monsieur Blackford who requires satisfaction, so only he who may withdraw without penalty. I can only allow him whatever satisfaction he may achieve. If any."

"You compelled him to take that position, I'm sure of it. What did you say?"

A flush rose in Sasha's face, turning the scar on his cheek to a streak of purple. "Why are you so certain the Englishman is blameless? Can you conceive of no reason why he might wish to remove me from his path?"

Stillness invaded her senses so she barely breathed. "You are saying he considers you an impediment?"

"Is that so difficult to believe? You are a beautiful woman of fortune and alone in the world — a ripe plum for the hands of a man without scruples."

"Ridiculous. Monsieur Blackford has shown no sign whatever of such an aim."

"But have you looked? Or have you been so intent on his instructions that you have not noticed?"

Abruptly, she was assailed by the memory of burning eyes above a leveled foil and the slow, suggestive slide of steel against silken steel. Heat bloomed in her lower body, rising in a tide to her face.

No, she refused to accept it. She and the Englishman were too far apart in thought and feeling ever to be anything more than tutor and client. The only thing which linked them was a single useless death and its consequences. When that was settled then there would be nothing, nothing whatever.

"Please don't look so, *ma chère,*" Sasha said, taking her free hand and holding it between his own. "I would do anything to spare you pain, even give up my honor if that were possible. I adore you, you know, and have been waiting my chance this evening to take my leave of you in case . . . in case events of the morning turn out wrong for me. I meant to be discreet, to say only what might live in your memory as a farewell later. But since you are aware of the meeting . . ."

"Don't," she said, her voice strained. "I can't bear it."

If he died it would be her fault since this meeting would not be taking place had she never embarked on her plan of vengeance. And if the Englishman was killed, what then? She would never be able to close the door of her mind on Francis's death.

"As you will." Sasha inclined his head, his

close-cropped hair glinting like silver wire in the gaslight. "Only promise me that you will do nothing so foolish as going to Blackford about this affair."

She felt as if a weight lay on her shoulders, pressing her toward the floor, while the ache of some deep internal chill made it difficult to think. Regardless, she had enough judgment to refrain from outright promises. "That would certainly be a mistake."

"Indeed. I trust you would have more dignity as well." He lifted her hand to his lips then drew her closer. "Now I must bid you good-night. You permit?"

She did not protest as he leaned to kiss her, first on one cheek and then the other. Afterward, he turned and left her. His stride was firm and strong, yet seemed to have less swagger than in the past. The words he had spoken rang in her head while she watched him cleave a path through the chattering groups, making for the door.

Dignity.

What did such a thing matter when the lives of two men were at stake?

To convince Maurelle that her nerves were overset and she wished to return to the town house at once was easy enough. Her friend showed every sympathy, gathering up their cloaks and ushering her homeward with the escort of one of her married friends and her husband who happened to be going the same way. That instant, caring response made Ariadne feel guilty even as she was grateful for it.

Once in her own bedchamber, she paced the floor with her cloak sweeping around her, trying to think of some way to contact the English *maître d'armes.* She had no trusted servant of her own to send with a message, and if she relied on the maid Adele, who had been attending her, she feared the news would be all over the city by morning. She had grown wary of the girl as well; she seemed to be of a curious disposition, asking too many prying questions. Solon would be the perfect go-between if she wasn't positive he would go to Maurelle at once with the request.

She could go to Gavin Blackford instead, but to venture into the Passage de la Bourse would pose grave risk to her reputation. While she was not as concerned as some with that aspect, she had no wish to become persona non grata in the city while her task was yet unfinished. Besides, any scandal in New Orleans was certain to follow her to Paris where she might one day wish to make her home again.

Perhaps she should just give up, allow the

duel to take its course. There was nothing to say that the Englishman would listen to her. What did it really matter if Sasha took the satisfaction she craved?

No, no, she could not bear that to happen. The risk required to stop it must be met. It was the only way.

Leaving the town house again at this hour was a problem in itself. Explanations and excuses would have to be made if a servant saw her go. Care was required then. Pausing on the gallery outside her room, she gazed along its length, from the straight stretch where she stood to the far corner where it turned at a right angle to continue along the L of the *garçonnière.* Nothing stirred, nor was there any movement in the courtyard below. The only other sounds were the soft rustle of a night breeze in the banana trees and the plaintive mewing of a hungry cat from the next street. Everyone seemed to have retired for the night.

Ariadne descended to the lower gallery and moved with silent care to the passageway which led under the house to the street. It was dark in the long tunnel. She could feel with her gloved hand the rough, handmade bricks that lined it, feel them underfoot through her thin slippers. She should have changed into more sturdy walking boots before leaving her bedchamber but had not thought of it and could not bring herself to turn back for them now.

The solid wood doorway loomed before her, made visible by an outline of light coming in around it. She felt for the metal bar which held it closed, lifting it carefully so it would not squeal. A moment later, she was in the street.

The night was cloudy and a faint mist hung in the air, making a nimbus around the street lamp at the corner. Her slippers were soon damp and muddy but made little sound, for which she was grateful. They would have to be replaced, but it was a small price to pay.

Pray God it was the only price.

The Passage de la Bourse lay a few blocks away, not at all an arduous walk by day. The dimness relieved only by the occasional street lamp made the banquette stretch to infinity ahead of her. The wind from the river was chill so she gathered her cloak closer as she hurried along. She also pulled her hood forward around her face to conceal it. Most of those on the street were men, and there was no point in making it easy for anyone to either recognize or accost her. As long as she kept moving, walking as if certain of her purpose, she should be all right.

At a cross street, she caught a glimpse of three ruffians reeling toward her. The trio were riverboat men from their clothes, dreaded *Kaintucks,* as they were known, who brought their corn and wheat, hogs and tallow downriver on keelboats, then proceeded to drink up their profits before toiling homeward again by land. They were said to be devils and no respecters of ladies, though they usually kept to the dives along the river or in the rougher area of the American section known as the Swamp.

Whipping back out of view, Ariadne took shelter in a doorway inset until they had crossed at the corner and passed on down the street. Only when she was certain they were gone did she set out again.

This was madness; she could admit it to herself if to none other. Her breath rasped in her throat and a stitch was forming in her side. She should be safe in her bed at the town house. Nonetheless, she could not turn back. Something inside her would not allow it.

At last she passed under the arcade outside the Hotel St. Louis, then turned and flitted across the street to enter the Passage which began opposite its main entrance. A barroom was still open at the far end; she could hear the music of a barrel organ and the low hum of male voices from that direction, see the light spilling into the street through its doors. Since that was a place to be avoided at all costs, she moved to the left, taking refuge in the shadows of one of the long archways that, in imitation of the hotel, fronted the buildings on both sides of the Passage.

As she stared down the long vista leading to Canal Street, she realized she had no idea which atelier, out of the dozens lining the throughway might belong to Gavin Blackford. A soft imprecation feathered her lips.

What was she to do? The ateliers were unmarked without doubt, since dwellings in the Vieux Carré had no numbers of any kind, much less identifying placards. She could hardly knock on doors until she found him. She closed her eyes and clenched her teeth as she sighed at her own foolhardiness.

"Your pardon, ma'am."

The speaker was a gentlemen who had turned into the Passage behind her, stepping around her where she stood undecided. He tipped his hat with a brief, curious stare before continuing along the arcade. Tall and wide across the shoulders, with an open countenance and firm mouth, he seemed to have kindly eyes. He was not French, she thought, but an American of a different breed from the riverboat men she had avoided. He might be from some upriver plantation or else the uptown section of the city, which meant he was unlikely to know her on sight or to see her again.

"Monsieur, a moment, if you please," she called after him.

He turned back with reluctance in every line of his large body. She thought for an instant that he suspected her of importuning him for a less than virtuous purpose. If so, her appearance, or perhaps her voice, must have reassured him, for he removed his hat and stood holding it against the side stripe of his pantaloons. "Certainly, ma'am. How may I be of service?"

Yes, he was most certainly American. The relief of it was staggering. Perhaps she cared more for her good name than she had thought. "Do you perhaps know the *maître d'armes*, Monsieur Gavin Blackford?"

"We are acquainted."

"Then you know where he lives?"

He was silent a moment, his gaze thoughtful in the distant light from the barroom. "You have business with him at this hour?"

"Business of the most urgent, monsieur. If

you will direct me, I should deem it a great favor."

"Yes, but will Blackford? I mean to say, if he isn't expecting you . . ."

She lifted a hand to push back the hood of her cloak, letting it slip down onto her back. "I feel sure he will speak to me regardless."

His eyes turned keen as he surveyed her face and the expanse of her shoulders exposed as the cloak's edges fell open. Lifting a hand, he rubbed it over his chin. "He might at that, since I would in his place. Come along, and I'll see about rousting him out for you."

She hesitated then took the arm he offered and moved into step beside him. Trusting that he would not lead her into some dark alleyway might be a grave mistake, but what else could she do?

At a house like all the others, of three stories with a wide balcony projecting out over the arcade, he stopped. He stepped up to the door beside the ground-floor apothecary and gave it a sharp rap. Some minutes passed. The American was about to knock again when the door swung open to reveal a tousle-haired youth still yawning and stuffing his nightshirt into his pantaloons.

"Blackford, at once. A lady to see him."

The boy gaped at her, apparently unused to female visitors. At a low word from the American, he recovered himself. Bobbing his head, he turned and disappeared up the dark stairway with much thumping of bare feet.

"I don't believe Blackford is asleep," her escort said, the ghost of a smile creasing his face into lines of startling handsomeness as he gazed down at her. "I noted a lamp still burning in his rooms."

She had also seen the light on the third floor. "I hope you may be right. I shall naturally absolve you of all blame if he objects to being disturbed."

"Oh, I don't mind that. It should be something, hearing what he has to say if he does object. The way the man talks is a pure wonder."

Somehow the thought did not promise the same entertainment value for Ariadne. The fluttering of nerves in her stomach made her feel a little ill and she pressed her fingers hard into the velvet of her cloak to prevent them from trembling. It was the effect of this unusual midnight excursion rather than any anxiety about what the man she had come to see might say, of course, but she would still be glad when the interview was done and she was safe in her bed once more.

Footsteps, brisk and even, were heard on the stairs. Gavin's voice preceded him from the dark stairway. "If I had but known you had a notion to send me bleary-eyed and blathering to the dawn meeting, Wallace, I would have put you under lock and key. Some men may swear to a night of sweaty fornication to ensure they go smiling to their graves but I am not one of them. Be the lady ever so lovely, I must —"

"A lady it is, and not a doxy," the gentleman addressed as Wallace interrupted in dry tones as Gavin appeared in the doorway.

The point was unnecessary. It was his recognition of her, she thought, that had stopped his words in mid-flight. She took a step closer to make certain of it.

"Decline," he finished, after a second's pause. "I must decline whatever the purpose and regardless of the lady."

"You haven't heard why I am here," she said, her voice not quite steady.

"It springs to the mind in images not unlike a toy soldier upon a cock horse. What maggot reamed out that fool Russian's brain that he marched off to tell you of our meeting?"

"He didn't. In fact, he asked me not to interfere when I taxed him with it. You are mistaken if you believe I am here on his account."

A glimmer of light from down the street flickered with blue fire in Gavin's eyes as he tilted his head. "Take care, madame. The alternative is that your concern is for me. Though it may please my vanity to suppose you care whether I live or die, reason refuses the leap." He looked suddenly toward Wallace. "I will see Madame Faucher homeward, my friend, unless you have a prior understanding or some other reason to stand all protective at her side."

The grin at one corner of the American's mouth vanished though it lingered around his eyes. "None in the world, in either case. I leave her to you, sir." He sketched a bow that was not without grace before touching the brim of his tall beaver hat. "I bid you a very good evening, madame. Blackford."

Watching the big American tuck his thumbs into his waistcoat pockets and stroll away down the Passage, Ariadne felt rather as if she had lost an ally. It was with a hollow feeling inside her chest that she turned back to Gavin. "My concern, as you phrase it, is for the useless nature of this dawn meeting between you and Sasha. How can it possibly benefit anyone? What will it prove?"

"It will illustrate the lack of wisdom in speaking loosely, particularly when the subject is blameless and female."

His quiet voice was freighted by some shadow of meaning that eluded her. "Female? You can't mean me. Or can you? Am I to understand that I am the reason for this challenge?"

"He didn't give you a full account, I see. Wise of him."

It had been foolish, rather, she thought, since Sasha might have guessed she would learn of it eventually. "I doubt he spoke ill of me for any reason other than to force this meeting."

"Oh, so do I," Gavin agreed on the instant. "But like the heretic who prayed only on Sunday, the result was still the same."

"And because of it, you would risk your life for my good name?"

He looked away. "I have fought for less. The point will be moot, however, if you remain here at my lodgings, all supplicating and forlorn. I would invite you inside except that might turn suspicion into certainty in the mind of any observer. Unless, of course, you intend to offer some sweet incentive for whatever plea hovers unspoken on your tongue. Then I should have to reconsider."

"If you expect to send me running home

with my hands over my ears at such a suggestion, you will have to try harder," she said, in spite of the hot color that flooded her face and the pulse throbbing in her throat.

He lifted his right hand, turning it in the pale light until she could see the ink stains that marked the fingers. "I was making my will, a tradition in this event. If you think me immune from the reflections attendant on such a task, you are in error. Mortality's malignant stare comes to us all, with or without sword in hand. If choosing between a sharp, quick death and some drawn out, black-biled fever or pus-wracked injury becomes necessary, most men would choose the first. But it is seldom welcome."

The pain fretting his voice was such an echo of the endless ache inside her for the same cause that her throat tightened into a hard knot. Driven by something more vital than the anger that had brought her out into the night streets, she stepped forward to put a hand on his arm. "Then stop this meeting," she said in low tones holding the very supplication he had named. "Send a message at once saying you withdraw the challenge."

"The time for that is past," he answered with his gaze on her white-tipped fingers.

"To withdraw now would be seen as lack of zeal for the fight."

"Why not as the magnanimous gesture of a man strong enough to brave the consequences?" The muscles of his arm under her hand were stone hard, but she did not think it was to support her or to impress her. It seemed to her heightened senses to be a sign of the restraint he held upon himself.

"Oh, but what if, by chance, you should feel some warm and scented welling of generosity, after all, some inclination to banish death's specter for the protector of your good name? Even Caesar turned his head while a gladiator destined for the circus maximus took a woman into his bed the night before."

For a scant second, she caught a glimpse of something in his face which sent alarm coursing through her veins. Was it real or only a trick of the uncertain light? No matter, it held her while she searched his eyes, trying to see it again. And in that instant, he moved, taking her arm and whirling her into the dark and narrow inset of the stairwell with her back against the wall and his body pressed against her from breast to knees. He smoothed a hand from her elbow to her shoulder then cupped her chin to tilt her head. His mouth, hot, scented with night freshness and the sweet and heady liqueur he must have drunk while making his last testament, came down upon hers.

Shock and fury exploded in her mind along with a surge of wild delight. This, this was what she had expected of him, what she required. Shuddering with the heat of his body against the chill of her own, with the abrupt gratification of overstrained nerves, she curled her fingers into the fabric of his coat. His lips were smooth, firm at the corners as they moved upon hers. His thumb brushed the corners where they met so her own tingled, throbbing as they swelled to meet his. There was unconscious mastery in his hold. The hard planes of his body enthralled her, incited a drifting impulse to be closer, to feel his weight, absorb his warmth. Hot triumph and something more spiraled up from somewhere deep inside her, mounting to her brain.

The sure touch of his tongue along the line of her lips made her gasp, allowing entry for his careful probing. He swept the silken underside of her lower lip, glided over the pearl-glazed edges of her teeth, and plumbed her warm, moist depths in a rhythm that hinted, beguiled. She met the incursion in delicate, startled exploration,

271

but was suddenly wary of its sweet flavor, its temptation. Boneless acquiescence hovered, sapping her will, threatening her purpose.

Without releasing her mouth, he shifted his hold, using one hand to find the edges of her cloak and slide his hand inside. His fingers outlined a breast, enclosed it, and sought its tightly beaded nipple. His gentle pressure upon that sensitive tip, the delicate way he rolled it with his fingertips, as if testing the ripeness of a small, sweet grape, caught her unaware with its certainty, its intimation of unlimited pleasure.

Never before had she felt like this, not on her wedding night or afterward, when the first pain of penetration was over and physical accommodation eased. Never had she been so overwhelmed by tastes, textures and touches, or the brand of hot, unbidden joy that unfurled in the deepest recesses of her body and mind. She was drowning in languor, drifting on the intoxicating surge of unexpected pleasure. Unfair, so unfair that this man should find its wellspring, should be able to unlock the source of her darkest, most alluring dreams. The betrayal of it struck her like a blow and a sob caught in her throat.

He raised his head, whispered a curse as

he released her. With meticulous care, he straightened the edges of her cloak, raised her hood to screen her features. Then he offered his arm. "Depravity comes in many forms," he said, his voice even, without inflection as he offered his arm, "but I have not yet sunk to the lowest of them. I prefer my women willing and heart-whole. Yes, and with their thoughts uncluttered by concern for other men. Forgive the experiment. It was not meant to harm either of us."

"I have not been harmed." Her voice sounded stilted in her own ears. She accepted his support because it was as necessary as it was polite.

"No. But you were not alone in that stairwell," he answered as he led her relentlessly back out into the Passage. "And you will not be on the field beneath the oaks in the morning."

SEVENTEEN

Gavin half expected to see Ariadne at the dueling ground in spite of what he'd said the night before; he did not put it past her to find some way of flouting public opinion and common sense by attending. A number of closed carriages sat off to one side, apparently the conveyances of spectators, but no females were in view. That she was not there might be owed to Maurelle's good sense or else fatigue due to her late-night excursion. It was just as well, either way. It gave him no pleasure to think the lady might rejoice in seeing him injured.

God, but what had been in his mind when he kissed her? The answer was *very little,* if the truth were known. He had thought, in his ignorance of her mettle, that Ariadne might have sent Novgorodcev to goad him into this ill-considered duel. It was only as she faced him with her plea to avoid it that he realized she was outraged because the

Russian seemed likely to steal the honor she craved, that of dispatching him herself.

His reaction to her presence, so unwary, so unprotected there at his atelier, had been predictable but no less stupid for all that. Now the scent and taste of her was embedded in his mind. It was a dangerous distraction.

He had come so close to taking her in blind, searing passion and a welter of crushed velvet and wrinkled skirts, like some street walker. Was it the conscious testing of her resolve which moved him, as he had thought, or sheer blind concupiscence? He wished he knew, wished as well that he could be certain he would have released her short of rutting consummation if she had not made that small sound of distress.

He could not be at all sure.

More than that, the mind-cracking effort it had taken to force himself away from her still sang in his blood like some ancient war chant. With luck, it might give him the edge necessary to face death while mounted on an animal whose most certain instinct was to avoid it. His one consolation was that Novgorodcev's horse, a big gray gelding with a white blaze, was unlikely to be better trained. Duels such as this one were not so common as to fill the stables of New Orleans with steeds trained to stand while someone tried to hack off their ears.

It was Caid who had supplied Gavin's mount from the selection he and his wife, Lisette, kept for their private use. The black stallion was a mixture of stock horse, plains pony and Arabian from the look of him, bred for stamina and speed, and trained to knee commands. Gavin had put him through his paces the afternoon before and thought he would do.

The dawn was gray and dripping, an introduction to yet another wet day. It made for uncertain conditions here under the oaks that splattered the ground with heavy droplets every time the wind stirred the branches overhead. How much difference that might make could well depend on the length of the meeting, which would dictate how much muck the churning of the horses' hooves created. Gavin was not inclined to prolong it and suspected the Russian would favor a fast outcome as well.

Novgorodcev wore gray to match the day and his mount, an excellent choice in the morning's uncertain light. What Nathaniel had laid out for Gavin included buckskin pantaloons and a double-breasted coat of royal blue with gold buttons so highly polished they seemed designed to invite a round-house slash from his opponent. Though Gavin deplored the boy's continued determination to act as his servant, he could only approve the choice. Flamboyant defiance suited his mood.

Nathaniel stood at Gavin's knee at the moment, in his role as second. Biting his lower lip, the boy watched the Russian circle the field at a fast clip as if to shake the fidgets out of the gray. It was an impressive performance if you were easily taken in by ramrod posture and military form allied to a horseman's bulging thighs under gray-dyed doeskin. Since the occasion was not a military review, Gavin reserved judgment.

The chief seconds huddled in the middle of the field in deep discussion. After a moment, they broke apart, each moving to rejoin his principal at opposite ends of the field. Novgorodcev trotted out to meet his man, while Gavin waited for Denys Vallier and Kerr Wallace to reach him.

The American's face was grave as he came to a halt. "The rules we're agreed on are basically the same as for any other meeting, as you may imagine," he said, keeping his voice low. "You will meet with Novgorodcev in the center of the field where you will exchange the usual salute. At the *on guard* command, you will stand ready. The signal to begin will be a dropped handkerchief, and this will start the first charge. Touches will remain above the waist. Any deliberate injury to a mount will be called as a foul and reason to end the meeting. The man who rides beyond the marked boundaries will forfeit the match. If one of you is unhorsed, the other will dismount at once and the fight will continue on the ground. Understood?"

"It's to be cut and thrust with the aim of brutal slaughter," Gavin said in agreement. "Though never let it be said it was unfair."

"You did challenge him." The reminder was spoken in even tones, though sympathetic understanding lay in the smokey gray of Wallace's eyes.

"With the utmost pleasure, and would again. So let us go trippingly toward this dance and the partner whose name is on our card."

He waited for no reply, but saluted Kerr, Denys and Nathaniel then put his heels to his mount and trotted out to meet the Russian. When the black's head was close enough to his opponent's stocky gray that the two horses seemed to blow into each other's nostrils, he stopped. Novgorodcev sat stiff and correct on his European saddle, his hair like silver spikes, his face a superior mask with his stiffly pomaded mustache hiding his upper lip and his eyes glittering like ice under his brows. Gavin swept up his blade in whistling salute, to which his opponent replied in kind. A moment late, the *en garde* command rang out, and they tightened their reins to the same tensile stretch as their nerves.

The handkerchief dropped, a white flag that plummeted, then caught a breath of air and settled slowly to the wet grass. Before it touched the ground, they came together, the horses shoulder to shoulder in a thudding impact that threw them back on their haunches. The Russian swung, a blow that would have severed Gavin's neck from his head had it struck. Gavin ducked, caught his opponent's blade with a heavy clang and rasping spurt of sparks, parried, thrust and was repulsed. Then they settled into the fight.

Novgorodcev was no weakling; of that there was little doubt. He depended on his strength, however, scorning finesse in favor of powerful moves of mechanical perfection. Instead of allowing his mount to aid his movements, he controlled it with rigid force. Grim as a blacksmith at his anvil, he hammered away, seeking to overcome with sheer rote labor. In less than a minute, Gavin could predict with minute accuracy exactly how he would attack, and when. By watching his opponent's eyes, he could also tell where the Russian would aim.

A fight with sabers, so it had been said, was like war. And in any battle, the man who used his brain had the advantage over one who depended on brawn. Gavin was inclined to put this ancient wisdom to the test.

He capered around the Russian on his lighter black, keeping his movements easy yet precise, as if in the dance that he had labeled this match. The tactic forced Novgorodcev to expend his strength in useless swings of his heavy weapon and tested his ability to maneuver the gray. It also gauged the Russian's grasp on his temper. The last was not without limit, Gavin discovered, and set himself to see that he surpassed it. An opponent who let his rage overcome him was a man half-defeated.

Their blades chimed and beat while they twisted and turned in their saddles, pulling their mounts hard around time and again, reaching with grunting effort. Gavin's muscles burned and sweat poured in runnels to thread through his brows, wilt his collar and soak his coat. His palm grew slippery upon the saber's hilt, and he snatched time while wheeling away from a particularly brutal slash to dry it on his pantaloon-covered thigh. Lather flew like spume from the horses, dotting the grass, flecking their boots. The ground churned beneath their hooves, becoming a green-brown morass underfoot, a pig-sty of mud in which the horses slipped and had to be held in to prevent them from falling.

Gavin could feel the boiling of blood-lust in his veins, hear the thunder of his heart-beat in his ears as a counterpoint to the rhythm of his blows against his opponent's sword. He saw the same half-crazed urge to kill in the feral stare of the Russian, felt it in his attack. In some distant part of his mind, he knew he should have a thought for how Madame Faucher might feel if he should kill her favorite, but he was too intent on preserving his own hide and pride to care what she might think.

Novgorodcev did care, or so it seemed, cared what his lady love might feel if he were defeated, cared that his pride might be tarnished. It animated his every stratagem, surged to the forefront when he saw, finally, that the match might be a draw. If neither man could be touched, then the seconds would call quits and the thing would be at an end.

The only way to change the outcome, the only path to victory, appeared to be by default, using cunning and deceit. Novgorodcev, desperate for the end he desired, chose that road without hesitation.

Gavin marked the pivotal moment by the narrowing of the Russian's eyes, his speculative glance in the midst of clamorous attack, his unconscious telegraphing of where he meant to strike the crippling, prohibited blow. He saw, and kicked the black stallion into a hard turn, dragging him away from the whining descent of that viciously misdirected sword.

It was not enough.

The Russian's saber point flashed as it cut into hide and muscle, laying open the black stallion's flank. The horse screamed, pain-maddened, as he erupted in kicking fury, bucking, side-hopping, leaping toward the boundary line which marked certain forfeiture.

There was only one thing to be done. Kicking free of the stirrups, Gavin sprang from the saddle.

The ground came up to meet him and he stumbled, slid in green slime, felt his feet fly out from under him. His breath left his lungs as he slammed down, landing flat on his back. His sword bounced from his grasp, turned end over end out of his reach.

By specific rules of the engagement, Novgorodcev should have come to a halt and dismounted to fight on foot. Instead, he spurred the big gray toward Gavin at a pounding run. His sword swung high in a glittering arc before beginning to fall, reaching, reaching. Shouts and yells rent the tree-shadowed sky. The seconds sprang forward at a run, their pounding footsteps lost in the earthshaking thunder of the gray's hooves.

Timing was an instinct, not a thought. Gavin waited, trying to catch his breath. At the last second, he wrenched over with a hard contraction of muscles, diving into a roll that carried him out of the gray's path. He felt the wind of the horse's hooves inches from his head, heard the singing whistle of the saber in the Russian's fist as Novgorodcev leaned forward and down for the blow, felt the tug as the blade sliced his coat at an angle across the back and to the side.

Novgorodcev flew past, began to turn mere yards away. The gray sidled, whinnying from the cut of the bit as he was jerked into a too-tight turn. Gavin leaped erect with the burning, reckless strength that flares up when rage and purpose merge. As Novgorodcev thundered toward him again, he side-stepped and lunged to grab his long coat-skirt. Swinging on it with his full weight, Gavin dragged the Russian from the saddle.

Novgorodcev came down in a flailing of arms and legs and unwieldy steel. Gavin caught his sword hand and twisted, jerking the saber free. Then he brought the heavy hilt down in a quick blow behind his opponent's ear with all his power and anger. Novgorodcev grunted, slumping to the ground in a sprawl while blood stained his white hair a sickly pink.

Gavin swayed where he stood. A trickle of something hot and wet was running down his back and over his left hip. He felt on fire from his neck to the backs of his knees. Pain colored his vision in shades of red, gathering in livid intensity as it burrowed into him. He saw Nathaniel coming closer, his face twisted and raindrops standing on his cheeks. Kerr Wallace was behind the boy though he seemed to be fading, moving in a ground mist of gray fog.

The mist reached out then, taking him down with it to muddy grass that had turned soft and warm. Yet amid the storm

in his ears, Gavin caught the powdery sweetness of woman's scent, felt the brush of a cool, smooth hand on his forehead while the low music of a woman's voice fell on his ears, chiding in tearful anger threaded with the husky rasp of horror.

Ariadne, he would swear it. Ariadne had come after all.

"Stupid, stupid men," she whispered for him alone, "to bleed and die for so little cause and be so *damnably* noble with it."

EIGHTEEN

Gavin lay in somnolent peace, watching the bright track of the winter sunlight as it fell through the French doors beside his bed. It pooled on a carpet of purest cochineal, red as blood and woven with a design of palm fronds in teal and viridian, fell across a duvet covered by cream and red calico, and reflected pink light into the shirred cream canopy of the tester above him. Warm in spite of the season, it made nothing of the small coal fire which burned under a mantel of sculpted rose marble.

He lay propped on two pillows while another raised one shoulder to take the pressure from his back and side, and covered in abnormal decency by a white linen nightshirt. The stitches in his side pulled with a vicious ache and the sheets on which he reclined had been starched and ironed to the point of irritation, but he made no complaint. He had been bathed, mended and bandaged, and was waiting for Nathaniel with his afternoon ration of red wine to rebuild his blood, a vintage straight from Maurelle's cellar as the sheets were from Maurelle's armoire. To find fault would be the rankest ingratitude. He was not ungrateful in any degree.

What he was, he recognized, was infernally curious.

It had not, at first, seemed at all strange to be installed in one of the best bedchambers of the Herriot town house with Nathaniel at his right hand and ladies in various stages of *déshabille* coming to hover over him at odd hours. He had been weak from loss of blood and so sunk in fever that he dwelled in some netherworld where dreams and reality swirled around each other, so entwined that it was impossible to pull them apart. Now that he was awake, he wasn't sure he wanted that separation. Some aspects of the dreams seemed worth keeping.

One in particular featured Ariadne in a nightgown and peignoir of lace-edged white lawn, her hair streaming down her back. She had leaned over him so he caught the scent of violets. The back of her hand had been smooth against his hot cheek and the concern in her eyes soothed some half-formed distress in his mind. She gazed down at him for what seemed a lifetime, her dark tresses shimmering with rainbow highlights as they spilled around them. Then she brushed across his lips with her fingertips, let them trail down his neck and over his chest until she pressed her palm to his heart as if counting its steady beats.

"Touché," he whispered.

Her lips parted on a gasp and her eyes turned liquid. He let his eyelids fall to close out the sight. When he looked again, she was gone. Gone, but the place where her hand had pressed burned like a brand.

Oh, but afterward, he had floated in a nightmare of being back at Maison Blanche once more following the duel with Francis Dorelle. Phantom pain throbbed in the jagged scar under his collarbone caused by a broken sword. He wanted to get up to see about the young man he had stabbed with his own blade in that freakish accident on the dueling field, but he couldn't move, couldn't speak, couldn't escape the fear that his opponent was dead and that he had killed him. It was a relief when sleep came down to smother the paralyzing anxiety.

It would be as well if he let the dreams go, after all.

The door on the opposite side of the room

creaked open, and he turned his head toward the sound. It was Ariadne, as if he had summoned her by his thoughts. She was well and fully clothed in a day gown of unrelenting gray, with her hair coiled in a tightly braided coronet on top of her head and a few stray spirals at her temples. A doubtful frown lay between her brows while she studied his face, allowing the silver salver holding a glass of wine which she carried in her left hand to come perilously close to tipping. He smiled before he could prevent the movement of his lips.

"You are awake."

It sounded like an accusation, he thought. "I can, if you like, pretend otherwise."

"Why would you do that?"

"Convenience? You could put down that glass, supposing it's still unspilled, and leave without having to speak to me."

"I can do that anyway." She glided across the room and deposited the salver on a small table within his reach. Her movements were swift, as if spilling the wine was not a concern, though he noticed that she checked for stray drops.

"It would not be a kindness — supposing, of course, that kindness matters to you. But no, you directed that I be brought here, which must have been well intended. It was you at the dueling ground?"

"You remember."

"It's the mystery that lingers, you see, almost as great a one as waking in your care."

"If you are trying to discover why I intervened, I do have an interest in the affair. Besides, all the rooms and wards at Charity Hospital and the Maison de Santé were taken by victims from the *Bluebell*."

He studied his hands where they lay, pale and lax, on the sheet. "A matter of charity then."

"It seemed little enough after the way you were . . . betrayed by someone who felt he was acting in my interests."

She moved to the window as she spoke, adjusting the draperies so the sun's rays did not strike across his pillow. Her face in profile appeared grave, with all expression carefully masked by perfect reason. The warm light shaded across her mouth, illuminating its perfection, reminding him that he had kissed those lips not so long ago and felt his world tilt on its axis. And would like nothing so much at this moment as to do it again. The vividness of that desire and unruly response of his body were ample proof he had begun to mend.

"The black I was riding, how does he

fare?" he inquired after a moment.

"He will recover so your friend Caid tells us, though with a considerable scar. Now I think of it, that's the same diagnosis your physician for the duel, Dr. Labatut, applied to his rider."

"No kindly coup de grâce for man or beast? We are both to be congratulated. And Novgorodcev, what of his fate?" Gavin kept his voice even, though these were questions that had plagued him since he had awakened an hour ago.

"He lives, though he might prefer otherwise. He is contrite beyond imagining for his loss of temper. That does not absolve him, of course, or prevent him from being scorned by all who hear of the duel. When the concussion you gave him will allow, he plans to take ship for Paris."

"Leaving you behind? A dire punishment for a moment's madness."

She swung to face him with a frown between her eyes. "You can say that when he almost killed you by as dishonorable a trick as can be imagined?"

His lips curved in wry acceptance. "A duel is not always a model of politeness and decorum. Besides, his incentive was great. He thought he was saving you." That was cutting a little too close to the bone, but he

291

had a great wish to know how she would answer the unspoken charge.

"From social ruin, you mean," she said with tilt of her head that caused the curls trailing down beside her face to shimmer in the light behind her. "I am not certain his motive was so exalted. He is a man who likes to command those around him."

"And you are not to be commanded."

Her smile was brief and tinged with self-knowledge. "A failing, but there it is. As he had no means to compel me to his will, he thought to remove my ability to disoblige him by removing you."

"Short-sighted of him, given the number of other sword masters in the Passage."

"Thinking ahead has never been his strong suit. Unlike some." The words were abrupt as she turned away from him, moving toward the door. "I must go. Your strength should not be taxed by too much conversation."

"Unlikely," he said, his voice dry. "Though too much time spent with your patient behind a closed door might not be wise."

She paused with her hand on the door handle. "I am not some young girl who knows nothing of the sickroom. My husband was ill for some time before his death. I seldom left his side since he preferred me to any other nurse."

"He was fortunate in his wife. But that was not my meaning."

"I am aware. Having brought you here for convalescence, I cannot think it matters how much or how little I come and go. The tattle-mongers will have us in bed together in any case. That is if they can be brought to cease talking of my part in your duel. If there is no freedom to be gained by being notorious, what's the point of it?"

She went from the room without giving him the opportunity to answer. It was just as well, since he could think of nothing to say. His brain was too engaged with the words she had spoken and the images they sowed like dragon's teeth in his mind, a score of new ones popping up for every one vanquished.

In bed together . . .

Her dark eyes holding his, her long legs wrapped around his hips while he plunged into her wet softness . . .

The sweet, hard berry of her nipple against his tongue as she moaned . . .

Her eyes glazed with passion, her skin like dew-kissed pearls . . .

She would be the death of him with her pronouncements and daring, her midnight visits and men's pantaloons. But that was, of course, her intention.

She wanted him dead.

It was not enough that he should die in some chance meeting or design ordained by others, no, not at all. She wanted to kill him with her own hands. So determined was she to have that pleasure that she was willing to nurse him back to perfect health in order to achieve it.

He was not inclined to allow it. Other pleasures, yes, but not that one.

Delirium, that had to be his trouble. He could not be right about her intentions. They could not be so deadly while she smiled with sweet reason and brought him wine and surcease for the doubts and fears in his mind.

Could they?

He had to be certain.

What better way than to play upon her sympathy and her sense of fair play? What better time than in this halcyon period of his recovery when she thought him too weak to be a threat?

He would test her resolve in the many ways that febrile imagination, lying quietly on starched sheets, could devise. It would be his pleasure and his pain. Mercy was something he could ill afford since the outcome was so vital. And if he was correct, if her purpose was as lethal as he supposed, then he would consider what to do about it.

He preferred not to be her enemy, but he could be, easily, if that was what she required.

Gavin had drunk the wine and lay turning the glass in his hand, watching the last drop roll around the rim as if seeking a way out, when the door opened again. He looked up, every sense tingling with alertness.

"Madame Faucher said you'd come to your senses." Nathaniel closed the door behind him and slouched across to stand at the foot of the bed. His face was flushed and earnest and doubt hovered in his eyes. "Are you all right? Anything I can get you?"

"I am, for the moment, swaddled in bandages and bemused by what I suspect was laudanum in fine Bordeaux so want for nothing." Gavin summoned a smile. "And you? You have been given a pallet somewhere?"

"In the room next to this one, a mighty fine bed with a whopping great roof thing overhead that looks like it might smash down on me in the middle of the night and a china piss-pot under it that's painted with pheasants." The boy grinned. "And I don't have to empty the pot."

"Your happiness is complete, I see. Have

you any idea how long I've been here?"

"Two days as of this morning, and the sun looks to set before long. You slept right through your back being sewed up. Madame Maurelle said it was a mercy you didn't deserve after making her heart stop the way you did, but I don't think she meant it."

"Let us hope," Gavin replied in light agreement. "Was Madame Faucher similarly concerned?"

"I'd be hard put to say. She mostly seemed mad."

"Mad? You mean angry?"

The young man nodded. "At you, for starters, and at the other idiot, as she called him, meaning the damn bastard who sliced you. At the sawbones for being so ham-fisted with his needle he was like to sew skin to backbone so she took it away from him. And at me, because I wouldn't let her strip off your clothes."

"I did wonder who accomplished that last part. Since it was you, I shall look about me for some reward, however inadequate it may be."

"No need. 'Twasn't her place."

"No. I agree most heartily. But if you managed to thwart an ambition held by that lady, you may aspire to anything."

"Oh, I don't think she really wanted the

296

job. She just thought the rest of us would let you bleed to death before we got it done."

"Ruining no end of linens in the process. I do understand." Gavin's smile was self-deprecating and secretly amused. "I will allow that the lady is above reproach. Or suspicion. You like her?"

Nathaniel's flush grew darker. "Happens as there's a bunch of ladies I like."

He referred to Lisette, Caid's wife, Gavin knew, also Juliette who was married to Nicholas, both of whom had earned his silent devotion. Not that it was difficult to achieve. Having been orphaned and put out on the streets at a young age, he revered all women, particularly those who smiled upon him. "But you may always add another."

"I s'pose."

"Especially one so attractive."

"She's not bad to look at and knows what people need."

Thinking of the oblivion-in-a-glass that she had brought him, Gavin could only agree. Abandoning his teasing of what appeared to be his young friend's blossoming infatuation, he veered to another subject. "Did Dr. Labatut indicate how long we will be dependent on Madame Herriot's hospitality?"

"Not that I heard. Madame Faucher said you're not to be moved until your back full of stitches come out."

"I am obliged to her for that as well." He could, he was almost certain, remove himself from the bed and the town house and make his way to his own atelier or, failing that, could convalesce with either Nicholas and Juliette or with Caid and his Lisette. He did not choose. Lying here on his side, if not flat on his back, seemed a perfect position from which to feel out the defenses of Madame Faucher before their secret and deadly duel of intentions commenced again. "It appears we have a week at least."

"A week for what?"

He should remember, Gavin thought, that his self-appointed nurse was brighter than most, in spite of acquiring his only schooling on the streets, or perhaps because of it. "Oh, to enjoy the luxuries of pheasant-painted *pots de chambre* and other such beguiling bits of luxury."

Nathaniel gave him a sidelong look. "And the company of the ladies?"

"That, too," Gavin answered, his smile seraphic with anticipation. "That above all else."

Nineteen

"You want me to what?"

Ariadne replaced the tongs she had used to add coal to the fire before she swung toward Gavin in his bed. The day had turned gray again beyond the windows and clammy coolness hung in the bedchamber given over to him. It was nothing to the strained chill in her voice.

"Is it too much to ask? An intimate service, I will agree, but I was certain you must have done as much for your husband many times."

An intimate service . . .

She would not think of such things. Nor would she think of the fact that he would not be lying there in need of shaving if not for her. She had wasted enough time in an agony of guilt over Sasha's dastardly trick that had brought Gavin Blackford to this pass.

"We are not so closely related," she said,

her straight gaze daring him to elaborate. "Besides, you have Nathaniel for such things."

"And a fine valet he is turning out to be," Gavin said as he lay with his hands piously folded on his chest and audacity lurking in the dark blue of his eyes. "Nevertheless, I shudder at the thought of his hand holding a razor at my throat. Past habits learned on the streets may overcome him. That is, if he isn't too worried at the mere thought to come near me."

"Nonsense. I'm sure he was never such a desperate criminal as to —" She stopped, alerted by the brightness of his eyes. "You spoke in jest. I might have known."

"Not about his state of nerves. He has refused to relieve me of my beard for fear of terminating the career of one he hopes will eventually advance his own."

"There is always Solon. I'm sure he has acted as valet to male guests in the past."

"Blancmange is nothing in comparison to the good Solon. He's too shaky by far. And so I turn to you."

This sword master was entirely too persuasive, she thought; she could feel the force of his will even as he lay supine and as outwardly docile as a saint. He was too charming and attractive as well, his gaze too piercing. Sparring with him in this way gave her the oddest sensation, as if her nerves were as tightly wound as a clock spring or she had taken too much wine so her heart raced with half-mad euphoria and her body tingled with some odd expectation. Why it should be so, she could not guess. A half dozen times in the days just past she had stood beside his bed, watching him sleep and wondering at the unfairness of it.

"I'm a female and virtual stranger, yet you would trust me not to be a cutthroat indeed."

He did not even blink at that suggestion. "Well, there is the matter of your experience. Unless you feel an attack of nerves coming over you as well?"

"I am not of a nervous disposition." She winced as she realized she had just banished her most viable excuse. Clutching for another, she went on. "Still, you must admit it's hardly what might be called a respectable service."

"As you pointed out before, your presence in this room is not respectable," he said with maddening logic. "What is this one small thing more? Of course, if you are reluctant to come so near . . ."

"I hope I am not that foolish."

His gaze turned watchful. "What of wary?

301

I did rather take advantage the other evening. If I apologize most abjectly would your mind be easier?"

She would as soon he had not reminded her at all. That kiss and its sensual magic hovered on the outer fringes of her mind, surging in upon her at the most inconvenient moments. She wished that it had never happened. She had been perfectly satisfied with the memories she carried of Jean Marc's mildly passionate embraces and the softness of his lips upon hers. Now the experience with her husband seemed tame and lacking in fire — his mouth too soft, too moist. Contrasting it with Gavin's kiss made her feel so heated that she moved further away from the leaping fire and let the paisley shawl of silk and mohair she wore slip from her shoulders to catch at the bends of her elbows.

"My mind is easy enough," she said.

"And quite made up? I do see. Yet here I lie with a beard of thorns that allows me no peace, much less comfort. Perhaps you will ask Maurelle to step in here so I may persuade her to divest me of it."

"She has not yet risen from her bed and is unlikely to do so for another two hours."

"I could, if forced, undertake to wake her.

Racket is something she can't abide as I recall."

She gave him a look of annoyance. "You would, too, even knowing she is quite worn out from entertaining those who came to inquire after you last evening."

Interest rose in his eyes. "I had visitors? Who might they have been?"

"At least a dozen sword masters have appeared in sequence, including your half-brother, the American who was your second along with Denys Vallier and your other friends who were at the levee some days ago. They were most concerned, but would not allow you to be disturbed."

"They are all consideration," he said, his voice dry.

"If you think they were kept from you . . ." she began with a frown.

"No, no, only that they may be wondering why they should not pay their respects at my own address."

"Maurelle made that quite clear, I think."

"A woman in a thousand, and quite handy with a razor, I have no doubt at all. If you will just ring for someone to fetch her?"

He meant to have his way. Polite but relentlessly persistent, he would not rest until someone shaved him. That he had chosen her for the task was suspect in the extreme. She could think of no reason for it unless simply that she was available and represented a challenge. Or perhaps he was bored enough to view instructing her in the use of a different kind of blade as amusing.

That he might find her attractive she rejected as scarcely worth a thought; ennui and propinquity could make any woman look good to a bedridden male. As for deeper motives, they could only apply if he knew who she was and what she wanted of him, and nothing in his eyes or his attitude suggested such a thing.

Why, then, was she so uneasy?

Yes, but what did it matter? She had been uneasy from the day she had met Gavin Blackford.

"Oh, very well, I will shave you." Grasping the bellpull beside the fireplace, she gave it a swift yank to summon a servant to bring hot water before she went on. "If you lose more blood than you have already, you will have only yourself to blame."

It was Nathaniel who brought the steaming brass can, and he who rummaged in Gavin's belongings, brought from the atelier, for the accoutrements of shaving. Laying the soap cup and brush beside the wash basin, he picked up a strip of heavy leather and stropped the straight-edge razor to shining sharpness.

A small smile curled one corner of the boy's mouth as he worked, a smile that made a frown gather between Ariadne's eyes. "*Mon Dieu,* Monsieur Nathaniel, do you find something comical about this business?"

"Oh, no, madame," he said, instantly wiping all expression from his features.

"You were grinning. I saw you."

The boy flung a quick glance at her patient. "It just struck me as funny. Monsieur Blackford lets me do nothing for him, but you now. . . ."

"But I?"

"You're different." Testing the razor's edge on his thumb, he gave a small nod of satisfaction before placing it beside the brush and soap cup.

"Obviously," Gavin interrupted, his voice soft. "That will do, I think."

"She asked."

"So she did, and you told her and are now done here. You may go and see to my laundry or whatever else needs attention."

"But I wanted to see how a female barber works."

"Mosquitoes pant for a taste of blood, but that doesn't mean it's allowed."

"All right," the boy said with a sigh, "I'm

going." He sketched a truncated bow in Ariadne's direction. "Ring the bell when you're done, madame, and I'll come to clear things away."

When the door closed behind Nathaniel, she glanced at the man in the bed. "He's very polite."

"He's Satan's own minion, a demon sent to be my plague and penance. But polite, yes." He paused, dismissing the subject of Nathaniel. "You could draw up a chair for your task, though I believe you will be more comfortable if you sit here beside me on the bed."

"Standing will be quite all right."

"As you prefer." He lay relaxed, patiently waiting for her to begin.

Contrary to Gavin's expectations, she had shaved Jean Marc only once or twice during the final days of his illness, when his valet had a day off. That had not been so very difficult a task as his whiskers had been thin and light around the small tuft of a beard he wore on his chin. Gavin Blackford's beard was much heavier. It covered the lower half of his face with shades of brown and red among the gleaming gold. The task was daunting, and that was without the necessity for coming close to him, touching him.

But wasn't this what she had wanted when she suggested to Maurelle that he be brought to the town house? She should be glad of the opportunity to come nearer to him. From that point of view, her refusal of a seat beside him was a mistake. It had been instinctive, she thought, based on purest self-protection. When had she grown so timorous?

It would not do to change her mind too quickly in his presence. He might begin to suspect she was up to something, even if he could not discern the extent of it. He was not a stupid man by any means; it would have been far better if he had been.

Turning from him, she busied herself by pouring hot water into the china basin then dropping a small linen towel into it. When it was soaked, she lifted it gingerly and squeezed a large portion of the water from it. Turning quickly, she laid it over the lower portion of his face and smoothed the edges down his neck.

Water was about to drip on his nightshirt. Hastily, she caught up a longer towel and spread it over his chest and his pillow to protect them. While the wet cloth softened the whiskers, she turned away to dip the shaving brush in water, then swirl it around and around in the soap cup to work up a thick lather. Finally, it was ready. She whisked away the wet towel and began to apply the soap.

It was impossible to avoid his mouth. She did not try after a moment, but quickly worked the lather into his beard with a brush. Once that was done, she used the pad of her thumb to skim over the smooth surfaces of his lips, removing the excess foam. A smear lingered on his lower lip and she wiped it again, slowly gliding her thumb over the firm yet silken surface.

His lips parted and she felt the swift breath he drew as it wafted across her fingers. Her eyes flicked up to meet his. A suspended look hovered in their blue depths, along with what seemed to be searing doubt. An instant later, his lashes came down and both were gone.

"Your fingers are so cool," he said, bringing one hand up from under the towel to wipe the remaining soap from his upper lip with his own hand.

"Does it bother you?" Concern for the wash of color across his cheekbones touched her, so she reached to lay the backs of her fingers against his forehead. "Perhaps you have a fever."

"I should not be at all surprised," he answered in dry tones. "You should not be cold, however. Warm your hands at the fire by all means. I can wait."

"I'm perfectly fine." She reached for the razor, glad of the excuse to turn away.

"As you will."

The straight-edge was a work of art in its way, the blade of Sheffield steel, the handle of ivory with Gavin's initials inlaid in gold. Smaller than many such instruments, it was well-balanced in her hand. It seemed fitting that a man whose life could depend on the quality of his sword should have an affinity for good workmanship in any blade.

"Second thoughts?" he inquired, his gaze watchful.

"Simply admiring the workmanship." She flipped the inlaid work toward him.

"It was made in Spain, a gift from my father on my sixteenth birthday."

"A proud moment, I imagine."

"Symbolic, yes, or it might have been if he had been present. It was handed to me by my valet."

His voice was without expression, but a shadow of bitterness lay over his face. Pursuing its cause, she said, "Your father was no longer . . ."

"Alive? Oh, yes, he was bonny and blithe, just away on one of his missions for the crown. That was how he added interest and importance to his days — his roles of landed gentleman, clubman, husband and father lacking something in that regard."

"At least you knew him," she said shortly. She had never had that privilege with her real father.

"Did I? The prattle of infants did not enthrall him. We, my brothers and I, were shuffled off to live with a grandfather who thought . . . But never mind."

"Go on. I should like to hear." Emboldened by his absorption in the past, she began with short strokes to rake the frighteningly sharp blade down the hard plane of his right cheek.

"The story is boringly common."

"Not to me."

Just beneath the area where she worked, a pulse beat strongly in the side of his lean neck. She glanced at it, then away again. How easy it would be to make a sudden cut with her weight behind it. Almost, it seemed that he offered that unprotected area, turning it to her in willing sacrifice.

She swallowed hard. No, no, something inside her forbade that easy end. It was too unfeeling, too much like murder. She must focus on what she was doing.

"You have a problem?" he asked, his voice dulcet.

"No . . . yes," she answered in some confusion, then grasped at the first excuse that came to mind. "I . . . think you may have been right about the position for this task. It's a little awkward to reach you from here."

"Come closer then."

To comply would be unwise, particularly in view of the banked heat in his eyes, but she could not back down now. Setting the razor aside, she pushed back the bed curtains which draped down from the tester, then dragged the mounting step to the head of the bed and climbed onto the mattress beside him. With one foot braced on the steps, she eased over the yielding surface a few more inches until she was almost against him.

If her jostling movements caused him discomfort, he did not show it. Rather, he lifted his arm to allow her closer access. When she was secure, he lowered it again, resting it across her bent knee with his lax fingers at the indentation of her waist.

"Better?" he asked, a husky note in his voice.

"Yes. Please go on with what you were saying." The words were a little breathless, but as much as she could manage.

Something flared like lightning in the blue depths of his eyes before his lashes came down to conceal it. "Where was I? Oh, with my grandsire, I believe."

His voice, melodious and lightly sardonic, came from much closer now, but she refused to look at him again. "So it was."

"Yes, well. My grandfather had failed to make a country squire of his son so determined to do better with his grandsons. My older brother Thomas, the heir, was elected to become the sportsman in his image, proficient in shooting, fishing and riding to hounds — when not riding roughshod over the tenants. To the old gentleman's great disgust, I was bookish instead, with a taste for astronomy and the study of the globes as the means of escape into a wider world. Swordsmanship, my preferred way of working off my aggressions, he considered effete and foreign, not quite worthy of an English gentleman. Which is probably why the affinity became so rooted in me."

"In defiance, you mean."

"Defiance of the most grim. Merry on the outside, dolorous as a hangman at the heart."

"But you were allowed to leave." The touch of his hand upon her was so distracting that she was not sure if what she said made sense. The heat of it seemed to melt away the layers of her clothing, the gray-figured India cotton of her day gown, the poplin of her stays and silk of her chemise. His clasp was meant, surely, to give her balance, but was so nearly an embrace that she was barely able to draw breath. That the trembling inside her did not communicate itself to her fingers was surely the miracle of the day.

"Allowed is not quite the term," he answered lightly. "Encouraged comes more readily to mind. Persuaded is another choice. Compelled might better apply."

The radiating heat of his body on her right side, with its quiescent, muscle-sheathed power, was fully as disturbing as his touch. It gave her the feeling that his stillness was by stringent choice rather than necessity. She sent him a quick glance before returning at once to her work. "You must have done something unforgivable."

"Astute and without remorse, a deadly combination in a lady." His laugh was short, a good thing since she was shaving carefully around one corner of his mouth. "But you are quite right. I killed my brother."

She paused while shock ran over her in a poisonous wave. It was a moment before she could speak. "Your elder brother, you mean? The heir?"

"Your opinion of me, I see, is no better

than that of my parents or grandparents. But no. The victim was my younger brother Sean, poor, darling child. He was an after-thought of my parents by several years, product of a fit of jealous assertion of hus-bandly rights when my father came home from Greece, Italy, Portuguese Macao or some such place to discover that my mother had taken the gardener into her bed. Or the baby may have been sired by the gardener. As there was no way to say with certainty, he was given the benefit of the doubt. He was dear and bright and his head was as gold as —" He stopped abruptly, as if his throat had closed.

"What happened to him?" She stroked the razor over his chin and down his neck with consummate care, as if anything more might increase the pain she'd heard in his voice. To learn something of his history made him less formidable somehow. That it also made him more human was something she didn't care to examine at the moment.

"He was playing with his toy boat on the ornamental lake that surrounded three sides of a ridiculous folly of a summerhouse built by some ancestor. He and his nanny had enjoyed an al fresco repast. She became ill afterward, so asked my elder brother to watch Sean while she ran to the house.

314

Thomas swore he delegated the task to me, as I was reading in the summerhouse according to my usual habit. In my concentration on my printed tale, so he claimed, I must have let Sean drown."

"No." The denial was a mere whisper, but definite.

He studied her, his eyes wide but his gaze not quite focused. "You seem very certain."

She was, though she could not say how. Was it something in his voice, or merely what she expected him to claim? Or could it be simply that she had seen his concentration and knew it to be fierce but capable of infinite expansion to include any movement or sound around him. "What really happened?"

"Farce and tragedy rolled into one and as sordid as you may suppose. I was not in the summerhouse, had never been there. I was, alas, involved at that moment in a mutually satisfactory rendezvous with the lady who was betrothed to Thomas. I could not betray her by claiming it, and naturally she could not speak for me without jeopardizing her future as my sister-in-law. It was better that I take the blame, accept the castigation and leave my grandfather's house. And that is how it was done."

Her hand slipped. That was all it was; she

315

was listening too intently, hearing not only the words but their plastered coating of grief and blame, pride and betrayal.

The blade nicked his neck above his Adam's apple. A bright bead of blood rose on his skin and hung there, shining in the morning light.

Sickness rolled over her in a cold wave. With it came the memory of how his side and back had looked as he lay on the field — a morass of flayed skin and bone in a welter of blood and mangled cloth from his coat and shirt. She dropped the razor, pressed her thumb to the small cut and held it tightly even as she squeezed her eyes shut.

"Don't," he said in hard command. "Don't think. It does no good."

"I didn't mean to do it." She looked at him with tears rimming her lashes. "Really, I didn't. I'm so sorry."

"It doesn't matter. Certainly it's nothing I haven't done and recently at that. It could even be," he added, "that I owe you some small recompense in blood."

Alarm struck through her. *He knew.* Somehow, he had discovered who she was, guessed her aim. She shook her head again, unable to comprehend it.

"For the cut to your wrist," he said, turning his head more toward her on the pillow.

"One injury is very like another. Some fester, some heal, but few are forgotten. Ours, I do trust, will leave no scars, at least none that are visible."

She met his eyes then while her heart slammed against her ribs as if trying to fight its way free. They were darkly blue, concealing in their swirling depths such vital secrets, such pain and remorse that she could feel herself being pulled into their vortex. He was eminently human and not without sensitivity, so had his sorrows and regrets as surely as she had her own. And who was to say whose were more dearly paid for or more difficult to bear?

She had sworn to kill him, sworn it in the fresh anguish of grief. The death of sweet Francis cried to be avenged. Yet how could she bring about the death of this sword master when she could not bear to see him bleed, when she felt the pain of the hurt she caused him in her own flesh?

"Forgive me," she said, leaving the razor where she had dropped it as she shoved away from him and off the side of the mattress. "I can't do this. Someone else must finish it for you."

"I will finish it," he said, taking the toweling from his chest to wipe the lather from his face.

She stared at him, caught by something in his voice, some inflection that made her wonder if they spoke of the same thing. He watched her, his gaze shuttered, features without expression. His was so very handsome even with a fleck of lather on his nose and a trickle of blood on his neck, and yet so implacable inside. His strength was not merely physical, not solely a thing of muscles and sinews and driving force. It was in his mind, that vital intelligence that shone from his eyes, sang in the words that tripped with maddening obscurity from his tongue and in the truths hidden in their snare.

Ariadne had thought to know more of him, to learn his weaknesses and turn them against him. It had never occurred to her that he might have none.

A sudden chill whispered across the back of her neck and feathered down her spine. With it came a desolation that crowded the back of her throat with the hot, salty ache of tears. She swung away before he could see, and moved to the door. It was only when she was safely on the other side with it closed behind her that she could breathe again.

TWENTY

Madame Zoe Savoie had no compunction about disturbing the Englishman. Like an unstoppable force of nature, she sailed from the salon where Ariadne and Maurelle had received her and, talking volubly all the way, shedding shawls and scarves and bits of feathers like so much flotsam released from her rolling waves of iridescent gray and aqua silk trimmed with silver braid, she traversed the gallery and swept into the sickroom. The parrot on her shoulder squawked and began to bob up and down as he saw Gavin. Once near the bed, he made a fluttering dive with clipped wings to establish a perch on the footboard.

"Napoleon and I have come this evening, *mon ami,* to smooth your pillows and raise your spirits," the diva announced, adding with a roguish smile, "the lift of anything else is entirely dependent on your mood and strength. Ah, but how unfair of you to look so wanly handsome on your pillows. It quite puts me out of patience with you."

"Napoleon doesn't seem to mind."

"Napoleon is male, so quite unaffected. Don't you agree, Ariadne, *ma chère?*"

The parrot, hearing his name, flapped his wings and puffed out his chest. Ariadne, smiling at his antics, said, "If you refer to being out of patience . . ."

"No, no, don't tell me the two of you are at outs already!"

"Certainly not. Monsieur Blackford is a guest here, as am I."

"Just so," the diva answered with a droll twist of her lips. "More than that, you are obliged to him for protecting your good name, even if that appears to have been useless since he is now a danger to it. But men are not at their best on their sickbeds, so I'm sure he's given you provocation. That is why I am here, to intercept it." She turned to Gavin, drawing a ribbon-tied box from the huge muff of sheared beaver that she carried on her arm. "Bonbons, chocolate of course, to sweeten your humor, *mon ami.* These are from Vincent's, so naturally too rich by far to be consumed all at once by an invalid. I shall help you dispose of them."

"You are too kind," Gavin replied at his driest.

"Am I not?" Her smile was wicked. "And I daresay Ariadne will be glad to lend her aid. All we require is . . ."

"Coffee, I think," Ariadne supplied as she went to pull the bell cord.

"Precisely." Madame Savoie flung her muff into the chair on the far side of the bed and proceeded to arrange it as a cushion. "Now we shall be comfortable and pass a little time, yes? But not too much, for nothing must be allowed to prevent the invalid from rising as soon as he is able. From his bed, of course, from his bed!"

If Ariadne had expected Gavin to be offended by the diva's risqué manner, she would have been disappointed. He held out his hand to Zoe with laughter in his eyes and accepted the quick kisses she pressed to either jaw before taking her fur-softened seat. Their exchange concerning Madame's next performance, her health and news of their mutual friends was quick, colorful and totally without pretense. They were friends of an uncommon kind, or so it seemed.

For herself, Ariadne was delighted to have Madame Savoie's presence to ease her way back into the sickroom. She had not been in it since the shaving incident the morning of the day before. She had been on the point of strolling in while pretending that nothing of moment had occurred on her last visit when saved by the diva's arrival.

And what had taken place exactly? Nothing more than an *attaque de nerfs* on her part, she saw in retrospect. It had passed, as such things did, and now she was quite prepared to take up where she had left off.

"I wonder if you had heard the rumor that your erstwhile opponent intends to quit the city?" the diva asked.

"It has been brought to my attention." Gavin directed his attention toward the chocolate box, pulling free the ribbon tie as if only half listening to his visitor.

"Word now is that the gentleman has reserved passage on the *Leodes* bound for Marseilles but due to repairs it will be some days before she sails."

"So his head is better?"

"It would seem so."

"Yet he languishes, unable to leave the scene of his disgrace."

"And visits sundry gaming dens where his capacity for drink has been duly noted, along with various remarks made concerning his regret that he was not permitted to finish dispatching you."

"Regret is no crime, nor is ambition."

Madame Zoe nodded so the feather on her hat bobbed around her shoulders. "Unless he acts on them. There were any number of *maître d'armes* present to hear him, and to remember."

"On whose behalf, you have come riding, *ventre-à-terre,* to put me on my guard? Or do you hope to pry me from my bed with the news?" Gavin held out half the bonbon he had taken from the box toward Napoleon, coaxing the parrot to come to him. "Though grateful for the warning, I can't think our Russian friend plans to continue the mayhem. For all he knows, a nice bout of gangrene or a putrid fever may save him the trouble."

The diva lifted dark brows. "There is a chance of it?"

"Not while I am tucked up in starched linen and nursed like an unweaned bunny in a nest of moss and mother's fur. Yes, and with chocolates to sustain me."

"Abominable man," Madame Savoie said without heat as she watched her pet waddle across the sheet and pluck the piece of chocolate from Gavin's fingers before nibbling it like a child with a cookie. "It would serve you right if I took back my offering."

"Which you might be able to accomplish," he said amiably, "if you care to engage in fisticuffs with a bird like a green eagle."

"Oh, I don't mind that, but it does rend

323

my soul to hear a baby rabbit cry."

Ariadne, hearing the low chuckle that sounded in Gavin's throat, was amazed. She could think of no one else who would have dared say such a thing to him or, saying it, have survived unscathed. Her estimation of the diva rose several notches. At the same time, it was fascinating to see that her patient was capable of laughing at himself. She had not thought it of him.

Other visitors had been in the house earlier in the day. Ariadne had not been present since it seemed clear they preferred her absence. Rather, she had allowed Maurelle to show them to Gavin's room while she kept to her own. Now he and Madame Zoe spoke of his friends, laughing at the things that had been said and the antics of the children that had accompanied them as if they were family.

Ariadne added nothing to the conversation, for what could she say? It was a relief when the café au lait arrived. Maurelle came with it, however, and naturally took upon herself the duties of hostess, seeing that everyone had a cup and also a small plate of rose-decorated china to hold their bon-bons and the candied rose petals that she had ordered to go with them.

"I met Lisette this morning at Barrière's

on Royale, and she mentioned that she had called here," Zoe said. "What did you think of her, Ariadne, *ma chère?* Is she not the perfect little mother, gathering her family of sword masters around her?"

"I'm sure she is," she murmured, her gaze on her coffee cup.

"It is she who holds them together, I do swear. Having no family of her own, she dotes on Caid's friends and their wives."

"No family? But I thought they had children."

"So they do. I was speaking of the sisters and brothers, the endless aunts and uncles and cousins to the last degree everyone seems to have here."

"Oh, yes, certainly."

"Madame Faucher is also alone in the world, or virtually so," Gavin said.

"Oh, but I thought —"

"No."

The word seemed freighted with warning. Ariadne saw Madame Savoie exchange a brief glance with Maurelle who only lifted a plump shoulder in a shrug that could have meant anything.

"My mistake," the diva said, unperturbed as she turned back again. "Though I tell you, it's an inspiration to see how Lisette has risen above all the talk of a few seasons

325

ago. Did you not find her congenial?"

"I barely saw her," Ariadne said a shade defensively. "My company was quite unnecessary."

Gavin turned his head on the pillow. "They slighted you?"

"Oh no, they were perfectly cordial."

"As only women can be when turning a cold shoulder toward one of their own. Shall I speak to them?"

His quickness was disquieting. "I pray you will not. They can hardly be faulted for feeling I share some blame in your injury."

"Even when it's untrue."

"I would not cause trouble between you."

"They would prefer to know how they've misjudged the matter."

"Still."

He did not answer, which effectively prevented her from guessing if he meant to abide by her request. That it should matter to him was, perhaps, the most disturbing thing about it.

"Where is Nathaniel?" Maurelle asked, glancing around the bedchamber as if she expected him to emerge from behind a curtain.

"He was growing restless at his confinement to a sickroom," Gavin said. "I sent him on an errand to relieve his tedium."

"One meant to save you from his ennui, I expect," she said placidly. "What a hand you are. But I suppose he will return before evening."

"Oh, without doubt, unless he's detained."

"Should he fail, you may always send for Solon to make you comfortable for the night."

Gavin turned his gaze to Ariadne where she sat still holding her coffee cup. She could feel its warmth on her face though she refused to meet it. "I'm sure," he said, his voice like silk, "that some arrangement may be contrived."

Madame Zoe, watching them, snorted and rose to her feet. "A perfect signal for my departure since my aid, unfortunately, will not be required." She picked up her muff, slipped it over her wrist and held out her arm for Napoleon to mount below the fur. "No, no, Maurelle, don't disturb yourself, I beg. Ariadne will see me out. Besides, I must just drop a hint in her ear as to how to handle a man who is flat on his back."

"Gently, I should hope," Gavin said.

"But not like a bunny," she returned at once with a droll smile and a kiss blown in his direction, "unweaned or otherwise."

As an exit line, it was less than satisfactory, at least to judge from the look on the diva's strong features as she walked along the gallery. Ariadne glanced at her, then back out over the railing to where the fretted leaves of the banana trees glistened with misting rain as they waved in the wind. Speaking in careful neutrality, she said, "If you are concerned about the care Monsieur Blackford is receiving . . ."

"No, no, that was a jest only. My thought was the opposite. I don't know what passes between the two of you, *chère,* but I would advise you to be on your guard."

A frisson ran along Ariadne's nerves, one she ignored with valiant effort. "I don't know what you mean."

"Do you not? No matter. Something about the way your patient looks at you when he thinks no one is watching concerns me. You will think me silly, I expect, but it calls to mind the drama of the opera. Death and tragedy, love and hate are everyday occurrences on the stage yet are based on the most common of human failings. People are so often predictable, you perceive. We behave in ways that come from inside us, from all the tangle of things we feel and dream, hope and fear. Sometimes we are civilized enough to rise above our more base emotions, but not often. We fail because we cannot see how what we do looks from the outside. We are lost in the terrible anger, the anguish and betrayal we feel. It fills our world and we will do anything to banish it."

Ariadne stopped, turning to her with her hands clasped in front of her. "What are you trying to say?"

"I'm not precisely sure, *ma chère,* or I would put it most frankly. I only know it isn't like Gavin to allow a stranger to care for him, nor to lie as watchful as some great cat waiting to pounce. Be very careful, for it is a dangerous game you play."

"I was not aware that . . ."

"Don't play the pretty simpleton with me. Others may believe you have the idle *envie* to learn fencing, but I am not so easily fooled. You want something of Monsieur Blackford, just as he wants something from you. It may be a mere itch for both of you, one easily scratched, but I doubt it. So I warn you again, take care. You may get whatever it is you are after, and find it is not what you want at all."

The operatic diva, magnificent in her disdain, swept around with her bobbing parrot riding her shoulder, and strode away down the gallery. Ariadne watched her go while cold dread settled inside her. There was something in what Madame Savoie had said, she knew there was, but what difference did it make?

It could not matter. She would allow nothing to matter.

A quiet footstep accompanied by the rustle of skirts sounded behind her. As she whirled in that direction, Maurelle exclaimed, "What is it, *chère?* You look as if you've seen a ghost."

"I'm . . . just a little chilled, perhaps." She tried a smile but feared it was not quite successful. "It's turning cooler, don't you think?"

"Was it something Zoe told you? What has she been saying?"

"Nothing of importance. Only . . . you said once, I think, that you accused Monsieur Blackford of being *épris.* It was a joke, wasn't it? You didn't mean it."

"He may find you attractive, but is quite aware of the line which separates you. It's unlikely he will overstep it."

Ariadne gave an unhappy nod. "So I thought. It's good to know you are of the same mind."

"Is that what Zoe was saying, that you should be wary of his advances?"

"Perhaps I misunderstood her."

"Or not. She is a romantic, our Zoe, under all her outrageous manners and sophistication."

"So likely to be mistaken, you mean."

"Or her views may be exaggerated." Maurelle linked her arm with Ariadne's and began to stroll with her toward the salon centering the main house as it fronted the street. "Be easy in your mind. Whatever she may think, matters can't be so very bad."

Ariadne was willing enough to be convinced. She moved with her hostess without resistance, though she glanced back once toward the bedchamber where Gavin lay. Yes, she would allow it, at least for now.

Regardless, the specter that Madame Savoie had raised, that Gavin might be stalking her like some great golden tiger, would not leave her mind. There was only one possibility she could conceive for it. He had discovered who she was in spite of everything, so had divined her purpose. Yet if that was true, why had he not confronted her?

He could have no reason for pursuing her, no need for revenge of the kind that drove her to meet him. What she might do need concern him very little; she had scant power to cause him harm. He was more than able to deflect anything she might try, or at least it must seem that way in his mind.

Still, she could not stop thinking about it as the evening wore on, wondering, guessing, going over every single word and action between the two of them. One moment she concluded that Madame Savoie was completely mistaken, the next she was positive she was right. She could settle on neither one nor the other.

One thing was clear. She must know how matters stood before she went a step further.

It was supper time, that late evening meal following some hours after the midday dinner taken at three o'clock, when she finally hit on a way to find out. Footsteps firm, smile grimly in place, she proceeded along the gallery toward the bedchamber allotted to Gavin with Adele carrying a supper tray as she followed along behind her. Knocking lightly on the door, Ariadne pushed it open and held it for the maidservant. Only then did she turn toward the bed.

It was empty.

Panic beat up into her mind. She turned quickly, searching the room with her eyes, half afraid she would discover her patient stretched on the floor where he had fallen out of bed.

Gavin was ensconced in a wingback chair before the fire with pillows cushioning his injured side and back and one foot thrust out toward the red-orange flames. A *robe de chambre* of dark Bordeaux-colored brocade wrapped him from his shoulders to the Turkish slippers on his long narrow feet.

He straightened, lifting his head from where it was propped on his fist with his elbow resting on the chair arm. "An auspicious evening," he said, his voice light and even. "Not only am I allowed to leave my bed, but it seems I am to have company for dinner. Can the excitement rise any higher?"

"Allowed?"

She moved forward as she spoke, directing the maidservant to wait with the tray while she pulled a table closer to the fire.

"By my devoted henchman here," he answered as Nathaniel rose from where he had been hidden by the back of the matching chair on the other side of the fire. "He was most strenuous in his objections on the head that too rapid a recovery might remove him prematurely from a household where he has neither to cook nor empty slops."

She gave a low laugh. "Strong considerations, I must agree. I rather thought I might relieve him of his duties, keeping you company while he has his meal with Maurelle."

Gavin glanced at the young man who stood by with hands clasped behind his back in an attitude of respect but a grin on his face. "What say you? Does the prospect of dining with Madame Herriot please?"

"If my manners are up to it — well, and Madame Faucher really don't mind taking my place."

"Your manners require no mending," she said warmly, "and I can't imagine your duties are beyond my performance."

"Then I'll leave you to it. Though I warn you he's soreheaded as a bull in a baiting ring."

"Is he now? I wonder why?" She half suspected the boy of teasing Gavin. If so, she saluted his daring in attempting it.

Nathaniel shook his head without answering, his gaze hooded as he followed the maidservant from the bedchamber.

Ariadne had more vital things on her mind than the byplay between sword master and apprentice. She gave it a few seconds of curiosity while taking the chair Nathaniel had vacated and disposing her skirts around her, then dismissed it from her mind.

How to embark on what she intended? She had thought something would come to her when she was in place, but she had been too optimistic. The silence in the bedchamber grew long, broken only by the quiet popping of the fire and the sound of a dray rattling past in the side street beyond the windows. She stared at the coals, but they burned brightly, offering no excuse for busy work, much less conversation. In her intent search for something to say, she started a little as Gavin spoke beside her.

"You have eaten?"

"Not . . . as yet."

"This abundance of food was surely meant for two then." He indicated the collection of silver dishes holding slices of roast chicken, blanched asparagus spears, small loaves of bread, crème brûlée, and the carafe of wine that went with them. "Please. Begin, if you will."

"The intention was to tempt your appetite."

"For which sentiment, I am grateful though I have little taste for food just now." He went on after a moment. "It's a reminder that I haven't thanked you for your care. I would include Maurelle, but know well she isn't at her best in the sickroom so has left most of it to you and Solon."

"None of us have been overtaxed. It's Nathaniel who has been constantly on duty."

"Which is why you determined to relieve him, another example of your thoughtfulness."

His words of appreciation made her feel distinctly guilty as nothing she had done, or very little at any rate, had been without motive. "I'm pleased to see you're improving. At least . . . I suppose you must be better since you left your bed."

"I was tired of it, to tell the truth. Too much bed rest is no great benefit with most injuries."

He shifted a little in his chair, as if uncomfortable with the discussion or perhaps with the soreness of his wound. She was not quite ready to leave the subject, however, having nothing else to take its place. "You have been injured before?"

"Like thorn pricks while gathering roses, it occurs around swords. As you know."

"This was something more than a thorn prick." She was obscurely glad to hear his description. The lack of convolution in his speech had begun to make her uneasy, as if he might be more tired or ill than he appeared.

"But of no more concern. Still, you did not join me, I think, to discuss my health or even to take Nathaniel's place. Why am I so honored?"

"I was persuaded you must be bored with your own company." For something to do while she waited to see if he would accept that evasion, she reached to break the end from the loaf of bread and began to nibble at it.

"Oh, assuredly, but I don't believe cross-ing swords with you this evening would be of benefit."

"Not if you mean literally." She frowned. "Am I to suppose you feel that's the only way we might pass the time?"

"If you have other joys in mind, then you must tell me plainly. Men of my stripe are not encouraged to suppose anything."

A short laugh left her. "Oh, please, as though that ever stopped you."

"Spoken by someone who is, of course, a model of propriety."

"Neither of us may make that claim, which should put us on equal standing."

He watched her through an ambush of gold-tipped lashes. "And that is something to be wished?"

"Merely a fact." How very controlled he was. She wondered what it would take to shake him. While she considered it, she finished her bread then reached for a plate and began to load it with a few slices of chicken breast, spears of asparagus and another piece of bread broken from the loaf. "Shall I cut your chicken for you?"

"I believe I can manage," he said, but made no move to take the plate she placed on the table near his elbow.

"You really are not hungry."

He turned his head against the back of his chair, his gaze darkly blue and penetrating. "My hungers are not so simple or so easily appeased."

What was there to say to that? What did he expect her to say?

It occurred to her to question if she could seduce him, not just in the physical sense but in mind as well. What better way was there to discover a man's weaknesses than by that ultimate closeness? How better to persuade him to lay aside his guard? Men and women were never more surely themselves, with all their faults and foibles exposed, than when they made love.

It was not as if she were some untried girl, nor was a liaison between them likely to be of any duration. It was what society must be whispering of them already after the duel fought in her name. What had she to lose? And what better time and place than here in this house while he recuperated under Maurelle's auspices?

Of course there was the small difficulty of his injury. It did not encourage explorations of a sensual nature, much less anything requiring more strenuous activity. He could barely move, after all.

"What are you thinking?" he asked, his voice soft.

She took a startled breath before forcing a smile. "Nothing of importance. Merely that . . . physical attraction may be the basis for most affairs, but there is more to the association between a man and a woman."

"Why, Madame Faucher, you do surprise me."

"Not that I have any great experience in these matters, you understand."

"Oh, perfectly." The agreement was dry but without conviction. "You were not tempted during your marriage?"

"Never."

"Not even with your Russian?"

"No."

"No?" he repeated, his eyes narrowed.

She thought he sounded almost incredulous. It might be a little odd, perhaps, given the nature of her marriage and Jean Marc's illness, but the prospect had never beckoned. She had been brought up to consider her marriage vows sacred and the sanctity of the home inviolable. More than that, she had met no one who made abandoning her virtuous stand seem worthwhile. Certainly, no man had ever stirred her blood to fever heat the way the man sitting beside her had accomplished with no more than a look.

"It still seems to me that some degree of trust and affection, some meeting of the minds, must be required," she said, continuing her reflective argument.

"Not," he answered, "with the majority of men."

"No?"

"No."

He should know if anyone did, she thought with a small frown between her eyes. "I did not, naturally, expect love to be a requirement, but surely the whole thing is rather empty unless . . . what I mean to say is, I don't see how men can simply remove their clothing and take a woman, any woman, to bed on the spur of the moment."

"It's a great mystery," he replied, his voice even, "like the tides or an eclipse of the sun. A few moments spent rising then falling, a few pleasurable seconds hidden away behind the brightness, and then they emerge, unchanged."

She must be depraved to be so affected by the images contained in the words that fell from his lips. For a flashing instant, she had seen herself in the arms of this man who had murdered Francis. How had she come to this, that it could seem not only possible but reasonable?

How had she come to be speaking at all of passion and love affairs? Was it because the subject was on her mind, or had he somehow drawn her into it by forcing her to defend her ideas? She thought the latter. Odd, but she had never before articulated her feelings.

Nor was it necessary to consider them too deeply just now, given that it was impossible to embark on any great intimacy this evening. She had time before any such fatal decision was made, time in which to discover how close she could come to him while he lacked the strength for physical consummation.

Surely he was incapable of it? It was impossible to be certain, of course, but she could not imagine that a man unable to shift in his chair without pain could take a woman into his bed.

He couldn't. *Could he?*

She must redirect her thoughts before he challenged her on them, picking them from the air in that unnerving habit that seemed his alone. It would be as well, too, if she could control her gaze which skimmed far too often over the firm, flat planes of his belly under its covering of brocade.

"You are so very English in your accent, your outlook and attitudes," she said in a rather desperate search for a change of subject. "How is it that you came to New Orleans?"

"I have a brother here, if you recall."

"Oh, yes." Nicholas Pasquale was his half brother. She had almost forgotten. It seemed vaguely possible that Gavin's attitude toward love affairs might stem in part from his father's wayward history in that area. "You came to visit him."

"My travels took me to where he was born, on the trail of a rumor that he existed. Eventually it led me here."

"What of your other travels? I mean, you can't have been so very old when you parted company from your grandfather, otherwise you would never have been expected to see after a younger brother. Where did you go from there?" She had no idea that he would answer the query, but it didn't hurt to ask.

"To London first, then on to Paris, Wiesbaden, Vienna, and finally to Rome and Rhodes before coming here. It was a grand tour, if you will, just of greater duration than most."

"Not so terrible an exile if you had the means to travel."

"My grandfather might have been inclined to favor Thomas, who must be considered a paragon of honor as the future heir to his titles, but he was not so lacking in charity as to send me off without a shilling. Second sons are usually destined for the church or the army, you know. An officer's commission was purchased for me. My father, in a belated show of responsibility, saw to it that I was posted to a ceremonial position with the Queen's Guard. Clattering through London, riding on parade in bearskin shako and polished boots bored me to the teeth. I resold my commission to finance the rest of my journey."

"At least you were not abandoned completely."

"No, though their generosity may have been because they guessed the truth. I would have preferred exoneration."

"Yes, anyone would," she said slowly, her gaze on the mask-like planes of his face that were glazed in red and blue light from the coal flames under the mantel. "You were in Paris. We might have met there."

"Unlikely." His lips curved in a self-deprecating smile. "My association with the correct and respectable of the city was not great."

"The bourgeoisie, you mean."

"Since that is the most imminently respectable segment, yes. I meant no insult, nor to suggest that I moved in more exalted circles. I did not."

She let that pass. "I expect you honed your swordsman's skills there as well."

His smile was brief. "Not on the overtly arrogant, though the temptations were many."

"But in the *salles d'armes,* perhaps?"

"There and elsewhere, notably Italy where the art of the foil and épée began."

"I did wonder how you came by the extra skill it takes to set up here in a *salon d'assaut.*"

"An accident, really, gained out of boredom, restless hardihood and youthful habit. As a pastime between bouts of dissipation, exercise with a sword had more appeal than gaming."

He was attempting, as before, to discourage her with outrageous claims. At least, she thought they were exaggerated. "So you came finally to New Orleans where you joined the select few."

"If by that you mean the *maîtres d'armes.*"

He made as if to reach for the wine carafe then halted with a wince. She forestalled him with a small gesture, leaning to lift the carafe and splash white wine into a crystal stem. She handed it to him while laying the fingers of her free hand alongside his to make certain it was in his grasp before she released it.

His skin was so warm, the tracery of gold hairs on his fingers crisp yet silken, their ridged calluses both fascinating and repellent. She could almost feel the turbulent flow of life inside him, feel it alter its rhythm to beat against the pulse in her own fingers. She was still, transfixed by the onslaught of fiery need. Lifting her lashes, she met his eyes and was lost in their crystalline blue depths.

He was so different from any man she had ever met, so hidden away behind a barricade of words and attitudes, so armored by skill at arms and intellect that it was impossible to tell who or what he was inside. And yet he was there, like some dragon in his castle, some beast in his lair. He was there, and he invited her inside. The question was whether it was to be protected or devoured.

A shiver ran down her spine, spreading chill dismay into her midsection. Before it could reach her fingers, she released the crystal stem and drew back. It was a relief to see that his grasp was firm enough that there was no accident. It was also oddly gratifying to watch him sip the wine, then turn his attention to the bread and chicken she had given him.

What ailed her that she should care?

With hands that were not quite as steady as before, she poured wine into the second stem on the tray and brought it to her lips.

It was an excellent vintage, as was only to be expected of anything from Maurelle's thick-walled cellar in the raised basement below the town house, but she was more in need of its restorative effect.

To cover that small, confused moment, she reached for a chicken wing, taking small bites and following them with wine. In the quiet while they ate, she could hear the distant murmur of voices from the dining room, which indicated that others had joined Maurelle and Nathaniel, and the sighing of wind around the eaves.

Before the quiet could grow too uncomfortable, she dredged from her mind a comment that promised to be fairly safe yet might be productive. "One hears much of a Brotherhood among the sword masters these days."

"One can hear anything."

"Yet you are very close, are you not, particularly those of you who are Maurelle's friends?"

"We have our small coterie, our circle within the larger circle of the Vieux Carré's social order. As Madame Zoe told you, it is Lisette, Caid's wife, who sees to it. If we are brothers in any sense, then she is the cause."

"It sounds as if she enjoys special affection."

"And is held in it by us all. Caid is fortunate in the lady he took to wife, though I could say the same of Nicholas, also of Rio de Silva, his friend who makes the fourth in our circle."

"But you do not seek to emulate them?"

"Remiss of me, isn't it?"

"Why would you say that?"

"Because," he said with a faint twist of his lips, "I am told it with great regularity by all I have mentioned. It seems the happily married require all their friends to join them in that state." He sipped his wine then sat staring into the glass. "What of you? Have you no thoughts of taking another husband?"

"Not at the moment."

"But one day you will, possibly for the sake of children if nothing else."

She had thought the same thing not long ago, still she gave a small shake of her head. "It seems a strange thing, to wed a man for the sake of his seed."

"No stranger than marrying a woman for the use of her womb."

"Someone spoke of my marriage in your hearing, I suppose?"

"It was a matter of passing interest."

What did he mean by that? Nothing in the quiet repose of his face or gleam of his eyes behind his lashes gave her any indication. "I won't ask who it may have been, but will say that those who are not intimately involved can have little idea of what passes between a husband and wife."

He watched her for a long moment. "Oh, granted," he said, the words so soft they barely stirred the air. "And we all have our secrets."

She glanced up, her gaze sharp, but he had turned away to stare into the fire again. Not a trace of emotion showed on the fire-bronzed planes of his face.

Nothing was there. Nothing at all.

TWENTY-ONE

Gavin watched the flames dancing over the coals behind the curling wrought iron grate while he considered the situation. It was bizarre to sit beside a woman who smiled and made conversation, poured his wine and appeared all solicitude, yet wanted him dead.

It was also strange to be alone behind a closed door with a woman who considered him harmless. At least, he would swear that was what was in her mind. She seemed so relaxed, as if she had no thought whatever of any designs he might have upon her. He was not used to being dismissed so easily.

More than that, he was not certain how many opportunities would be provided for the purpose he intended. His time here was limited after all, and the lady's charity toward him was unlikely to survive his recovery. It was doubtful it would last beyond the moment when she realized he was able to move about on his own.

He had not intended that she should know he could leave his bed. Another visit from her today had been unexpected.

Why was she here? He had been reasonably certain he knew her purpose which was to see him hale and hearty again so she might annihilate him herself. He did not make the mistake of thinking that her anger with Novgorodcev was any indication of concern for his welfare; it was almost certainly for the Russian's treachery in usurping her prerogatives. If anyone was going to kill him, it would be she.

He was perfectly willing to allow her to try. He only reserved the right to defend himself in any way that seemed likely to serve. That included exploiting the sensual awareness that hovered in the air around them, a current that seemed to both fascinate and repel the lady who attended upon him. He wondered what it might take to make it more evident.

His fingers opened without conscious direction, allowing the glass he held to fall. It struck his brocade-covered thigh, tumbled over the edge of his chair toward the floor.

Ariadne moved so quickly that it was almost as if she had been waiting. Sliding from her chair in a silken billow of skirts, she went to one knee to catch the crystal stem before it struck the floor.

"Brava," he said with unstinted admiration as he met her dark gaze where she knelt at his feet. "I thank you for the rescue, and Maurelle will thank you as well."

"It was luck, I assure you," she said on a low laugh.

"You didn't think but only acted. I feel sure you could now catch any sword thrown your way."

A flush rose in her face though her smile was crooked. "Do you? How very . . . kind of you to say so, *monsieur le maître*."

"It should be interesting to see when our sessions resume."

"Let us hope that's before I forget everything I've learned to this point."

She shifted a little, as if preparing to rise. He prevented it by putting out his hand to take hers. Removing the glass from her cool fingers, he set it on the table then reached to cup the soft plane of her face in his hand. "You will be a swordswoman extraordinaire. I only wonder what you will do with what you have learned."

If he had ever doubted her intentions, the color that flooded her face at his words would have convinced him. The ludicrous thing was the answering surge of heat in his groin. Or was it really so extraordinary that the fillip of danger should draw him like a wasp to honey, to this woman, this moment, this sublime chase? The risk of the game was what attracted many to the life of a *maître d'armes,* himself among them. Hazard as an aphrodisiac was not that different, when all was said and done.

He should resist; that much was clear. It would not benefit him to succumb to whatever she intended.

Merely to benefit was not his purpose, however. He wanted to know — could not be denied knowing — just how far she would go. Would she give herself to him in pursuit of her perfect vengeance or would she draw back before the final sacrifice? Did she intend some betrayal while his guard was down? Or was her purpose to weaken his resolve, making it more difficult for him to protect himself against her when the time came?

That last was not so far-fetched, he knew. It was a hard man who could harm a woman in a match with swords, an even harder one who could even think of killing one who had just left the warmth of his bed.

He couldn't do it. That being so, he most certainly should end this here, now, before it really began.

Too late.

It had been too late from the moment he had turned and looked into Ariadne's angry black eyes on the evening of *Réveillon*. She was a challenge he had no wish to resist, even if he had the resolution for it.

If it was a duel she wanted, then she would have it. The rules would not be standard, nor the weapons. Conduct for it would be as honorable or dishonorable as she chose since he would follow her lead. The battle was joined from this moment, and would not end until one of them was defeated.

She wanted him dead. What he wanted was her capitulation, her admission that she had no cause to hate him, no will to strike the final blow. He wanted her warm and willing in his bed, wanted her to want him — to want him *alive*.

Drawing her to himself, he lowered his mouth to her lips. How tender they were in their generous curves, and how temptingly sweet with their flavoring of wine. He remembered their taste, yet something inside him ripped open at their merest touch, sending pure and desperate longing racing through his veins. Their delicate line opened on her swift, indrawn breath and he swept inside, gathering impressions and flavors as if addicted to their precious elixir.

He wanted to drown in her, spend count-less hours learning these gentle surfaces, teaching her to open to him as a flower unfurls its petals to the sun, to join him in offering homage to the heated rays of desire.

There was no time, no time.

Instead, he allowed his fingers to drift down the turn of her jaw, feather across the pulse that throbbed in her throat before seeking with his thumb the small hollow at the base of her neck. Her skin was soft, so warm with its elusive hint of violet scent. Soft, too, was the fichu she wore of finest lawn.

The urge to pull the fichu from her neck-line, exposing the gentle curves it hid from his sight, shook him with its strength. To be denied when he was so close was almost insupportable. But he would not startle her with the desire that beat in his blood, ham-mered in his heart, flooded the lower part of his body. She was, he thought, untried in many ways concerning the passions of men, and especially of her own; he could sense it in her hesitancy even as he felt her arousal. How could it be otherwise when she had her knowledge of such things at the hands of an older, sickly husband?

Such limited experience was what made her think his injuries rendered him harmless. He would not deny her the comfort of that misjudgment. At least, not for the moment.

Still, her tiny forays between his lips were intoxicating, as if she would take the lead, become the seductress. And her hands . . . she had placed one on his thigh for balance while grasping his shoulder with the other. Did she have any idea what she was doing to him, the least guess at what the proximity of her warm fingers mere inches away from the hard heat and weight of him did to his control?

The muscles across the back of his neck tightened into iron bands. A red haze gathered at the edges of his vision. The palm of his hand burned as he spread it over the fullness of her breast, feeling the tight budding of her nipple while cursing conventions and the past, the lack of true privacy and too, too many layers of cloth and restrictions.

Dear God, but she was like a flame in his grasp, searing in her heat that purified his very being even as she threatened to destroy him. He wanted her as he had never wanted anything in his life, wanted to sink with her to the floor before the fire, to cover her with his hot, shivering flesh while she moaned, nude and immodest, beneath him, around him. He wanted eons in which to seek out every sensitive plane and hollow of her body and make it his, to find the sites of greatest pleasure and lavish them with caresses until she cried out for more, for surcease, for him.

He wanted to be absorbed in her in a tumult of the senses, hot, tight, and silken as they rode with gliding ease, meeting and parting, twisting with fervid joy and desperate friction, in an endless pummeling of heart and mind and body that mounted to oblivion and beyond.

Impossible, impossible for now. Still, there was one thing he could do, for her, for himself. Leaning back in the depths of his chair, he drew her with him so she came, awkwardly, to rest across his lap.

"I'll hurt you," she whispered against his throat.

"Pain, they say, is necessary to school an intelligence and make it a soul." He smiled into her hair while stray wisps tickled his eyelids, smiled to think she should care, even as a matter of politeness. "It doesn't hurt so much as letting you go would rend me at this moment."

"If you are sure . . ."

He was, and so he gathered her close, fitted their mouths together once more. That she came to him, shivering as she accepted his tongue, sliding one hand to the turn of his neck, made his heart swell in his chest even as he pushed from his mind all question of her purpose, of methods, of reason.

The glide of her fingertips delving under the rolled collar of his dressing gown and open neck of his nightshirt, skimming down along his collarbone, was an incitement. That she wanted to touch him scattered thought, so he almost forgot what she would find. Until he felt the catch in her breathing and her tentative exploration stopped.

"You've been hurt before," she whispered against his throat.

Her fingertips lay upon the puckered scar where the broken blade of her foster brother's sword had plunged into him in their twice-damned duel. It burned under her touch, throbbing as it had not in years. "I am sometimes unlucky in my meetings."

"I'm sorry," she said, and turned her head to press her lips to the tortured flesh.

She didn't mean to absolve him. It felt that way regardless, a kiss of benediction that banished pain. His throat ached, and his heart swelled so his rib cage could hardly contain it.

Reaching for her skirt hem, he lifted it, gathered its fullness, piled it and her petticoats in her lap. He ran his palm over the silk of her stockings and the firm contours they covered, brushed over the lace of her garters and higher, until he could slip his fingers between the open edges of her feminine split pantaloons, until he could brush the skin of her inner thighs that was more silken still. Invading with exquisite care, he sought the small, hidden triangle of curling hair and the soft folds within that were silkiest of all.

Warm and moist, swollen and tight, her flesh was like the holiest of grails, her fine curls the most amazing of treasured fleeces. Gently questing, he captured the center of her with the heat and firmness of his palm, plundered it with delicate thoroughness yet near mindless need, fingering the small bud of her femininity that swelled under his ministrations while she moaned into his mouth.

His breath rasped in his chest, his back and side burned with the strain he placed upon them; the stitch line stung with the perspiration that seeped to the surface of his skin. Still he would not stop, could not until he had probed deep inside her moist heat, until he felt her stiffen, shuddering on a gasping cry before she turned boneless in his arms.

Resting his forehead against hers, breathing in ragged difficulty, he held her until the tripping, stumbling rhythm of his heart grew calm again and sanity came to mock him with the crucial question of just what he had done. Yes, and who was more the victim, the lady or himself?

He released her with the creak of reluctant muscles, then straightened her crumpled skirts, brushing them into place again. "Forgive me," he began.

"No. There is nothing which requires . . ."

"I don't regret the past few minutes," he said, his voice not quite even, "only the need to end them. Nathaniel will be returning. Who he may bring with him, not even I can guess."

"Oh. Indeed."

She stirred, uncurled her fingers from the tight grasp she held on the lapel of his dressing gown, making a small, oddly touching attempt to smooth the brocade she had crushed. She sat up then. Her eyes met his for a long instant while wild rose color bloomed across her cheekbones. Such vulnerability, such doubt and confusion lay in their depths that compunction washed over Gavin in a hot wave. He touched his tongue to his lips. "Perhaps we should talk, *chérie*, about these secrets we all keep."

"No, don't. I'm not sure I can, not now."

Her lashes flickered before she turned her head away. Grasping the arm of his chair, she levered herself erect without touching him any more than was necessary. She shook out her gown while he watched, touched her hair, tucked in a few stray hairs. Gathering her dignity around her like a beloved shawl, she stepped away to what must seem to her a safe distance.

What had just happened changed nothing for her, he saw that clearly. Why he had expected that it might, he could not have said, though he was still disappointed. "I am grateful," he said evenly, "for the company at dinner. You must come again."

She did not look at him as she answered, though her color deepened, even touched the tips of her ears which gleamed, beguilingly, through the curls that spiraled around them. "Perhaps I will, since it has been so instructive. You are ever the consummate tutor. It may be you will have another lesson for me."

His brows drew together over his nose. "I did not mean to mock you."

"Did you not? It turned out that way nonetheless. I will remember, never fear."

He was left with nothing to say while she went quickly from the bedchamber. He sat quite still for long moments while her footsteps faded. Then, clenching his teeth against the drawing ache of his stitches, he poured more wine and sat turning the glass, frowning into the fire. By the time Nathaniel returned, the wine bottle was empty and the crystal stem lay in shining, sharp-edged pieces on the marble hearth.

His self-appointed valet-cum-nurse came to kneel before him, picking up the broken shards of crystal. Intent on the chore, he asked, "You have an accident or a tantrum?"

"Either way, a replacement is owed Madame Herriot."

"And Madame Faucher, what is owed to her?"

Gavin directed a hard stare at the back of the boy's head. "What do you mean?"

"She looked upset when she came outa here. Yeah, and like she'd been in a hurricane."

"No one else saw?"

"Happens not. I was sitting down in the courtyard. "Don't much like cheese and nuts, so was having a smoke while Madame Herriot and the others got done. Monsieur Nick was at dinner, you know, and Madame Juliette."

"I am obliged for the information. But you were speaking of Madame Faucher."

"Saw her goin' along to her chamber as if

361

the fiends of hell were after her. So what went on up here?"

"Nothing of importance or that the lady did not invite."

"You certain-sure?"

It was a question that had exercised his mind without results during these past several minutes. "Any error can be founded in a truth. How then can we be certain of anything?"

"You can."

"Your faith might be touching were it not so damning."

"You are." Avoiding his gaze, the boy moved away to the bed where he began to straighten the covers.

"Chivalric and morally pure as a young knight of old. What a pity the lady doesn't know she has a champion. Though how you learned your attitude toward women while living on the street is more than I can see."

"I learned it from Madame Lisette and Madame Juliette along with a tad more grammar. Yes, and from you." Nathaniel returned to stand in front of him, straight and tall with the firelight behind him. An unlikely avenging angel, but an effective one. "Are you ready?"

"As ever." Gavin used the arm the boy offered to hoist himself from the deep chair, accepting its support as he eased toward the bed. Settling on the mattress, he closed his eyes.

A short time later, he dismissed his helper to his adjoining chamber for an hour or two of the privacy they both required. The boy's words remained with him, however, routing the healing sleep he might have managed.

What if Nathaniel was right and he was wrong? What if he had misjudged Ariadne? He had condemned her on scant evidence. It could be mere coincidence that she was closely connected to Francis Dorelle. That she had refused to allow him to dispatch her enemy for her could be a matter of pride rather than because it was physically impossible for him to challenge himself.

What if she did not want him dead? What if all she had offered with his dinner had been companionship with no trace of seduction in it?

If that was all that had been in her mind, then he had insulted an innocent lady and led her down the path toward corruption. He had taken her kisses and her sighs and turned them into something he could not bear to look upon.

If he was wrong, then he owed her an *amende honorable* with whatever weapon she might care to choose. There must be a way to discover if it was required. He had only to find it.

It was a quest at which he could not fail for the consequences were much too grim. He would meet the lovely Ariadne on any ground she preferred, if that was the way it must be, but his heart shrank inside him at the thought of facing her with nothing to prevent injury to either one except a few layers of linen and his best intentions. Sterling objectives on his part had not, in the past, prevented tragedy.

He was still staring into the cream-colored sunburst of cotton fabric that lined the tester above his bed, when a knock came on the door. It was brisk and totally without diffidence. To guess who it heralded was easy, given Nathaniel's report of the dinner guests.

"Come."

Nicholas Pasquale, with the prerogative of a half brother, had already advanced three long steps into the bedchamber. Glancing around, he found a straight-backed chair against the wall that he pulled forward, then turned and straddled. "Still wrapped up in sheets and nightshirts, I see," he said, crossing his arms over the back and giving Gavin a thorough appraisal. "Nothing like the care of a female household to keep a man flat on his back."

"You wound me," Gavin said in mock protest. "Malingering is the last thing I would attempt under such strict supervision."

"Yes, I'm sure Madame Faucher is formidable, though we all know Maurelle has nougat for a heart. If she had not, you would be elsewhere. And complaining about it."

"Is that how you see the lady, as formidable?"

A wry smile curled Nicholas's mouth as he shook his head. "The description is Juliette's. She was most impressed with the report of her generalship in getting you loaded and hauled here from the dueling field."

"But she doesn't care for her?"

"Oh, that doesn't follow at all. Madame Faucher may be lacking the gentle disposition of my lady wife, but Juliette admires her prodigiously, having no prejudice against ladies who know what they want and do their utmost to get it. Beneath my Juliette's smiles and willingness to please lies a will of iron, I do assure you. She merely prefers using sweet reason to have her way."

"Which you prefer to allow, being no more eager for a fight."

Laughter leaped into the rich brown of his half brother's eyes. "It's so much more . . . pleasurable that way, you see." He sobered. "Are you malingering, in truth, or have you some fever or putrefaction of your wound to keep you here?"

"Neither. It's a question of will and wiles."

"So I suspected. Juliette believes you have some veiled purpose of a Machiavellian nature that may rebound on your head."

"Being something of a conspirator herself, according to her husband, she won't reveal this suspicion?"

"Doubtful, I should think," Nicholas said, the smile fading from his eyes. "She believes in signs and portents, you know, so feels Ariadne Faucher has been sent to lead you from the labyrinth of your own dark design, a savior like her namesake."

The Greek myth had not been far from Gavin's thoughts since meeting Ariadne. It was not surprising to hear someone else had made the association. "I am no Theseus of old, hanging onto a piece of thread for my salvation."

"You must argue that with Juliette. Still, I would not say she is wrong. I learned better months ago."

Gavin let it pass, but the image would not leave his mind. It remained while he told his half brother, his only real confidant in the city, something of what he intended, also while he asked, again, after the black stallion from Caid's stable that he had ridden in the duel. It was there as they spoke of the latest developments concerning the annexation of Texas as a state, principally the addition of Southern-born John C. Calhoun to President Tyler's cabinet as Secretary of State following the death of former Secretary Upshar in the calamitous explosion aboard U.S.S. *Princeton* while it was being inspected by the president's delegation. Calhoun seemed certain to sign any annexation treaty presented to him, but it was questionable whether the senate would approve it with the Mexican government declaring that as tantamount to a declaration of war.

If this last event came to pass, as had long been expected in New Orleans, then the legions that tramped back and forth every week in the Place d'Armes would finally march away, courage high, down the long road to Mexico.

Gavin was not anxious to see war happen. In the first place, the exodus of these would-be soldiers would leave the Passage de la Bourse extremely quiet. Then he had no particular wish to see the men he faced on the fencing strip in his salon buried in Mexican sand or returned to the city in a preservative bath of raw rum. As for going himself, this was not his country, therefore loyalty did not require it nor intelligence recommend it.

When Nicholas, his concern and curiosity satisfied, went away again, Gavin returned to his perusal of the tester above his head. His thoughts were not on war or its possibilities, however, but on Ariadne as a Greek goddess, daughter of the sun god Helios of Crete, gowned in flowing white draperies over unconfined curves and with her hair drifting in a dark cloud around her. Imperious, tempting and possibly kind, she seemed to beckon. But if she had a life-preserving thread to offer, she kept it hidden. And it was impossible to see what lay behind her smile.

Goddesses, insofar as he remembered from his study of their stories while learning his Greek and Latin, were not known for their mercy.

TWENTY-TWO

It was on her return from a fitting with Madame Pluche for her mourning wear two days later that Ariadne saw Sasha for the first time since the duel. He approached her on the street just outside the dressmaker's house, tucking his cane under his arm and sweeping the banquette with his hat as he bowed to her and her companion, Madame Zoe Savoie. "What a joy it is to see you, my Ariadne," he said when greetings had been exchanged and the requisite pleasantries broached and dismissed. "I so longed to come to you before I go, to explain this affair with the Englishman and my conduct which must seem unforgivable. But you surely see how it is, the difficulties, when he is there in the same house."

"Yes, of course," she said to deflect what could be embarrassing excuses. "You really are leaving?"

"With the greatest reluctance, you may be

369

sure. My dear one, only say you will join me for the return to France. I shall be the happiest of men in spite of my disgrace."

"My plan has always been to remain here through the *saison des visites,* as you know. I'm sorry, but I cannot change it at a moment's notice." She tried to keep the coolness from her voice but wasn't sure she managed.

"Because of the events on the dueling field, yes? I know not what came over me, I swear to you. It was madness, I think, because the Englishman seemed so certain of having you."

"Did he indeed?"

"He spoke so slightingly, with such calculation, during the exchange which led —"

Madame Zoe, waiting until that moment with a look of determined patience on her face, reared back her head as she spoke in interruption. "You are certain of that, monsieur? It does not sound like the Monsieur Blackford that I know."

Sasha barely glanced at her. "You were not there, madame. I was, to my eternal regret."

"But it was you who forced the duel upon Gavin, you who sought him out at his atelier for that purpose. Those who were there say you gave him no choice except to issue a

370

cartel, and used references to Ariadne to achieve it."

Ariadne had guessed something of the matter, but this was the first time she had heard it confirmed. Madame Zoe, as the sword masters called her, being on terms of friendship with them and their wives, doubtless had sources of information denied to her.

"The heat of the moment, as I said before," Sasha proclaimed with a wave of his hand, as if brushing away an annoying fly. "The exact words I do not recall, merely that the exchange grew so insulting it could not be endured."

"But it was Blackford who challenged you," Madame Zoe insisted with lifted brows. "I believe it must have been he who heard something which required redress."

"Really, *madame,*" Sasha began.

"Never mind, the thing is finished and can't be undone," Ariadne said, overriding his protests as she held out her hand to him. "All that is left is to wish you godspeed on your journey and good fortune on your landing."

"You are kindness itself, as always," he said taking her fingers and lifting them to his mouth, his lips hot through her glove. "It may be I will give myself the pleasure of

371

taking a more formal leave of you before I sail. When is it that Monsieur Blackford removes to his lodgings?"

"As to that, I can't say. He was most grievously injured."

Sasha gave a disparaging shrug. "I barely touched him, I'm sure, and the flow of blood makes these things appear worse than they are in fact. Besides, men of his stripe heal with astonishing ease."

To argue was pointless and might make it appear her concern was more personal than it should be. "You must do as you think best."

"I shall, madame, never fear," he said, his pale blue gaze hooded. Releasing her, he tipped his hat and nodded a farewell to Madame Zoe. He strode away down the banquette with his shoulders back, swinging his cane forward like a weapon with his every stride.

"A dangerous ass, that," Madame Zoe said as she stared after him, "but an ass all the same. You would think one of his canes had been shoved up his — but never mind."

"Do you think so?" To Ariadne, he seemed merely pompous and overly fond of having his own way.

"Those who do not see themselves and events as they are, who can't recognize that others may have a different view, are always dangerous. They so often must force matters to conform to their desires, removing anything that stands in their way."

"Or anyone? Sasha tried that and discovered it did not work."

"That doesn't mean he won't attempt the same again."

A shiver feathered down the back of Ariadne's neck as she considered how unfit Gavin was as yet to face another such threat. Abruptly, she was glad beyond words that Maurelle had insisted he recuperate at the town house. Not that his life was so important. No, it was simply that she wanted no other injury he might sustain to be upon her head. If that seemed a bit ridiculous in light of her vowed intentions, then she could not help it. It made a difference in her mind.

"Perhaps I am wrong," Madame Zoe said as she adjusted the long bottle-green shawl she wore, throwing an end over one shoulder with theatrical aplomb. "We must hope so, yes? If we cannot feel that joy and pleasure will always triumph over death and destruction then we might as well all slit our wrists and be done with it."

Beneath her flamboyant manner and sense of fashion, the diva was a wise woman,

Ariadne reflected. Not so long ago, she might not have seen it, or, seeing, appreciated it. What had changed? She thought it might have something to do with the easy manners and laissez-faire attitude of the New Orleans French Creoles. Or maybe the change was in herself, she didn't know. She was glad of it, regardless.

"What say you to a pastry to take the sour taste from our mouths, *chère?*" Madame Zoe nodded toward a *pâtisserie* with its blue and gold window decor just down the street. "I feel the need of a crème coronet, and there are tables on the sidewalk so we can't be accused of plying the oldest trade by seating ourselves inside without a male escort."

"An excellent idea, and a coffee to go with it, I think. I'm a little chilled."

It was a pleasant interlude, made even more agreeable by the stories told by the diva. She regaled Ariadne with the fraught courtships of the sword masters who were Gavin's friends, particularly that of his half brother, Nicholas, which seemed to have taken place in the midst of a horde of street boys. He and his Juliette were currently trying to entice the youngsters into the newly endowed St. Joseph's Orphanage which Nicholas helped to support or else find positions for them, such as Nathaniel's with Gavin. Their luck was spotty, since the boys were not always ready to give up the freedom of the streets. In the meantime, the sword masters seemed to have appointed themselves their guardians, keeping an eye on their movements, protecting and correcting as necessary.

The impression Ariadne gained was of a unique solidarity among the masters at arms. She had thought of Gavin Blackford as living in isolation, like an outcast. This increased perspective on the fullness of his life was disturbing.

She parted company with the opera singer, finally, at the entrance to the Herriot town house. Walking through the tunnel-like entranceway, she removed her bonnet of fine Italian straw shirred inside the brim with pink silk to match her gray and pink walking costume, then tied the bonnet strings in a bow and looped them over her arm like a basket while she began to loosen the fingertips of her pink gloves. She was almost at the end of the passage, where it emerged into the courtyard, when she heard a rhythmic beat and clang that had become all too familiar. She stopped, standing quite still, listening for long seconds before continuing with quickened steps. By the time she reached the open court, she was almost running.

What she expected to see, she could not have said — Nathaniel holding the stairs against Sasha at the sword point, perhaps, or even Gavin protecting himself at all costs. She did not expect to see Maurelle's injured guest conducting a lesson in the open air, moving gingerly back and forth over the slate-gray paving stones that were damp with the first droplets of a blowing mist while his lilting voice mingled with the whisper of the rising wind in the tattered leaves of the banana tree.

"What is the meaning of this?" she demanded, coming to an abrupt halt with alarm jangling at her nerve endings like a servant's bell. "Are you trying to kill yourself?"

Gavin spared her the briefest of glances while parrying in tierce. At his signal, then, the two men stepped from their guard positions and turned to face her with foils in hand. "Nursemaid or scold, we are undone by your concern," he said with a wry smile. "The idea was merely to limber stiff muscles and prevent dead monotony from claiming another victim."

"Told you she wouldn't like it," Nathaniel said in accusation.

"And who is supposed to stitch you back up like an unraveled seam if you go too far?" she demanded. "It isn't the kind of needle-work at which I excel. Or enjoy."

His eyes turned brightly blue with amusement allied to what seemed startled acceptance. "You really are responsible for the row of silk knots down my back?"

"Since the doctor's stitches looked like shoe lacing."

"I don't mean to complain, but . . ."

"Then don't." Annoyance made her voice shake.

"Oh, I recognize the ingratitude, but it's a matter of sleeping, you understand. If you could see your way to making them more comfortable . . ."

"It's too early to remove them, as you should know if you have as much experience as you claim."

"Five full days, almost six with today. A lifetime."

"Not long enough," she insisted. At least he seemed to have caused no damage. The white bandaging which covered the stitches, faintly visible under the linen of his shirt, showed no seeping spots of blood. His face was a little flushed but that could be from exertion. His breathing, though deep enough to cause an obvious rise and fall of his chest, did not seem labored.

He appeared, in fact, to be amazingly fit as he stood there in his shirt sleeves and pantaloons, with his hair tousled into unruly strands of gold, and Turkish slippers on his feet. More handsome than he had any right to be, able to take on his portion of the known world and more, he left her breathless, shaken to the core, and incensed that he could do it with no intention of affecting her whatsoever.

Or was that strictly true? Something bright and hot in his eyes sent the blood tripping along her veins while memory blossomed inside her of his mouth upon hers, his bandage-wrapped chest under her spread fingers, and his hand, oh, his hand beneath her skirts . . .

The same memory was in his smile, his eyes, the sudden tightening of his grasp on the hilt of his foil. It lay between them like a thrown gauntlet, impossible to ignore, dangerous to contemplate, exhilarating to anticipate.

And she did look forward to what might come next. It was like a bout on the fencing strip, attack and parry, move and counter-move, defense and riposte in a time-honored dance that moved inevitably to a single conclusion, a similar, ultimate penetration.

When?

She could not tell. She only knew that it would happen. It must. There was no other way unless she withdrew from the sensual *phrase d'armes* which held them. That she could never do, not and remain true to her vow.

"If you are well enough to instruct Nathaniel," she said slowly, "it may be that we can continue our lessons by tomorrow evening."

Gavin considered her with an unblinking gaze for long seconds while swift thought moved behind his carefully schooled features. Or so it seemed to Ariadne, though the impression vanished scant seconds later.

"Yes, of course, madame," he answered, inclining his head so light caught in the gold waves of his hair even in the overcast gray of the afternoon. "Or it could be tonight if you wish it."

Tonight. Did he mean . . . ?

It was impossible to know what he meant. He was far too armored inside himself to be so easily read.

Her smile was cool, or at least she hoped that it might appear so. "I do wish it, Monsieur Blackford. I wish it very much."

"Your pleasure is ever my goal," he answered with bright audacity and a sweeping salute of his sword.

He meant that exactly as it sounded, she knew that much with absolute certainty for she had experienced the full demonstration of it. Heat surged into her face in a blinding rush, and the urge to slap him was so strong that she almost wrung her kidskin gloves from her hands. Turning with conscious grace, she moved toward the stairs, speaking over her shoulder. "Until our usual hour, then, Monsieur Blackford."

"I shall be waiting."

No doubt he would be, she fumed to herself as she mounted to the main floor. He thought she would melt into his arms as she had two nights before, would turn to him in glad surrender for the hot, sweet fervour of his kisses and incredible knowledge of feminine responses. He expected her to succumb for the unsuspected tumult of passion he could arouse in her, an upheaval such as she had never known in her marriage. He was wrong. It would not end as he intended tonight, not if she could help it.

It was later, while dressing for dinner, that it came to Ariadne what this night might portend. The advantage in this match would be hers. At the moment, while Gavin was still recovering from his injuries, she could move faster than he, was possibly just as strong. She had been looking for a weakness of personality or habit. It had not occurred to her that she would ever have a chance of physical equality.

Gavin had known. That was why he had hesitated earlier, she thought. What did that suggest? Could he suspect her purpose after all?

No, surely not. It need only mean he knew she had been angry and remembered her penchant for attacking in a temper. Why should he think anything more than that? Their foils would be blunted and bodies protected by padding, after all.

Was this finally the culmination of her plans? Could she abandon all scruples in order to best him?

Women were said to have no honor in their dealings with men, but that was because they were unequal in most encounters. They could not afford to be choosy in the measures they used to even the odds. Even so, she was reluctant to take the way which lay open to her. That instinctive aversion was the most troubling aspect of the coming contest.

The rain began once more in earnest as night fell. Endlessly drumming on the rooftop, it poured down as if it meant never to stop. It streamed from the eaves into the courtyard in silver runnels as Ariadne left her bedchamber just before midnight and walked down the gallery toward the *garçonnière* chamber that had become their fencing salon. Lightning flashed, white tinted with gold, showing the courtyard paving below running ankle-deep in water that channeled in a millrace toward the entry passage and along it into the street. Wind-blown mist swept in upon the gallery floor so she walked close to the interior wall. Regardless, the moist freshness was welcome against her skin.

She felt on edge, already overheated in spite of the freedom of her body in her man's shirt and pantaloons. Her shirt grew damp and limp, and she felt her nipples tighten with the contrast between her warmth and the night coolness, yes, and something more that she would not name. For an instant, she had an almost overpowering urge to turn back to the quiet safety of her bedchamber, to her corset and petticoats.

Too late.

Gavin lounged in the doorway ahead of her, one shoulder propped against the frame as he watched the storm. He straightened, sketched a bow as she came closer.

"A wild night," he said. "We will be lucky if the candles stay lit."

His voice held some minor note that, like the pure sound of a violin, raised echoes inside her. It was infuriating to feel her nipples tighten still further, becoming almost painful as they pressed against the linen of her shirt.

"I'm sure we shall manage," she said in clipped tones.

"And if all else fails we can proceed in the dark," he answered, backing away a step, indicating with a brief gesture that she should enter the long room before him.

The glance she gave him was searching as she brushed past. Whatever he meant to imply was hidden behind the polite cast of his features. Still it lingered, disturbingly, in his smile.

He did not look incapacitated in any way. He appeared, in fact, remarkably hale and hearty. If she had not known about the long red line that stitched its way down his back before curving around toward his waist, she would never have guessed. Nevertheless, she did know.

"You are quite certain you are capable of this lesson?"

"Your concern unmans me," he said with a lifted brow. "We might, if you prefer, find other ways of passing the time."

She could feel the flush that mantled her throat mounting to her forehead. To conceal it, she began to don her mask and padding that lay ready. "So you hinted before. I'm not sure that would be wise."

"Wisdom being something to be desired? I had not thought it."

His mood of irony was catching, or so it seemed. "The inclination," she said with precision, "comes and goes. At the moment, it is in ascendancy."

"Spirit over flesh, I do see. You will tell me, I hope, if there is a shift."

"I'm not sure I will," she said over her shoulder. "You are far too sure of yourself already."

"A fallacy. Where you are concerned, I am not sure at all." He went on with the barest of pauses caused in part by the need to assume his own protective covering. "Will you choose your weapon?"

He had stepped to the table where the foils were laid ready, she saw as she turned to face him. "I have no preference. You choose for me."

"Trust indeed, or perhaps depend on chivalry to give you the better blade of the two."

The smile she gave him held real amusement since something of the kind had crossed her mind. "Fairness, rather."

"Oh, I am always fair."

That seemed to suggest that he was not always chivalrous. "I am forewarned."

"So you are," he murmured as he tried the blades in turn before swinging around with one in either hand. "So you are."

She caught the foil he tossed her because she was expecting it. Immediately, she turned away from him toward the long stretch of canvas that appeared a dirty gray in the uncertain glow of the fluttering ranks of candles on their stands. Her movements deliberate, she donned protective gear, as he was doing, then took her place on their makeshift piste.

How familiar it had become to face him there with the prescribed distance separating them, to salute him, then cross his blade, letting steel kiss steel in a first touch like two lovers meeting. If he was less strong than before, it was not readily apparent in the feel of his foil against hers. That contact was as powerful and as certain as ever.

In that instant, she was reminded of his lesson in control meted out not so long ago. A deep drawing sensation assailed her at the memory, and she tightened the muscles of her abdomen against it. Such things could not be allowed to matter. She forced it from her mind, forced everything away from her except the glittering tip of the blade before her and the rampant will of the man who held it. That last she must not forget, now or ever.

Was she ready? Doubt of her skill assaulted her. She was a relatively new pupil of this ancient art, when all was said and done. But if her skill was lacking, it meant nothing more dangerous than another defeat at his hands.

They began, as always, at Gavin's signal. It was like a dance, a centuries-old *pavane* of advance, parry and riposte in measured rhythm. Each movement called for its counter; each step matched and mated, as graceful as any set of movements between a man and woman. Their shadows moved over the floor, met and parted on the walls. The smoky air currents in the room shifted with their swift lunges, joined with the wind that swirled in the open French doors to make the candle flames sway and flatten before either dying away or leaping high again. The bell-like chiming of their blades echoed against the walls, music with a marked beat that broke now and then into a passionate counterpoint, sliding down a grating scale of steel into attunement.

Abruptly a gust like a small tornado swirled into the room, shivering the candle flames burning nearest the door. They hopped, fluttering on their wicks an instant before several of them went out, leaving black tails of smoke. That left only a half-dozen to guide their movements.

Gavin raised a hand to signal a halt and stepped out of position. He said nothing about the diminished light, however.

"You're holding back," he said, the words hollow from behind the mask that concealed his features.

"No more than you." Her answer was a trifle breathless from exertion. She could barely see his eyes through the metal grid. Across from the door, a silver-branched set of six candlesticks had only two candles left burning. Their acrid smoke drifted in the air along with the scent from the courtyard of rain-drenched tea olive. She coughed briefly as it caught in her throat.

"Don't."

"Don't?" For an instant, she thought he meant her attempt to clear her breathing.

"Don't hold back." He indicated with a flick of his foil tip that they would resume the guard position.

How could she not? The question plagued her as they began again. The foils in their

387

hands, though neither as heavy or lethal as the sabers used in the dueling field match between Sasha and Gavin, were jangling reminders in the back of her mind. That bout had ended in blood. She could not stop thinking of the moment when Sasha's sword had flashed down, slicing across Gavin's back. She had expected he would be decapitated, maimed, crippled for life. Every move he made now, every lunge, must cause him pain. How could it be otherwise?

He was no less powerful for it, that much she was forced to admit. Still he was not the same. His timing was off, lacking the effortless coordination of body and mind he had shown before. His recoveries were slower, more a matter of driving intelligence than instinct. He kept to his set position as much as possible, and he did not take the advantage he might have of her mistakes. He seldom attacked at all, letting her come to him, letting her set the pace while he defended, always defended.

She could strike. The means was at hand. They were alone and the house was quiet around them. All she had to do was surge into an attack, using the blunted end of her foil to rip through his padding. It could be done.

Gavin would retaliate in kind; she could

expect no less. No matter, her greatest chance of besting him was here, tonight, and she could not be sure it would ever come again. She had suspected it before and was doubly certain of it now.

It was impossible. Something inside her rejected that devious victory. There could be no satisfaction in defeating him under such circumstances.

Defeating him?

She meant to kill him, not just to best him. Yes of course she did. Her aim had not changed.

Had it?

Where was the burning hatred that had sustained her for so long? What had become of it?

Her closeness to Gavin Blackford might have been a costly error. Before, he had been a fiend in human form in her mind. Now he had taken on the guise of a man with all the attendant possibilities for good as well as evil. He had shown himself kind and caring and eminently honorable as well as proud; he viewed the world with as much tolerant amusement as cynicism.

What was she to do? Her arm ached, and her mind was weary. This fight was going nowhere, gaining nothing, proving nothing beyond the grim endurance of the man who faced her. The shuffling of their feet and snick of their blades were slowing. They could barely see in the flickering gloom.

Another candle flame sputtered and died in a curling plume of smoke. Ariadne raised her hand, said quite clearly, "Stop."

"Madame?"

He stepped back and stood watching her through his mask, the point of his foil trailing on the floor. She wondered briefly if it was because he could no longer lift his arm. "You are not fit enough for this, I think. I should not have suggested it."

"Generous of spirit as well as valiant — though I wonder what I can have done to make you think me unfit."

"It was you who taught me to read my opponent."

"And if I say I was holding back for other reasons?"

She tested the timbre of his voice but no shadow of purpose or emotion layered it. "What could they be?"

"To see what you have learned, perhaps, or what you would teach me."

Surprise shook a laugh from her. "Teach you? That doesn't seem likely."

"You have shown me that the female of our species, unlike the male, is selective when she hunts, and retains the ability to reason in the heat of pursuit."

"I can't think how you came by that revelation." Or at least she chose not to.

"You could have taken me in these last few minutes. The puzzlement of it is why you refrained."

Thunder rolled in the night beyond the open door, followed by a flash of lightning that painted the courtyard in shades of blue and silver. Wind whipped into the room, lifting the edge of the canvas strip on which they stood, swaying the draperies at the window, extinguishing the last of the candles.

Darkness closed around them. Outside, the banana and palm trees thrashed and clattered. Blown rain spattered onto the gallery floor. The clash of fretted impulse and need inside Ariadne was no less violent. She dropped her foil so it thudded to the canvas then rolled onto the hardwood floor with a hollow clang. "I still can," she said, and began to walk toward him while dragging off her mask and tossing it aside, removing her chest padding and letting it drop. Her footsteps were almost soundless in the windswept night.

"No doubt," he answered, "if your weapon is ancient wiles flavored with sacrifice, irrational but glorious. And I could well allow it. But will you be glad in the morning?"

"I don't know. Shall we see?"

When she did not falter, did not turn back, he dropped his foil, divested himself of mask and padding in his turn, then set his feet. White-faced in the dark, with silver lightning reflected in the blue of his eyes, he watched her come ever closer. When she was a mere step away, he opened his arms and gathered her to him.

It was what she craved in that rebellious portion of her mind that refused to consider reason or consequences, past or future. She wanted him, needed to be held, ached to be loved with a desperation that would have been humiliating if she had thought he guessed it. But how could he when she had given no sign she could recall, had not known it herself, had even thought otherwise, until this moment?

Yes, and what harm was there in it, after all? To feel desire was a natural, even a necessary, part of life. It meant nothing beyond the moment. And if she could not seek his death just now, she might still discover a way to make him know the pain of loss she felt when she thought of Francis.

That anguish was in her kiss as he lowered his head to take her mouth; it crowded her throat with tears. Nonetheless it was comfort she sought from him as she leaned into his strength, pressing her breasts to the hard planes of his chest, feeling the hard musculature of his thighs against her own that were shockingly unprotected without her skirts.

She slid her hands to his shoulders then around the strong column of his neck, tangling her fingers in the thick gold silk of his hair where it met his spine. Applying pressure, she deepened their kiss in a swirling clash of tongues and an agony of yearning.

He splayed long aristocratic fingers over her back, clasping her flesh as if to impress the feel of it into his brain, then smoothed downward until he captured the curve of her hip, kneading the resilient softness, drawing her more firmly against his hard heat. And by slow degrees, he took her down with him, down to their knees and then lower to the canvas strip where he shoved aside masks and padding and weapons, making room, making a bed of what had been their battleground.

Yet, in its way, it was an arena of combat still, as they fought their way out of boots, shirts, pantaloons and such unmentionables as they had chosen in anticipation of the unfettered exchange of touches with a foil.

Splendidly naked, they lay bathed in the flashes of lightning and fine spray of blown rain through open doors while they traced with delicate care and diligent longing the sheen of muscles, curves of breasts, glint of fine, curling hair. They did not notice, didn't feel the power of the storm as they cupped and tasted, trailed kisses over hot skin, spread their palms to gather sensation or to feel the turbulent throb of the blood that raced in their veins.

Ariadne was on fire. Her heartbeat thundered in her ears. Like a child learning forbidden secrets, she felt wicked yet enthralled, daring and damned. Beneath it, she was aware of how magnificently made was the man who lay with her, his broad shoulders, taut waist wrapped with muscle, flat belly, lean flanks, hard thighs and restrained power. It thrilled her, left her drugged with longing.

His touch was magic, as if he understood without word or gesture the exact place to kiss, to touch with tongue or clever, clever fingers. His features reflected wonder, his unhurried movements suggested that he intended sybaritic gratification of every pleasure. Gently searching, he removed the pins from her hair, spread the long tresses around her, over her like a dark net through which he sought the tightly knotted peak of her breast. The heat of his mouth, the hot flick of his tongue followed by tugging, insistent suction, took her breath, made her tremble, made her arch her back for more. He stifled her low moan with his mouth, a sign of tender concern that embarrassed yet incited her. Half mad, she clung to him, sliding her hands over his arms, his chest, avoiding his bandaging but seeking the sword-like projection of his body that in its scorching silk over steel promised surcease.

Finally, when they were both shaking, thighs quivering and breath rasping in their chest, they fitted their bodies together, pulsing firmness into moist, welcoming softness. Moving in a parody of advance and retreat, parry and riposte, they strove together as if only one of them could be the victor.

Ariadne took him inside her, absorbing his power as he strained with bunched muscles and fierce, thudding, hot-eyed effort. She took him until her being shattered, coalescing around him in rhythmic pulsations. She cried his name, arching against him with muscles so locked in violent joy that she could not move, would not allow him to stir — until he kissed her hard, fast and deep, then dragged free, rolling away as his own shuddering completion overtook him.

He had been less lost in his paroxysm of pleasure than had she. He had thought to withdraw, preserving her from the consequences of their joining, from the possibility of a child that might have trapped him, trapped them both.

That thought had not crossed her mind from start to finish, perhaps because it had never been a factor in her marriage. It was a stunning realization.

Lying there on that gritty canvas fencing strip, unclothed, replete, her hair spread in a tangled mass around her, thighs open, bereft, she was no longer certain who had taken whom in the moments just past. And she was afraid, deathly afraid of what she might feel, after all, when morning came.

TWENTY-THREE

The note was brought to her in bed with her café au lait. Tucked under the small silver pot of hot milk by Adele, it had no doubt been put there in return for a handsome *pourboire*. Ariadne thought for an instant that it might be from Gavin, an apology for the night before, another assignation, even a declaration of how he might feel toward her. Her fingers were not quite steady as she broke the seal, unfolded the stiff paper.

It was from Sasha.

He had a matter of grave importance he wished to discuss with her. If she should chance to be walking in Cabildo's arcade this morning, it would be his great pleasure to stroll a few minutes in her company. The situation being what it was, it would be best if her only companion was the usual maid carrying a shopping basket for her purchases. He was her devoted etc . . . etc. . . .

It was a rendezvous he suggested, no more and no less. Why he could not simply call upon her, Ariadne could not see. Maurelle might not be in complete charity with him after his conduct on the dueling field, but she was too indolent to refuse him admittance or be actively spiteful once he sat in her salon. The likelihood of his being forced to confront the man he had injured in such a discreditable manner was slight. Gavin had, in the main, kept to himself; certainly he had not run free about the town house.

The places he *had* appeared rose up in Ariadne's mind in brilliant remembrance but she forced them down again. She would not think about the night before, of making love on the canvas-cushioned floor of the dark *garçonnière* chamber like some common *putain* without modesty or discretion. She would not, no matter how it made her stomach muscles flutter or how overheated she became. Fiercely, she concentrated on the note once more.

A matter of grave importance.

What did Sasha mean by that? If the issue was really all that dire, surely he would have come to her. It was unreasonable to expect her to go to him.

She had gone to Gavin the night before — and see where it had gotten her. Lifting a hand, she rubbed at the ache between her eyes.

The two of them had donned their clothes again and left the practice chamber, separating at the door of her bedchamber since she had a pressing need to put herself back to rights, to brush her hair, remove her men's garments and bathe before bed. But she wasn't going to think of that, or of the kiss he had placed upon her brow, his smile, his bow, his whimsical voice quoting some fragment of a poem as he backed away a few steps before walking down the gallery to his own chamber.

Sweetest love, I do not go,
For weariness of thee.
Nor in hope the world can show,
A fitter love for me;
But since that I
Must die at last, 'tis best,
To use my self in jest
Thus by feign'd deaths to die.

It was, she thought, from the indefatigable scribbler, Donne. But what on earth had he meant by it? Why give her a poem with its reminders, its echoes of pain due to her foster brother's interest in meter and rhyme? Why declaim a fragment that spoke of death

399

unless it was because it also spoke of leaving a lover.

She could not untangle the mystery, certainly could not accept that he felt himself to be a lover in truth. The intimate moments they had shared had nothing to do with love. They did not, even if she could go only a few moments without reliving them.

She wasn't going to do it again. No, not now.

Nor would she go to meet Sasha. To encourage him was pointless and perhaps even a little cruel. Whatever ostracism he might be suffering while waiting for his ship to post its sailing orders had been brought on by himself. The dastardly slash at Gavin's mount, clearly against the set rules of their engagement with sabers, had been his decision, his betrayal. She sympathized with his isolation but could not condone the action that led to it. If he still hoped she might change her mind and leave the city with him, then he must be disappointed. She was out of all sympathy with him.

Oh, but did she really want Sasha to come here, where he might come face to face with Gavin? What if a meeting led to another confrontation?

It might be as well if she saw him, after

all. The small outing would get her away from the town house for a short while. If she left at once, she could stop on the way to see if the dressmaker was finished with her gowns. She would also have a little more time to compose herself and decide what she would say, how she would act, when she saw Gavin again.

She would dress then, and go. Now, at once. And all the rest of it could wait until she returned.

Sasha was standing ramrod straight, hands behind his back, when Ariadne caught sight of him. His attention was on the legion that tramped up and down the parade ground of the Place d'Armes before the Cabildo. The wonder was that he had not found an excuse to join those who drilled there. He would not, she was almost certain, be the only gentleman of foreign birth to offer his services.

"The military still appeals, I see," she said as she drew near. "Perhaps you should embrace it again."

He turned and a smile shifted the cast of his features from coldness to warmth as he swept off his tall hat and executed a bow with a sharp crack of his heels. "Perhaps I shall, if I am ever allowed to return to my country. Though I would prefer to embrace you. You are looking especially well this morning, like a rose in bloom."

The somewhat shopworn compliment was, she thought, on account of her walking costume of dark rose velvet trimmed in black; still something in his face made her acutely self-conscious. It was ridiculous, for he could not know how matters had changed between her and Gavin. "You are too kind," she said, even as heat swept up her neck to her face.

He glanced around her. "You came without a maid?"

"The girl Maurelle assigned to me has been a little too interested in my comings and goings, I think. I sent her back to the town house with a gown completed by Madame Pluche. But never mind that. I trust all is well with you, and this grave matter you wish to discuss is not too drastic?"

His smile faded, leaving his pale blue eyes watchful. "No, kind madame, I am well. The time has been set for my departure from this accursed city, which pleases me mightily you may be sure. My ship sails in less than two days so this is good-bye. Yet I cannot leave without . . . that is, I have such concern for you. This is why I inquired after your maid."

"I don't understand."

"You must guard your good name, and your person. You must be warned."

"Warned? About what?" She searched his face but could see nothing there beyond his usual pride and overbearing interference.

"All is not as it seems with this Englishman. He takes advantage of the good nature of Madame Herriot, and of you, madame."

There it was again, that oblique reference to matters that were intensely private. Or was she being far too sensitive? "Please. I closed his wound with my own hands. I know how it was."

"But you are not used to such things, cannot be aware of degrees of severity. Truly, it was no great thing to such a one as this swordsman. He would have been up and about the next morning if left to himself."

"It's of no importance since he has now risen from his bed," she said. "No doubt he will be leaving us soon."

"Then now is the time of your greatest danger. I plead with you to take care, my Ariadne. He is a demon of the most diabolical sort, bent on deceiving you. He means to have you, no matter what he must do to achieve it."

"Really, Sasha." In spite of the protest, she put a hand to her throat where her high collar, fastened by a large cameo, suddenly seemed too tight.

"I assure you it is true. He was heard to say it in conversation with his brother, this Pasquale who is also a sword master. He thinks you are using these lessons between you as a ruse to injure him, even to kill him, in retaliation for the death of your loved one."

Her heart leaped in her chest, beating frantically against her ribs under the compression of her corset. "How do you know? Who told you this thing? Surely you could not have overheard them yourself?"

"I must confess to having an emissary in Madame Herriot's household. The young maid you spoke of, Adele, has been reporting to me whatever she might see or hear that concerned you."

"You . . . you paid her to inform on me?"

He stepped forward to take her gloved hand and hold it to his chest. "Forgive me, I beg of you. You must know how important your welfare is to me. I could not understand this business of fencing lessons with the Englishman. You had changed so since Paris, you were not yourself. I thought grief had made you deranged in the way that sometimes happens with widows left alone in the world. I had to know what was happening with you. I had to protect you, don't you see? Everything has been to protect you."

He believed what he was saying, she thought, he really did. That did nothing to soothe her outrage. She was appalled, even sickened as she wondered if what had passed between her and Gavin the night before had been reported to him.

"My welfare is not your concern, Alexander Novgorodcev!" She snatched her hand from his grasp and balled it into a fist so tight it endangered her glove seams. "You had no right to set a spy upon me. You say I am not myself, but what of you? You have behaved as no gentleman should — having me watched, attempting murder under the guise of an affair of honor, hacking at an unarmed man. How could you do these things?"

His features contorted as if with anguish. "For you, my Ariadne, always for you. You were slipping away from me, I could feel it. I would do anything to keep you for my own."

"*Mon Dieu!* This is not the way."

"You prefer the tactics of your swordsman? This one who worms his way into the house where you stay, enticing you into his bedchamber so he might be alone with you in the dark, putting his hands . . ."

"Stop!" she exclaimed, her voice shaking with anger like none she had ever known before. "What you have done is beyond vile. Since you have confessed it to me in your own words, you will not be surprised when I tell you I never want to see you again. Take your ship and go. And if ever we are in Paris again at the same time, you will keep your distance. You will stay far away from me or, I swear by all the saints, I will come after you with my sword!"

Sasha stared at her with his features drawn and anger and grief clashing in his eyes. Then he drew himself up. "As you wish, madame. Go back to your precious Englishman. Be his doxy or whatever he wills. It may be all you deserve."

Swinging around on his boot heel, he strode away from her with the wide skirt of his coat flapping about his ankles. She watched him go while sickness roiled inside her.

Gavin knew.

She had thought he might suspect, but no more than that. It had not seemed possible he could have discovered her purpose when she had told no one. How had he known? And for how long?

It must have begun on the day she had

seen her sister and stepfather taken from the steamboat. Her shock and horror had been so great she could not hide it, though she had tried, she had tried.

He knew, and had set out deliberately to deflect her vengeance. He had seduced her, had used her softer emotions to possess her in what had seemed passionate accord while he felt only triumph. She had been a challenge for him, no doubt. How it must have amused him to turn away her hatred, transforming it to desire.

He had almost succeeded. She had almost let her violent intentions toward him slip away. She had come close, so close to forgetting what he had done, in her concentration on how he made her feel.

Yes, yes, she had thought of seduction in her turn, had used his apparent attraction to her for her own ends. Maybe this was no less than she deserved, as Sasha had said. No matter, it still hurt. It hurt more than she had dreamed possible.

How very strange that was when she felt nothing for the English sword master beyond the ardor he had so carefully awakened inside her and, perhaps, some small gratitude for revealing to her the sensual union possible between a man and a woman. He was an attractive man and she appreciated his intelligence, but that was all.

Surely that was all.

She could not be in love with him. She refused to consider it. She despised him, and with excellent reason. He had killed Francis, plunged his sword into his chest and stopped his heart. And he had come close to taking her heart as well, along with her body and her claim to the chaste faithfulness of a widow who had known duty and affection but never passion.

She would have retribution. This terrible anguish that took her breath, squeezed her heart and blinded her with acid tears demanded it. She would kill him for what he had done. If that did not ease the pain of his treachery, it would at least restore her self-respect.

Oh, but could she do it? Could she really kill him?

If he stood before her at this moment, she was certain of it. Her rage and pain went that deep. About later, she could not be so certain. Still, something must be done.

What was it he had said on the night they met, something about a woman's revenge? She stood frowning down the Cabildo's long shadowed arcade with its dark slate paving marred by patches of mud as she considered it. Then she had it. A woman's reprisal, so he had claimed, was more subtle than a man's but more devastating because of that subtlety. Yes, that was it.

She had scorned the idea at the time, but what of now?

What if he was right after all?

Twenty-Four

Ariadne stood at the French door of her bedchamber listening to the rain that fell in the dark street below, the endless winter rain. It seemed like a minor refrain running through the days since the New Year, since she had met Gavin Blackford. It reflected her somber mood, she thought, echoed the gray desolation of her expectations.

She was waiting. Her plans had been made, everything was in readiness. She was not quite sure what would take place, knew only that this farce between her and the sword master would soon be over. It felt odd, not quite real, that it should be so. She moved, breathed, gave orders, bathed and dressed, yet it seemed that she stood outside herself, watching as if she were someone else entirely.

Something deep inside her warned against what she was about to do. She refused to heed it. She had lived with this need for revenge, this determination to have it for so long that it was a part of her. What would she put in its place if she let it go? How would she fill the emptiness?

A carriage rattled past in the street below, its top shiny with wet, its side lantern casting a moving glow on the lower wall of the house across the street. The driver huddled on the seat, a miserable figure under a limp-brimmed hat that dribbled water down his back. As it passed along, she saw a kitten in a window across the way, with a candlelit room behind it. The small gray tabby mewled plaintively as he watched a sleepy pigeon on the windowsill before him. The faint sound mingled with the music of a piano-forte as some virtuoso further down the street practiced a Mozart concerto.

It was easy to see out because only a single candle burned in the room behind her. That was not only highly convenient, but by strict design.

Light spilled from the windows of Maurelle's salon further along the street-side balcony, laying geometric designs on the canvas-covered floor and showing the rain that spattered in its collected puddles. Her hostess was busy there, Ariadne thought; Maurelle had mentioned having letters to write. No guests were with her on this dreary evening unless it was Gavin and, perhaps, Nathaniel. Ariadne didn't actually know where the sword master was at the moment. He could be reading or playing cards as easily as visiting with his hostess. She only knew it had been arranged that he would come to her at this time. And so she waited.

One moment she was alone, the next he was there. It was the draft from the door as it opened from the inner gallery, stirring her robe, dipping the candle, that warned her. She turned to see him with one hand on the doorknob, the gray light turning his hair to the hue of tarnished gold coins, leaving only a vague impression of his frock coat and cravat, pressed pantaloons and polished boots.

He had dressed for her. The knowledge threatened to close her throat before she lifted her chin, breathing deep.

His gaze was dark blue with appraisal as he scanned her rather elegant *robe à la Française* with its lightweight silk fullness and her dark hair that flowed over her shoulders and down her back. It paused on the fine batiste folds of her white nightgown, edged with black lace like a mourning handkerchief at neckline and ankle-length hem, that peeped through the robe's open

412

front. "A casual affair, I perceive," he said, his voice deeply musical. "I would have complied most happily, but your invitation did not specify."

"An oversight. It doesn't matter. Please come in."

The rings holding the draperies of gold-fringed bronze silk rattled as she turned to pull them over the window, shutting out the dusk. Releasing them, she moved to stand in front of the fire that burned in the grate. The warmth felt good on her back, though that was not her purpose. The firelight, she was well aware, faithfully outlined her form through her thin night clothes. She knew because she had already checked the effect in the cheval mirror which sat in the corner next to the bed.

Gavin noticed, of that there was little doubt. Closing the door, he came forward, his tread light and wariness in his eyes.

At least his attention was upon her.

She feared he might take her in his arms, given the warm nature of their last meeting, last parting. That was a risk she preferred to avoid. Stepping to one side, she sank onto the seat of one of the pair of armchairs before the fire and indicated that he should take the other.

Eyes narrowed a little, he dropped soundlessly to the cushioned surface with the control allowed by smoothly flexing muscles. "Not a night of tender fornication, then, or even an hour? I shall survive the disappointment, but pray to know the reason. Or have we come, finally, to a reckoning for past favors?"

"Past injuries, rather."

"That does sound ominous."

"It should." Leaning so the cascading swath of her hair hid her movements, she picked up the rapier which lay on the far side of her low chair. It whistled softly as she whipped it around and leveled the shining point straight at his heart.

He did not so much as glance at it but kept his gaze on her face even as he brought both hands up and away from his body. "Poetic justice, as it were," he said in soft recognition. "Press home, *chère,* if that is your dearest wish. I could have stopped you long before now had it been mine."

"So I've discovered. Why did you let it go on? Unless it was for the — how did you style it? Tender fornication?"

"A delectable prize, admittedly, even spiced with hatred, flavored with intrigue. How was I to resist? But no, that was not the purpose. It seemed you were due recompense. Not perhaps, in the form of my skull to wear on a ribbon against your breast, sublime a resting place though it might be, but in some degree. The trick was to allow it without causing a matching remorse."

"You thought I would regret injuring you." She rose to her feet, made a brief, lifting motion with her rapier to show that she intended he should stand as well.

He complied, all languid grace, following as she backed away from the confined area near the chairs toward a clearer space at the foot of the bed. "Hope, they do say, springs eternal." His smile was wry at the edges. "I was optimistic enough to think you might change your mind."

She almost had for a short while, she thought as she faced him. That was a moment of weakness it was best that he should never know. "Or arrogant enough."

"I believe I also explained the travails of repentance to you," he went on as if her insult touched him not at all. "It seemed as well if you were not required to share that burden."

"Share?"

"To cause a death, any death, lies heavy on the conscience of a feeling person. Your foster brother's weighs on mine. I trust mine would weigh on yours. Not, I do realize, as a personal loss but in the way the final moment of even the lowest creature touches us, as a harbinger of our own."

"You killed him." The words fell from her lips in stark accusation. She had meant to be less obvious, but the thought had been too long in her mind for anything less than plain speaking. Without removing her gaze from his, she reached behind the bed's footboard, retrieved the rapier secreted there earlier, mate to the one she held, and sent it spinning toward him.

Gavin caught the glittering blade by its hilt, gazed down at it for a long, considering instant. Sweeping it up in a salute then, he inclined his head. "Let us give him his proper name, your foster brother. Francis, it was, Francis Dorelle. He was so young." He paused, his lashes shielding his gaze. "I suppose Maurelle told you how it came about."

"She did of course." Ariadne shrugged from her robe, leaving only the gathered fullness of her nightgown that fell from its high yoke edged in black lace. It gave her more freedom of movement. If it proved a distraction to her opponent, that was all to the good.

His gaze not quite focused, his pupils wide in the dark, Gavin removed his frock coat and tossed it aside. "Maurelle was not there when the challenge was issued so can have only a second hand account of it. Shall I tell you how it happened?"

She wanted to deny him that right, wasn't sure she could bear to hear. But to refuse might mean that she would never know the exact nature of that tragic duel. Assuming the *en garde* position, holding her blade steady so he might cross it with his own, she said, "It was over a poem, I believe."

"Not just a poem but the fact that it was dedicated to a lady who was — well, let us say her affections were directed elsewhere." In answer to Ariadne's signal, following her initiating beat, he met her blade, tapping against it with no intent to overpower, nothing more than the force required to turn it aside in the barest of engagements. "This was Madame Lisette, now married to Caid O'Neill," he went on conversationally. "She was, and is, special to those who fight for a living in the Passage de la Bourse because she makes for us a home of sorts, a circle where we are always welcome. But that is beside the point. Francis had written her another of his poems and meant to declaim it in the moonlight below her window. Unfortunately, he had taken several glasses of brandy to gain courage for this literary serenade."

"You are saying he was drunk. He never

417

drank." Angry at that claim which must be a lie, she swirled into a sudden attack with solid purpose behind it. Her rapier slid, abruptly, past his guard and caught his left shirt sleeve, passing through it with a harsh whisper of tearing cloth. A thin line of red appeared on the pristine white fabric.

Shock drove her back in haste, also the fear of some dreadful reprisal. It did not come. Instead, he stepped out of the guard position, transferred his weapon to his left hand and touched the splayed fingers of his right to the slit, glanced at the blood.

"Satisfied, madame?"

She was stunned at the ease of that touch; never had she expected it. She had thought to wear away at his stamina that had been weakened by his injury, or perhaps achieve some small victory by dint of feminine trickery, but that was all. Sickness rose inside her as she eyed the red stain. Beneath it ran a thread of suspicion, however, one made more certain by the set look on his face. More than that, she was close to learning, finally, the details of a meeting that had baffled her for long years but never more so than in the past few days.

She met his gaze with steel in her eyes. "No, monsieur."

"As it pleases you." Face impassive, he

gripped his sword in his right hand again.

"*En garde,*" she said, sinking into her swordsman's crouch that fluttered her hem around her ankles. When he assumed his own guard position in grim-faced compliance, she tapped his blade with a musical clink. "Now. You were saying?"

They had done this so often, the beating back and forth, gently, experimentally, that it almost seemed natural. Certainly, it was inconceivable that there should be danger in it. That it could, she was almost certain now, was true for only one of them. And it was not her.

"You say he did not drink," Gavin went on after a second. "Doubtless you are right. If he had been more in the habit, he might have held his liquor better or been more wary of the consequences. As it was, he objected to being interrupted in his intentions. I thought I was protecting the lady's peace and good name in the absence of my friend Caid by ordering him off. I could have been more tactful."

"He refused to go so you challenged him."

"He refused to go, I made sundry scathing remarks concerning his efforts with a pen, and he challenged me."

"But that was . . ."

"Madness on his part, yes. He knew it,

419

but pride prevented him from backing down. I could not refuse his cartel without further damage to his twice-damned, abominably sensitive *amour-propre,* and so —"

The acid self-condemnation in his voice raked across her nerves leaving them raw. "So you met him. Rather than damage his poor pride even further by forcing him to live with defeat, you killed him."

"Yes, if you like." The words were stark, unforgiving.

Ariadne did not like it. Temper drove her forward again. He parried, whirled into a riposte, hesitated. This time, she caught the moment when he broke his timing, deliberately faltered to allow her blade to slip past his own. A rent appeared in the linen gathers at the top of his shoulder. Another red stain appeared on his shirt.

Rage shook her. It was rank condescension for him to allow her to injure him without standing and fighting as if she were a worthy opponent. She would not have it. As he stepped out of position, she did not wait for him to ask if she was satisfied. Voice stark, she said simply, "No."

He appraised her, his face implacable before he gave a single hard nod.

Once more, they approached each other. This time she was more cautious, reining in her temper, watching his every move. Regardless of how much she wanted to slash and hack at him, she would not attack with force. They traded forays, parrying in seconde, in quarte, in sixte, the ripostes crisp, every counter precisely timed, perfectly executed.

It was exhilarating. Beyond her purpose and the outcome she envisioned was an odd pleasure in facing off against Gavin Blackford. She had worked hard to come to the point where she could hold her own with him, at least as long as he was not in deadly earnest. Regret brushed her that it must all end here, the lessons, her quarrel with him, their clash of tempers and tempered steel.

He was frowning, she saw, and was almost certain it was not entirely in concentration. She must act soon, she was sure of it; he was far from dense, could read her much too well. Choosing her moment with care, she skipped forward in a sudden attack, met his parry, then hesitated in her turn, allowing her guard to grow slack just as she was driven back by a particularly fast and economical riposte. His blade was a flash of silver, a blur as it came toward her, slid into the batiste of her nightgown, barely missed her left hip.

His virulent oath singed the air. "God's

teeth, woman, what do you think you're doing? I might have gutted you."

It was true in its way; he might have done real damage had he been slower in his responses, less agile in the turn of his wrist. "What? You object to being allowed a touch? It seemed only fair given those you allowed me."

"You think I'm humoring you."

"I know it."

"Protect yourself then, *ma belle*."

It was what she wanted, wasn't it? She should have been happy. Instead, she shivered inside with a sudden chill that did not blend well with her frantic excitement. His eyes had an icy gleam behind their gold-tipped lashes; his mouth was set in lines of forbidding sternness. Whatever his game had been, he played no longer.

They came together with the clash of steel against steel; it clicked and clanged, slid and scraped while fiery sparks dripped down like rain. Within moments, Ariadne's brow was damp with perspiration and she could feel a slow trickle between her breasts. Her wrist was numb from the jarring power of his strokes communicated through her steel and the muscles in her arm tingled, beginning to burn. She breathed in quick gasps, grunting with effort, and she didn't care. This was a true duel and she gloried in it. He was holding nothing back and it was a thing of magic and miracle that she could meet his steel, return his attacks, execute a sudden, wrenching move or two that made him step back and square his shoulders before he began again.

The pace was measured yet incredibly fast. There was little time to think or prepare. It was war with no quarter, a battle of nerves and will and stringent, unwavering intention. She made a riposte that opened his eyes, then she was driven back, breathlessly defending. Seconds later, she heard fabric tear, felt cool air around her shins. Instantly, he retreated, stood waiting, ready for what she would do next.

Ariadne looked down at her feet in their soft slippers. She could see them because the hem of her nightgown with its frill of black lace had been cut away at her knees as cleanly as if with a dressmaker's scissors.

Was the desecration in retaliation or warning, or was it, just possibly, an attempt to make certain she did not trip on her hem this time? She could not tell, though she looked up, staring at her opponent for long seconds. His eyes were empty of all emotion there in the gloom lit only by firelight and a single candle. It was as if he had retreated from her, from the bedchamber and what he was doing in it, from what might be required of him here in its feminine confines.

Was this the way he looked on the dueling field when he faced another duelist? Did he retreat inside himself so he might not be touched by what he was forced to do?

Forced. Why had she put it that way in her mind?

Abruptly, she realized he had not finished his account of the duel with Francis, did not want to go on with it any more than he wanted to continue with her. He didn't want to remember what had happened that fatal morning. That made her only more determined to hear everything he could be brought to tell her.

Lips tight, eyes narrowed, she came to the guard position once more. Skipping forward, her breathing ragged, she attacked as she railed at him. "Francis could not have been a match for you in any sense during your meeting. You were just arrived in town, or so I'm told, and had not become a sword master. But you were not without experience — certainly you had more maturity. Why in God's name could you not have simply drawn a little of his blood and declared yourself satisfied?"

"For the same reason this farce continues," he answered, executing parry and riposte with fierce skill. "I was not allowed the opportunity. It had rained the night before, the grass was wet. He made a wild swing that snapped his sword in half as it struck mine. He slipped, fell forward. My sword —" He stopped, and for a second, his hand used normally for balance clenched in a fist that touched the scar he carried high on his shoulder.

A scar she had kissed. A scar Francis had given him.

"I am sometimes unlucky in my meetings."

Pain gripped her. With it as a goad, she skimmed her foil under his arm, felt it catch shirt, bandage, skin. Then he was gone like a ghost, swinging away, coming back at her in a flurry of steel mesmerizing in its power and beauty, lethal in its control. When he drew back this time, the lace was gone from the yoke of her gown. More than that, a capped sleeve had been sliced so it barely clung to one shoulder, threatening to expose her.

"Satisfied *now?*" he asked again, his voice strained, not quite even.

She could feel his gaze on her bare skin, feel her near nakedness like a blow to the pit of her stomach. She had thought to retain a veiling of respectability in the flowing folds of her nightgown made by modest nuns. Now it was being stripped away from her. Whatever protective benefit it possessed had almost vanished. The question was how much farther he would go. Yes, and what he would do when she had no protection at all.

Her hands were shaking, her throat unbearably tight. The wild tangle of emotions inside her, anger and despair, terror and excitement, made her feel ill. She had been a fool for embarking on this desperate gamble. Now there was no way out.

His blood, the blood she had shed, gleamed wetly red in the candlelight. It added to her illness. What if he had been without fault in Francis's death? What if she had hurt him for nothing?

Lowering her sword but keeping the hilt in her clenched fist, she met his eyes. "Why?" she demanded. "Why did you agree to have me as a client? Was it simply to mock me?"

"No, no. For the sake of your *beaux yeux,* of course, and because we are so alike, both caught in the ultimate snare."

"Which is?"

"Oh, nothing dangerous, merely self-pity."

"Self-pity!"

"You thought it grief?" He reached out

with the tip of his sword to flick away a bedraggled scrap of black lace that still hung from her hem. "You missed Francis, I don't doubt, but did you truly mourn him there in France where you had journeyed, so blithely, when he left you alone? Did you yearn to have him with you or only long to know that he was safe and whole, living the life of the bon vivant to which he so grandly aspired? Was it him you missed or only your dream of home, that place where you might always be welcomed and adored instead of being shuffled off like some stray that did not, never could, belong?"

Her heart hurt, crowding against her chest walls. The back of her nose burned with a thousand unshed tears, each one of which told her he was more right than he knew. Or perhaps not. He had said, after all, that they were the same. "You have no home either," she said in quiet discovery.

"No. No matter how great the longing. Still I have discovered from the examples of my friends that it is better to live as if there is no pain, to find another dream to take the place of the one abandoned. Like great lumbering swamp turtles, we all carry our homes with us. They are invisible, but our own. Within them we are free to squat like ignorant peasants in hovels, spitting at fate, or to make them into palaces of our own design."

He was a shadow touched with gold before her eyes, a wavering ghost edged with tears. She swallowed hard before she could speak. "I don't want to forget Francis."

"Nor will you, not as long as you breathe — and what other immortality is there for any of us? Neither will I forget him."

She shook her head, an uncertain, almost aimless gesture. "You have scars enough as reminders."

"And will have more, of a certainty. That is still more tolerable than being beyond pain or love or life."

"Yes," she whispered, and turned away, trailing strings of black lace as she moved to put her foil on the nearest table, holding it there with both hands until she was certain it would not roll off, could harm no one by falling. It would have to be cleaned. But not now, not now. Her mind shied away from the thought, much less the task.

Drawing a deep breath, she said, "You will need medical attention."

"Nothing you can't supply."

"I don't . . . I'm not sure I can."

"It would be as well, perhaps, if no one else knew of our . . . exchange of opinions."

Better for her sake, he meant. "If this was

the farce you called it in the beginning, isn't that taking it a little far?"

"To the last degree, yes. But then, that will be the end of it, I should imagine."

Yes, it would have to be. There was no place for them to go from here. Her purpose was ended, as was his.

Yes, the end of it.

She glanced around, her gaze settling finally on the wash stand with its pitcher and bowl. "Then if you'll remove your shirt . . ."

"As you wish, madame," he agreed, his voice soft with final acceptance. "Always as you wish."

TWENTY-FIVE

The urge to apologize bubbled up inside Ariadne like a spring released from some hidden cavern. But that was ridiculous, to flay him then regret the damage and the pain.

His cuts were not deep; he had seen to that. It was hardly surprising, considering that he had allowed them, allowed himself to be hurt in the misguided hope that she would own herself satisfied. He had, in a way, harmed himself, so why should she be sorry?

Except, of course, that it was she who had begun what might have ended as a deadly game. Or had it ever really approached that level since he had been in control from the instant she handed him a sword?

Why had she not realized that he would be? The answer was that she had, but hoped it might be counterbalanced by his old injuries and her wiles. That was where she had made her mistake, in trusting that his attention could be diverted in such a fashion. Or had she thought he would be deterred by her womanly softness? Had she counted on it?

She didn't know. She hoped it wasn't so since that argued she had meant to kill him without danger to herself. But how could she know? The chance that it would make no difference whether she was male or female had always been present.

Oh, but that was mere specious reasoning. She had known. He had let pass a thousand chances to harm her over the past days. Why should he start this evening, after they had been lovers?

She had, without doubt, been a little mad since learning of Francis's death. The things Sasha had said this morning had only added to it. How incensed she had been to think Gavin had made love to her while knowing exactly who she was and what she wanted of him, that he had tried to use her emotions to deflect her purpose. Yes, and had succeeded.

What she had done was worse. It was unforgivable. There was no point, then, in seeking absolution.

She was silent as she sponged away the blood from his cuts and wrapped them with bandaging, being careful not to touch his hot skin with her bare hands. When she had tied the last small, flat knot, she stepped away from him. "Your shirt is ruined. Again."

"So it is. And here I am, half naked, gamboling around your pristine bedchamber like a satyr in search of female prey. And there you hover, a half-naked nymph uncertain whether to run or succumb."

Hot color surged into her face. "The thought never crossed my mind."

"No? Little else has exercised mine while you so diligently bound up my wounds. It's become a habit."

"You mean . . ."

"I do mean," he agreed, his smile wry. "It's the usual result of a man facing death, the urge to reaffirm life after he has survived. It seemed you might recognize it, if not share it."

"How can you, when I just tried to kill you?"

"Perverse of me, isn't it? But no more perverse than you binding me up to heal and then slicing me open again."

"Don't!"

"I could always hope it was for the sake of healing me a second time, since my excuses for claiming Maurelle's hospitality were scabbing over far too well. A few more could have meant a joyous extension for Nathaniel. Yes, and for his maître."

"I'm sorry," she cried, the words torn from her by guilt and the soft goad of his words.

"Don't be, please, for it's another insult," he said, fingering a bit of dangling black lace that hung down from her rent neckline, lying over her breast so his knuckle grazed the nipple into a tight bud of anticipation. "Healing was the subject, not compensation for being wronged."

"You are not the only one who has been hurt."

He met her gaze, his own darkly blue. "Nor did I say that the healing would be one-sided. I will make for you a poultice of caresses and concern, hold you until the sweet land of forgetfulness is found, if you will undertake the same."

But what of afterward?

The question hovered in her mind but she did not let it reach her lips. There could be no afterward; they were too different. Too much lay between them. He would return to his atelier and his male clients who understood all the desperate measures of the dueling game. She would pack her things and the little dignity she had left and return to Paris, to Europe, some place where forgetfulness was permanent. They would become strangers again as they had been so short a time ago. If they ever saw each other in years to come it would be merest accident. If she heard his name finally, after a few decades, she would shake her head, unable to recall his face, his touch, his smile, the way the light gleamed on the golden strands of his hair or turned the laughter deep in his eyes to blue magic.

Or perhaps not. She might never forget, might always remember the time spent in his arms, the infinite pleasure of his inventive love-making, the pure, drugging ecstasy of becoming lost in him. And if she did not fail to remember, then she might never forgive herself if she refused this last, bittersweet apology of the flesh.

Her gaze meandered down his face, over the perfectly made planes until it rested on his mouth. She put her hands on his shoulders, lightly, almost tentatively as she swayed toward him. He caught her around the waist, lifted her to sit upon his lap so she lay against his chest while he rocked her, burying his face in her hair. Then he rose and crossed in quick, not quite steady strides, to the bed. She felt the feather mattress give under her, felt it sag to his weight.

He dropped down beside her, tearing away the last, hanging threads of her nightgown's capped sleeve, pushing it from her, removing her slippers. She helped him divest himself of boots and pantaloons and all the rest. Then they came together, heated skin to heated skin, her breasts flattened against his chest, her belly against his, their legs intertwined. The strutted heat of his maleness nestled at the notch of her thighs, a silken rigidity, perfectly accommodated.

She was painstakingly aware of his injuries. His care was directed elsewhere but was no less meticulous. She sighed and shivered with a rash of goose bumps under his sure hands and inventive mind. He murmured a litany of praise and pleas that was like quiet music, an arpeggio of desire. And between them there was no dissonance but only a slowly mounting dedication to the moment.

Taking her hand, he lifted her arm away from her body, his gaze roving over the curves of her waist and flank. "Your skin shimmers as if sprinkled with crushed pearls," he said in quiet wonder. "To mar it would be sacrilege. Are you sure I didn't touch you?"

"You didn't," she whispered. "You wouldn't."

A shadow moved over his face. "Only by

accident, but accidents happen."

"They do." She released her hand, touching the jagged scar that ran from his neck to his collarbone. "To all of us."

"Forgive me." Taking her hand again, he lifted it to his lips and turned the palm up, placing a kiss there, then laving the sensitive surface with the wet heat of his tongue.

A quiver ran over her while tears rose to her eyes. She bent her head to hide them, pressing her lips to that last part of his scar she could reach, whispered against that discolored, yet silken, skin and the muscled firmness underneath. "Without reservation."

Placing her hand on her hip, he traced her spread fingers and the curves beneath it, gently licking as if at some sweet confection. Nor did he stop there. Raising higher in the bed, he eased her to her back and rolled between her thighs to hold them open. Trailing small, hot kisses across her abdomen, he nuzzled an instant, blowing hotly into the fine curls between her legs, then angled down over the joining at her groin to reach her knee. There he licked and smoothed with delicate precision until she writhed under him in ticklish, half-mad abandon. When she could stand no more, he began again, spanning her slender waist with his hands, testing the satin surface of her abdomen, the tops of her thighs, and between. With utter faithfulness, soothing her small gasps and cries with sure caresses, he followed the same path with his lips.

His breath upon the delicate, many petaled opening of her body was warm, moist, incredibly sensuous, impossible to avoid as he held her. She caught her breath with the wonder of it, then closed her eyes and stifled a low moan as she felt the hot wetness of his lips and tongue upon her. Drifting in a purgatory of delight, she discovered how very abandoned she could be. She gave him greater access, touched the gold silk of his hair in token of permission, in beguilement at his knowledge of a woman's body, in wonder for the unrestrained intimacy of his ministrations. At the center of her being there was a hot, melting sensation and a tense emptiness that only he could assuage. She gave him her most exacting concentration in hope that he would accomplish it.

He did not fail her. Imperious, maddeningly deliberate, he laved her, tasted her, applied gentle suction until she was mindless with acquiescence. With firm hands, he cupped her flesh, holding her to him, caressed in slow circles, rolled the nipples of her breasts between his fingers with infinite care. Pleasure flowed in endless tides inside her, eddied and whirled into hot pools until her senses reached such a painful pitch that she twisted in his arms with her breath sobbing in her chest.

Her very skin felt on fire. The muscles of her abdomen and her thighs tightened, quivering. Her blood tumbled through her veins so swiftly that she felt dizzy with it. Her every gasping breath was a cry. Turning her head from side to side, she caught his shoulders with trembling hands. An instant later, she felt his bandage and released him with a moan of self-reproach for the hurt she must have caused him.

She raked her fingers through his hair instead in the enthralled need to touch and hold. Tangling her fingers in the thick strands at the nape of his neck, she drew him upward.

With a soft sound in his throat, he caught her hands, opening her arms wide as he moved inside them to gather her close. He buried his face between the tender mounds of her breasts, pressing a kiss there before turning his attention to the nipples that were beaded with need.

His body was so firm, so hot and rigid against her. She moved against him, delighting in the heaviness, inhaling his masculine scent mixed with the faint spice of his shaving soap. Desire rose like an intoxicating vapor to her brain. She wanted him closer, felt herself swell toward him while her innermost being waited in liquid suspension.

He brushed his lips across her cheekbone, feathered her eyelids as if to taste the slight saltiness before he drew back, hovering above her. His voice was strained, not quite even, as he spoke. "Hiding from this consecration is cowardly, sweet Ariadne, and unbecoming in a goddess. Will you not open your eyes and see who holds you?"

She wanted to refuse. It hovered in her mind along with a protest for the interruption, for the loss of his caresses, his so very able ministrations. Something in his voice would not allow it. More than that, she did not lack courage, would not slight him in what had become her recompense.

Still, her lashes jerked as with palsy before they obeyed her will, lifting until she could meet his gaze. How bright it was, how limitlessly blue yet marked by pupils that were so wide and dark that he appeared drugged with passion and some desperate longing that glazed his eyes with pain. "I know well who you are, Gavin Blackford, and will never forget you."

He breathed lightly, if at all. "Hail and

farewell? I do see. *Partir, c'est mourir un peu,* to part is to die a little, or so it's said. Then let us seek together the small and glorious death that is nothing of the larger one."

The ache inside her swamped thought, blotted out the world and everything in it except the dim bedchamber and its soft feather bed shadowed by flickering firelight. Her voice barely stirred the air as she answered. "It shall be exactly as you wish it."

His hold tightened while his vision lost focus. "If every parting is a death, then every return should be a resurrection," he said, the words perfectly even. "Prepare yourself, for this may be a promise you will regret."

Hard on the words, he eased into her, penetrating her engorged flesh in a purposeful and heated slide. He filled her, stretching her resilient softness to the utmost. A wordless cry rasped her throat. Sliding her hands down the ridged muscles of his flanks, she grasped his hips, holding him against her while she took him deeper, embracing him with spasmodic internal contractions.

His breath hissed through his teeth in his grasp at control. His eyes were closed now, squeezed shut, while his mouth set in a hard line. Then he began to move, swirling in abrading contact, testing her depths with small forays, withdrawing against the resistance in her every muscle only to plunge forward again. With every movement he came closer, and closer still, to a conscious rhythm, found it finally in an implacable beat as full and steady as a thudding heart.

Rapture gathered inside her, spilled over to pebble the surface of her skin with gooseflesh, bathe it in a dew of perspiration. Tentatively, she moved with him, against him, gasping at the perfect union, the sounding touches that ignited a fiery gladness inside her. It spiraled higher, too strong to be denied or encompassed alone. He felt it; she knew he did, could sense it in the fierce expression on his face, the shuddering effort of his muscles. They plunged with it, rocking while the mattress jounced on its rope supports, creaking in protest. Her breasts brushed his chest in tingling abrasion; the flat hardness of his belly was sublimely hard against her own softness. Her very bones were dissolving, her body becoming infinitely malleable as if it would conform entirely to his shape, absorb him until they were one. And the ecstasy of it rose higher, reaching, reaching for something just beyond her grasp.

Still, they surged upon each other in a frenzy of yearning, holding with panting breaths and tender, aching bodies, seeking to deny the future that glimmered just out of sight.

He scooped her up with one hard arm beneath her, holding her against him while he rolled onto his back with her hair twining around them. Setting her on top, he pulled her down, down onto his swollen member. She cried out with ecstasy for the deeper penetration, deeper melding.

It was primal joy, an eternal physical indulgence that obliterated rank and position, time and place. They hovered, striving with locked muscles and racked breathing. Somewhere inside her, Ariadne felt the insidious gathering of unbearable tension. She moved back and forth upon him in a liquid slide until her every muscle jerked and quivered and her very skin felt on fire.

Abruptly, Gavin heaved above her once more, lunging with his hard, swordsman's muscles, delivering shuddering impacts. She arched upward, welcoming, wanting, needing every stroke. He gave her what she required, throbbing and powerful inside her, his every movement fueling the wondrous rush that mounted, irresistibly, to her brain.

It swept in upon her, a miraculous upheaval that banished differences, united minds, hearts and bodies. Stunning in its force, it held her immobile while her heart cried out in silent wonder and desperate, unending grief for all that was impossible, impractical, and too, too final.

With a last plunge, generous in its thoroughness, he allowed his own pleasure to overtake him. Surrendering, they clung, breathing hard, forehead pressed to forehead, connected from breast to ankle. They did not let go, even when the moment passed and their hearts slowed, beating in muffled synchronization.

He eased to his side at last, hovering above her with his head propped on the heel of one hand, drawing her against him. The flickering candlelight burnished his arm where it enclosed her, turning it to bronze, glinted with tiny gold lights on the dusting of hair along his legs. His hand was tinted with shades of yellow and gold, pink and peach, bronze and ivory and blue from firelight as he began to caress her once more.

It could not be — or could it? She felt him stir against her, felt the languid resurgence of her own acutely sensitive responses. She turned her head to stare at him, searching his face. He returned her gaze with one lifted brow and a faint smile curving his mouth.

Yes, he could. He would. And so would she. Closing her eyes, swallowing salty tears, she turned toward him, pressing fully against him while hiding her face in the curve of his neck. Neither noticed when the candle died and the firelight faded into the night.

TWENTY-SIX

Gavin came awake with a start. Alert yet unmoving, he surveyed the dim room where dawn was just seeping in around the edges of the window draperies. He was in Ariadne's bed still, with her slender form pressed to him in a way that caused his body to stir in turgid response. That was what had roused him. It was beyond exasperating. He had no control where she was concerned. And never had he needed it more.

He had slept more soundly than in weeks, months, perhaps even years. The fire had flattened to dull gray coals. The candle on its stand was only a puddle of cold wax with a black curl of wick. The rain had died away. No sounds came from the rest of the house, not even from the kitchens in the courtyard below. He did not usually leave his departure from a lady's bed so late, but it seemed his timing might still be adequate.

Raising on one elbow, he began to slide from under the covers. He stopped abruptly. A long strand of Ariadne's hair tethered him to the bed, wrapping around his waist. Carefully, almost hair by hair, he pulled it free then lay caressing it between his thumb and forefinger. It was so silky, with a faint scent of violets. Lifting it called attention to the long swath that draped her like black lace. Through that dark veiling, her skin shone with an unearthly gleam, picking up hints of pink and blue from the dawn light. He was irresistibly reminded of the way the long strands had swirled around her as she feinted and parried, now concealing, now revealing her curves under her fine night-gown. He had avoided, most assiduously, any chance of cutting the silken length as he slashed at the edging of black she wore. That would have been as much a sacrilege as causing a mark on her amazing skin.

Dear God, but she had been magnificent in her wrath and lethal intention. It had been worth every slice, every drop of blood he shed — to see her, to face her with the firelight behind her giving him tantalizing glimpses of how little she wore underneath her fancy robe. That was before she had removed it and handed him a sword.

He should have expected it. That he had

not was mere self-delusion. He had dared think the intimacy they shared had meant more, that it moved them beyond such things as past injury.

His mistake. He had paid for it in full this time. Or so he hoped. It was impossible to be sure.

It was also impossible to say what had brought her to him at the end of it. Was it the inevitable farewell, as he suspected? Or was it, just possibly, the *coup de grâce,* the final touch of a woman's less obvious vengeance?

It might well be deadly, more deadly than anything she had done with a blade, more deadly than she could ever be allowed to know.

Setting her hair carefully aside, he eased from the bed. It was the work of only a moment to step into his pantaloons, ease into his frock coat and vest and pull on his boots. His shirt was beyond repair and he could not find his cravat. He left them behind as he stepped silently to the door.

He did not mean to look back. In fact, he intended deliberately to refrain.

It was impossible to resist that one last glance, an indelible imprint in his mind's eye that he could carry into eternity. With the way out clear before him and fingers on the handle, he turned his head.

Ariadne lay unmoving, huddled on her side with the sheets pulled around her as she watched him go. Her eyes were wide and liquid, almost black, in the soft morning light. She met his without expression, without the least sign of what she might want or expect from him.

Nothing, she wanted nothing. He had no part in her life, certainly none in her future. So he sketched a bow with as much grace as he was able, and as little conscious irony.

"Ingratitude, you think, departing without kiss, promise, favor or yet more repetition? The first is insufficient, the second unwanted, the third inappropriate and the last unwise. What is left then except a sensible exit and my most sincere compliments. You were a worthy opponent, *ma chère madame.* None has ever been more so."

She made no answer, but then he expected none. With extreme resolution, he passed from the room and closed the door softly behind him. Then he walked, one foot in front of the other, along the gallery and out of the Herriot town house.

He could have stayed. He could have slept until mid-morning in his bedchamber before gathering up his belongings and Nathaniel, making his goodbyes to his hostess and leaving in decent order. But then he could not have been certain he would go at all, nor that he would keep to his own bedchamber.

No, it was better this way. He would send a note to Maurelle with apologies and a request for Nathaniel to retrieve all that was required and return to the Passage. If there must be an end, then let it be clean and let it be now.

Discretion, he had found, was often a decided handicap. It might save a great deal of public embarrassment, but its effect on private pain was another matter altogether. He had no memory whatever of walking the blocks to the Passage de la Bourse, could not recall who he saw or whether he acknowledged friend or foe.

When the sun rose finally on a clear and bright day, Gavin saluted it with the last of a *demi-bouteille* of fine Napoleon. Removing his booted heels from the window sill of his own bedchamber, he rose from his chair, stretched and sighed, then set about the day he had outlined for himself during his hour of introspection.

He bathed, shaved in cold water and changed his clothes, then left the atelier. At the firm of Bourry d'Ivernois on Chartres, he purchased a fine lawn nightgown that was edged in delicate Italian lace, though its trim was most assuredly not in black. Since he could not have it delivered without causing unwanted speculation, he carried the paper-wrapped package away with him. Some blocks away from the shop, he paid a street boy two bits to deliver it to Madame Faucher at the Herriot town house. By the same messenger, he sent his note to Maurelle and summons to Nathaniel. That done, he went in search of breakfast.

He was not hungry by any stretch of the imagination; still it seemed best to order his day in the accustomed manner. Besides, he was at loose ends with no clients scheduled, due to his supposed incapacitation, no appointments with friends, no visit or lesson with a certain widow in black lace.

Black widow, lovely, deadly and entirely too . . .

No, he could not allow her into his thoughts. She had no place in the life he had made for himself with its masculine company and pursuits. In a day or two, when he was a little less sore from his sundry cuts, he would take up his accustomed schedule again. Work and obligation would assure that she seldom crossed his mind. Everything would be as it had been before.

Everything. Something. Or possibly nothing.

He had finished his breakfast of poached eggs and shredded ham on a bed of creamed spinach when he looked up to see Nathaniel bearing down upon him. The boy's face was set and he carried a paper-wrapped bundle under his arm. Reaching the table, he slapped his burden down upon it, then put his hands on his hips.

"Good morning," Gavin said, all affability. "Did Madame Herriot give you breakfast? If not . . ."

"Why'd you sneak off without me is what I wanta know," the boy interrupted with mutiny in his eyes. "What've you been playing at?"

"Playing?" Gavin fingered the paper of the bundle on the table before him. He did not remember it being quite so slick or so yellow-brown.

"You and Madame Ariadne were at it again last night. I heard the swords clanking, though you never said nothing about another lesson. She went after you, didn't she? What'd you do to set her off?"

"You wouldn't, I suppose, believe me innocent?"

"Not with the rattlesnake tongue you got

on you. You said something. I know you did."

"My main fault, insofar as I can recall," Gavin said, pushing the bundle to one side, "was an excess of caution. Well, and the unpardonable sin of being alive."

Nathaniel frowned with a shake of his head, then nodded at the package. "You not gonna open that, see what she sent you?"

"I know well what it contains. I sent it to her this morning."

"Not that one, you didn't. I saw what you're talking about, saw the maid take it to her room while she was out. This one she gave to me when she come in, just as I was leaving."

Gavin stared at the boy a second, then pulled the bundle toward him and tore it open.

A shirt lay in the wrappings, pristinely white, of finest, smoothest linen, meticulously hand-stitched. She had replaced the one she had destroyed. Their impulses, it seemed, were curiously identical. It gave him an odd sensation under his breast bone, like the first numbness of a sword thrust, before the pain begins.

He should return it. He would, except he could be sure the nightgown he had sent to her would arrive back at his atelier before he did. Better to let it go, to accept this example of her generosity as the parting gift it was no doubt intended. Though how he was to ever wear it, he could not say. A hair shirt as a reminder would be as likely.

"Well?" Nathaniel demanded.

"The lady merely replaces the shirt the Russian destroyed," Gavin answered with deliberate mendacity. "No doubt she felt responsible, seeing she was the cause of the meeting."

"Didn't know she felt that."

"Nor did I. Never underestimate the generosity of a lady, *mon vieux*." Gavin got to his feet, left money on the table, gathered up his package. "It can be, and often is, quite lethal."

"She's packing, you know, leaving New Orleans."

"Is she. For Paris?"

"Didn't say. Wasn't my place to ask."

"Like mummers at a funeral, we worry overmuch about our proper place even if no one else notices," he said, almost to himself. Glancing at his companion's set face, he went on. "You came to appreciate her while we were in residence, I think."

"She'd guts. When she saw a problem, she did something 'bout it 'sides sit around and moan. She made you sit up and take notice, something I never thought to see."

"So she did," Gavin murmured.

"You liked her, too."

"I was an admirer, if you will."

"More than that."

"For what good it may do me. We do fully understand our places, you and I, from so much thinking on it."

Nathaniel gave a moody shrug, but did not contradict him.

The day did not improve as it progressed. Gavin could settle to nothing. Leaving Nathaniel to his unpacking at the atelier, he went out again.

He made the rounds as on other, more usual days, visiting two or three salons of his fellow masters on the Passage. He drank their wine, watched the young dandies practicing on the strips, smoked a cheroot or two while lounging on the balconies in the welcome sunshine. He joined various discussions on the topics of the moment, deflected questions about the duel with Novgorodcev, and spoke of his particular friends, Caid and the Conde de Lérida, also his brother, Nicholas. Scathing, reproving and enthusiastic by turns, he strolled here and sauntered there, frittering away the time. No matter where he went or what he did, it seemed he should be some place else, that he had left something undone. He felt as if he waited for some event, some appearance, some message that never came.

At the oddest moments, while holding a glass of claret, nibbling an olive or watching a flower seller carrying nosegays of violets in a tray on her head as she passed along the street, he was assailed by images of Ariadne. The color of her lips, the sweet taste of her, her violet scent haunted him. The least tiny thing could send him tumbling into a sensual morass where he held her in his arms while the world shattered around them. It was a true obsession, he thought, one born of the shared remembrance of a young poet who had died too soon. Yes, and of passion forged in expiated anger. This was no gentle thing of hearts and flowers, bluebirds and honeysuckle. It had something wild in it, and something that grieved while saluting life and joy. He missed it, missed his clashes with Ariadne as he might miss a limb, and even, possibly, his beating heart.

Soon she would be gone. Perhaps he would find some kind of peace then, some deeper healing.

Or perhaps not. It had occurred to him in the sunrise hour, and again at moments of supreme self-disgust during the day, that he had not withdrawn at the zenith of his pleasure in her arms. He had been too enthralled by the way she felt and moved under him, against him, the pulsating glory of her, the incredible way she encompassed him. What if she carried his child? What then?

Nothing, nothing would come of it. How could he think otherwise?

She would rid herself of the babe, or else rear it in some out-of-the-way place. She might pass it off to a woman who, like her own foster mother when she was given away, had no child of her own. She could dispose of his child and he would never know.

He would never know.

It was Kerr Wallace who found him on the balcony of the Croquère's salon, alone and morose, as evening began to fall. "Well met, my friend," the large Kentuckian said, clamping a hand on his shoulder, "Rio said I'd find you here."

Gavin winced away from the greeting, his breath hissing through his teeth.

Kerr lifted his hand as if he had touched a hot stove. "Hell, but I'm a clumsy idiot. Forgive me."

The injury he had touched was more recent than the dueling slash he spoke of, also less explainable. Gavin let it pass. "The lost has been found, the straying gathered home. You had some reason for searching me out?"

"Rio seemed to think you were at loose ends. I wondered if you might like to change your mind about signing on with the Legion?"

"Hieing off to war while the bands play, old men cheer and women cry? That is, if the happy event ever comes to pass. It's a thought. But my bent doesn't yet turn in that direction."

"Should be a good fight."

Gavin gazed past Wallace's shoulder at the sky that was streaked with layers of rose and lavender and gold, and where a flock of pigeons wheeled in delirious pleasure with the lilac flush of the sunset under their wings. The bells from St. Louis Cathedral were tolling the Angelus, which had, no doubt, startled them into flight. The air was cool and as soft as a woman's caress against his face, as intoxicating as a night of love.

"Oh, certainly," he agreed with utmost politeness. "On foreign soil with overextended supply lines and against foes that know every rock and hot sand wallow and count scorpions among their relatives."

"It won't be that bad."

"No, it will be worse. I thought you pragmatic and dedicated to your own quest, my friend. You even said so, as I recall. Of what use is a uniform and marching orders to you?"

"A way to get to Mexico without fanfare? And without having to rake up ship's fare, either, truth be told. I've learned the man I want has been seen there."

"If you break ranks to find this elusive foe, and are captured, you'll face either Santa Ana's firing squad or else the hangman's rope reserved for deserters. You'll do better to take to the road disguised as a muleteer with a fat wife and two baskets full of little muleteers."

"A fine idea. Now if you'll only point me toward the wife market."

"You're too literal, my friend."

"And you're too obscure," Kerr said cheerfully. "I'd suggest you dressing up in a skirt and bonnet for the job, but fear the suggestion might get my throat cut for me."

"Nothing so plebian," Gavin replied. "It would be an exercise in precision, rapiers at dawn with all the usual witnesses, seconds and doctors, the exquisite preparation and requisite courtesies. Then I would cut your throat."

"I might let you do it, too, just to see such

folderol. No. Really, Blackford, have you no yen for adventure, no urge to see the Rio Grande and the army you've been preparing men to fight for these many years?" He made a sweeping gesture with one long arm. "Is your life in the city so fascinating that you can't bear to leave it all behind for even six months?"

It was a point. "You believe it will be over in that time?"

"Washington assures us of it. So does Sam Houston, when he isn't doing his dead-level best to prevent hostilities guaranteed to deplete his treasury before Washington gets its purse out of its pocket. If it ever does."

"I'll consider it," Gavin said.

"Capital." Kerr lifted a hand as if he meant to slap his shoulder again. Then he remembered, for he spread his hands and shook his head. "I'll look forward to hearing from you."

They were still there on the balcony, in a cloud of blue smoke and brandy fumes, when Nathaniel found them. He shouldered out of the crowded salon, almost tripping on the balcony threshold. "Monsieur Gavin! I been looking everywhere for you. A message has come, brought by Solon."

Gavin felt his heart rate increase to a thunderous beat. He took the square of ivory paper, broke the wax seal and extracted the missive. Maurelle's elegant scrawl made little sense for a moment. Then he caught its style and the message leaped from the page.

"What is it?" Kerr asked, his features alert as he straightened from where he lounged against the railing. "What's happened?"

"It's Madame Faucher." Gavin's voice was grim and he began to move before the words left his mouth.

"Madame?" Nathaniel's voice slid upward on the scale with the query.

"She's gone."

Wallace caught up with him in two long strides, and Nathaniel was on the Kentuckian's heels. "What do you mean, gone?"

Gavin dodged a white-coated servant passing glasses of burgundy, stepped between twin dandies dressed with absolute sameness down to the monocles attached to their lapels. "Vanished. She hasn't been seen since she went out on an errand just after midday. Her bonnet was found on the rue de la Levee, just down from the steamboat office. Solon picked it up while searching for her, since he recognized the black ribbons she'd added a couple of days ago. Maurelle asks if by chance, or mischance, she is with me."

"I never!" Nathaniel said in outrage.

"Failing that, she fears she may have been abducted."

Wallace increased his pace. "I do see your urgency."

Gavin made no answer. It was not that he had no words, but that they were, every one of them, far too profane to utter and far too personal to be heard.

TWENTY-SEVEN

Ariadne stepped from the office of the steamboat line with her head down as she pushed the ticket she had just purchased into the drawstring bag on her arm. Her features were set in lines as somber as the gray velvet walking costume trimmed in black braid that she wore. She had so much to do. The vessel would be leaving in less than four hours. The captain, having been delayed in his departure already by the constant rain, would not wait for her.

A man appeared in front of her just as she reached the banquette. She side-stepped instinctively, and would have passed around him if he had not touched her arm.

"Where are you going in such haste, *ma chère?* Dare I hope you plan to sail on the *Leodes?*"

"Why, Sasha," she said in surprise as she raised her eyes to his face where his mustache lifted with a pleased smile. "I thought you had gone."

"In the morning, without fail, since the rain seems to have cleared so the pilot can take the ship downriver without running her aground. And you, madame?"

"I'm sorry to disappoint you, but I will be taking the Natchitoches packet." She gave a small shake of her head. "My mother left the city, you know, carrying my stepsister and stepfather home for . . . for burial. I should have gone with them, but could not make up my mind to it until now."

"A sudden decision." The scar on his face took on a purplish hue as hope faded from his eyes.

"Slow, rather. It . . . seems to take considerable time for me to know my own mind." For an instant, she thought of Gavin as she had seen him last, inclining his golden head in farewell as he left her. A knot rose in her throat and she swallowed, taking a shallow, difficult breath against the pain of it.

"You are determined to remain in this benighted country."

"As you say. Paris is so far away. And I do have family here, after all."

A nun in a flowing habit and flying veil was coming toward them on the banquette. Sasha glanced up then took Ariadne's hand and placed it in the crook of his elbow as he moved with her out of the way. It seemed rude to disengage immediately. She allowed her fingers to remain in his grasp as he began to stroll down the street.

"You could have family in Paris as well," he observed in his rumbling bass. "You have only to become my wife."

"Please. Don't let's go over this again."

"You are a stubborn woman."

"Agreed. Once I do know what I want, I'm not easily diverted from my chosen path."

"And your path now leads to the Englishman." He leaned forward to see under the brim of her bonnet.

"How can you say so?"

"Can you deny there is something between you?"

"Oh, indeed there is, if you mean dislike, even hatred." She would not think of what else there had been — the hard strength of his body, the brush of skin again skin, the feel of him inside her. Yes, and most of all, the desolation in his eyes as he turned to leave her.

"The other side of the coin of love, so they say."

"They are optimistic if not downright foolish."

"Are they, my own?" he asked with ponderous dignity. "He is not your usual sword master, low of birth and devoid of manners. He might have made you a husband."

"Please," she said a little desperately. "We should be saying our good-byes since we have met so providentially and will be going our separate ways."

"We did that, as I remember." His grip tightened on her fingers where they lay on his sleeve, and he smiled down at her with sadness and something more in his eyes.

"But this time it's certain. My boat will leave before sunset. I must return to Maurelle's to pack my trunks and reach the dock."

"Will you not stop with me for a small moment, long enough to have a coffee and pastry at some table on the banquette?" He was staring ahead of them, frowning a little as if he sought such a place for their refreshment.

"I'm sorry, truly I am, but there is no time."

"It's such a small thing to ask. I will not keep you overlong."

He was leading her further along the rue de la Levee where began the barrel houses and other such unsavory places catering to the sailors, backcountry boatmen and longshoremen. It was not a particularly dangerous street as long as she had a male escort, but neither was it one she would have chosen as a route to Maurelle's town house. As they approached an intersection, she turned her footsteps automatically in the direction of the cross street that would take them back to a more respectable thoroughfare.

Sasha walked on, tugging her with him as if he had not noticed her preference. She stopped, setting her feet, putting pressure on his arm. "This way, if you please. I really must get back."

"It will be closer if we use the rue St. Louis." He glanced up the street once more, his attention on a hackney that negotiated the corner a few blocks away then rattled toward them at a terrific pace.

"It's the same either way, and I don't care for this area."

"Please, *chère,* only a few extra minutes of your time. We have so little left to us."

Something was wrong. If the oddness of his manner had not told her, the alarm that skittered along her nerves would have done so. Regardless, she wasn't sure enough of it to make a scene.

"Oh, very well. Shall we say a small coffee then, at the *pâtisserie* on Royale?"

"No, you were quite right, *chère.* I have a

better idea."

He wasn't looking at her as he spoke, but watching the hackney that hurtled toward them. In a moment, it would be even with where they stood. She frowned as she saw Sasha lift his hand in a signal for the vehicle to stop for them. "Really, this isn't necessary for so short a distance."

"I insist," he said as the hackney driver hauled on the reins, slowing the horse between the shafts. "You did say you were pressed for time." Before the vehicle had fully halted, he urged her forward, reached to open the door.

Instinct made her hang back. "No, truly, these hackneys are usually dirty and smell vile. I prefer to walk."

He paid no attention as he looked up and down the banquette. It was empty except for a few street boys playing marbles. Abruptly he snatched her around the waist, hefting her against his hip as he hauled her closer to the hackney and jerked open the door. Bending, he thrust an arm under her knees, lifted her against his chest and threw her inside.

White-hot pain exploded in her temple as her head struck the door frame. Her bonnet cushioned the blow but was ripped off as its black ribbons gave way on one side. She plunged toward the floor, caught her elbow on the seat with a numbing blow, landed between the seats.

Before she could right herself, Sasha leaped inside, slammed the door shut and shouted to the driver. The man yelled and cracked his whip. The hackney started with a jerk and careened away down the street, its wheels grating on the muddy paving and the clatter of hooves echoing back on the buildings on either side.

Fury boiled up inside Ariadne. She dragged herself up in the swaying conveyance, trying to get her feet under her. Before she could find her balance, Sasha seized her hips and jerked her down on the seat beside him.

"What are you doing?" she demanded, straining against his hold. "Stop this hack and put me down at once!"

He laughed, a harsh sound in the back of his throat. "I don't believe so, *chère*. I begged and pleaded with you countless times but you did not listen. I followed you across the world and you do not see me. Now it will be as I say."

"Don't be a fool. You can't force me to accept your proposal." She pushed her elbow between them, shoving at his thick chest.

Snatching her closer again, he pinned her arm against him, his hot breath against her ear as he answered. "Can I not? You may be glad of it after a night or two spent together."

"You are deluded if you think this will make me care for you."

"Care? My foolish one, I will have you whether you care or not. I have lost my country, my birthright, my family and my honor, but I will not lose you."

She was stunned, outraged, disbelieving, but she had not been afraid until that moment. This was Sasha who had escorted her to musicales and the opera and on drives along the boulevards of Paris. Sasha, whose proposals she had refused and pretensions she had depressed a dozen times over. Always before, he had bowed and accepted her refusals. Why not this time?

"You can't do this," she said, forcing the words through the tightness in her throat.

"Who is to stop me? You have no husband, no father, no brother to come after you. Your swordsman might have interfered had he stayed, but he left, or so I'm told. There is no one. You will be mine."

"Where," she began, then stopped, moistened her dry lips, began again. "Where are we going?"

A rough chuckle shook his chest even as he spread a large hand over her ribs, pushing upward until his splayed fingers captured her breast. "You dare to ask? Such courage, *chère.* It's what I've always admired in you. Among other things."

Dread expanded inside her like yeast set too near the fire. He was bigger, stronger, and flushed with the triumph of the moment. He had the advantage of his immovable hold gained by surprise. She did not think he meant to force himself upon her while they jostled back and forth in the hackney with its cracked leather seats and fetid smells of sweat, rancid hair oil and illness. It would be better if she saved her strength for the time when she might need it more.

Snatching a glance out the window, she saw they were rolling past the Place d'Armes, the rounded bell towers of the cathedral and the stalls of the market which lay just beyond. If they did not turn soon, they would leave the confines of the Vieux Carré to enter faubourg Marginy in the Third Municipality. But no, they were swinging onto the road that paralleled the river and its docks. It took only that to tell her where they must be headed.

His ship, he was taking her to the *Leodes,*

bound for Marseilles. Oh, but surely the captain would not allow him to bring an unwilling woman on board? There were laws governing such things, after all.

Rumors abounded of women who disappeared never to be seen again, whispers of females sold into slavery in the desert countries beyond the Red Sea. If that was possible, then it must be managed in some fashion. She had no idea what kind of ship the *Leodes* might be, or how law-abiding its master.

This was infamous, unendurable. She stole a glance at the hackney's rusty door handle, wondering if she could reach it before she was stopped, calculating her chances of jumping out, leaping beyond reach of the fast-turning wheels.

"I wouldn't try it," Sasha said. "You will not like making the sea voyage ahead of us with broken bones."

"I quite see the difficulty," she answered, her voice a too accurate reflection of the chill inside her. "Release me, and I will undertake to sit quietly until we arrive."

"I have your word?"

She agreed, though it struck her as ironic that he would accept it in the midst of this abduction and after just admitting his own lack of honor. Still, she was grateful to be free of his grasp. Rubbing her wrist where he had grabbed it, she sat staring out the window as respectable dwellings gave way to rough dives which in turn became mere shanties half-buried in swamp muck.

On the other side of the rutted track, the river could be seen running at yellow-brown flood stage after the long days of rain. Boats of all varieties — from flatboats and keel boats that depended only on river current to the fastest of steamboats — were tied up to rough wooden docks. Ocean-going vessels, both sailing ships and steam packets, ordinarily made their landings closer to the city center. The rain and high water had slowed loading and unloading so many of these were anchored in the river, waiting their turn at the dock or else standing by for the pilot necessary to make their way downriver to the gulf. If Sasha was to sail on one of these, it seemed clear they must be rowed out the short distance to the ship. At some point along this stretch, then, they should be meeting a dingy or longboat supplied by the *Leodes.*

At a furtive movement beside her, she glanced back to Sasha. He was taking a flask from his coat pocket and removing the top. That he should require a restorative was not greatly surprising. It was a hazardous venture, taking her as his captive, and she would not make it easy for him. It had occurred to her already that a ship's master who could be swayed by money from one person might just as easily be swayed toward another for higher payment.

Sasha was not drinking from the flask but studying it as if dubious of its use. His teeth were clamped together so the muscle in his jaw made a lump under the purple-red streak of his scar. Carefully, he laid aside the top he had removed before turning to her. As he shifted, the liquid inside gurgled and its sickly, familiar smell wafted to her.

Laudanum.

"If I were to ask you, most politely, to drink this, I don't suppose you would comply," he said, his gaze calculating yet mournful.

"Certainly not!"

"I didn't think so."

She guessed what he intended an instant before he reached for her. She whipped her head away, but he was too fast, too close, too big. His shoulders blocked her into the corner of the carriage and he thrust a heavy thigh across her knees to hold her down. The flask knocked against her lips as the hackney bounced into a pothole, bruising them as she struggled. She fought him, raking his neck with her nails, clawing at his hands. But he caught her forehead with his free hand, forcing her head back against the seat before shifting his big, sweating palm down over her eyes and nose, cutting off her air so she must breathe through her mouth. The lip of the flask struck her mouth again, grating against her teeth as he shoved it between them. The vile liquid, a strong tincture of laudanum in brandy, dribbled from the corners of her mouth, wetting her cloak. She choked, coughed, but was forced to swallow. When the flask was empty, he released her and sat back, breathing hard.

Ariadne coughed, wheezing as she tried to clear her throat. Impotent fury shook her as she wiped her face with hard swipes of her trembling hands, brushed at the wetness on her cloak and bodice. If she had possessed a sword at that moment, she would have run him through without a second thought.

How much of the narcotic liquor had she drunk? She had no idea. Enough to make her helpless for whatever he intended? Enough to kill her? It was certainly enough to make her sleep. Already, she could feel the numbness creeping in upon her.

She put her head back on the leather seat, gazing at the black roof of the hackney. Hope of escape was gone. Even if she got away from Sasha, she could not run far. What would become of her? No one knew who she was with or where he was taking her. She would simply disappear. After a while, she would be forgotten.

What did he intend? She had not allowed herself to consider that point in detail. Would he hold her prisoner, abusing her in all the ways a man could use to coerce a woman until she agreed to marriage? She did not think he would actually do her permanent harm but there was no way to be sure of it. Then what? What kind of life would it be after they were wed? He professed to love her but it could be a lie. Even if he did, it would not make him an acceptable husband, not when she cringed at the mere thought of being at the mercy of his hands, his mouth and hard, rutting body. Once he was master of her fortune, he need not keep her alive under the prevailing laws of many European capitals. She could be disposed of in any number of convenient ways.

She might never see New Orleans again, never see Gavin Blackford. She would never be able to tell him how truly sorry she was that she had hurt him, never be able to tell him how her stupid heart had come to love him while she had planned his defeat in her mind. Or was it she who had been stupid and her heart wise?

She closed her eyes, unable to bear her thoughts. While the hackney rocked on along the rutted and muddy road, a gray swamp mist rose up around her and closed off the light.

Twenty-Eight

Ariadne woke by degrees, rousing only to drift away again. Once, her bed was hard, slimy and smelled of dead fish as it bounced beside a high wooden wall painted dark blue with a maroon line near the top. Another time she was being carried with her head hanging down and her legs held tightly at the knees while the world swung in sickening sweeps. She rallied briefly as she was lowered into a narrow, coffin-like space and covered with a scratchy blanket, but dark nothingness came down again.

Now she stared at a soft glow not far away, watching it without real curiosity until it slowly became a whale-oil lamp burning in a gimbaled support. It was a ship's lamp, for it moved with the gentle sway of a vessel at anchor.

She was on a ship, and it was impossible to imagine that it was anything other than the *Leodes*. In the morning, it would hoist sail and move slowly down the river to the gulf, on its way to Marseilles. That was what Sasha had said, wasn't it? Her mind was so fuzzy she could not be sure.

He was nowhere to be seen. The cabin was empty, insofar as she could tell without lifting her head from the hard pillow of the bunk where she lay. She could hear the creak and groan of the ship, but nothing more. Most of the crew was on shore leave, she suspected, as this was their last night in port. Surely they would be returning before too long. She had a sense of time having passed, perhaps several hours. Darkness had fallen, making the lamp necessary.

She had missed the Natchitoches packet, might never make that upriver journey.

She pushed up on one elbow, pausing as her head swam. After a moment, she tried again and was able to shove away the blanket of rough brown wool that covered her and sit up on the bunk's edge. It took another minute or two for her senses to clear. Gingerly then she put her feet on the floor. Her half boots had been removed but that was all, she realized as her skirts settled around her ankles. Praise heaven for small mercies.

It was possible she should be thankful as well for the laudanum that befuddled her mind. If not for its effects, she might now be completely naked and lying under the swinish Russian nobleman she had considered her friend. What had he told the captain to account for her presence? Had he said she was ill or perhaps out of her head? Had he simply called her a drunken whore? Or had it been unnecessary to call her anything at all?

Urgency gripped her. Sasha would be back shortly to check on her, she suspected. She held on to the bunk support, concentrating desperately on finding her balance and the rhythm of the ship's movement upon the river current.

Three large trunks lined the wall on the cabin's opposite side. They belonged to Sasha for she recognized his crest, and it was his coat in the military style which lay over the back of the chair drawn up to the table. He had apparently thought her incapacitated enough to leave for a time, possibly while he conferred with the captain or even enjoyed a drink in his company.

When he returned, he would expect to find her in his bed where he had left her. She required a weapon, had to have one before he reappeared.

The room was devoid of anything sharp or heavy, contained nothing that might slide or come loose in bad weather at sea so there was nothing she could use for defense. Even Sasha's dog-headed cane was missing; he must have taken it with him. The only items in the pockets of his coat were a pair of gloves, ticket stubs and a pocket watch.

Letting the coat fall back on the chair, she turned to his trunks, took a step toward them then stopped. It was one thing to go through his outer wear, but something else to delve into his more private belongings. It seemed flagrant meddling, like rifling through the drawers of a house where one was a guest.

Such scruples were all very well, but Sasha had forfeited any right to expect them from her. She had to search everything.

The trunks were locked.

Ariadne stood biting the inside of her bottom lip for a long moment, wondering if she could leave the cabin without being discovered. Could she find where she had been hauled on board? Was it possible to climb down to whatever small boat had been used to transport her from the shore?

What if she were seen? She would be worse off than now since Sasha was certain to watch her more carefully.

There was nothing for it but to pick the trunk locks. They should present no great difficulty since so many things — knife boxes, tea and spice caddies, journals and jewelry cases — had similar locks and keys were often misplaced. She dropped to her knees beside the first trunk, felt in the heavy, sliding knot of her hair to pull out a pin and set to work.

What she expected to find in the baggage, she was not sure. Another cane, perhaps, since a man often had a spare in a different wood in case his favorite did not match all his clothing. A set of dueling pistols was not impossible. A razor was almost a certainty, as was a stick pin with a sizeable shaft. Any of these would do. Anything at all.

Her fingers were shaking by the time the lock clicked open. She listened a moment to be certain no one was coming, then lifted the lid with care to prevent its hinges from squeaking.

Nothing, there was nothing in the first trunk except frock coats and trousers and nightshirts. She lifted everything out to be certain, then set back on her heels amid the piles of clothing as disappointment threatened to overcome her.

She had no time for tears and despair. Sniffing, wiping underneath her eyes, she listened again then turned to the next trunk. This one held Sasha's soiled laundry, a large portion of it wrapped around a box of some fashion, one long and narrow of the kind used for dried fruit. Shuddering with revulsion, she pushed it away from her while she turned to the last trunk.

She set to work on the third lock in a fever of haste. It was stiff, or perhaps her fingers had grown clumsy, or the hairpin was a little bent. She couldn't manipulate the inner works. Somewhere not too far away, she heard a gust of masculine laughter. A door or hatchway slammed and footsteps sounded, approaching the cabin. She clamped her teeth together, desperately jimmying at the lock, shaking it as she tried to find the magic slot that would make it open. Or perhaps it was her hands shaking.

The lock wouldn't budge, and the heavy, measured treads were coming closer. Her normal dexterity seemed to have deserted her. The laudanum that coursed through her veins was making her slow and stupid. She whispered an imprecation that became a sob deep in her throat.

The footsteps were nearly at the door. There could be no doubt to whom they belonged. She had to . . . had to . . .

Suddenly her brain revolved like a cast iron mechanical toy to present a magical image. Drawing breath on a sharp gasp, she whirled back to the second trunk and its soiled shirts and underdrawers. She scattered the clothing, pulled out the long box she had felt but not seen.

Not a box of dried fruit at all. It was a flat sword-case of polished walnut with laurel leaves and fleur-de-lis in gold leaf around an incised crest. Its closure, intricate but without a lock, sprang open at her touch. She flipped back the lid to reveal a set of matched dueling swords, polished sabers with cleverly wrought hilts of silver inlaid with gold.

These were the sabers Sasha had used in the duel. One of them had sliced open Gavin's back. The very sight of them brought hot tears to her eyes while her stomach roiled.

The door was opening behind her.

She drew a fast breath, grasped the hilt of one long and heavy sword and lifted it from its blood-red velvet bed. With it held in both hands, she rose, bracing her feet as she faced the doorway.

"*Mon Dieu, chère.* What are you doing?" Sasha stepped over the high threshold but came no further. Color mottled his face, his pale eyes narrowed to a glitter and he seemed to swell like a bull preparing to charge.

"You should not have left these with me." She flicked the saber case briefly with one toe. "Not if you didn't want me to arm myself."

He breathed audibly through flared nostrils, as if trying to control his rage. "Now that you have, what do you intend?"

"I'm leaving. You will back away from the door so I may pass."

"Suppose I refuse."

"I don't advise it."

"What will you do? Am I to believe you will slice me open like a melon? No, no, you won't do that. It isn't in you."

"I'd have said you would never stoop to abduction. That was wrong, just as you are wrong now."

"Don't be foolish. What you have there is not your light foil but a cavalry weapon, meant to slice off arms and heads and . . ."

"And lay open the flesh of horses and men?" she interrupted. "If you don't shrink from it, why should I?"

"You are not trained for it."

"How much training is required in order to kill? My lessons with the English *maître d'armes* were most thorough, I assure you." That was purest provocation, but she could not help herself.

"So I imagined," he said, the scar on his

face like a streak of fire. "But you are not a man. It's too heavy for you."

"You hope so."

"No really. Come, be reasonable. You will hurt yourself."

He took a step toward her. She lifted the saber to waist height, directing the point at his midsection. "I am perfectly reasonable. Allow me to leave, and neither of us will be harmed."

"Oh, *chère,* you think you can be a danger to me if I choose not to allow it?" He took another step.

"I've warned you."

He was uncomfortably close in the small cabin now. Armored in condescension, he seemed to be considering how best to regain control of the situation with no thought that it might be impossible. "Don't be melodramatic," he said in hard tones. "I am not your indulgent Englishman, fascinated by the contrast between your beauty and your threats. Give me the sword."

"I don't believe so." Had Gavin been fascinated? Had he really?

Sasha's mouth tightened. It was a warning, if she needed one. Abruptly, he reached out to catch the end of the saber, jerking it toward him.

Her reaction was instant. She pulled back

485

as she stepped away in smooth recovery.

He cursed, slinging his hand that was suddenly streaked with blood. He stared down at it then looked at her with incredulity in his face. "You cut me."

"What did you expect from such a childish trick? Back away, Sasha. Back away and let me leave."

"Don't be foolish. I love you, have loved you these many years. We will be married, resign yourself to it. All will be well once we are far from here. You care for me, I know you do. We can be happy if you cease fighting and accept it."

He feinted, as if he meant to plunge around her. She whirled to prevent it. "If you think so, you have never known me," she answered him, shaking back a loose strand of hair from her face. "I have no use for another husband."

"Unless it's the Englishman, yes? It's he who stands in my way. I should have killed him while I had the chance."

"You are mistaken." She put weary conviction into the words.

"Am I? You would have tired of widowhood and accepted my proposal if not for this fixation with him. Yes, and what about this cold Englishman? He sees your fire and your passion and seeks to warm himself with them. You dance around each other armed with foils as if to defend against the feeling that draws you together and I can do nothing to stop it. It is sickening, sickening, I tell you."

He was talking to distract her. It might be impossible to ignore what he was saying, but it was a tactic two could use. "Wrong again. Gavin Blackford is far from cold."

"Indeed." Sasha's chest swelled. Abruptly, he ducked his head and lunged for the sword case at her feet.

She had three choices; she saw that in the split second allowed for a decision. She could strike a killing blow, slashing across his neck and back as he had served Gavin. She could dart away, allowing him to gain a weapon she must face when he came up with it. Or she could use the seconds while he snatched up the weapon to escape from the room. The first was beyond her, as he had said, the second dangerous. The third had been her object all along. Before Sasha's hand touched the other saber, she was sliding from the cabin, spinning around, running down the dark and narrow corridor toward the companionway with the faint glow above it that was an open hatch.

He shouted a curse. His heavy footsteps pounded behind her. Breathless, half-blind in the dimness, she snatched her skirts from under her feet and scampered up the steep steps.

Fresh air met her at the top of the companionway, and damp, windblown night. The man on watch turned from where he stood with the light from the binnacle gleaming on his face.

"Catch her, you fool!" Sasha shouted as he emerged from below.

The sailor stared with his mouth open. He seemed to want no part in cornering a woman with a saber in her fist. Face pale under its sun-blackening, he backed away with his hands held in front of him as if to ward her off.

Ariadne had no time to worry about him. Sasha was bearing down on her with the weapon that was peculiarly his own flashing before him. Though she scanned the deck in wild hope, she could see nowhere to run, no way off the ship except the rope ladder that dangled over the side. Whirling, with the wind blowing her skirts around her like sails and unfurling her hair from its loose knot so it flew out behind her like witches' tresses, she faced him. She brought up the saber in *en garde* position.

Sasha skidded to a halt, eyes wide as he stared at her. Then he gave a short laugh.

"So this is how you would have it."

"How else?" She watched him with care, her mind already slipping into fencing mode, judging, weighing, planning ahead. Her head seemed to have cleared, her drug-induced cloudiness of mind swept away by rage and the cool night wind.

He whipped up his saber in salute then faced off against her. "As you will."

No canvas strip, no marked limits existed for their bout. The only piste available was a stretch of deck hemmed in on one side by the ship's rail and on the other by a clutter of coiled ropes, barrels and kegs, saws and bung hammers not yet cleared away for embarkation. Yet the makeshift strip was not that different except that it rocked with the wind and the river's flow. They circled slowly in it, Ariadne keeping her distance since Sasha's sword arm was longer. She must let him come to her, she thought; anything else would be mere stupidity. She hoped he would try to overpower her by strength and fury alone. It would give her something to counter, something to turn against him.

He allowed no delicate preliminaries, no initial moves to feel him out as in fencing with foils. One moment he was easing around her while she turned to keep him in sight, the next he lunged at her in fully extended attack.

She parried, slid into a riposte that sent him leaping back with a black scowl between his brows. He paused a long moment, then came at her with the clanging force of a workman wielding a sledgehammer.

The shock of his heavy blows against her blade shuddered through her wrist again and again until it was numb. Still, she countered every one, catching them in seconde, in quarte, in sixte, always retreating, leaving him nothing to strike except her steel.

She saw almost at once why he had chosen the saber for his meeting with Gavin. With it, he was a strong and menacing fighter, mechanically correct in his movements. He had no grace or intuition, however, and he brought little intelligence to the bout. He was using his saber as a cutting weapon with little thought to its point. Intent on beating her down with sheer, flamboyant might, his movements were high and wide, as if he expected no real response.

She set her feet and performed a sudden stop cut in counterattack that sliced across the top of his sword arm. He bellowed and stumbled back. While he raised his arm to suck at the cut, she skipped away again with her skirts blowing around her and the blood singing in her veins.

How glad she was for all the exercises Gavin had made her do, the endless repetitive movements that now let her react to the man in front of her without conscious thought while her brain evaluated, planned. She saw why Gavin had stayed as much as possible beyond Sasha's reach during their passage at arms on horseback. It had been to wear him down until he could be met with something approaching finesse.

Her breath rasped in her throat. Fear and excitement, the advance and retreat, routed the last vestige of laudanum fumes from her brain so she felt as sharp and unyielding as the blade in her hand. Anger, that deep-buried rage she had brought with her from France, burned high inside her again, fueling her every movement. She felt so alive, as she had felt vividly alive during her meetings with Gavin. The difference was that this was real, with consequences that might be past bearing.

Would Sasha really hurt her? Would he kill her? He wanted to marry her, needed to marry her for her wealth and to salve his ego, but the purpose that flared in his eyes seemed so dire he might have lost sight of such things. At this moment, he wanted only her defeat, her surrender to his will and design.

She half-expected some trick, some stratagem or sudden display of skill that would bind her blade and send it flying from her hand the way Gavin had managed. It didn't come. Sasha simply advanced upon her again and again, forcing her back, making it necessary for her to watch behind her while breathlessly defending.

They had collected an audience. It was not large, the night watchcrew and a man who was almost certainly the ship's captain. She thought they were exchanging bets, was sure she heard a call or two of encouragement for her if only in jest. For all that, they would surely follow Sasha's orders to keep her on board. They thought her his woman, it seemed, and there was no time to explain their error.

Somewhere in the darkness along the shore where the levee ran, a commotion arose, shouts and cries from around a dray drawn by a mule team. A dingy was being launched, she thought. Cargo to be loaded? More passengers embarking? She had no time to look though other passengers might mean allies for her. Every iota of her attention was directed toward the whistling steel that flashed before her, striking endlessly from the wind-blown dimness lit only by the dim ship's lanterns fore and aft, the binnacle's light and star shine. Even her one brief glance allowed Sasha to plunge toward her in a low attack. Parrying in prime, she managed a riposte that ripped his coat skirts before she spun away, out of reach again.

She was tiring. The laudanum had taken more from her than she realized and she was not seasoned to this after only two short weeks. Her shoulder ached, her elbow was on fire and she could hardly feel her wrist. Still Sasha came on, a true bull of a man, charging, ever charging.

She didn't want to take his life. He was unfeeling and arrogant and a clumsy imbecile, but he had been faithful in his fashion. She had known him so long, knew his grief for his exile from his homeland, how much he missed the family he had left behind — his uncles and cousins, his little sister and his parents. She knew his tastes in music and food, what made him laugh and the way he sometimes shed a tear at tragic opera. She had seen him drunk on Russian vodka and gallant as he sipped champagne. Even if she could, she did not want to cause his death. Yet how else was she to escape him?

It was this realization that dragged at her, stealing her strength, dimming her fervor, leaving her with despair.

A murmur ran over the onlookers. They were staring somewhere behind her, to her left. She could not look, for Sasha was bearing down on her once more. She retreated like blown spume before the wind, difficult to touch, evading capture, never there for the vicious swipes he directed at her. Whatever it was that had attracted the attention of the others, Sasha had seen it, she thought, for he redoubled his efforts. Slashing, thrusting, he came at her, forcing her to leap back, to twist and turn on nimble feet, hardly daring to look where she stepped.

Her foot came down on a coil of rope. The big hemp strands rolled under her. Her balancing arm flailed, and she stumbled back. With a sharp cry tearing her throat, she began to fall.

TWENTY-NINE

Gavin sent Nathaniel to call out the Brotherhood, to race from one house to another requesting the aid of Nicholas and Caid, Rio and Croquère and any other sword master who might be inclined to help in the quest to find Ariadne. She might yet be discovered in the dim confines of some emporium fingering laces or purchasing chocolates, but it seemed unlikely. Maurelle was not of an excitable nature. If she was alarmed over her guest's disappearance there was reason.

His friends arrived one after the other, their faces serious, their purpose more so. Nathaniel did not return with them. Gavin noticed the absence even in his rapid-fire organization of the search effort. It was not like the boy to disappear when needed. There was no time to consider it. The first priority was to discover what Maurelle knew concerning Ariadne's movements.

It was precious little. According to her hostess, she had gone out some hours before without giving her intended direction and without a maid or other escort. Solon had seen her leave, but could only say that she wore a gray walking costume with the bonnet he had found, and that she had seemed in a hurry. She had been on foot and carried a reticule on her wrist.

"She said nothing to you of her plans?" Gavin asked with a frown.

Solon, standing beside Maurelle's chair, shook his head. Maurelle made a helpless gesture as she stared up at him with red-rimmed eyes. "She was so quiet, had very little to say this morning after breakfast. But then, she has not been particularly forthcoming since she arrived from Paris. Something has been weighing on her mind. I thought . . . I guessed what it might be but could not bring myself to accuse her. It seemed so impossible. Now this is what comes of it."

"She mentioned no errand, no one she meant to visit, no fitting at her dressmaker, no sighting of a new bonnet or the arrival of an interesting shipment of dress goods?"

Maurelle gave a slow shake of her head, a movement Solon copied in his turn.

"Did she have immediate plans to leave

496

the city?"

"She said nothing of it to me. I rather hoped she might be reunited with her mother and the rest of her family, but . . . oh!"

"I know of it. You haven't been indiscreet."

"Yes, so kind of you to absolve me." Maurelle looked away though relief drained the tension from her shoulders so she sagged a little in her chair.

"She had no communication from the Russian?" Gavin continued, his voice relentless.

"None that she spoke of, but she has been so secretive, as I said before."

"You've seen nothing of him today?"

Maurelle shook her head again, sighing.

Solon, lifted a finger, his dignified face grave. "I saw him, monsieur. He walked past on the street while I was directing the cleaning of the banquette. I would not have noticed, perhaps, except that he stared so hard at the house. After that, I saw him twice more. I regret to say he may have been awaiting a message from someone in the house."

"From Madame Faucher?"

"I think not, monsieur."

Maurelle sat up straighter in her chair as she looked at the butler. "If you know something, Solon, please speak plainly."

The elderly butler compressed his lips, staring at a spot above Gavin's head. "The young maid Adele has suddenly acquired new slippers and a knot of fresh ribbons. I regret to say she may have been keeping him informed on . . . on certain matters of interest."

"Alors," Maurelle exclaimed in annoyance. "I will have a strong talk with her."

Anger spread its heat along Gavin's nerves before he suppressed it. His gaze on Maurelle, he said, "You know Ariadne better than anyone. Is it possible she went to Novgorodcev, that she left the city with him of her own will?"

"Without her trunks? Without the new mourning clothes just delivered or even a brush for her hair? You cannot be in earnest."

He allowed himself to breathe again. "No, I see what you mean. Did he take his leave of you? Did he mention, by chance, that his ship was ready to sail?"

As she shook her head, Solon cleared his throat. "Perhaps the shipping offices . . ."

"My thought exactly." Gavin rose to his feet, reaching for his hat and cane. Ariadne's bonnet had been found not far from where most of these were located.

"You must find her," Maurelle said, her face set in lines of apprehension. "She is so young really, though her seriousness makes her seem older. If anything should happen to her, if Monsieur Novgorodcev should harm her, I will never forgive myself."

"Don't distress yourself," Gavin said quietly. "I shall find her, and if he is with her . . ."

"You will take care, yes? Your wound, it can't be perfectly healed."

Gavin made no answer. There was nothing to be said since it could not be allowed to matter.

In the event, it was Nicholas who discovered the correct shipping office for the *Leodes*. Novgorodcev's name was still on the passenger list, and the three-masted schooner would raise anchor in the morning. Its master was not known for being choosy about cargo, the crew he signed on or the passengers who occupied the cabins.

The information did not mean the Russian had anything to do with Ariadne's disappearance. Still, it suggested certain things. Gavin, receiving the news, frowned at his half brother.

"You were able to discover the ship's berth?"

Nicholas inclined his head with such

conviction a light brown curl slid forward onto his forehead. "You aren't going to like it."

"Nothing I've heard encourages me to dance for joy. Tell me."

Nicholas did, and he was right. Gavin didn't like any part of it, from the down-river location of the *Leodes* to her mid-river anchorage. It was entirely too suggestive of a fast run for the gulf.

Still, it was left to Nathaniel to present the most telling news. While they were busy with ship's offices and other avenues, he had been canvassing the street boys who had once been his confederates.

"Monsieur Gavin," he called out as he came at a lope toward where Gavin and Nicholas stood on the rue de la Levee. "They saw her, Wharf Rat and Cotton, not two blocks from here. A man with white hair threw her in a hack and drove off. She was kicking and fighting like she didn't wanta go."

It sounded like Ariadne. "Why didn't they come to me at once?"

"They didn't know her until I described her to them. And they didn't know you cared."

Gavin met the boy's level brown eyes since he was as certain as any man could be that the last comment was Nathaniel's own. "I care," he answered in hard tones. "Which way did they go?"

"That way," he said, waving toward the Place d'Armes and the lower reaches of the river which lay beyond. "Bastard was in a hurry."

"How long ago?"

"Four, maybe five hours."

Anything could have happened to her in that length of time, Gavin thought as remorse and rage filled his chest, pressing against his heart. The possibility she might have gone willingly had hovered in his mind in spite of what Maurelle had said. The news from the street boys indicated otherwise. He should have known.

Ariadne had fought. He hoped she had the will to keep on fighting. And the strength, especially the strength. She was no match for the Russian if he chose to force himself upon her.

It seemed unlikely he would not.

Gavin banished the images that rose at the thought. They would not help him, nor would they benefit Ariadne. No matter what happened to her, it would not change who or what she was, nor would it change his feelings toward her.

He required a vehicle. It might have been

possible to pick up a hackney near the Hotel St. Louis, but that would mean retracing his footsteps and there was no time. Instead, he stepped into the street to flag down a dray with a four-mule team and empty wagon bed. The driver was more than happy to have his custom, especially in light of the Mexican silver dollar he caught as it was flipped in his direction with promise of more. They all piled in, Gavin, Nicholas, Caid, Kerr, Nathaniel and Croquère as they flocked from every direction. The jehu holding the reins stood up, cracked his whip over the heads of the mules, and they were off.

They lumbered along the streets, rattling over the ballast-stone paving, splattering mud from potholes, careening around other drays and more sedate carriages. Soon the Vieux Carré and its gaslit streets were left behind.

Night was falling and the dray had no side lanterns. It was a miracle the driver managed to keep the great wagon between the water-filled ditches. He did not slacken his pace, but hurtled down the road, a danger to life and limb, dogs, cats, chickens and anything else that crossed their path.

They passed a number of steamboats, a keelboat or two and a few ships tied up to the levee, rocking with the river's current.

They were mere shapes in the dark with lanterns at stem and stern for visibility and little else to distinguish them. Gavin had almost decided they had missed the *Leodes* when she appeared, rising from the mist beginning to gather on the river's surface, floating on the reflected glow of her lanterns in the water.

They drew up and piled out. Caid walked to the water's edge and hailed the ship, but no sign came that he had been heard. A fight of some description was taking place on deck, or so it appeared. The meager crew formed a knot amidships. Yells and calls came across the water, sounding thin and high as they carried on the night wind.

The ship swung slightly on its anchor chain. Gavin's attention snagged on a flutter of gray and white. He narrowed his eyes, making out a pale face. As the figure moved, the flutter became a woman's skirts. The silken skein of her hair flew out around her, shining in the faint lantern light.

He needed nothing more.

He had found Ariadne.

It was then he caught the clang of blade against blade, saw the flash as lantern glow slid along a length of steel. Icy fear struck deep inside him, piercing his very soul.

To wait for a boat was impossible. Gavin

shrugged from his frock coat, ripped his cravat free and threw it aside, bent to drag off his boots.

"Monsieur Gavin?"

He paid no attention to Nathaniel's worried query. With his eyes on the ship, he raced back along the levee several dozen yards, gauging how much distance he must allow for drift in the fast-moving current.

"No!" Nathaniel shouted, starting after him. "You can't . . ."

He gave the boy a single long look across the space which separated them. Turning away, he hit the racing waves in a shallow dive.

The chill of the water took his breath, stung the cuts down his back and on side and shoulder with a ferocious bite. He paid no heed. Pushing away pain, thought, fear, chance, doubt and all else from him, he swam for the ship. Nothing mattered except reaching it.

Waves slapped him in the face but he hardly felt them. The vessel riding at anchor was his goad and goal. He heard nothing except the rush of the river and his heartbeat. Plowing steadily through the water, stroke after stroke, he hardly dared look ahead for fear the laggard progress would sap his will. A frantic chant echoed in his head and whispered across his lips with every surging thrust of his arms that drew him nearer.

Stay out of his reach, Ariadne. Keep your distance. Stay out of his reach.

Abruptly the ship's side towered above him. Some few feet along its beam, a rope ladder dangled from a break in the railing. He caught the line that trailed from it, pulled himself toward it until he could reach the drooping rungs, then he swarmed upward with his stocking feet slipping in the river water that poured from him. Even as he climbed, he could hear the fight almost directly above him, catch the grunts of the combatants, the yells of the spectators. A moment later, he pulled even with the deck while scanning the open space for Ariadne.

She was mere yards away, retreating before the clanging fury of Sasha's advance, desperately parrying when she could not evade. She was failing, it seemed, half-blinded by her hair, hampered by trailing, flapping skirts as she met the mighty blows of the Russian's steel. How she had sustained them so long was beyond his comprehension.

In that same encompassing glance, he saw the trap that had been set for her, saw her trip, start to fall.

"To me! Ariadne, to me!" Hard on the shout, he grasped the top rails on either side of the opening and surged aboard, settling on the deck with his legs set and his toes gripping the teak planking.

She saw what he wanted, knew what was required. The knowledge sprang into her face even as she fell. She unclenched her fingers from the saber she held and sent it spinning toward him.

He caught it, fitted his hand into the grip even as he leaped to intercept Sasha's extended attack. Fiery sparks spewed from their blades as they clanged together, scraping edge to edge. Gavin plunged into Sasha's guard, meeting him *corps à corps,* body to body, as they strained for mastery. Then Gavin, summoning the power of righteous fury, threw the Russian back on his heels.

Novgorodcev jumped forward again, his face purple with rage. Gavin met him with a hard, fast parry and riposte. And suddenly the match took on a vicious edge. The beat was harder, faster than it had been before, the clanging blows resounded over the water with a brutal ring.

Gavin felt the concentration of the dueling field settle over him like a mantle. It fit him well in spite of the clinging wetness of his shirt and pantaloons and the dank, muddy-smelling water that ran from them to streak the deck, regardless of the pull and burn of his stitches. Deliberately, he called on every iota of poise and skill he possessed, every sublime advance and deadly stratagem.

Ariadne pushed to her feet and backed out of the way; he was aware of her movement on the periphery of his vision. He was glad to have her beyond the strike zone since it left him with more room, more freedom of motion. He was able to give his complete attention, for these few moments, to the Russian.

Sasha Novgorodcev was grim of face, his teeth bared under his bristling mustache. Blood dripped from a cut on his arm that Ariadne must have given him. It stained the leg of his pantaloons, spotted the damp deck. He advanced, hacking, once, twice, three times, until Gavin curbed his aggression by attacking every time he came near in his offensive. From that point he held the initiative, upsetting with threat, early parry and footwork that negated the Russian's attempts to gain ground.

Desperation rose in Sasha's narrowed eyes. With it came a glow of cunning, a tensing of muscles.

He could not have indicated his intention more clearly if he had shouted it from the ship's main mast. Gavin was ready as the Russian took a running leap in a powerful attack. He side-stepped, leaving him to engage nothing but air.

Sasha veered to his right, came to a stumbling halt then slewed around in panicked haste. Gavin knew such a chance might not come again. His strength was not infinite, and he could not trust the captain and crew not to intervene. This must be ended, here and now.

He lunged into an advance as swift and lethal as an arrow. The point of his saber took Sasha in the shoulder, driving him back while he howled like a wolf in pain. Gavin withdrew, then bore down on him again until he stumbled, sprawling on the deck in the same way he had forced Ariadne to fall. In an instant, he leaned over the Russian. He ripped the saber from the other man's hand then flung both weapons in a wide arc. They turned end over end, flashing in the dim light, before plunging into the river.

"Bastard," Sasha said from where he lay with blood seeping through his fingers where he clamped them to his wound. He turned his head, calling out to the ship's crew. "Get him! Take him now!"

The seamen stirred, glanced at their captain who rapped out an order. They got to their feet, pushed from where they leaned on the masts and rails, started forward in a milling group.

Gavin turned to Ariadne, reached her in a few steps and caught her arm before swinging with her toward the rail. "You swim?"

She shook her head, her eyes dark as they held his, as calm as if they were alone on the deck, as though they could not feel the vibration under their feet of the seamen jogging toward them.

He had not expected it. Few could swim in this city surrounded by water, especially few females. "Will you trust me to see you to shore?"

He saw the struggle in her face, the questions in her eyes. Could she rely on him to get her off this ship, to keep her safe? Though she might not know it, she had already shown her trust in the most supreme manner of which she was capable. She had thrown him her weapon, disarming herself because she expected him to be a better match for Novgorodcev. That knowledge was like molten gold inside him, warming him, strengthening him.

"I will."

His smile was a brief yet fervent salutation. An instant later, he swept her to the rail opening, paused to take her in his arms. Behind them, he heard Alexander Novgorodcev crying out, calling to Ariadne with despair like a groan of pain in his voice. Then Gavin plunged headlong with her, heart to heart, into the river.

The going on this return journey was harder, much harder with the need to keep Ariadne afloat and her face above the washing waves. The fog drifting around them made it difficult to see the shore. He could hear the shouts and calls behind them but dared not look back to see if a boat was being lowered. Nor could he find the will to look ahead, to see what the other swordsmen might be doing on the levee. Nothing mattered except the next hard stroke of his one free arm, and the next and the next.

Nothing could be allowed to break through the control he held on his will and mind, not the drift of blood, warm compared to the river water, from the slice along his back that had split open during the fight, not the slow draining of his strength that threatened to fog his brain. He could not stop, couldn't afford to rest though his muscles clamored for it, urged him to turn and float even if he and Ariadne both sank beneath the silt-filled waves. He breathed with conscious effort against the burning agony, the laboring of his lungs and dizzying thunder of his heart. He was slowing; he could feel it. His arm grew heavier each time he lifted it. The powerful kicks that should have sent him surging forward seemed barely to stir the water behind him.

"Let me go." Ariadne's voice was a hoarse whisper from where she lay with her face in the crook of his arm and her body trailing alongside his, trying to help kick, so closely matched she might have been a part of him.

"No."

"My skirts are dragging us down and I can't unfasten them. You can . . ." She stopped, coughing in a spasm as a wave washed over her, before going on in a breathless rasp. "No need for . . . for both of us to drown."

"Both or neither." He had no breath for a better answer.

"You . . . you've done enough. I can . . . make it from here."

She couldn't. He knew it and she knew it, which meant it was an excuse, a sop for his conscience if he should do as she suggested. "Sweet, unacceptable sacrifice — I would do the same . . . if I could. It would be right."

"An ultimate injury, gladly taken?"

"Poor Ariadne . . . caught between monsters, both crying out, 'Live for me.' "

She had begun to struggle, as if she would free herself from his grasp. He tightened his hold.

"You are no monster," she said on a gasp, even as she pulled at his constricting arm.

"No angel, either. I will choke you like a mewling kitten before . . . before I'll let you go. One death is as good as the other."

She was abruptly still. He swam on while black curses filled his head for his threat that had banished trust, his promise that made him a monster in all truth.

It was then he heard the dip and swirl of paddles and the sluicing whisper of a craft shooting over the water. He redoubled his effort, not to avoid pursuit, but to reach the skiff that ghosted toward them. It eased alongside. He saw Nicholas and Caid bending over the side. Hands reached, taking Ariadne from him, dragging her, sodden skirts and all, into the rocking boat. It was his turn then, and the rescue was not gentle. Somewhere in the middle of it, he shuddered, cringing at the ripping of another few inches of stitches. Curling in upon himself in the bottom of the boat, with his wet head resting on Ariadne's knee, he closed his eyes and accepted, at last, that neither death, sacrifice nor polite, soul-scarring murder would be necessary.

What followed afterward was a confusion of voices and movement, exclamations and shouted orders, none of which came from him. He was transported back to the city with intemperate haste and a great deal of painful jostling, then left at his atelier to the brusque solicitude of Nathaniel and Nicholas. A sawbones came with a needle larger and sharper than any foil to reset his stitches. Then he was left alone with a hot brick at his feet, the smell of laudanum in the air, and his unanswered questions concerning Ariadne's whereabouts lying around him like singed moths around a candle flame.

He slept and roused and slept again, sipped broth, stared at the window near his bed, watched clouds skim past and birds loop their way through them in ecstatic flight. He damned Nathaniel for a cow-handed oaf in the morning when he attempted to shave him and called him his savior in the evening when he appeared with steak and a glass of ale. He was being stubborn and oafish, knew it, and did not care. Above all, he waited, though for what he could not say.

It came on the morning of the fourth day, when he was half mad with inactivity and doubt and the suspicion that his friends, when they deigned to visit, were keeping something from him. The form was a note on thick parchment, closed with a wax seal of French blue impressed with an Athenian owl. The direction which had brought it to him was in the fine, sloping hand of a lady.

Nathaniel gave it to him on his breakfast tray. Gavin drank his café au lait and ate his hard roll before reaching for the note and breaking the seal. Even a condemned man was allowed a meal before his sentence was carried out.

It was not the note of farewell he expected. It was, instead, a summons.

Gavin pushed the tray aside, shouting for Nathaniel.

Dressed finally in a tobacco brown frock coat, buff trousers and a new beaver hat of impressive height and sheen, he left the Passage. He crossed rue Royale on his way to the street where lay the town house of the Widow Herriot, the present address of her guest, the daring Madame Faucher.

The lady had rare courage, he thought. She would not give him his congé, his final dismissal as her sword master, in a note. Rather she had resolved to face him with it.

To smile, perhaps, and give him her hand. To thank him for his intervention and speak a clear but personal farewell.

It was a surprising consolation.

THIRTY

Ariadne was packing when Gavin was announced. She had not thought to see him so soon, had expected to wait until evening perhaps, when he might reasonably be expected to be free. So little news had come her way about him that she thought he must have returned to his usual pursuits, his round of clients and manly pleasures. Maurelle had been maddeningly vague on the subject, though Ariadne knew she sent often to learn how the Englishman was faring. She said merely that he was no worse for his dip in the river or the reopening of his injuries, but seemed to have recovered as was usual in a man of health and vigor.

It was most unsatisfactory.

Ariadne had thought Gavin might pay a courtesy call on Maurelle, if not on her. She had given him little reason to feel concern for her sake, of course, but he might have pretended out of mere good manners once he presented himself. She had been abducted, after all, even if few knew of the circumstances. She might have been prostrate with nerves or in the throes of morbid decline.

He had not appeared. It might have been worrisome if she had not known he was in fine health.

If he would not come to her of his own inclination, then he must come at hers. Certain things still required to be settled between them before she could say goodbye. It might not be comfortable, that interview, but she refused to take the coward's way out by leaving matters unresolved.

Moments after she came to that conclusion, her note had been written and handed to Solon for delivery.

Rising from her knees in front of the trunk now, she shook out her skirts of lavender broadcloth striped in white and black over a black underskirt. She smoothed her hair, pressed her lips together to make them pinker, then walked as calmly as she was able along the gallery to the salon.

Gavin turned as she entered, putting his back to the fire that burned in the grate and clasping his hands behind him. His smile was polite, his composure as impenetrable as a brick wall. He was a little pale, she thought, but gave no other sign of the events on board the *Leodes* or afterward. Still he seemed to glow like a work of art in gold, brown and ecru, with the dark blue of his eyes a brilliantly cool contrast. The knowledge that this rare swordsman had held her, made love to her, burned through her from her head to her heels, a lightning strike of pleasure that held her rooted where she stood. Her gaze touched his mouth, his hands, while a tremor ran down the back of her neck, catching her unaware.

"Madame," he said, inclining his head.

As if released by the low resonance of his voice, she jerked into movement. She glided toward him, determined to match him in imperturbability if it killed her, to behave as if nothing untoward had ever occurred between the two of them. "Thank you for coming so promptly," she said. "Has Solon offered . . . ?" She stopped as she saw the balloon glass holding a dark gold liquid which sat on the mantle behind him. "I see that he has. Excellent. Won't you please be seated?"

"I would as soon stand," he replied. "Executions are traditionally met in an upright position."

She gave him a narrow look. "Why would you say such a thing?"

"Expectation based on experience?"

"Both of which are wrong. I only asked you here to . . . to express my appreciation."

He tilted his head, his gaze watchful. "For?"

"Coming to my rescue, of course. You may consider it nothing, but I do not."

"I haven't said so."

"Said what?" she asked in exasperation. She had not meant to take this tone. Why did everything between them have to descend into a quarrel?

"That it was nothing, preventing you from being taken from us."

"You saved my life, I believe."

"I doubt the danger was of that nature," he answered, his eyes blue slivers between his narrowed lashes.

"You think Sasha would not have killed me?"

"He meant to make you his, whatever the means. That was all."

"Assuming, of course, that he had the skill you once displayed of disarming without injury," she snapped. "But you were not there. He would have killed me, I do believe, to prevent me from leaving him. Yes, and especially from going to someone else."

"Still you faced him with a saber."

"As did you, if I remember correctly."

"That was different."

He was truly angry. Beneath his quiet veneer of elegant indifference, he was furious with her. It had taken a moment for her to see it, but the recognition seemed to ease something cold and hard inside her. "It was the only weapon available." She shrugged. "I dared it because I had been taught well, particularly in the area of strategy. It was ill luck that I fell."

"It was a trick, and his doing alone. He meant you to fall, would have been upon you in an instant."

"I might have dispatched him first if you had not appeared. What were you thinking of, to demand the saber from me? You might have been killed, fighting him so soon after being wounded."

"What were you thinking when you gave it to me?" he asked, the words even.

She lifted her chin in defiance. "Very little, if you must know. It was, as you have harped upon so often, purest instinct."

"As it was my instinct to prevent you from causing his death. You will be far better off to remain among those who can still revere life without reservation."

"So you said before." She turned from him, moving away, trailing her fingers along the back of the brocade settee before the fireplace while cogent thought moved in her mind. "Your aim from the beginning of our acquaintance seems to have been to prevent me having a death on my conscience, even if it was your own."

His smile was brief. "As efforts go, it seemed more worthwhile than most."

"But why? Oh, I understand that you aren't anxious to forfeit your life, but surely there was more to it."

"Do you really not see?" He tilted his head, his gaze considering. "You were the very embodiment of life and purpose while I was lost in an endless round of death and aimless days. It seemed teaching you the art of the sword with its myriad painful ways of causing harm might convince you to abandon your need for revenge. Of course, I didn't know that I was your quarry."

"You soon learned."

"I guessed, a different matter," he said in correction. "It required proving."

"Which you set about with underhanded methods."

"As you pointed out, it was my skin at stake."

She lifted her hand, clenching it into a fist. "And your skin that you allowed me to slice at my leisure, finally, for Francis."

"You misjudge me. It was not at all for

Francis. Rather, it was to prove, if need be, that you were not made for taking life but for giving it."

"A salutary lesson." She paused, looked away from him. "And you were right. I could have killed Sasha, you know, when I first faced him with the saber in the ship's cabin and later, when I slashed his arm instead."

"Then it was worthwhile."

Worth the pain she had given him, he meant. She swallowed hard. "Is that why you didn't finish him when you had the chance, because of this aversion to killing?"

"You might say so, though I also thought he could mean something to you. Besides, he roused my pity, wanting you so badly. He called after you, you know. I hear him in my dreams, Othello crying for his Desdemona — though it was worse for him since you were merely lost to him instead of safely dead."

"There, you see? You did think he would kill me."

"Reason says he would not have struck the blow — but men are not always reasonable in their jealousy."

She released a long sigh. "I'm glad you let him live. It was a generous impulse."

"Or a most dastardly punishment, who

can say? He has been forced to leave the city without you. The *Leodes* sailed two days ago. He was on it."

"You're quite certain?"

"My friends in the Passage made it their business to know."

"For your sake."

"And yours."

Restless, driven, she walked to the window and stood with her back to him though she saw nothing beyond the wavy patterns of the thick, greenish glass. "There is something I don't understand, something I've been puzzling over since I came, finally, to see that you knew who I was and what I intended. Why didn't you just tell me what happened with Francis, that his death was nothing you could have prevented?"

"Maurelle knew, and I was sure she must have given you the details," he said as he turned toward her. "If you chose not to believe her, why would you believe me?"

"No," she said after a moment. "I don't suppose I would have, not in the beginning."

"Then I was guilty, you see. I injured his young pride, interfered in his effort to praise a lady. My reasons were, perhaps, inadequate for the offense. Some recompense was owed. As I could not render it to him,

523

then. . . ."

"Then you would allow it to me."

"If you required it."

"It seems I did, though I might have been less bloodthirsty if I had known you had been injured as well. Maurelle never mentioned that, or your regret."

"Some injuries are best kept hidden so they, and their cause, can be forgotten. As for my regret, a sword master reluctant to meet other men, one haunted by past kills, becomes a target with every man's hand raised against him. I am not that fond of deadly meetings."

She turned, drawn by the rasp of old anguish in his voice. "But you allowed me to see the scar."

"It seemed a fit lesson in what not to achieve. But I was silent for another, less exalted reason."

"That being?" Her frown was perplexed.

"It seemed likely you would abandon our sessions with a sword if convinced your foster brother's death was unavoidable."

"But why should that matter? Unless . . ."

"It was not the money for my services," he answered her unspoken thought with the ghost of a smile curving his lips. "I needed the lessons to continue. I was only alive when I was here, facing you in your man's garb that showed you as more womanly than any petticoat could, seeing the possibility of my death in your eyes."

She met his gaze, noting the certainty which rested there, seeing, too, the opaque self-protection that gave away nothing more. Forcing words through the constriction in her throat, she said, "I might have handed it to you in a moment of rage before I knew you. But not . . . not afterward."

The realization of what she meant leaped into his face, the understanding that she would never have been able to cause his death once they had made love. "In spite of everything?"

"Yes, in spite of it all."

She waited, thinking he might answer the declaration, that he would say something more, something that she could depend on for a tiny hope of a future. The moment stretched, filled by the ticking of the mantel clock, the muffled sound of traffic in the street, the voice of Maurelle's cook humming in the kitchen below. He did not look away but his gaze turned even more stoic than before, as if to conceal some pain beyond imagining.

A piece of coal turned to ash in the grate with a small, shattering whisper of sound. Ariadne let go the breath she had been holding, turned sharply away. She put a hand to her mouth then brought it down again.

Lying on a side table was a long, narrow case of polished ebony inlaid with ivory. She had placed it there earlier in the day to have it on hand for this occasion. She moved to it now, taking it by the silver handles set into each end and carrying it to the settee. "You may not recognize this," she said as she sprang the catch and lifted the lid back then waved at the contents, "but I am persuaded you will be familiar with the weapons."

He glanced down, his gaze impassive as it moved over the swords she had kept concealed in her room, over their silver and black enameled hilts and the silver chasing on their blades. "Indeed."

"They have been cleaned, at least the one with traces of your blood. I thought — I hoped that you would accept them as a gift, and as my surety that any need I ever had to be avenged against you for Francis's death is ended."

"You sent for me for this, to present a parting gift?"

His voice was devoid of emotion, the muscles of his face rigidly controlled. Her gaze on the hard line of his jaw, she said, "I suppose you might say so."

"You gave me a shirt."

"And you gave me a nightgown. We are even on that score."

A chill smile flickered at one corner of his mouth. "I thought you might intend to return it this morning."

She should have done so, had told herself a hundred times that she would. Instead, she had worn it these past nights, wrapping it close around herself because he had touched it, perhaps thought of her in it, pictured it against her skin. "It was not a gift but a replacement," she said, the words abrupt. "A sign of damage repaired."

"So it was." He shot his cuffs, holding out his hands in an open gesture.

He was wearing the shirt she had given him. A tight, hard ache squeezed her heart and she gripped her hands together as she fought a vital need to smooth them over the silky linen and the warm muscles of his chest and shoulders which lay beneath it. "Besides," she said, dragging air into her lungs along with the scent of new linen and clean male, "I have need of the nightgown for my journey."

"When do you go?"

"In two days, though I will return before the end of the season."

He lowered his arms, his eyes narrowing. "So soon?"

"I would not impose on my mother for more than a week or two on a first visit."

"Your mother." He hesitated, went on. "You are going upriver?"

"You thought I was returning to Paris?" She held his gaze, trying to decipher it. "But there is nothing for me there. And it was you, I think, and Madame Zoe, who convinced me of the importance of family. I was enraged with the world when I first saw my mother at the benefit. Since then, I have had time to consider many things, including her plight all those years ago. How could I bear not knowing more of her, nor meeting all my sisters?"

"You are no longer alone."

"So it seems." It was gratifying that he remembered what she had said, could see now what this meant to her.

He gave a slow nod, returned his gaze to the case of matched swords. His voice hard, he said, "I'm sorry. I must refuse your gift."

It hurt. She had not expected that, had not really thought he would refuse. She was forced to clear her throat before she could speak. "Why should you?"

"Many reasons, among them their high value, my pride, and the implication."

"Implication?"

"That you will no longer be my client. That our late-night lessons, and all that went with them, are at an end."

He thought she was dismissing him. Her heart stuttered in its beat before settling into a quick throb that made the blood surge in her veins. Reaching out with an idle gesture, she took the hilt of one sword and lifted it from its velvet bed. "Is that of such moment?"

"Is the moon queen of the night? Does its light pour down to make men mad and women weep for what might have been?"

"You think I might weep for you?"

"No, no, only for the idea that it could have been different."

She lifted the rapier, pressed its point to his coat front where his heart beat beneath the layers of broadcloth and linen. "And will you long madly for me?"

He met her gaze. Light, like a candle advancing from the darkness, rose to gleam in the depths of his eyes as he saw the tears she made no attempt to hide. "If I say yes, what will I use to guard against whatever you may do?"

"You refused my gift, so have forfeited mercy. You must take up the twin of this sword and face me."

"And if I disarm you?"

"You are welcome to try." She held the blade loosely as she waited, hearing the sincerity of her declaration echoing in her ears.

He did not disappoint her. Moving more swiftly than the eye could follow, he lifted his arm, brushed aside the sword point and swirled around the blade to take the hilt and twist it from her grasp. If she had been in earnest she could have countered, could have beat his arm aside and driven high and inside, piercing his unprotected chest.

She was not. Releasing her grasp, she let him take the weapon, saw it glint with reflected silver light as it was tossed to the settee beside her. She swayed, already moving toward him as he pulled her close.

"There is more than one kind of disarmament, my Ariadne. I have no weapon, no defense against you, have had none since the night I took you for my client. In this time, you have been the sword pointed at my heart but also my shield and my buckler, my most certain protection against self-imposed exile, a misspent life and death that comes at the end. The old gods, laughing, set us one against the other in hope of mayhem and instead we give them hope. You give them hope, for in forgiveness is glory. Still I dare more."

"What do you dare?" she whispered, touching his face with the very tips of her fingers, trailing her thumb along the firm line of his bottom lip.

"I dare ask if the portion of a younger son can suffice for a French Creole lady or if, like Hercules, there is some further task I must perform, some test I must pass to win my place."

"What place is that?"

"At your side, in your arms, in your heart."

Trailing her hand down to his cravat, she slowly closed her hand upon it, using it to draw his head down. "We French Creoles are fond of our gentlemen who do not sow, reap nor toil. All that we require of them is sweet words, good lineage. Yes, and honor."

"I would not be your pensioner."

"Then be my buckler, my shield and my soul in turn, for I refuse to let you go. And my instinct is not yet honed to such brightness that I can always guess what you require."

"You," he said against her mouth. "I only require you. At my side, as my fencing partner, as my love and most beloved wife."

His mouth was hot and demanding on hers, and the sweep of his tongue inside, against hers, set her senses aflame with such

531

scorching heat that she clung to him in consuming need. His desire matched hers for she could feel its hard strength against her, feel the shudder that passed over him, taste the promise.

It was enough, Ariadne thought as she closed her eyes and melted against him with her own whispers of love. Neither of them wanted or needed full surrender from the other.

But they might, if they were very lucky, achieve it anyway.

ABOUT THE AUTHOR

Since publishing her first book at age twenty-seven, *New York Times* bestselling and award-winning author **Jennifer Blake** has gone on to write over sixty historical and contemporary romances. She brings the seductive passion of the South to her stories, reflecting her seventh-generation Louisiana heritage. Jennifer lives with her husband in northern Louisiana.